PENGUIN BOOKS

THE WARLORD

Richard H. Dickinson is a graduate of the United States Military Academy at West Point. After taking advantage of a unique opportunity to be commissioned in the United States Air Force, he spent twelve years as a hurricane hunter and air traffic controller. His duties included penetrating into the eyes of forty-five hurricanes, flying into radioactive debris clouds from nuclear explosions, and surveilling incoming Russian ICBMs over the North Pacific. Author of *The Silent Men*, he lives in Seattle with his wife, Amy Solomon.

THE WARLORD

RICHARD H. DICKINSON

PENGUIN BOOKS

PENGUIN BOOKS

Published by the Penguin Group

Penguin Group (USA) Inc., 375 Hudson Street, New York, New York 10014, U.S.A.

Penguin Group (Canada), 90 Eglinton Avenue East, Suite 700, Toronto,
Ontario, Canada M4P 2Y3 (a division of Pearson Penguin Canada Inc.)

Penguin Books Ltd, 80 Strand, London WC2R 0RL, England

Penguin Ireland, 25 St Stephen's Green, Dublin 2, Ireland (a division of Penguin Books Ltd)

Penguin Group (Australia), 250 Camberwell Road, Camberwell,
Victoria 3124, Australia (a division of Pearson Australia Group Pty Ltd)

Penguin Books India Pvt Ltd, 11 Community Centre,
Panchsheel Park, New Delhi – 110 017, India

Penguin Group (NZ), cnr Airborne and Rosedale Roads, Albany,
Auckland 1310, New Zealand (a division of Pearson New Zealand Ltd)

Penguin Books (South Africa) (Pty) Ltd, 24 Sturdee Avenue,
Rosebank, Johannesburg 2196, South Africa

Penguin Books Ltd, Registered Offices:
80 Strand, London WC2R 0RL, England

First published in the United States of America by Rugged Land, LLC 2004
Published in Penguin Books 2006

1 3 5 7 9 10 8 6 4 2

THE LIBRARY OF CONGRESS HAS CATALOGED
THE HARDCOVER EDITION AS FOLLOWS:
Dickinson, Richard H.
The warlord / Richard H. Dickinson
p.   cm.
ISBN 1-59071-017-7 (hc.)
ISBN 0 14 30.3589 4 (pbk.)
1. War—Fiction.   2. Afghanistan—Fiction.
3. Adventure stories, American.   I. Title.
PS3604.1455W37 2004   813'.6
QB133-2038

Printed in the United States of America
Designed by HSU + Associates

TO

THE WARRIORS

OF

SPECIAL OPERATIONS COMMAND

IN

AFGHANISTAN

AND

THE WORLD OVER.

UNITED STATES ARMY captain Louis Salam looked the Afghani warlord directly in the eye, bypassing the bastard's interpreter, and shook his head no. Salam and the warlord, Raz Khan, sat at a scarred wooden table inside a flat-roofed, dirt-floor, mud-brick hut in the remote mountains of northeast Afghanistan. The view out the window was spectacular, but the interior of the hut was squalor in shades of brown. Everyone had stopped talking, and the squawk of a small color TV filled the silence. The thirteen-inch Toshiba sat in a corner on top of the cardboard box it came in. Two black cords trailed from the TV out the window—one to a gas-powered generator and the other to a satellite dish on the roof that was pulling down a CNN broadcast. Salam glanced over at a snowy image of Tiger Woods sinking a putt. The vibrant green of the course was almost hypnotic compared to the dirt colors inside the hut. Back home seemed like a distant planet to Salam.

Raz Khan stared at him, his thick black mustache deepening his scowl. He raised his hand and extended all five fingers to show what he wanted. Five Hummers. Plus $100,000 in cash. All of it courtesy of the US taxpayer.

Well, he could go fuck himself, Salam thought as he shook his head again. Khan isn't gonna get it. Not for what he's offering.

Like all these warlords in Afghanistan, Khan was as patient as he was stubborn. After all, these people were the ones who had invented haggling. Salam knew the drill because he'd been through it many times before with other warlords. Khan would keep Salam here a week if he could, negotiating this thing to death, his *mujahadeen* body slaves bringing in tray after tray of those little glasses of *chai*, hot tea, until Salam finally gave in just to get the hell out of there and give his kidneys a rest. But Louis Salam wasn't your average G.I. Joe. He was a Green Beret, highly trained in Special Ops, and a Lebanese-American to boot who spoke fluent Arabic, Pashto, and Dari, the archaic dialect of Farsi, which happened to be Raz Khan's native tongue. The United States Army did not have a lot of guys like Salam.

Salam's grandfather, who had owned a jewelry store—first in Beirut and then in Chicago—had been a hardball negotiator just like these Afghani Ali Babas. Once, when Salam was seven years old, he had bet on a Cubs game with his grandpa. The wager was a Milky Way, his absolute favorite candy in the world. His grandfather kept the candy bar in his shirt pocket during the game. The Cubs lost to the A's in ten innings, and Grandpa won the bet. Salam was convinced that the old man would just give it to him because he was the kid and kids get candy, but his grandfather didn't play it that way. Instead he slowly unwrapped the Milky Way bar and ate it right in from of his little grandson. All of it. Didn't even offer to give him a bite. The old man had savored every last speck of it with spiteful delight, so now whenever Salam dealt with the warlords, he treated them as if they were his old son-of-a-bitch grandpa.

Khan's high-beam stare didn't waver. Unlike his *mujahadeen* followers, he shaved occasionally so that his black walrus mustache remained prominent. He looked to be in his late fifties or early sixties but could have been younger, Salam figured. The harsh sun and unrelenting terrain tended to age the locals before their time. Khan had a thick, stout build, but not fat. He wore a large gray-blue turban on his head and a drab-green flak jacket over a knee-length white *shalwar* shirt and voluminous black pants.

Khan was the leader of a faction within a larger faction of the Tajik tribe. This was the way of the tribes in Afghanistan. Their loyalty, even to their own tribesmen, was liquid at best, and each warlord grabbed as much power as he could. So, outsiders never knew where these tribesmen stood. Today they might be your ally, but tomorrow they could be your enemy if it suited their purposes. To them an ally was only as good as the assets he offered, and today Khan aimed to squeeze the United States, his professed ally, for as much as he possibly could. He, in turn, would offer information as to the location of a large Taliban unit rumored to have crossed over the Pakistan border and into the region. That could definitely mean trouble for US forces. Of course, in the world of the warlords, Khan might have planted the Taliban rumor himself so that he might have something to sell.

Yusef, Khan's interpreter, top lieutenant, and number one ass kisser, stood just behind his boss. He raised his five fingers just in case Salam had missed the point. "Five Humvees, one hundred grand," he said in perfect American English.

Yusef looked like your typical *muj*—gaunt face, dark deep-set eyes, dirty-face black beard, the ubiquitous wool *pakul* hat on his head, which all the men in Afghanistan wore. But Yusef had lived in the United States for several years and had actually attended UCLA for a while. He'd dropped out for some reason, which invalidated his student visa and forced him to go back home. He could imitate several American regional accents, and he liked to use them to annoy Salam, switching on the fly from an Alabama good ole boy to a "Hava'd Ya'd" Boston Bruins fan to a southern California surfer dude. Salam suspected that providing annoyance was Yusef's main function because Khan's English was good enough that he didn't need an interpreter.

Khan's ever-present "companion" sat by his side, a blank-faced ten-year-old kid named Hajji who seemed to be an idiot savant without the savant part. A potato had more personality than Hajji, and Salam thought the boy might actually be mentally impaired on some minor level. Khan took Hajji with him wherever he went, but Salam couldn't pinpoint the nature of their relationship. He'd been told that Hajji wasn't Khan's son. More like Khan's pet from the way the warlord constantly stroked his back and rubbed his shoulders. It creeped Salam out whenever he saw them together. Salam decided their relationship had to be something sick, which made it that much harder for him to deal with Khan.

Everyone in the hut carried a weapon, including Hajji, and they kept their weapons close at hand, but this was the norm in Afghanistan, and most of the time it didn't particularly upset anyone. Khan wore a 9mm sidearm. A sniper rifle on a bipod was set up on a small table, pointing out the window. A Soviet-era AKS-74U submachine gun hung from Yusef's shoulder. Salam kept his M4A1 assault rifle across his knees. But what *did* concern Salam was Hajji's weapon. The kid always seemed to have an AK-47 assault rifle with him, and he kept his finger loosely curled on the trigger *all the time*. The kid definitely seemed brain-damaged enough to frag someone without giving it a second thought, and Salam was obviously pissing off Khan, refusing to give him what he wanted. Salam hoped the kid wouldn't try to please his Big Daddy by putting a few rounds through the nasty American's face.

Khan raised his hand again, showing his five fingers.

Salam shook his head and wondered if maybe it was time for a counter-offer. Negotiating with these bastards was always delicate business. If you showed your hand too soon, you could lose it, but you couldn't wait them out either. Khan might withhold the information about the Taliban unit out of pure spite, and he knew this matter was time sensitive. If Taliban soldiers actually had entered the area, they'd be on the move. The longer Salam and Khan dicked around over a deal, the greater the chance the Talies would slip away.

Salam extended five fingers. "Five Toyota pickups and ten thousand dollars," he said, stating his counteroffer.

Khan's bushy eyebrows crumpled with displeasure when he heard the word "Toyota." He glared at Salam, insulted by the offer.

"Take a minute and think about it," Salam said. He turned his head toward the TV, where a housewife mopped her linoleum floor, having a goddamn orgasm over the sparkling, lemon-scented results.

Khan and Yusef conferred in low grumbles. Salam expected Khan to come back with the rag-head guilt trip—*Why do you insult me with such an offer? Am I not a man in your eyes?* It was the kind of bullshit tactic his grandfather would have used. Guilt the other guy out to soften him up, then pounce.

Khan relaxed his face and lowered his gravelly voice. "Where are you from, Salam? I am curious."

What was this? The good cop routine?

"I was born and raised just outside of Chicago," he said in clipped military fashion. "Now stationed with the Fifth Special Forces group out of Fort Campbell, Kentucky."

Khan waved away the military info. "No, no, no. Tell me about your upbringing, your parents, your family."

"Is that pertinent to this negotiation, sir?" Salam felt himself getting hotter. He didn't mean for the "sir" to slip out—it was habit.

"I am curious. Your name is Arabic, no?"

"Yes, that's correct."

"Your parents were born where? Lebanon?"

"Yes. I believe we've covered this territory before."

"So you were brought up with the Koran?"

Salam could feel the blood rushing to his face. "Again, is this pertinent to the matter at hand?"

Khan smiled paternalistically. "You are a Muslim—"

"I am an *American*," Salam said, cutting him off.

"America is where you live," Khan replied. "What I want to know is where your *soul* resides?"

"Excuse me?"

"God." Khan pointed to the ceiling. "Do you have a place for him in your life?"

"I believe in God," Salam said. In fact he had not been inside a mosque since his freshman year in high school. He'd tried Catholicism a few years ago, but only because he'd gotten serious with an Italian girl who never, ever missed church on Sunday. Her family had big problems with her dating a Muslim guy, and basically she wasn't willing to buck her family. After about a year and a half together, they broke up.

"*Why* do you believe in God?" Khan persisted.

"Because I do."

"A lot of very bad people say they believe in God."

"We've gotten off the subject, General Khan," Salam said.

Khan grinned. "I sense that you are not comfortable with the topic of God."

Salam cleared his throat. Enough, he thought. This God bullshit was getting on his nerves. "General," he said, "I'm uncomfortable with you bringing up God when what we're really talking about is vehicles and money and you trying to shake me down for as much as you can get in exchange for information that so far is unverifiable and may in fact be a crock of shit."

Khan's brows furrowed. "Crock? What is a crock? "

"Let me finish, General. "As a representative of the United States Army, I'm empowered to offer you *something* for this alleged information you're peddling, but I'm not gonna pull down my pants, bend over, and say come on in. You understand what I'm saying, General? Forget about the Hummers. You're not gonna get 'em. Five Toys and ten grand is my best offer. You're basically getting something for nothing, General. I suggest you take the deal."

Khan's hawk eyes glinted under his bushy brows. He didn't like being talked to this way, not at all. Hajji looked agitated and uncertain, his finger tightening on the trigger of the AK. He was hardwired to his Big Daddy's moods.

"If in fact," Khan said, "you have ever read the Koran, you did not pay attention, Salam. Respect—"

Yusef the interpreter gently interrupted. "General? " He nodded toward the television.

Salam looked at the TV and saw the words "LIVE FROM THE PENTAGON," at the bottom of the screen. Secretary of Defense David Riordan stood at a podium, a gang of reporters sitting before him. His signature rimless eyeglasses flashed under the hot lights. As usual, he didn't smile when he spoke, and when he did smile, it was more like a warning sign that he was going to blow.

"... all in the interests of global security," he said. "Now I won't be taking any questions as I have to leave immediately for a meeting. Save it for General Monroe. General? "

General Jackson Monroe stepped up to the podium. Riordan cupped his hand over the microphone as he whispered something to the general, then left the stage followed by two stone-faced young men wearing department-store suits and earpieces.

"Good morning," General Monroe said, showing a small smile in contrast to the secretary's high-school principal demeanor. This earnest but not totally humorless expression had become Monroe's trademark. He cut a forceful figure, square-shouldered in his uniform with close-cropped graying hair. Salam guessed that he was fifty-something, but the man showed maturity rather than age.

Of course, it didn't hurt that Monroe was black, Salam thought. He'd always felt that Monroe used his race to advantage, not blatantly but subtly and very effectively. General Monroe projected such an image of competence and perfection that white people didn't dare criticize him for fear of being labeled racist. Officially he was the Pentagon liaison with the Senate Armed Services Committee, but more than that he was the media's favorite general and the Army's—well, the "Old" Army's—poster boy.

Yusef went over to the TV and turned up the volume.

"I'll take any questions you have about my upcoming trip," Monroe said.

Reporters raised their hands and called to him by name. Monroe pointed to a middle-aged woman reporter in the middle of the audience. "General, are you going to Afghanistan to gather information for the Pentagon or for the Armed Services Committee?"

"Both," he said. "My aim is to get a firsthand look at what's going on there. As you know, Special Forces troops have done a commendable job there. Taliban and Al-Qaeda forces have been effectively squeezed out and kept at bay, keeping Afghanistan free. But our job will not be complete until a duly elected government can take power and rule without interference. To that end, I've been asked to observe and make recommendations."

The reporters clamored to be recognized.

"Yes," Monroe said, pointing to a petite blonde in a dark pants suit. She had shoulder-length hair and sharp features. Waspy pretty, Salam thought.

The young woman stood up and identified herself. "Brie Richards, *Washington News*," she said. "General, when you refer to the establishment of a 'duly elected government,' are you saying that the United States will be committing additional ground forces and conventional artillery to safeguard that government? And if so, how big a presence will that be?" She flashed a hint of a smile at him as she took her seat.

"Brie, at this time we don't know if any additional forces will be needed in Afghanistan. We do know that the country is in a precarious position right now. The existing government is weak. The warlords are jockeying for power. The Taliban forces that have been driven out could pick up reinforcements outside the borders and attempt to reinfiltrate the country at any time. Special Operations Forces are without question the best at what they do, but they can't do everything. Their numbers are limited. They very well may need conventional support to maintain what we've achieved there, to deter outside forces, and to keep the peace internally."

Yeah, blah-blah-blah, Salam thought. Monroe sounded like every other heavy-metal guy Salam had ever heard, singing that same old song: Call in a cast of thousands—no, hundreds of thousands—with tons of tanks and artillery and that'll solve all your problems. A huge standing army that's slow as shit. Great idea, General, Salam thought sarcastically.

"Yes?" Monroe said on the screen. He picked a round-faced white guy who wore thick glasses.

"Dennis Kates, *Cleveland Sun*. General, you're scheduled to testify before a joint committee of Congress in two weeks, regarding the proposed Frye-Yoder Act. Do you anticipate that your findings in Afghanistan will influence your testimony with regard to the act's proposed reorganization of the military?"

Monroe's expression turned serious. "Influence my testimony in what way?"

"If enacted, Frye-Yoder will dismantle Special Operations Command and put Special Forces troops under the direction of the regional commanders who aren't all big fans of Special Forces."

"Mr. Kates, if you mean to say that Frye-Yoder will *reduce* the role of Special Forces in the military, I think you're under the wrong impression. To my understanding, the Frye-Yoder Act simply aims to reorganize and streamline the administration of the various commands in order to eliminate duplication of services and, of course, save taxpayers money."

"But isn't it true that if Frye-Yoder is enacted, Special Forces, such as the Navy Seals, the Army Rangers, Green Berets, Delta Force, etcetera, will be used only at the discretion of the regional commanders instead of as a strategic force unto itself? That sounds like an overall reduction to me."

The general smiled. "That's not my understanding of the bill's intent."

"But, General—"

"I'm afraid we have to move on. Are there any other questions? Yes."

Monroe pointed to a young man in a light gray suit. "William Traeger, *Houston Register*. Can you give us some specifics regarding your trip to Afghanistan, General?"

"I leave tonight and I expect to be back by the beginning of next week. I'll be meeting with General Graydon who, as you know, is in command of our forces in Afghanistan. I also hope to meet with the head of the Northern Alliance, General Zyrous Mohammed."

"The warlord?" Traeger asked.

"We prefer the term 'indigenous commander.'" Monroe smiled, and a ripple of laughter drifted through the audience. "I'd like to be able to give you more details about what I'll be doing once I get there, but the country is still a hot zone, and so I can only say so much. I'll be making a full report to Secretary Riordan and the Armed Services Committee when I return, and I will tell you what I can at that time."

Other reporters called out to be recognized.

"I'm sorry, ladies and gentlemen, but that's all the time I have for questions right now." He flashed his patented tight-lipped grin. "As you know, I have a plane to catch."

Salam exhaled a bitter laugh. Kiss my ass, motherfucker, he thought. "You don't have a fucking clue about Special Forces," he muttered at the screen.

"You don't have a fucking clue about Special Forces," Yusef said. He parroted Salam's words exactly—tone, accent, spot on.

Khan roared with laughter, pointing at the Green Beret's startled face. Yusef laughed, too, but young Hajji just looked confused.

The warlord stood up and dragged his chair to the sniper rifle by the window. He sat down and leaned over the table, holding the stock in his left hand, his right index finger on the trigger. He peered through the scope, taking his time to set up the shot.

"Hajji," he said.

The boy leapt up and ran to Khan's side. "Don't move it," he told the boy in Dari.

Khan gingerly removed himself from the rifle and instructed the boy to take his place, telling him what to do to find his mark.

Salam looked out the window. He didn't see what they were aiming at until he adjusted his focus and scanned the mountainside farther away. About 150 yards off, a young boy around Hajji's age was walking on a narrow path. A frisky yellow dog was following him, playfully jumping up on him, falling behind, running ahead, doing anything it could to get the boy to play. The boy carried something on his shoulders, but he reached out to pet the animal every time it came within reach.

Salam's heart started to beat faster. "What're you shooting at?" he asked.

"The dog," Khan said, keeping his eyes on his pupil.

"Why?"

Khan gave Salam a hard look. "Do you think I am a cruel man?"

"Why kill a dog for no reason?"

"For practice. We need good fighters. We do not need pets." Khan turned his attention back to Hajji.

The dog kept running back and forth around the boy.

"But what if you hit the kid?" Salam said.

Khan cocked an eyebrow and glanced back at Salam. "What do you mean? I don't understand," he said in Dari.

Yusef jumped in and answered for Khan: "Collateral damage."

Salam said, "But the kid could end up—"

Khan ignored him. "Shoot!" he ordered.

Hajji obeyed instantly. The crack of the rifle was sharp and sudden inside the hut.

Salam moved closer to the window to see the result. In that moment the dog, which had been lagging behind the boy, suddenly dropped to its haunches. Blood stained its yellow flank. Salam couldn't hear from this distance, but he was sure the poor animal was yelping frantically as it dragged its useless hind legs. The dog would bleed out a slow death. The boy dropped his load and stared down at his wounded pet, frozen in horror and confusion as he tried to figure out what had just happened.

Khan stroked Hajji's scalp approvingly as he stepped in front of Salam, blocking his view out the window. "So," he said, peering into Salam's eyes. "What are we going to do about my Hummers?"

2

THE REPORTERS at the Pentagon shouted out questions as General Jackson Monroe left the stage, even though they'd been asked repeatedly to refrain from turning press conferences into free-for-alls. The current administration preferred a little more decorum from the press corps than previous administrations had, and Monroe concurred with that policy. As far as he was concerned, journalists served little purpose when it came to reporting on military matters. They usually got their facts wrong even when experts spoon-fed it to them. Monroe trusted only a select few to deliver his message the way he intended it to be delivered.

As he entered the hallway just outside the press room, he caught the eye of his personal assistant, Second Lieutenant Kevin Reilly. The lieutenant had blazing red hair and pale blue eyes, but the calm maturity of his expression negated his boyish looks. "Catch Brie Richards before she leaves," Monroe said to him. "Tell her I'd like to see her for a moment."

"Yes sir." The lieutenant headed for the press room to fetch her without bothering to salute. No one saluted inside the Pentagon. If they did, that's all they'd be doing all day long since everyone here was military.

Monroe checked his PDA while he waited. He had two meetings here at the Pentagon that afternoon and a dinner party that evening at Senator Yoder's home in Georgetown. The dinner party was the important appointment.

"General?" Lieutenant Reilly called out as he reentered the hallway—Reilly's heads-up for Monroe to close his PDA because the reporter was coming.

"General Monroe," Brie Richards said, shouldering past Reilly and walking briskly. She extended her hand as she came toward him. "Will this be on the record?" She grinned at him, keeping it light, even though her question was serious. Getting statements on the record from someone of Monroe's stature almost guaranteed a byline on the front page.

"Neither on nor off," he said. "I wanted to offer you a seat on my transport to Afghanistan."

Her eyes widened and a strand of hair fell over her brow. She quickly swiped it back into place. "For an interview? An exclusive?" she asked, trying not to sound anxious but failing miserably. "Or to cover. . . ?" She let her sentence trail off, afraid to say the words.

"I'd like a journalist to accompany me to Afghanistan to cover my trip. I respect your work, and I like how your newspaper covers major events. Your reporting is usually fair and accurate. That's why you're my first choice, Brie."

She looked a bit weak-kneed for a moment. He had just offered her a journalistic jackpot, the opportunity to be the only reporter covering this story. She'd be inside a hot zone with a major player. Monroe enjoyed watching this usually knife-edged professional turn to mush. It was a nice feeling, a concrete reminder of how much power he actually had—and with a woman, always more enjoyable. A quaking male junior officer is one thing, but a swooning female is somehow more satisfying. He knew he had that effect on women, particularly well-educated young white women who'd had limited contact with powerful black men. Power, after all, is the ultimate aphrodisiac, he knew, and he thought at this very moment she found him very attractive. No doubt about it.

"Do you need to talk to your editor about this?" he asked.

"No. . . well, yes, I have to tell him, but I'm sure there won't be a problem." That strand of hair fell over her forehead again. She hooked it behind her ear, clearly annoyed with it.

"Good," Monroe said. "I'll have a car pick you up at twenty-one hundred hours. That's nine o'clock."

"I know," she said, flashing a confident grin and regaining her composure.

Monroe looked her in the eye and held her glance until her grin turned bashful and she looked at the ground. Now it was his turn for a grin. He wondered how old she was. Not yet thirty, he guessed. He wondered why she hadn't gone into television journalism. She certainly had the looks to be an on-camera personality. Blonde, clear skin, attractive features. Her voice was a bit high. Maybe that was it.

"I assume I should bring rugged wear," she said. "Hiking boots, jeans..."

"Lieutenant Reilly will put you in touch with my office. They'll advise you on what to bring." Monroe made eye contact with the red-haired lieutenant who acknowledged with a nod that he knew what was expected of him.

Monroe shifted his gaze back to Brie Richards. "I'll see you tonight then. But if for some reason, your editor decides that—"

"I'll be there," she said, making it definite.

"Good. Until then," he said and turned to go.

"Oh, General?" she said. He pivoted on his toe, reversing direction to face her. "Yes?"

"I assume I may bring along a photographer."

"By all means." He looked past her to Reilly. "Make arrangements for an additional passenger from the press."

"Yes sir."

Monroe turned around and continued on his way. Photo op, he thought. Even better, photo ops taken by an independent photojournalist. The press is always leery of shots taken by Army shutterbugs. This will add to my credibility, he thought.

"To the end of SOCOM," Senator Walter Frye said in a hushed voice so that his other dinner party guests didn't hear him. He hoisted his glass of scotch.

"To the end of SOCOM," said the three men clustered with him, clinking their glasses but keeping their voices down.

The senator had the long, loose-fleshed face of a basset hound. Political cartoonists occasionally portrayed him as a floppy-eared dog. But tonight he was a happy hound, his eyes sparkling and his smile confident.

Lobbyist Alan Hooper stood to the senator's left. He had a round doughy face and a round doughy body that even the best cut dark suit couldn't conceal. The hair on his head was little more than blond peach fuzz. He looked like the kind of guy you sent out for coffee, but in fact he was one of the most cutthroat lobbyists in Washington, an attorney by training and a boa constrictor by trade. Over the years he'd represented all of the major arms manufacturers, including Boeing, Raytheon, and GE. His current job was working the strings behind the scenes to make sure Frye-Yoder got the support it needed to become law.

Army general John McCreedy was one of the Joint Chiefs of Staff. Although only fifty nine years old, he looked considerably older. His weathered, craggy, and pockmarked face resembled a coral reef. He was a big man, tall and heavy in the chest. In his huge hands, his glass seemed more like a delicate teacup. He had an infamous bark and wasn't shy about using it when it came to shouting down the Secretary of Defense and his staff of brownnosers. McCreedy was the most prominent of the heavy metal generals, the holdovers who believed in traditional war craft. To McCreedy's way of thinking, Special Forces troops amounted to a bunch of hot dogs, glory hounds, and guerrillas in the worst sense of that word. The heavy metal crowd firmly believed that wars were won the same way they had been won in the days of the Roman Empire and long before that—with overwhelming troop force, overwhelming field artillery, and a clear means of exit.

Jackson Monroe stood between Hooper and McCreedy. Like General McCreedy, he wore his dress uniform and sipped a scotch on the rocks. Both generals had come of age in Vietnam, but Monroe had been a noncom drafted into the Army after dropping out of Benjamin Franklin High School in north Philadelphia. The Army trained him to be a sniper, and in Vietnam he was one of the best. Too good, in fact. On a misguided mission into Cambodia, he took out a man he thought was a high-ranking North Vietnamese leader but in fact was a dirty ARVN officer, one of our supposed allies. A clean head shot at eight hundred yards, but that was the only thing clean about it. Monroe nearly lost his life getting out of Cambodia, and his partner on the mission did lose his. An ugly incident and something Monroe preferred not to think about if he could help it.

After going through West Point and holding various administrative and command positions in the Army, Monroe felt that he'd gotten beyond that nightmare, far beyond it.

"Gentlemen," General McCreedy said, "we are on the threshold of returning our fighting forces to their former glory. And to that I say, amen."

Hooper quickly scanned the senator's parlor where men in dark suits and women in evening wear chatted in small groups. None of them appeared to be under the age of fifty. A carved ice swan surrounded by tall sprays of white gladiolas and spider mums graced a side table. Waiters in tuxedos circulated the room with silver platters of hors d'oeuvres and flutes of California sparkling wine, which were taken only by the ladies. The men went to the bar set up in the corner for hard liquor. It was a smallish affair, forty-two guests in all. Most, if not all, were emphatic supporters of Frye-Yoder, but Hooper, as always, was cautious. Every American was entitled to know their goals, but the manner in which they would achieve those goals was nobody's business but theirs.

"I caught your news conference on TV this afternoon, Jackson," Senator Frye said to Monroe. "It was fortunate that the secretary had to leave early. Gave you center stage. We could have done without that pain in the ass from the Cleveland paper."

"The one who asked me about the realignment of Special Forces?" Monroe said, then shrugged. "I assume his editor is infatuated with the tough-guy stuff. It's pathetic really. It's as if we're threatening to take away their G.I. Joe dolls."

The men chortled, General McCreedy louder than the others, which made Hooper scan the room again to see who might be listening.

"I think you handled him well, Jackson," Senator Frye said. "You have the touch. If it had been any of us, that reporter would have latched on like a pit bull and never let go."

McCreedy huffed. "I would've had him shot."

Hooper's eyes opened wide. "General, please," he whispered, nodding toward the crowd. "You never know who's..." He let his words trail off.

"Yes, yes, yes," McCreedy said, lowering his voice, "but let's not act as if we were doing something bad here. As it stands now, the military hierarchy is as confused and cockamamie as the wiring in a Harlem tenement building."

"Yes, General," Hooper said, "but your choice of words—"

"Fuck my choice of words!" McCreedy fired back, his eyes bulging. "Streamlining the military and making it more efficient is nothing to be ashamed of. Anyone who thinks so has his head up his ass."

"Or up the secretary's ass," Monroe quipped.

The men laughed, even McCreedy, who'd just been so fired up. McCreedy drained his glass and rattled the ice cubes. "Gentlemen, my ice is lonely. I'll be right back." He headed off toward the bar.

Hooper turned to Monroe. "Jackson, before I forget, I've outlined a few points that I think would be important for you to make during your testimony. I've sent them to your office and they'll be waiting for you on the plane tonight."

"Alan, if I know you," Monroe said, "you've written out an entire script for me."

"Well, no, Jackson, I would never be so presumptuous as to—"

"It's all right. You don't have to apologize. Just as long as you left me a few pauses for a sip of water here and there."

Hooper feigned humility. "Jackson, I would never dream of telling *you* how to deliver a speech or give testimony or christen a ship—"

"That's Navy work, Alan," Senator Frye said. "Jackson is Army."

"One hundred percent," Monroe said. He took a sip of his drink and let the warmth of the scotch trickle down his throat. He smiled at Hooper and Senator Frye, and they smiled back. Personally he had little use for Hooper. The man was a lawyer and had all the undesirable qualities associated with that profession, and as a lobbyist it only multiplied. And like all politicians, Senator Frye was primarily motivated by his unquenchable desire for endless reelection. He came from a state with more defense contractors than any other except for California, which was the home state of Congressman Yoder, the bill's cosponsor. Yes, the Frye-Yoder Act would create jobs in their districts, lots of them, and jobs equaled votes.

But Monroe didn't give a rat's ass about these men's individual motivations and ambitions. The results that Frye-Yoder would achieve were what really mattered—a return to traditional military values. Special Forces had a place in modern American warfare but not a leading role. They were supporting players in a larger arena, although their proponents at Defense didn't want to accept that. Small elite teams were flashy and admittedly sometimes very effective, but they did not win wars and that was the bottom line. Being fast and light was good in concept but unreliable on the battlefield, and that had been proven throughout history. SOCOM's successes in Afghanistan over the years were commendable, but had they secured the entire country? Could they with such minimal personnel? Of course not.

The guerrilla lovers at Defense liked to refer to the officers who had cut their teeth in Vietnam—men like Monroe and McCreedy—as the "heavy-metal guys," but Monroe took that as a compliment. American heavy metal overwhelms enemy forces. Heavy metal preserves the lives of Americans in uniform on the battlefield. Heavy metal achieves and *maintains* victories.

"Are you still with us, Jackson?" Senator Yoder said. "You look like you drifted away from us for a moment."

"No, no," Monroe said, "I was just thinking about something."

"Would you like to share it with us?" Hooper asked. He was smiling, but he was also prying. Hooper had been treating Monroe like a hothouse orchid that might wilt and spoil before he got it to show. Hooper was a worrier, but there was no need for him to worry about Monroe. He was squarely on board with Frye-Yoder, and he would pull out the stops and use all his powers of charm and persuasion at the congressional hearings.

General McCreedy headed back toward them, navigating around the delicate Georgetown ladies like a battleship in a swimming pool. He had a fresh drink in his hand and a deep scowl on his face. Something was wrong.

As soon as he was safely within their huddle, McCreedy started hissing like rattler who'd been stepped on. "What the fuck is *he* doing here?" he said, glaring at Senator Yoder. "Did you actually *invite* him?"

Deep frown lines appeared around the senator's mouth. "Who are you talking about, John?"

"Him!" McCreedy nodded toward the bar.

Monroe turned around to look and immediately knew who McCreedy was talking about. Retired general Otis Vandermeer was chatting with an elegant woman of a certain age in a flowing white dress. Vandermeer wore a dark gray suit, white shirt, and a maroon print tie. He was laughing at something the woman had just said, but the joviality of his face didn't exactly match his keen gaze. Vandermeer saw everything, and Monroe knew that for a fact. Nothing had ever gotten past Vandermeer. Not in Vietnam, and not at West Point, where he'd been posted after the war. No one knew this better than Monroe because Vandermeer had taken him under his wing and turned him into a soldier and an officer. If it weren't for General Vandermeer, God knows what would have happened to Monroe. Either dead in Cambodia or dead on the streets of north Philly, where he would have ended up if he hadn't decided to make the Army his career—a decision strongly suggested and shaped by General Vandermeer. Vandermeer was a good man and an inspiring leader. Too bad he'd been brainwashed by the Dark Side, Monroe thought, the pro—Special Forces contingent at the Pentagon. He was a vociferous supporter of SF and in recent months a frequent guest commentator on television, constantly singing the praises of SF gains around the world.

"And who's that woman with him?" McCreedy growled under his breath as he glared at Vandermeer and the woman in white.

"That's my wife," Senator Yoder said. "Ellen is an old friend of General Vandermeer. *She* invited him."

McCreedy rolled his eyes to Hooper. "Will this be a problem?"

"I don't think so. It's just a party."

McCreedy leaned into his face. "Hooper, in Washington a party is never just a party. Even I know that."

"That's very true," Hooper said, "but..." He noticed Monroe walking away. "Jackson! Where are you going?"

"I'll be right back."

"Let's think about this before you say anything—"

But Monroe was already heading across the room toward General Vandermeer. It would be rude and disrespectful to ignore him. Plus, it might be useful to talk to him. Monroe might be able to discern which way the wind was blowing over on the Dark Side.

Ellen Yoder had just excused herself and moved off to mingle with her other guests. But before she departed, Vandermeer already had his eye on Monroe as he approached. Monroe shifted his drink to his left hand and extended his right. "General Vandermeer."

Vandermeer shook his hand with a firm grip. Except for a little less hair on his head and a little more bulk on the body, Vandermeer looked pretty much the way he always had. "General Monroe," he said.

Vandermeer kept Monroe's hand in his grip as he scrutinized him with those all-seeing eyes. But there was a warmth behind the penetrating gaze. "How've you been, Jackson?"

"Excellent, sir. And yourself?"

"I'm terrific. It's not every day that my mere presence puts a four-star's shorts in a knot." He raised his glass and smiled at General McCreedy across the room.

Monroe couldn't help but laugh.

"So," Monroe said, "what's the good word from the secretary's office?"

Vandermeer brought his drink to his lips and stared at Monroe over the rim of the glass. The warmth disappeared.

3

THE HUMMER'S ENGINE revved loudly as it surged over a nasty hump in the dirt road, its front wheels leaving the ground. Salam's butt lifted off his seat as if he were riding a mechanical bull in a Texas honky-tonk. The vehicle landed hard, but nothing it couldn't take. Salam straightened the steering wheel and looked in his side mirror just in time to see the Hummer right behind him jump the hump, front wheels free-flying, like a whale breeching the waves. Green Beret sergeant Butch Proctor was driving that one. Salam hoped to hell Raz Khan was watching from somewhere up in the mountains. This was what he wanted, after all, a road monster that would put his rival warlords to shame.

The dirt road went into an incline, but it was graded smoother along this stretch, so the ride was a little easier. They were at the base of a mountain, heading for the village where he had met with Khan the day before. The interior of Salam's Hummer almost looked new even though it wasn't. He'd ordered two privates to make it clean enough to eat off of, and they'd done a pretty good job. He and Proctor were heading back for round two of his negotiations with Khan. His plan was to dicker a little more, then offer the bastard one Hummer, not the five that he wanted, and up to ten Toyotas, plus twenty grand tops for up-to-date info on the Taliban unit that had crossed the border. But he was pretty sure that once Khan saw Proctor's Hummer, he would be wanting that one, too. Salam also knew that he'd probably give it to Khan if the miserable goat turd coughed up the intel he wanted, but Salam would delay delivery of the second vehicle until that intel could be verified.

Salam looked in his mirror and could see Proctor's wraparound sunglasses glinting through the windshield. Proctor's head was so big he looked like he was wearing a helmet even when he wasn't. He was built like the Rock, huge chest and arms that tapered to a trim waist and powerhouse legs. When he wasn't smiling, he looked like the ugliest cuss in the Army, and Salam had ordered him not to smile once they got to Khan's village. Salam wanted Proctor to be the evilest snake-eater these ragheads had ever seen just to help move this negotiation along.

"You feeling ugly today, Proctor?" Salam said into his wireless headset microphone.

Proctor's voice came back in Salam's earpiece. "Yes sir, I am," Proctor said. "I am one ugly motherfucker."

"Are we gonna get what we want today, Proctor?"

"Yes sir."

"Is Khan going to get what *he* wants?"

"Yes sir. In the short term."

"And how's that, Sergeant?"

"Ali Baba does not deserve such a fine American vehicle, sir, not for keeps."

"So what's your idea? That we steal it back before he puts his name on it?"

"Or before he paints it in those wild hippie colors these people like to paint their trucks. That would be a goddamn shame, sir."

"No danger of that, Proctor. The *muj* see themselves as warriors. Only civilians do those tie-dye paint jobs."

"They still shouldn't have such a fine vehicle, if I may speak freely, sir. This is an SF-worthy vehicle. The *muj* should keep riding their little mountain nags and Jap pickups. It suits their style."

"Thanks for your input, Proctor. But when we get there, you let me do the talking, okay?"

"That was my plan exactly, sir. I'm just the mean-ass motherfucker. That's my job."

"You got it, Sergeant."

Salam kept his eye on the road and saw a blind curve up ahead. "Curve," he said into his mike.

"Roger," Proctor responded. "I see it."

In the rearview Salam could see Proctor slowing his Hummer down to a crawl. A blind curve is a perfect setup for an ambush. It was standard field procedure to send the lead vehicle in alone so that the whole convoy isn't bushwhacked. If the first one takes fire, at least the others can figure out a response from safety. Proctor pulled to a stop, bringing up a cloud of dust behind him. Salam eased up on the accelerator and proceeded with caution.

As he entered the curve, a huge boulder on his right soon blocked the line of sight between him and Proctor. Voice communication would be the only way to alert Proctor of trouble. The road dipped, then took a sharp curve to the left. More boulders blocked the view ahead.

"'S' curve," Salam said into the mike, informing Proctor of the terrain.

Proctor's voice came back in his ear: "Roger."

Salam removed his sidearm, a 9mm Beretta, from its holster and held it while he drove. If necessary, he could return fire immediately and give himself precious seconds to get to his rifle, which was on the passenger seat. He moved toward the second curve. His mouth was dry, his throat full of dust.

"Approaching second curve," he said.

"Roger," Proctor said. "Quiet on this end."

Salam maneuvered his Hummer around a two-story pile of boulders on his left as he took the curve. As soon as he came around the boulders, he saw a pickup full of *muj* up ahead in the middle of the road, three sitting in the bed, at least two in the cab. The men in the back of the truck had their rifles hitched over their shoulders. They stared at Salam, but they didn't seem particularly alarmed, and Salam was immediately suspicious. He didn't like their casual posture. They could be the decoys.

Salam hit the brakes. "Five *muj* in a Toy stopped in the middle of the road."

"Roger. Whose *muj* are they?"

"Don't know yet."

One of the problems with fighting in Afghanistan was that the *mujahadeen,* no matter which side they were on, didn't wear uniforms and looked pretty much alike. Deep tan complexion, full beard, flat-top *pakul* hat, long vest over a blousy shirt, and big baggy pants. The lucky ones had flak jackets. The Taliban *muj* had the courtesy to wear black turbans and a minimum of four-fingers worth of beard, but in a place where you could suddenly become anybody's enemy and not even know it until they opened fire at you, American soldiers had to be wary of every indigenous soldier.

One of the men in the back of the pickup slapped the roof of the cab. Salam switched the Beretta to his left hand and grabbed his rifle off the seat. The *muj* weren't moving any faster, but that alarmed him more than if they'd been scrambling. They were up to something, Salam was convinced. He glanced over his shoulder, assessing his chances of backing around a curve at high speed because the road wasn't wide enough for a fast turnaround. If trouble started, he'd have to take fire, return it, and hope that Proctor could cloverleaf around the road and hit these bastards from the other side so that together they could squeeze the Toyota's position like a pimple.

The passenger door of the Toyota swung open. Someone was getting out. Salam turned the wheel of the idling Hummer, ready to block the road laterally. If a firefight started, he'd get out of the vehicle and use it as protection.

A slender bearded man wearing a turban and a desert tan flak jacket got out of the cab and started walking toward the Hummer. A submachine gun on a strap hung from his shoulder, bobbling loosely as he walked. Salam's eyes darted from the man's hands to the other *muj* in the truck. Salam's foot hovered over the accelerator.

The man waved. He smiled, showing a row of teeth through the black beard. He called out, "So what's happening, dude?" The accent was pure American.

"Fuck," Salam muttered under his breath. It was Yusef, Khan's right-hand man.

Proctor's voice materialized in Salam's ear: "Talk to me, Captain."

"Hold your position," Salam said. "I think we're okay here, but hang tight until you hear from me."

"Gotcha."

Yusef walked up to the driver's window. "Captain Salam," he said, "long time, no see."

Salam nodded toward the men in the truck. "What's this all about? You guys gonna block the road all day?"

"Why? You got someplace you gotta be?" Yusef grinned. He loved speaking "American."

"Khan is waiting for me," Salam said. "You don't want to make me late, do you?"

"The boss can't see you today."

Salam frowned. "What do you mean he can't see me? We have a meeting set for this morning."

"You *had* a meeting set for this morning. Something came up."

Salam looked Yusef in the eye. "If this is some kind of bullshit bargaining tactic, tell him to forget it. The deal's off."

But Yusef wasn't listening. He was checking out the Hummer. "Hey, is this one of the ones we're gonna be getting?"

"I said, forget about it. Save the bullshit for someone else." Salam set down his rifle on the seat and put the Hummer into reverse.

"No bullshit, man. Khan's busy. For real."

"Doing what?"

"He's with Zyrous Mohammed."

Salam didn't believe him. "Doing what?"

"Going someplace, getting ready for the conference."

"You're a lying cocksucker, Yusef."

One of the men in the pickup truck called to Yusef in Dari and pointed up the road. Four vehicles were coming down from the mountain: two pickups, a light troop carrier, and a white Jeep Cherokee. They were moving at a pretty good clip, raising a lot of dust and staying in close formation. Several men were posted in the backs of the two trucks, bouncing with the ruts in the road, each one holding a rifle.

"Would you pull over to the side, Captain?" Yusef asked in a snotty tone. "These people have to get through."

"Yeah, right away, *sahib*," Salam said sarcastically. He took his time putting the Hummer into forward and pulling over, and he deliberately didn't go as far to the right as he could have. He wanted to make the convoy slow down to pass.

The convoy did slow down as it approached the parked Toyota. The two lead vehicles—one of the pickups and the troop carrier—slowed to a crawl when they came up to the Hummer. The vehicles were inches from Salam as they passed. Grisly fighters eyeballed Salam suspiciously. Salam made eye contact with every one of them.

The Jeep, which was third in line, waited for the first two vehicles to pass before it proceeded past the Hummer. Salam spotted Raz Khan in the backseat on the near side. The warlord nodded to Salam and gave him a crooked, fuck-you smile. His brain-dead pet-boy Hajji was next to him in the middle. On the far side was a middle-aged man with a striking profile, short beard, and a mass of dark, short-cropped curls on his head. He looked Salam in the eye, nodded, and touched his forehead with two fingers, the local version of a salute. Salam got the sense that this gesture was sincere, unlike fucking Khan's greeting. But it wasn't until the Jeep had passed that Salam realized that the man in the backseat was Zyrous Mohammed, the leader of the tribal coalition. Salam had never actually seen him in the flesh before.

Goddamn, Salam thought. So that's the man.

"Proctor, you there?" he said into his mike.

"Ready and waiting, Captain."

"V.I.P.'s coming through. Let 'em pass."

"If it's Khan, I'll whip out my dick and piss on him first."

Salam laughed at the thought of Proctor dousing Khan as he passed. "Do whatever you want to Khan," Salam said. "Just don't hit the other guy."

"How come?"

"We need him."

4

REPORTER BRIE RICHARDS and *Washington Times* staff photographer Jane Norcross sat side-by-side in the rear section of an Air Force C-17, heading for Afghanistan. Brie, petite and blonde in her late twenties, wore an open-neck white cotton blouse under a tan pants suit. Her laptop blinked on the fold-down table in front of her. Notes jotted on a lined, yellow pad trembled on her lap.

Jane Norcross was thirty four, tall and lanky with blunt-cut, jet-black hair and no makeup but eyeliner. She wore green cargo pants and a black t-shirt. Her beat-up black camera bag lay under the seat in front of her, the toe of her hiking boot right up against it. She never let that bag out of her sight. A 40-gig iPod weighed down her breast pocket, mini earphones in place. She'd been listening to the Clash, but the CD had finished ten minutes ago, and she wasn't listening to anything now. Bored out of her mind, she sighed, knowing there were nine hours of flight time to go.

"There he is," Brie whispered excitedly in Jane's ear. General Monroe exited the bathroom at the front of the plane. For the umpteenth time Brie started bubbling in her seat like a little fountain, which annoyed the hell out of Jane. Brie had a fucking orgasm every time she saw Monroe, as if the old guy were Lenny Kravitz or something.

Brie waved to the general. Fifteen rows of officers and assistants hitching a ride to the hot zone sat between Brie and the general, but she somehow managed to catch Monroe's eye. He smiled and nodded to her. As soon as he turned away and went back to his seat, Brie grabbed Jane's forearm, digging her fingers into Jane's biceps. "This is great," she whispered. "We are *so* lucky to be here."

Jane shrugged and pulled her arm out of Brie's grip. "It's just another assignment."

"Another assignment? Are you crazy?"

"I sincerely doubt that we'll see any action when we get to

Afghanistan," Jane said. "Bigwigs like Monroe never go near the front. It's too dangerous. Too real."

"Exactly!" Brie said, her eyes popping out of her head. "They don't want him anywhere near where he could get hurt because he's too important." She lowered her voice. "I've heard a rumor from a good source that he's going to run for president in eight years."

Jane couldn't have cared less. "I wish I had a joint," she murmured.

"Jane, this guy could be president of the United States someday. And we're here alone with him. No other press at all. This is the kind of contact we'll be able to take to the bank some day."

"Just what I want. Photo ops in the Rose Garden. The president with the king of Luxembourg, born-again assholes, retarded kids from the Special Olympics—"

"You are so cynical."

Jane shrugged. "I live for the good shots, Brie, the ones that show you something real, not the shit they want you to see. That's all I care about."

"You're a typical photographer."

Jane squinted. "What's that supposed to mean?" She didn't like being categorized.

"All you know is what you see," Brie said. "No concern for content, just visuals."

"Hey, it works for me." Jane exhaled impatiently, looking up at the ceiling. "You don't have a joint on you, do you?"

"Of course not! I don't smoke pot," she whispered. "Not since college."

Jane nodded, "I'll bet you were pretty cool back then."

Brie looked down at her notes and went back to her work. "Fuck you, Jane," she muttered.

"Only if you buy me dinner first, Brie."

Jane pulled out her earphones and stared down the length of the cabin. The seats up front where General Monroe sat weren't set up like a commercial passenger jet. Banks of seats lined the sides of the plane, backs toward the walls. The junior officers sat in those. These guys were the drones studying reports, talking on their sat phones, pecking into their laptops. "First class" was a cluster of about a dozen seats in the center of this space. This was where General Monroe and the other big honchos sat, and from the solicitous way the others treated him, Monroe seemed to have the biggest dick of the bunch. She'd noticed that no one below a two-star sat in that section. Monroe was a three.

Jane wished she could go up there with a camera and take some candids, but she and Brie had been given orders to stay out of that section unless invited, which sure as shit wasn't going to happen. Normally that wouldn't stop her from trying, but her cabin mates in the economy section were Special Forces guys in desert camos, Green Berets and Rangers who were ready to rumble with the enemy, and to these guys the press counted as enemy. One of these apes had nearly tackled her when she'd gotten up to go to the bathroom and made the mistake of heading for the one up front. Assholes, she thought.

She glanced over at Brie typing away on her laptop but had absolutely no interest in reading whatever it was she was writing. Jane looked around at the granite-faced SF boys in the seats all around her, but they had no interest in her. Cute little Brie was obviously their type because they kept sneaking looks at her. Clearly she was the one who gave them hard-ons. Jane knew she was much too dark and edgy to be attractive to these huah Hulks.

She closed her eyes and sunk down in her seat. God, I wish I had a joint, she thought.

"Ms. Richards? Ms. Norcross?"

Jane's eyes shot open the moment she heard that familiar silky deep voice. General Monroe stood right over her, his hand on the seatback right in front of her.

He extended his hand to her. "We haven't actually met, Ms. Norcross," he said. "I just wanted to come back and introduce myself."

"Nice to meet you," she said, shaking his hand. It was warm, dry, and unexpectedly large. She studied his face. He had deep chocolate brown eyes. Kind but determined eyes. The relaxed expression of his face almost contradicted itself—it said, I'm really a nice guy down deep but do not fuck with me. He had a little too much flesh under the chin compared to the SF boys. Generals must have it too good.

"Is everything all right back here?" he asked. "Is there anything either of you need?"

"Oh, we're just fine," Brie said, beaming like a one hundred-watt bulb.

"I know I've promised you an interview," Monroe said to her, "and I haven't forgotten. Once we're in country, we'll get that scheduled."

"Thank you, General."

"And, Ms. Norcross, if there's anything in particular you'd like to photograph, tell Lieutenant Reilly and we'll do our best to arrange it."

"Thank you," she said. "I will." She sounded like a suck-up, just like Brie, but she knew that's how journalists got what they needed. It wouldn't be the first time she'd made nice with someone she didn't give two shits about just to get access. Who was she kidding, she had done more than that.

"We'll be landing in Gardiz in about eight and a half hours. Again, if there's anything you need, just let us know."

He moved on to the SF boys, chatting them up. He tried to be casual with them, but in his presence they stiffened up. It was all "yes sir" and "no sir." Jane thought maybe they acted this way because they were hard-ass fighting machines who breathed propane and farted fire. Or maybe they just didn't like him. It was hard to say for sure.

Jane closed her eyes and pressed on her iPod. Joe Strummer started belting out "London Calling." She still wanted a joint.

When Monroe got back to his seat, he unpacked his laptop and checked the e-mail he'd downloaded before he'd left. He scanned the list of unread messages, the senders all familiar and not unexpected, but one grabbed his attention. It was from General Vandermeer. Monroe slid his finger across the touch pad to select and open it. He furrowed his brow pensively as he read the message:

Dear Jackson,

I was most disturbed to see you with Frye, McCreedy, and that lobbyist Hooper tonight. It's no secret that there's strong opposition to the role of Special Forces in the military, and there are some—you included, I'm afraid—who would like SF to disappear completely. Your feelings are understandable on one level. The Cambodian incident was indeed regrettable, and I in no way mean to minimize it, but I would hope that you are not condemning SF for something that happened nearly forty years ago.

I consider you an intelligent man, Jackson, and so I am asking you to make an informed, intelligent decision in this very crucial matter. Before throwing your weight behind Frye-Yoder, take a good hard look for yourself at what SF has achieved in Afghanistan. Talk to people over there, get out in the field, get the facts. You know how I feel about heavy metal, so I don't expect you to take my word for it. All I'm asking is that you do the fact-checking and make up your own mind.

Sincerely,

Otis Vandermeer

Monroe stared at the screen for a few moments, then moved the cursor to the delete icon and tapped the touchpad. Vandermeer's message disappeared. Monroe went back to the list of unread e-mails and selected one from Alan Hooper.

General,

I've just received word that there will be a tribal conference taking place in the NE mountains while you are in Afghan. The warlords tried to keep it quiet, but as I'm sure you know, attempted secrecy sometimes ends up becoming the best (or worst) publicity. We think it would be very helpful if you could attend. Photos ops with warlords, one on ones with major players, handshakes, allies in arms, all-around good-will, etc. Will forward more info as I get it. If you have any questions, get back to me.

Best,

Alan

Monroe dragged the cursor to the save button and tapped it.

Eight hours later Monroe sat at a polished wood table in front of a plate of bacon and eggs at the American airbase in Gardiz, Afghanistan. He was in the private quarters of the regional commander, General Bill Graydon, who sat to Monroe's right at the head of the table. Tall and big-boned with a long horse face, Graydon kept his hair so short it was nearly shaved. From what Monroe had heard, Graydon was an affable sort and well liked by his men. Slightly younger than Monroe, he had been at West Point when Monroe served in Vietnam as an enlisted man. Monroe attended the Point later after his tour of duty in Nam. They were both three-stars.

Monroe sipped his coffee, waiting for the caffeine to give him a recharge. He didn't have time to give in to jet lag. He wasn't going to be here that long.

He speared a piece of bacon on his fork, brought it to his mouth, and chewed thoughtfully as he stared out at the airfield where an F-16 was just taking off. He followed it with his eyes as it lifted off the ground and started gaining altitude. Large fluffy white clouds drifted across the perfect blue sky. In the distance to the east, the mountains loomed. They had a unique reddish hue that Monroe had never seen in any other mountain range. A rugged and remarkable panorama.

Monroe washed down the bacon with more coffee. Graydon was respecting the quiet, no doubt thinking that Monroe needed some down time after the long trip. He was wrong.

Monroe got right down to business. "I've been informed that there's a tribal conference taking place somewhere in the mountains this week," he said.

Graydon nodded. "Up in the northeast about midway between the Tajikistan and Pakistan borders." He sipped from his coffee mug.

"Who's attending?"

"The usual suspects. At least the ones who aren't actively screwing each other at the moment."

"Is that a problem?" Monroe asked.

"Big problem. Within a single tribe, you've got factions within factions within factions. Thank God we've got Zyrous."

Monroe squirted catsup from a squeeze bottle into a corner of his plate.

"Without Zyrous there would be no Northern Alliance," Graydon said. "He's the only warlord the other ones respect." Graydon put down his mug. "Well, respect may be a bit of an overstatement, but he gets their attention. For the most part they listen to what he has to say, and for that alone he's pretty valuable. Without him, these people would spend more time fighting each other than fighting the Talies and Qaeda."

Monroe leveled his gaze on Graydon. "I want to go."

Graydon was just bringing his mug back to his lips when he stopped and looked at Monroe. "Where? To the conference?" He laughed through his nose as he took a sip.

"I want to go," Monroe repeated firmly. It wasn't a request.

"That's crazy, Jackson. Do you know how many problems that would cause?"

"I want to go," Monroe stated flatly.

"My best flight crews are out on extended missions right now. I couldn't—"

Monroe cut him off. "This isn't a combat mission. I'll take whoever's available." There was a steely glint in his eyes.

Graydon put down his mug and leaned on his elbows. "Is this gonna be a pissing contest?"

Monroe said nothing, but his unwavering stare made it clear that he wasn't going to back down.

"Jackson, I don't know you all that well, but we're the same rank so I'm gonna speak plainly with you. You're an assistant secretary, and the Armed Services Committee loves you, so the Pentagon has to love you. I've already gotten word from CENTCOM to give you whatever the hell you want. I realize you're swinging the bigger dick here."

"Let's not make this personal," Monroe said.

But Graydon raised his finger, indicating that he wasn't finished. "Let me just tell you this, so that afterward you can't say you weren't fully informed. I was invited to that conference myself, but I declined. You want to know why? Because it's being held at a fortress that dates back to the Middle Ages. It's so remote, security cannot be guaranteed up there."

"We have the technology and the weaponry to—"

"*Fuck* technology and weaponry. Maintaining your security would only be part of the problem. I don't know who's been briefing you, but these warlords are a very touchy bunch. *Your* presence at *their* conference could be misinterpreted a hundred different ways. Diplomatically you could end up doing much more harm than good."

"In war, feathers get ruffled," Monroe said. "In time, it's all forgotten."

"Not here, not in Afghanistan. Shifting loyalties doesn't begin to describe how two-faced these people can be. We're convenient allies right now, but if any of these warlords see an advantage to siding with the Taliban, they'll do it. They don't give a shit about oppressive religious regimes. It doesn't affect them."

"That's not how our government views the Northern Alliance," Monroe pointed out.

Graydon's cheeks took on some color. "Of course they don't," he said, raising his voice. "But they should, goddamn it!" When he realized that he'd been shouting, he abruptly shut his trap.

Monroe scooped up some eggs on his fork, not even looking at Graydon. He was waiting for the man to calm down so that he'd fully understand what he was about to say. He cleaned his plate, taking his time about it, watching another F-16 take off. Across the airfield an AC-130H Spectre, a fat monster of a gunship, was being towed into a hangar for maintenance. Monroe calmly sipped his coffee, finally looking at Graydon over the rim of his mug. He enjoyed this.

"I want you to arrange for my transport to the conference, Bill."

Graydon hadn't simmered down all that much, but he had to sit on his temper. Monroe calmly sipped his cofffee. Eating crow didn't make for a very nutritious breakfast, he thought.

"General," Graydon said when he got himself under control, "if that's what you want, that's what you'll have."

"I'd also like someone to accompany me who speaks the tribal languages and knows his way around the warlords."

Oddly, Graydon's face relaxed a bit. "I will give you my best man," he said.

"Thank you. I'm sure he'll be invaluable." Monroe wasn't sure, but he thought Graydon's eyes might be smiling. He let it pass. After all, this wasn't a pissing contest. Monroe knew that he'd won before they even shook hands. "So what's this man's name?" Monroe asked.

5

"TEN-HUT!" Captain Salam called out and saluted as Generals Monroe and Graydon strode into the shade of the hangar. The other eleven men in Salam's Green Beret A-team stopped what they were doing and faced the generals. These were the Berets who would be escorting Monroe to the tribal conference, and they were busy preparing for the trip.

Monroe held the men at attention as he walked slowly in front of them, giving them a good once-over. He didn't like what he saw. The men had all saluted, but they were lackadaisical by Monroe's standards, not exactly what he expected from an elite unit. Of course, this was the SF way. Blood-and-guts bravura took precedent over discipline. Individualism was rewarded in SF. They knew how to work as a team, but their ultimate allegiance was to their unit, not to the Army as a whole.

Monroe prolonged the moment, making them hold the salute like a dog trainer making a mutt remain in sit-stay. He wanted these soldiers to know that he was not impressed by them or their reputation, certainly not the way they were dressed and groomed. Every man had a full beard, ranging from dirty-face short to Abe Lincoln long. They also had a flair for Afghani fashion, adding native flourishes to their basic uniforms. They seemed particularly fond of patterned scarves and those ubiquitous taupe-colored *pakul* hats. They should have cleaned up to see a real three-star.

"At ease," Monroe finally said.

The men dropped their arms and clasped their hands behind their backs, widening their stances. Monroe stepped among them, disdainful, and that's when he noticed it, the medal, a gold star superimposed over a wreath with a spead-winged eagle on top. A Congressional Medal of Honor was pinned to the chest of the sergeant standing next to Salam, a burly black man with a scruffy patch of facial hair. Monroe's first thought was that he shouldn't be wearing medals on his fatigues—medals were reserved for dress uniform—but then he realized. This was for his benefit, to see how he'd react. Army tradition demanded that everyone, regardless of rank, salute the man wearing the Medal. Rank was immaterial in its presence. A five-star would be obligated to salute a cook if he had been awarded the Medal. These jokers might have thought they had reinvented the wheel with this prank, but they hadn't. Monroe had heard stories about this at West Point. Forcing a flag rank to salute an enlisted, it dated back at least as far as the Spanish-American War.

Without hesitation Monroe snapped off a salute to the sergeant whose name tape said "Dover." The man's right hand was bandaged, the last three fingers in curved metal splints.

As Monroe dropped his salute, he glanced at Salam, but Salam stared straight ahead.

"Sergeant Dover," Monroe said, "how did you come to earn the Medal, if I may ask?"

Dover cleared his throat. "Sir, I took out a few Talies."

Graydon stepped in. "Exposing himself to enemy fire, Sergeant Dover ran through a minefield rescuing three wounded men."

Monroe nodded, uninterested. He had seen more valor on money giving days in Vietnam.

"Then," continued Graydon, "he defended against two Taliban units attacking from different directions, while administering emergency aid, saving two soldiers' lives, though he himself was shot. He counted both units, killing eight hostiles, in order to provide a safe LZ for evacuation. The wounded men, including Dover, are doing fine now."

Dover was uncomfortable with the accolades until one of the Berets grunted "Huah!" which prompted a chorus of similar responses. Dover was looking down but grinning.

Monroe glared at the back row where the first "huah" came from. He despised this kind of frat-house behavior. It exemplified everything that was wrong with the SF mind-set.

"Gentlemen," General Graydon said, "I'm sure you all recognize General Monroe. As you know, you will be escorting him to the Northern Alliance tribal conference, and—"

"And," Monroe took over, "you will assure our exit."

Monroe smiled, but the men remained granite-faced. He was sure they'd understood the reference.

The Berets had been packing their gear and ammo when the generals walked in. Just outside the shade of the hangar, two pilots and their respective flight engineers had been checking the two HH-60G Pave Hawk helicopters that were baking in the sun. Two big piles of clear plastic were on the ground near the helos. The flight engineers had been folding them when the generals arrived. Curious as to what they were, Monroe walked back into the sun toward them.

"What are these?" he asked the first pilot he came to. The pilot was a thin man with pronounced cheekbones and a prematurely gray crewcut. The tape over his pocket identified him as "Jenks." Double silver bars gave his rank.

"Sir," Captain Jenks said, "these are fuel bladders."

Monroe stared down at them. "We're going to need these?"

"Yes sir, it's very possible that we will. The air is pretty thin where we're going, sir. Getting off the ground with a fuel load could be near impossible. What we'll do is unload as much fuel as we can spare so we can get off the ground, then suck it back up before we leave."

Monroe looked down at the bladders again. Each one had a thick, coiled black hose attached to it.

"Thank you for the explanation, Captain. Carry on with what you were doing."

"Thank you, sir." Jenks saluted. It was a crisp, professional salute, which pleased Monroe.

Nice to see that they're not all infected with SF fever, Monroe thought as he headed back into the hangar.

"General Monroe," Graydon said to him, "this is Captain Louis Salam. He's the man I was telling you about. You'll be in good hands with him."

Salam was standing at attention next to Graydon. His posture wasn't exactly ramrod straight. Monroe stared at Salam and said nothing. According to what Graydon had said, this was the best man in his command. Salam spoke the languages and more importantly understood how the tribesmen thought. He was supposed to be extraordinarily effective in dealing with the warlords, a highly valued skill set. Well, that was a mark against him in Monroe's book. Graydon had obviously given Salam too much authority. The general should have been dealing with the warlords himself and by himself. Letting a captain negotiate for him sent the wrong message. Americans were not *mujahadeen*. Army is a hierarchy for good reason.

"Pleased to meet you, sir," Captain Salam said. "I had hoped to meet you sooner, but I was detained in the mountains. Speaking for my team, we all look forward to working under your command."

A half-smile crept under Monroe's cheek. *My* command, he thought. My command, indeed.

Salam was clearly waiting for Monroe to extend his hand. It was customary in less disciplined military circles for a ranking officer to shake hands with the junior officer who would actually be leading the impending mission, but Monroe didn't subscribe to that kind of familiarity with the troops.

"I'm happy to have you working for me, Captain," Monroe said. "I'm sure our association will be productive and effective."

"We will guarantee it." Salam ventured a smile, which immediately rankled Monroe. This kind of informality had not been granted nor was it welcomed.

"Captain Salam, we will not be needing your full A-team," Monroe said. "Cut it in half. Six Berets will be sufficient."

"But, sir—"

"Do you have a problem with that, Captain?"

Salam glanced at Graydon, hoping for help, but Graydon held his tongue. Salam pressed his lips together and looked straight ahead. "No sir. I do not have a problem."

"Good, now I—"

"But I fail to see the purpose of splitting our unit," Salam interrupted.

Monroe leveled his gaze on Salam. Salam didn't flinch. "Were you given permission to speak freely, Captain?"

Salam paused for a moment before he responded. "No sir."

"Do you have something you need to say?"

Salam glanced at Graydon again, but Graydon wasn't about to get in the middle of this. "Yes sir," Salam said. "I do have something I need to say, sir."

"Then go on, say it."

"In my opinion, sir, undertaking this mission with half strength is inadvisable. The fortress where the conference will take place is in dangerous terrain. No one really controls it. Your safety and the safety of your party cannot—"

Monroe cut him off. "Captain, this 'mission,' as you put it, is not to assault the fortress. It's not a combat mission. I have been invited to attend a conference of our *allies*. We are their *guests*."

"Sir, we're talking about the warlords. They cannot be completely trusted. . .as hosts."

"Are you saying, Captain, that you know better than the president of the United States and the secretary of state and their many advisors who constructed this alliance?"

The hangar was silent. The other Berets and the specialists assigned to this mission stood at ease but perfectly still, listening with great interest to this exchange, each man privately rooting for Salam while knowing very well that a captain could not possibly get the better of a three-star.

"General," Salam said, "no disrespect intended, but the president and the secretary of state and all their advisors are two continents and an ocean away. We are here, and we deal with these people. Every day."

"So you know more than the president?" Monroe said coolly.

"No sir. I didn't mean to imply that, sir."

The chickenshit was backing down, Monroe thought.

"But what I do know is significant," Salam continued. "And I want to give you every benefit of my knowledge, sir."

The suppressed grins on the faces of Salam's men were almost audible, like squeaky hinges.

Salam was clever. He had scored on a general. But Monroe knew enough to keep the ball in play. Scoring a point—no matter how spectacular—did not decide the game.

"I'm grateful to have the benefit of your extensive knowledge, Captain. Please fill me in on the intricacies of dealing with the warlords. Educate me."

"Right here, sir?"

"Right here."

Everyone waited for Salam's response. The faint drone of an F-16 high overhead filled the silence.

"May I speak freely, sir?" Salam asked.

"Please do."

"Then speaking freely, sir," Salam said, "the warlords are assholes."

"Captain!" General Graydon barked, about to reprimand Salam, but Monroe held up his hand to stop him.

"Continue, Captain," Monroe said. "I'm listening."

"The bottom line, sir, is that the warlords and their men cannot be trusted. Their loyalties blow with the wind. They are not committed to a unified, democratic Afghanistan. They're out for themselves to the exclusion of all other interests."

"Then it's our job, Captain, to reeducate these 'assholes,' as you put it," Monroe said. "We have to show them the benefits of true cooperation."

"With all due respect, sir, that's what we've been trying to do."

"And we will continue to do that. So to that end, we will put our best foot forward at this conference, Captain. We will not go in there like an invading force. We will not take a full A-team. Your men will dress in full Army-issue uniform to show our guests the stellar products of a democratic government. You and your men will also shave and get proper haircuts before we leave."

Feet shuffled, echoing in the cavernous hangar.

"Sir," Salam said, "the beards give us credibility with the *muj*, particularly the religious ones. To them a shaved face is a godless face."

"Accepting diversity among peoples is a big part of democracy. If they truly want to be democratic, they'll deal with us as we are."

Salam was silent, but it was obvious that he didn't agree.

"America is the most advanced culture the world has ever seen," Monroe said, "but you seem to think we should accommodate a civilization that's still living the way it did in the tenth century."

"No sir, I agree that there is no advantage to living like the *muj*."

A few of the men laughed. Even General Graydon cracked a smile.

"Then I'm going to *take* your advice," Monroe said, "and order you and your men to stop living like *mujahadeen*. Pick the men you want, get them groomed to specifications and in proper uniform. We are not going to this conference to fight. We are going as representatives of the United States, and we will look and act like representatives of the United States. Is that understood, Captain?"

Salam let out a long breath. "Understood, sir."

"My assistant Second Lieutenant Reilly, a female reporter, and a female photographer will be accompanying us. Accommodate their inclusion, Captain, which should not be a problem now that our number is where it should be."

"Yes sir."

Monroe scanned the equipment spread out on the floor of the hangar—ammo boxes, assault rifles, duffels, medical kits, rations, and storage containers—but one thing immediately caught his eye. Money. A black duffel bag right behind Salam's boot was unzipped and open, its contents in full view. Thick, shrink-wrapped packets of dollar bills— one-hundred-dollar bills—filled the bag.

Monroe pointed at the cash. "What's that, Captain?"

Salam had to turn around and look down to see what he was referring to. "*Baksheesh*, sir. Bribe money. It sometimes comes in handy dealing with the warlords."

"Leave it."

"But, sir, money is a necessary tool here. It can be a lifesaver."

"Not on this mission. Leave it behind," Monroe said. "That's not how I do things. Do you understand?"

Salam paused. "Understood, sir."

"Good." Monroe spoke to the whole group. "Proceed with your preparations, men." He turned on his toe and headed out of the hangar, walking toward the helos. He was glad he'd gotten this out of the way before they'd left. Salam might be cowboy hero under Graydon, but he was going to be on a short leash while under Monroe's command. Better to rein him in here than out in the field.

6

THIS IS FUCKING LUDICROUS, Salam thought.

He crouched low on the deck of Starwood 1, the lead Pave Hawk, holding a strap in one hand and his rifle in the other, afraid that he might actually lose it on this insane roller-coaster ride. The rotors beat furiously, the helo making frequent small dips and pitches as it worked to maintain altitude in the thin air. The woman reporter, the blonde, was wetting her pants she was so scared. Sergeant Proctor, right next to him, looked down at the mountains from the open bay. He'd been rolling his eyes and shaking his head all the way up here because he knew this was fucking insane too. So did everyone else on board, including Sergeant Amberson from Salam's now bisected A-team, Steve Jenks the pilot, and Corporal Rudge, the flight engineer.

Salam could see Starwood 2 about fifty meters ahead in the lead position. Everyone on that helo knew this was nuts, too...except for maybe that photographer chick and Monroe's lackey, Second Lieutenant Reilly. Green Beret sergeants David Carpenter, Tim Mokely, and Wally Bainbridge were on 2 along with pilot Rob Landry, the intel officer Andy Vitelli, and that pimply flight engineer—Salam couldn't remember his name.

Salam glanced back at General Monroe, sitting in the jump seat and taking in the scenery. He wore dark aviator shades, acting like Douglas fucking MacArthur. The big difference was General MacArthur knew how to lead men in the field. Salam only knew that Monroe gave a good press conference.

It was mid-afternoon, and the camel-hair mountains glowed almost purple. The colors of these mountains changed remarkably throughout the day. By sundown they'd be a deep reddish brown, like the surface of Mars.

Proctor caught Salam's eye and nodded. The helos had just cleared a range of peaks, and suddenly there it was, the fortress. Salam had to admit he was impressed. He'd heard about this place but had never actually seen it. It seemed medieval. Like everything else in this country, it was made out of baked mud bricks and its color blended right in with the mountains. As they flew closer, he could see crenellated battlements atop the walls with round turrets at each corner and a huge courtyard, at least 250 yards long and half that wide. More recent structures had been built inside the walls, and as they approached, he could see hundreds of *muj* clustered around the structures like an infestation of ants.

As they moved in closer, Salam could see two light gray circles about six feet in diameter on the courtyard floor. From the color, he guessed that they'd been made with ash, which stood out against the dusty brown of the courtyard. A couple dozen *muj* on horseback raced around, scrambling between the circles that were on opposite sides of a marked field. The horses were the funny-looking, short-legged native breed, ugly as hell but sure footed on the mountain passes.

Brie Richards leaned forward in her seat, tapped him on the shoulder, and pointed down. "What are they doing?" she shouted in his ear over the racket of the rotors.

"They're playing *bazkashi*," he shouted back. "It's the national sport, sort of like polo."

"The circles are the goals?" she asked.

He nodded. "And the ball is—"

"A headless goat," she finished.

Salam was surprised that she knew. Everyody knew everything now about Afghanistan, since the war. The rotten goat carcass didn't seem to disturb her, which kind of disappointed Salam. He'd wanted to break the news to her and see if she hurled. Maybe she would have hurled on Monroe's nice pressed khakis.

"Captain Salam." The chatter of the two pilots had been in Salam's headset all during the flight, but Steve Jenks, flying this helo, addressed Salam. "The *muj* have cleared a site for landing. They're waving us in. Permission to land."

Salam looked down at the cleared landing space and the three men signaling them in with homemade landing paddles. He looked over at Monroe, who also wore a headset. The general gave him a nod.

"Take us in," Salam said.

"Roger that."

The helo moved forward, then made a ninety-degree turn to the left, hovering in place as it started its descent. Starwood 2 hung back, waiting for Starwood 1 to land. Monroe had insisted that his helo land first—hoping to make a big entrance, no doubt—even after Salam had advised the opposite. If any kind of trouble emerged, Salam would have preferred to have the general in the air for a fast escape. Escorting a senior officer—particularly a very senior officer—was a touchy situation. Normally the commander of the unit, i.e., Salam, ran things because he knew what to do. The senior officer usually sat back and relaxed, confident that the Army had produced a junior officer with enough brains and balls not to fuck it up. But General Monroe micromanaged—not everything but enough to make Salam crazy because he didn't know when to defer to the general and when to just do his goddamn job.

The helo descended slowly and touched down with a double bump. The rotors were still turning, kicking up a cloud of dust.

"Cut the engine," Monroe said into the headset mike. "Too much dust for our hosts."

Salam ground his teeth. Who the fuck cares if we get the *muj* dusty? he thought angrily. Those rotors should be turning, engines running. What if something happens? What if they have to evacuate fast?

The engine noise started to dissipate, and gradually Salam could hear what was going on around him. He unbuckled his harness, checked the safety on his rifle, and stood up, prepared to disembark. Amberson, who'd been stationed on the other side of the helo opposite the open bay, checked the safety on his MP5-A5 submachine gun. They both thought the same thing—cover fire just in case things got crazy.

"Gentleman," Monroe said as he stood up and brushed off his jacket, "shoulder your weapons. These are our *allies*," he said pointedly, looking directly at Salam.

"Yes sir," Salam said. He hitched his weapon over his shoulder. Amberson and Proctor did the same, Proctor furrowing his brow at Salam to show his disagreement.

Monroe moved up behind Salam. "So what have we got here, Captain?"

Salam blinked, dumbfounded by the question. This was a hell of a time for a briefing. Salam had assumed that Monroe would have done his homework long before he got here. As Starwood 2 landed, Salam could see dozens of *muj* just beyond the dust cloud, waiting to swarm like bugs on a couple of Twinkies.

"Well, sir," Salam said, "what we've got here—as I'm sure you know—are contingents from every major tribal group in the country, some who inhabit territories that cross into the other 'stans—Pakistan, Uzbekistan, Tajikistan—"

"Yes, captain," Monroe interrupted, "I know what the 'stans are."

"Yes sir. I was just going to add that you'll find representatives from the Pashtuns, Tajiks, Uzbekis, Aimaks, Hazaras, Kyrgyzs, Baluchis, Pamiris, Nuistanis—"

"Tell me about Zyrous Mohammed. What are your impressions?"

"He's the head of the largest faction within the Pashtun tribe. Right now he's the glue that holds the Northern Alliance together. That can all change next week, but for the past year he's been the big Kahuna. The other tribal leaders respect him, even the ones that don't particularly like him."

"Does he have any rivals?"

"They're all rivals, sir. Each warlord thinks he's king."

"How secure is Zyrous Mohammed in his position?"

"I'd say he's pretty secure for now. The other warlords do listen to him, but from what I've been hearing, he's getting some flak from within his own faction. My sources tell me his second-in-command, a guy named Raz Khan, has been bellyaching about him, stirring up trouble within the Pashtuns. I don't think Khan's got the muscle now, but he might try to make a move somewhere down the line."

"What's this Khan like?"

Salam couldn't help but look at Proctor, who was already making a face.

"Khan is a real pain in the ass, sir," Salam said. "If he were in charge of a faction that big, he'd be a nightmare for us."

"Do you think Zyrous can hold him off?"

"Yes sir, I think he can. Zyrous is very popular."

"What's he like personally?"

"Personally? I haven't had any actual face time with the man. He's a bit elusive that way. But he's a very good speaker and very charismatic in public. I heard one warlord refer to him as Afghanistan's JFK."

Monroe frowned. "Yes, I've been briefed on all that. I want to know what *you* think of him. Gut reactions."

Salam was surprised and flattered that a three-star, especially a hot dog like Monroe, gave a shit about his opinion. "Sir, I think of Zyrous Mohammed as the 'good warlord.' He's as unpredictable and irrational as all the others, but at least he's good to his word. If he looks you in the eye and makes you a promise, you can take it to the bank. I can't say that about any of the others. Just my opinion, sir, but without Zyrous, this coalition would be useless to us. They'd spend more time fighting each other than the Talies and Qaeda."

Monroe nodded. "Thank you, Captain. I appreciate your thoughts."

"Anytime, sir." Salam glanced over at Proctor who raised his eyebrows. Maybe Monroe wasn't such an asshole after all, Salam thought. Maybe he was just half an asshole.

"General?" Lieutenant Reilly ran over from Starwood 2 and stood outside the open bay. "The welcoming party is here, sir."

Hundreds of *muj* had gathered in the courtyard to see the famous American general. It was a sea of bearded ragheads and pakul-heads, all of them carrying rifles. A few of the warlords stood at the front of the mob. Salam figured the others were sulking in their quarters, pulling attitudes. He had no doubt that some of them would insist on Monroe coming to them. But Zyrous Mohammed arrived front and center with

Raz Khan by his side. As usual Khan had his boy Hajji with him, his hand resting on the boy's shoulder.

The passengers from the other helo had disembarked and were waiting for General Monroe to lead their party. The three Berets from Starwood 2—Carpenter, Bainbridge, and Mokely—had spread out to protect their party, but their weapons were pointed up—Lieutenant Reilly's order, no doubt. The photographer chick was already snapping pictures without asking. Salam knew she was going to be a problem the moment he'd laid eyes on her. Corporal Vitelli, the intel officer, just stood there with his thumb up his ass, looking like he'd just sucked a lemon. He impressed Salam as the kind of guy who washed his hands a lot. The flight engineer from Starwood 2, the pizza-faced corporal, had stayed on board the helo with Landry, the pilot. Corporal Rudge would be doing the same with this helo.

Monroe crouched down on the lip of the chopper bay and conferred in private with Reilly for a moment.

Reilly turned to Salam. "Captain," the lieutenant said, "which one is Zyrous Mohammed?"

Salam looked out at the welcoming party. "The guy in the middle," he said. "The one with the dark curly hair and nothing on his head. He's a little better-looking than the rest of these sand rats."

Reilly conveyed the information to Monroe.

"Okay, let's go," Monroe said to the group. He stood up and hopped out of the helo, which pissed off Salam. His men should have gone first, Reilly and Monroe knew that. How the hell were they supposed to protect him if he went running out like fucking Miss America?

Salam, Amberson, and Proctor hustled to form a perimeter around the general as he walked toward Zyrous Mohammed. The warlord had a placid face, but his eyes were intense. He looked directly at Monroe, a slight smile on his thin lips. Khan, on the other hand, had that wise-ass smirk that Salam had come to hate. Monroe walked toward them, and the Berets fanned out around him. Zyrous walked forward, extending his hand. Salam scanned the crowd, looking for trouble. He moved closer to the general, ready to lunge if he had to. Monroe extended his hand to Zyrous.

"Gentlemen," Reilly said, rushing up from behind and motioning for the Berets to move off. "Make way, make way."

Reilly hustled the photographer up to the front, physically moving Proctor and Amberson out of the way.

"What the fuck?" Proctor grumbled under his breath.

Amberson scowled at the lieutenant.

Reilly got the photographer to the front just in time for Monroe's and Zyrous's handshake. The photographer clicked off shot after shot, and Monroe knew how to milk it, hanging onto Zyrous's grip longer than he should have so she could keep shooting. The man was a pro in front of the camera. Square-jawed, tight-lipped smile, glint in the eye—a living, breathing photo op, tailor-made for the front pages.

"Motherfucker," Proctor breathed with disapproving awe.

Monroe kept pumping Zyrous's hand. "I'm so happy to meet you, General Mohammed," he said.

"I am so pleased to meet you as well," Zyrous said in heavily accented English. "I have read very much about you, General. I have heard that you are an expert marksman, that you are a sniper."

Monroe seemed a little taken aback. "Well, yes, I started in the Army as a sniper, but I wouldn't say I'm an expert anymore."

No shit, a sniper, Salam thought. He hadn't known that about Monroe. Heavy-metal guys usually don't cotton to snipers. That's SF work. Extreme SF work.

Zyrous grinned at Monroe. "We have a special surprise for you, General."

"Oh?"

The photographer kept snapping shots.

"What is it?" Monroe asked.

Zyrous pointed up to the high wall that surrounded the fortress. The sun was blinding.

7

MONROE, ZYROUS MOHAMMED, and their respective aides and followers stood on the ramparts of the fortress. The courtyard was down below on one side of the wall, a magnificent panorama of the mountains on the other. A cool breeze wafted in from the snow-covered peaks, fluttering the fabric of the Afghanis' scarves and voluminous pants.

The narrow walkway on the rampart teemed with *mujahadeen*. Zyrous wore a cryptic Mona Lisa smile as Monroe waited for his "surprise." Monroe was curious but not as unsettled as Captain Salam seemed to be. Monroe knew from experience that different peoples had different customs, and he was willing to be patient. Despite the proliferation of weapons present, he did not feel ill at ease. Despite Salam's frantic warnings, Monroe saw the warlords and their soldiers as allies and he intended to treat them as such.

A ripple traveled through the murmuring crowd as one of the *mujahadeen*—an older fighter with a salt-and-pepper beard and a deep scar across his forehead—pushed his way to the front. He carried two rifles, one on his shoulder and one in his hand. Zyrous nodded, pleased with the man's arrival.

"General Monroe," Zyrous Mohammed said, "please accept this humble gift."

The old fighter passed the rifle in his hand to the warlord. Zyrous balanced it on his palms and presented it to Monroe with great ceremony.

"Thank you so much, General," Monroe said as he accepted the gift.

He could hear Brie Richards's stage whisper behind him as she prompted Jane Norcross to take more pictures. Indeed this would make a good shot, he thought. It would show goodwill between the United States and the warlords. More importantly it would show him as the personification of that goodwill.

The rifle, a vintage bolt-action Mannlicher, had a wooden stock worn down from use, but it had been carefully polished to a deep whiskey finish. The rifle had seen a lot of use. From the look of it, it might have actually been in service during World War II. Monroe was very impressed. Unfortunately someone had jerry-rigged a modern scope onto it, a ten-power Unertl with a bullet drop compensator, more than adequate for long-range targeting. Monroe liked the heft of such a fine old instrument in his hands. Examining the tiny scratches on the forestock, he wondered about its history. Who had owned it? How many had it killed and who were they?

Brie Richards called out to him, "How about a demonstration, General?"

He looked over at her, grinned, and shook his head. "Oh, it's been a while since I've handled one of these," he said.

Reilly was standing right next to her. The lieutenant had an uncanny way of conveying his feelings without altering his expression. Monroe sensed that Reilly was in favor of Monroe firing the weapon. A good photo op, no doubt. Reilly was media savvy and had worked summers for his uncle, Alan Hooper, through high school and college until he had signed up for ROTC. Monroe occasionally asked for Reilly's input when it came to shaping his image.

But then Monroe caught Captain Salam's eye, and from the grim look on his face, Monroe deduced that he did not approve of something, which didn't surprise Monroe. Salam disapproved of this entire trip. But Salam didn't understand its purpose, and, of course, he didn't need to. His job was to keep the men in uniform in line and make sure their brief stay at the conference was safe and comfortable. That's all.

"General Monroe." Raz Khan stepped forward. "Like you, I am a shooter," he said in heavily accented English. "But not good like you. Still, I want to shoot with you. A—how you say?—a contest."

Monroe maintained an even expression on his face, even though Khan conveyed an unsettling presence. Something about him was insincere. And a little too obsequious. And what about that boy who never left his side? A boy that age should be more mischievous, more independent, but this child seemed strangely needy.

"What kind of contest did you have in mind?" Monroe asked Khan.

Khan pointed into the distance toward the mountains. "Look there. You see the man with the white flag?"

It took Monroe a moment to locate the man Khan wanted him to see. The man stood on a rocky ledge below their position about eight hundred yards away. His clothes were gray and brown, which blended in with the mountain landscape. A white rag was tied to the barrel of his assault rifle, and he waved it slowly from side to side, high above his head.

"You see the targets?" Khan asked.

Monroe had to use the scope on the Mannlicher to locate the targets. He spun the focus with his middle finger until a pair of clay urns came into view. They were set on a flat boulder about five feet apart. The man with the flag stood off to the left about fifteen feet away. The urns, reddish brown, like the rocks around them, nearly disappeared into the background as a cloud moved off the sun.

Monroe lifted his face from the scope. "As I said, I wouldn't call myself a marksman anymore," he said.

"I am not either," Khan said with a toothy grin. "I just do it for enjoyment."

"I think you're being modest, sir," Monroe said, but Khan didn't understand the word "modest." A tall, younger man who'd been standing behind him translated and Khan roared with laughter.

"Come," he said, motioning to Monroe, "we will play."

Khan opened his arms as he walked forward to shepherd Monroe along. Monroe cooperated, not wanting to look awkward or mistrustful, especially with a camera present. The boy walked on Khan's right as the warlord touched shoulders with Monroe. "Friendly competition," he said. "Maybe I will win. Maybe you."

Monroe had experienced this kind of instant camaraderie from men many times before. It was a staple of the D.C. dinner party circuit. But the most blatant experience he'd ever had came in the summer after he'd graduated from West Point and found himself on leave in Istanbul. A rug merchant in the Grand Bazaar had held him "hostage" for three hours, cajoling him, enticing him, browbeating him, plying him with endless cups of sweet strong tea, using every tactic he knew to get Monroe to buy a rug. Monroe had absolutely no intention of buying a rug that day and was just there to see the ancient, exotic marketplace, but he became fascinated by the man's inventiveness and stamina, so he stayed just to see where it would go. The rug merchant didn't succeed in making a sale, but Monroe wound up with a bursting bladder and a headache that lasted into the next day. It was a lesson he'd carried with him ever since: Know what you want and what you don't want. Resist the hard sell. Learn how to say no and stick to it.

The crowd parted for them as they moved along the rampart, and to Monroe's surprise, an intricately patterned tribal rug was spread out on the ground in front of a one-by-six-foot slit in the wall where it met the floor. It reminded him of the Turkish rug merchant who had instructed his assistants to roll out rug after rug after rug until they were just a dizzying blur of colors and patterns in Monroe's mind. Khan looked over his shoulder and motioned to one of his men, who rushed to the front with another rifle as well as an extra bipod for Monroe's rifle. The man quickly set up Khan's rifle on the rug with the barrel pointed out the slit.

Monroe recognized Khan's weapon instantly, a British-made Parker-Hale M-85 with a fiberglass stock in a camo pattern and a Schmidt & Bender scope—not a weapon for casual shooting on an occasional Sunday afternoon. Monroe's Mannlicher was a '65 Mustang, perfectly adequate. But the Parker-Hale was the Hummer of sniper rifles with a dash of Jaguar thrown in for pedigree, a serious assassination mechanism. When he looked up, Khan grinned at him with smarmy friendliness, a lot like that rug merchant in Istanbul.

Zyrous looked on with an expression of detached amusement. He was a hard one to read, Monroe thought. The man had a regal presence but was in no way intrusive or overbearing. He seemed wise and thoughtful, an old soul in a younger man's body. Monroe guessed that he was somewhere in his forties. Khan appeared to be at least ten years older, but he had none of the charisma of Zyrous. Not surprisingly Zyrous was the leader of the Northern Alliance—Zyrous had real substance; Khan was a rug salesman.

"Please," Khan said, pointing to the rug, "take your position, General. Shoot first if you wish."

But Monroe looked to Zyrous before he did anything. He wanted to forge a relationship with the top gun, not the underling.

Zyrous indicated the rug with his open palm. "We would be honored to see your skills, General," Zyrous said, bowing his head slightly. "But please do not shoot the man." He pointed to the soldier with the rag on the end of his rifle. "He is from my tribe." Zyrous kept a straight face for only a moment.

Everyone laughed.

Except for Salam.

There was nothing to laugh about. He didn't like this setup one fucking bit. Three Berets up on the wall with Monroe and three down in the courtyard with the helos. Not nearly enough men. If the shit came down, they'd be eating it. And Khan with a gun in his hand made him very nervous.

Monroe and Khan got down on the rug and took their sniper positions, flat on their bellies. Monroe smoothed out his pressed khakis as best he could before settling in.

Don't wrinkle your pants, General, Salam thought sarcastically. You're gonna have a hard time finding a *muj* dry cleaner up here.

The sound of Jane Norcross's incessant picture-taking clicked and whizzed in his ear like a pesky mosquito. These were gonna be some pictures, he thought. Two big-ass old guys lying side by side on a rug.

Proctor nudged his arm and handed him a pair of binoculars. "My money's on the Parker," he whispered. "Twenty bucks says Khan makes it in two."

Salam took the binoculars and found the targets. He didn't want to bet on Monroe on principle. Plus, he'd seen Khan shoot, and the son of a bitch was no slouch. On top of that, he had the go-to weapon. But Proctor was a good guy, and a little wager now and then made life interesting. Salam would bet on Monroe, but he wanted the points.

"Monroe in three," Salam said under his breath.

Proctor scowled at him. "Why?'

"He's out of practice. Khan's not."

Proctor made a face but relented. "Okay. You're on."

Monroe squinted down the barrel of his rifle, bracing the stock with his shoulder, face pressed to the cheekpad as he set about to find his zero. "Ready," he said after a moment.

Khan nodded his appreciation. "I am impressed, General. Some men take much longer to prepare."

Monroe didn't answer him. His shot was set up so he wasn't going to move. He took shallow breaths, doing as little as possible so that he didn't screw up his shot.

Salam watched the clay urns through the binoculars. He could feel the breeze on his face. Monroe must have been waiting for it to die down, he thought, recalculating his trajectory to compensate for the wind. Salam prepared for a wait—the old man said he hadn't done this in a while—but surprisingly Monroe squeezed off his shot right away. The rifle made a brittle crack in the cold air, the recoil jolting the general's body. A split second later a puff of pulverized rock rose from the cliff behind the urns. Monroe's shot hit too high by at least five feet.

Khan set up his shot, taking his good sweet time about it. Finally ready, he pulled the trigger. His gun gave a louder report, which startled Brie Richards and made her flinch.

Jane Norcross, who kept her camera to her face, hissed, "Yes!" at the sound of the gutsier report.

Salam kept his eye on the urns and saw another puff of powdered rock about a foot and a half to the left of the urn on the left.

"Close but no cigar," Salam whispered to Proctor.

Proctor snorted.

Monroe adjusted the windage and elevation knobs. Salam kept his eyes on the urns, secretly pulling for Monroe despite the fact that he couldn't stand the guy because right now he was the underdog.

Crack! Monroe fired.

His bullet went high again. Salam saw where it hit the rocks. Monroe had practically duplicated his first shot. Maybe his eyesight, Salam thought. After all, the guy was over fifty. But then again so was Khan.

"Too bad," Khan said, his face pressed to his weapon. He'd watched Monroe's miss through his scope. "Perhaps Allah is not smiling on you today, General."

Khan took less than ten seconds to find his zero and pull the trigger.

Bam!

Salam peered through the binoculars. The urn on the left shattered. The top half was gone, the bottom just a jagged fragment. The man on the cliff waved his rifle and his free arm frantically to verify the hit. The *muj* up on the wall cheered and whooped like coyotes, shaking their fists in triumph and celebration.

"You would have thought he'd knocked a homer over the Green Monster at Fenway," Proctor grumbled, laying on his Boston accent thicker than usual.

Khan nodded with satisfaction as he pulled himself to his knees. "Allah is smiling on *me* today," he crowed.

"Congratulations," Monroe said. He started to get up off the rug.

"Stay, stay, General," Zyrous urged. "You are our guest. Please shoot again."

Khan shot him a dirty look as if Zyrous were deliberately trying to steal his thunder, but Zyrous ignored him. Monroe got back down into position and readjusted the knobs.

Come on, Salam thought with his eyes to the binoculars. Come on, General. Score one for us.

Monroe took his time before he pulled the trigger. Salam's eyes were glued to the remaining urn.

Crack!

Salam's heart stopped in the split second it took for Monroe's bullet to cross the long distance to the cliff. He willed the bullet to find its target, willing the urn to break.

But it didn't.

The shot hit low, striking the rocks about ten feet below the urn. Monroe had overcompensated.

Fuck! Salam thought.

The *muj* cheered for Khan, who pumped his fist over his head. Monroe stood up and congratulated him. They shook hands, both men smiling broadly for the camera.

What the fuck was wrong with him? Salam thought. Didn't Monroe know he'd lost?

Jane's camera kept whizzing and clicking, annoying the hell out of Salam. Proctor looked over at him. Proctor had won the bet, but from the bittersweet look on his face, he clearly would have rather lost the twenty and have their guy kick Khan's ass.

When the photo op finally ended, Monroe picked up his rifle and motioned for Proctor to come forward. "Sergeant?"

Proctor stepped lively and saluted. "Yes sir."

"Stow this for me." He handed Proctor his gift.

"Yes sir." Proctor hitched the sniper rifle over his shoulder. "Do you want it in Starwood one, General?"

"That'll be fine."

Proctor caught Salam's eye as he turned to go. Salam was fuming. He didn't like Monroe treating his A-team like errand boys.

8

THAT NIGHT, after a feast of roasted goat and couscous, the *mujahadeen* representatives at the conference assembled in the courtyard to hear the warlords speak. Monroe, their honorary guest, sat on a metal folding chair on a makeshift wooden stage with several of the top warlords who mainly smiled and nodded to him because they didn't speak any languages in common. Except for a sickle moon hanging over the mountains, the sky was a blank canvas of midnight blue. The courtyard thrummed with hundreds of men, their burnished faces illuminated by dozens of burning torches. It was a restless crowd, and though Monroe didn't completely understand the particulars of the shifting relationships within and among the factions, their collective edginess created an unmistakable tension.

Monroe had agreed to address the assembly. Unfortunately he was fighting jet lag and struggling to stay alert. Even the extra-caffeinated soft drinks he'd been guzzling since he'd arrived weren't doing the trick anymore. Still, he wasn't worried. He'd made speeches at black-tie galas on less sleep. Anyway this wouldn't be a long speech, just a rousing show of support—brothers in arms, strong allies, common goals, freedom for all peoples, that sort of thing. He just hoped he didn't look tired and haggard when he took the dais. Jane Norcross was odd, and he wasn't sure if she could be trusted to do the right thing. Monroe hoped Brie was keeping her in line, making sure she snapped solid shots that conveyed the right message as opposed to the kind of artsy, off-beat candids that could be embarrassing or worse, damaging.

He suppressed a yawn as he scanned the crowed. The scene could have come right out of the tenth century if it weren't for the automatic weapons and the flak jackets. The torches cast an eerie, other worldly glow over the proceedings. The crowd moved continuously, faceless bodies slipping in and out of the shadows. Brie and Ms. Norcross stood at the edge of the stage with Lieutenant Reilly and one of the Berets. Brie wore a *pakul* at a stylish angle. Ms. Norcross was in jeans and a thin t-shirt with only a pocket-laden fisherman's vest keeping her from completely offending the more religious Muslims in the crowd. He'd told Reilly to get her to cover up a little more, but she'd apparently disregarded the request. Captain Salam was posted at the side of the stage, just a few feet away. The other Berets took positions around the courtyard, two of them up on the wall. Salam had insisted on men up there, but Monroe didn't like the impression it made, that the Americans didn't trust the warlords. Monroe had gone along with it only because Graydon had assured him that Salam knew the territory and besides, he was just too tired to argue the point.

Brie Richards was doing all she could to get his attention, but he deliberately ignored her. A sweet girl and very pretty in that well-bred, Southern way, she knew how to flirt subtly to get what she wanted. Monroe had to admit he'd found her very attractive when he first met her, but she was a kid compared to him, and he loved his wife too much to embarrass them both with a meaningless affair. Still, the attentions of a woman in her twenties are never unwelcome to a fifty four-year-old man. When he finally looked at her, she flashed her million-dollar smile. He nodded back, offering the slightest of smiles. He certainly didn't want to encourage her.

The warlords on stage with him ran the gamut from surly to unctuous, but they had all been very welcoming to him. Surprisingly Raz Khan had not yet arrived. However, Khan's lieutenant, Yusef, the young man who spoke English so well, was conferring in private with Zyrous at the side of the stage. From the looks on their faces, Yusef seemed to be making excuses about something to a clearly displeased Zyrous.

Khan finally arrived, pushing his way through the crowd to the front of the stage, calling out in his native language as he approached. He stopped dead when he realized he was pressed up against the backs of the two American women. He scowled and pushed his way around them, climbing to the stage with more agility than Monroe expected from him. But Monroe knew not to equate a gray beard with diminished skills. Quite the contrary as Khan had proved earlier up on the ramparts.

Khan took his seat next to Monroe, and Yusef immediately hopped off the stage and disappeared into the crowd.

"My apologies," Khan said to Monroe. "A small crisis."

"Is everything all right?" Monroe asked.

"Oh, fine, fine. All fixed now. No problem."

Monroe nodded, not knowing what else to say. It would be impolite to prod for more information.

Zyrous went over to Monroe. "I will say a few words first," he said. "Then I will introduce you, General."

"That's fine," Monroe said.

"Our men are very excited to hear what you have to say," he said. "They know you are a hero to America. They want you to be *our* hero, too."

"It makes me very happy to hear you say that," Monroe said. He knew Zyrous was bullshitting him, but at least Zyrous had a nicer way of doing it than Khan. Zyrous would fit right in if he ever found himself in Washington.

Zyrous walked to the front of the stage and raised his arms over his head, calling for silence. Instead he received wildly enthusiastic cheers that lasted at least a full minute. Monroe tried not to seem too impressed. Considering the tenuous bonds that kept this coalition together, this was an extraordinary response. All the intelligence reports agreed that Zyrous might just keep the Northern Alliance together, and for what it was worth, Captain Salam concurred with that assessment.

Suppressing another yawn, Monroe glanced over at Salam, who scanned the crowd, his expression terribly stern and grim. Salam was distrustful beyond reason, Monroe felt, and that's why Monroe did not take all his advice at face value. Whether his attitude resulted from his upbringing or his experiences here was immaterial. Monroe wondered if perhaps he was just negative by nature, knowing that this attitude would surely keep Salam from rising above his current position. In any given situation Salam immediately saw the bad side but lacked the vision to see beyond that. He was a tactician rather than a strategist, and that would hold him back in the Army. The Northern Alliance certainly wasn't perfect, comprised of flawed individuals, but the fact that it existed at all was useful and potentially beneficial to the United States. Salam obviously didn't see it that way.

The cheering started to die down. Zyrous silenced them with a hawk-eyed look, his expression changing instantly from benign to fierce. He had the profile of a bird of prey. He started to speak in Dari, his penetrating voice reverberating off the mud-brick walls of the fortress.

Salam climbed onto the stage and crouched down beside Monroe. "Would you like me to translate, sir?"

"Yes, please."

"He's greeting them tribe by tribe, mentioning each warlord by name," Salam said.

Zyrous raised a clenched fist and shook it at the night sky as his voice boomed through the courtyard without the benefit of a microphone.

"'*We* are Afghanistan!'" Salam translated. "We are not the Taliban. We are not Al-Qaeda. We are the *real* Afghanis!'"

The crowd erupted, fighters yelling until they were hoarse, waving their arms and shaking their weapons furiously.

Zyrous raised his hands to quiet them down and continued his speech.

"'Together we are strong,'" Salam translated. "'In the past the world has picked us clean like a carcass in the desert, but no more.'"

More wild cheers, louder than before.

"'The sadness of our history will not come to pass ever again. We will rule and thrive in what is rightfully ours. We are the just and the righteous. And we have the United States with us.'"

Another wild outburst of cheers.

"'The United States of America is our brother,'" Salam interpreted. "'And a united Afghanistan is *their* brother. Their enemies are *our* enemies, and our enemies are *their* enemies. We will fight together as a family of brothers and emerge victorious.'"

The uproar doubled in intensity. Monroe focused on one *mujahadeen* who stood at the skirt of the stage, a broad-shouldered man with a wide face and a flat nose. The man bellowed his support, his deep voice cutting through the clamor, but oddly he didn't look joyous, his expression tough and no-nonsense. Monroe noticed that many of the *mujahadeen* lacked enthusiasm. With war such a constant in the history of Afghanistan, they seldom had much to celebrate.

Zyrous continued his speech, holding the assembly in his thrall. Salam dutifully interpreted, speaking in Monroe's ear. But Monroe, still exhausted from the trip, only half listened. He gazed out at the crowd, his attention wandering, going from face to face, most of them indistinguishable in the shadows. He scanned the high walls, where more torches burned. The two Berets stood thirty yards apart on the wall facing the stage. Monroe stifled yet another yawn, struggling to keep his eyes open, knowing that it would be his turn to speak next. He rubbed his eyes and blinked them back into focus. He rolled them right and left, and that's when he noticed something.

On the wall to his left, near the corner, about forty yards away. In the weak torchlight, he thought he saw a rifle barrel poking out from one of the crenellations. He didn't trust his eyesight in this light, and the Berets must have checked the ramparts before the event began, he told himself. Nevertheless, in Vietnam he'd been trained to spot a hide.

He opened his mouth, about to mention his suspicions to Salam when he thought better of it. It's the fatigue, he told himself. Just my imagination.

But he couldn't take his eyes off that spot. The torchlight was too weak to make a positive identification, but he could swear he saw something up there, something barely discernible in the flickering flames.

"Captain," he said to Salam, speaking into his ear, "did your men inspect the entire wall—?"

Bam!

The crack of a gunshot instantly silenced him. He saw the muzzle flash up on the wall where he'd been looking. Salam immediately got in front of him to protect him. The crowd went silent for a split second. Zyrous collapsed onto the stage in a broken heap. The front of his head and half of his face had exploded, his exposed brain glistening in the torchlight. His closest aides immediately ran to his side, blocking Monroe's view. But Monroe didn't need confirmation. No one survives a headshot like that.

The sound of the shot echoed in Monroe's mind. *Bam!. . . Bam!. . . Bam!. . .*

The Parker-Hale, he thought. Khan's gun.

"Stay with me, sir," Salam was saying. "Stay close."

The crowd of *mujahadeen* suddenly became an enraged mob, the roar of their raw emotions pitiful and frightening. Monroe could feel the volume reverberating off his skin.

Khan's lieutenant Yusef jumped up onto the stage and started yelling to the crowd in Dari, his face a devil mask in the fire light, his eyes wild. He pointed up at the wall where the shot had come from, then pointing back at Monroe. Yusef shouted in Dari, but Monroe picked out one word, "American."

Monroe stood up. "What's he saying, Captain?"

"He's saying that we did it, that we shot Zyrous. He's repeating it in Pashto and Uzbeki. He's riling them up."

Yusef turned and faced Monroe. "You!" he shouted in English. "You did it! You ordered your men!"

Salam removed his sidearm from its holster and pressed it into Monroe's hand. "You may need this, sir," he said.

Mujahadeen swarmed the stage. Monroe noticed the man with the broad face and the fierce look as he mounted the stage with several others, leading with his assault rifle. The crowd wanted revenge.

"Sir? *Sir?*" Salam had to shout to be heard. "I suggest we evacuate, sir. May we evacuate, sir?"

Images spun before Monroe's eyes.

"Sir, may we evacuate?" Salam yelled. "I need an answer now, sir. *Sir!*"

9

SALAM GRABBED the general by the upper arm and led him to the rear of the stage, where they jumped off. Proctor met them there. He had his MP5-A5 in his hands, but so far no one had started shooting.

"The women," Monroe said. "Where are the women?"

"Don't worry about them, General," Proctor said. "We've got them covered. Let's worry about you."

Salam barked into his headset microphone: "Starwood One and Two, start your engines. Repeat, start your engines. We're getting the fuck out of here."

"No," Monroe said. "Rescind that order. We can't leave now. I saw a sniper up on the wall. We have to tell them."

"The *muj* aren't in a talking mood right now, sir." Salam started moving toward the helos, hustling Monroe along with him. "Please stay close, sir."

Proctor and Salam altered their positions and made a General Monroe sandwich, Proctor leading and facing forward, Salam trailing and facing backward, Monroe pressed between them.

On the stage, Yusef had gotten hold of a bullhorn. "Do not let them escape!" he yelled in Dari. "Do not let them escape!" he repeated it in Pashto, then Uzbeki, then Tajik.

The front line of *mujahadeen* had overrun the stage and was charging hard. Salam detached a concussion grenade from his belt, pulled the pin, and tossed it.

"Here," he growled at the *muj*. "Go fuck your mothers."

The grenade hit the ground and skittered to the feet of the charging *mujahadeen*.

BOOM!

The force of the explosion threw Salam into Monroe's back. Toppled *muj* rolled on the ground. The ones still standing backed off, but Salam knew that would only be temporary. Monroe yelled something at him, but he couldn't hear what the general said, deaf from the explosion. He felt as if someone had wrapped wet towels around his head. He knew it would take a few moments for him to regain his hearing. In the meantime he kept moving backward, shoving Monroe along.

He glanced over his shoulder and saw the rotors of the two helos beginning to pick up speed.

"This is Gator One," Salam shouted into his mike. "Where are you and what's your status, Gators? Talk to me, all of you."

The voices came back one by one in his ear.

Gator Two was Proctor. "Gator Two right in front of you, Gator One, marching the general double time."

Amberson: "Gator Three on the steps coming down from the north wall."

Mokely: "Gator Four right behind Gator Three."

Bainbridge: "Gator Five with Lieutenant Reilly and the lady reporter. We're clear of the mob near the west wall, circling wide to get to transport."

Carpenter: "Gator Six with the photog, ten yards to the left of your position, Gator 1, heading for transport."

Salam looked right as he stepped backward. Gator Six was dragging Ms. Norcross by the collar of her vest. Camera to her face, she snapped off as many shots as she could.

Stupid cunt! Salam thought angrily. She's gonna get him killed.

"Use your grenades as needed," Salam said into the mike. "Fire your weapons only if fired upon."

A few moments later another concussion grenade went off at the back of the crowd near the north wall, followed by the low *thwump* of a smoke grenade. Thick yellow smoke filled the air. It didn't take long before Salam couldn't see the north wall at all in that sector. Gators Three and Four, who were farthest from the helos, wanted to create some chaos, so they could carve an exit path for themselves.

Automatic gunfire in three-shot bursts crackled from somewhere in the distance, but the whipping of the rotors prevented Salam from determining the point of origin. It really didn't matter. Every one of those sons of bitches had a weapon. It wouldn't be long before they all started firing.

"Return fire at will!" he shouted into the microphone.

"Rescind that order," Monroe shouted in Salam's ear. "I mean it." The general had turned around completely and stopped running.

Salam ignored him, pretending he couldn't hear. He plowed his back into Monroe and forced him to move.

Increased gunfire came from the *muj*, single shots and short bursts. "Gator Two, change positions with me. Make 'em sorry they weren't born women."

Proctor fell back and took the rear position as Salam took Monroe's arm again and pulled him toward the nearest helo. Proctor used his weapon skillfully but judiciously, firing in bursts within a ninety-degree wedge. He wanted to scare them off more than effect maximum casualties, but if things got any hairier, he'd do whatever was necessary to secure their escape.

Salam looked past Monroe and saw Carpenter still struggling with that damn photographer who wouldn't stop trying to take pictures. Just shoot the bitch, Salam thought.

"Positions and conditions," he shouted into his mike.

Their voices came back in order.

"Gator Two with Gator One, making *muj* Swiss cheese."

"Gator Three approaching Starwood Two from the west."

"Ditto Gator Four. We're together, Captain."

"Gator Five inside Starwood Two with Lieutenant Reilly and the reporter."

"Gator Six approaching Starwood One on your flank. This civilian is one pain in my ass, Captain."

Salam wanted to tell Carpenter to leave her. Instead he said, "Do whatever you have to, Gator Six. She'll be thanking you later."

Now that he knew where all his men were, Salam used his remaining three grenades, first the concussion, then the two smokers. He pitched the concussion into the midst of the charging *muj,* and the explosion left a bald spot in their attack. He quickly tossed out the smoke grenades, but the beating rotors of the helos blew the yellow smoke away from where it was needed. Another concussion went off farther down the line, then a second and a third. His men gave the *muj* an old-fashioned Fourth of July. The main body of attackers hadn't penetrated the area around the helos yet.

"Everybody on board," Salam shouted into his mike. "Pilots prepare for takeoff."

"Captain," a new voice came through his headset. Lieutenant Landry, one of the pilots. "This is Starwood Two. We're still attached to our bladder, Captain. Most of our fuel is offloaded."

"Starwood One reporting," Jenks, the other pilot, said. "Same sit, Captain. We won't get very far on what we've got."

"Can you get us out of the fortress?" Salam shouted. Enemy fire picked up again. He spun around and returned fire.

"We can get out of the fort, but then what?" Jenks said. "Can't land in the mountains."

"And we sure as hell can't stay here," Salam said. "Prepare to take off on my order. Everyone on board on the double."

Smoke swirled in the rotor wind. Stray bullets tore up divots in the dirt. The *muj* yelled and screamed like a mob of rabid baboons. "Come on, General," Salam shouted to Monroe. "Run!" He grabbed a fistful of Monroe's jacket and made a run for Starwood One. He tried to force the general into a broken-field run, but the old man resisted. The shortest distance to your own funeral is a straight line, dickwad, Salam thought.

By some miracle or just sheer *muj* incompetence, Salam and Monroe made it to Starwood One. Monroe dove in through the bay, and Salam helped him up, pushing him across the deck on his belly. Salam jumped in next and crouched on the deck, firing at the *muj* on full auto as Proctor scrambled on board. The taste of fuel fumes clung to the roof of Salam's mouth and burned his throat. Big as a sea lion, the bloated plastic bladder sat underneath the helo, still attached to the fuel tank. Gunfire had already punctured it in several places where small geysers gushed. Rudge, the flight engineer, worked on disconnecting the bladder from the tank. Salam kept firing into the charging crowd to give him cover.

"Status," Salam shouted into his mike. "I want everyone accounted for."

"Gator Two right with you, Gator One."

"Gator Three on board Starwood Two."

"Gator Four on board Starwood Two."

"Gator Five also on board Starwood Two with Lieutenant Reilly, the reporter, and our pilot. Gator Six has just climbed aboard, but he's been wounded. His leg."

"Where's the photographer, Gator Five?"

"No sign of her, Captain."

"Fuck!" Salam said.

Then he spotted her, running in a crouch across the terrain between the helos.

Stupid bitch is gonna get her ass blown off, he thought. And she deserves it.

Somehow Jane Norcross made it to the open bay. "Is the general here?" she shouted. But as she asked the question, she spotted him in the back, scrambled onto the deck, and started taking pictures of him.

Salam felt like shoving her back out. Her drag-ass antics had gotten Carpenter shot. Salam scanned the interior of the helo to see who was there. Monroe and the shutter bitch crouched together, out of the line of fire. Proctor, down on one knee, fired out the open bay. Vitelli, the candy-ass intel officer, sat in a jump seat by himself, looking very annoyed. Rudge, who had come aboard, sat up front with the pilot. The other flight engineer, the pimply corporal with the white-blond high-and-tight, crouched between them up front.

"Corporal!" Salam roared.

The kid spun around to face Salam. "Sir." His hands trembled.

Salam wondered if this kid had any combat experience other than on a GameBoy. He read the name tape over the pocket of his coveralls. "Corporal Canfield, what in the *fuck* are you doing over here? You're supposed to be with Starwood Two."

"Yes sir. I know, sir. I . . . I was just visiting when. . . when—"

"When the shit started to fly?"

"Yes sir."

"You had better hope your helo gets off the ground and gets those people out of here or I'm holding you personally responsible. You read me, Canfield?"

"Yes sir. I understand." He shook like a puppy in a thunderstorm.

The acid smell of fuel choked the air inside the helo.

Salam did a mental recount to make sure everyone was accounted for, then gave the green light. "Gator One to all personnel. Everyone is accounted for. Let's get the hell out of here."

"Roger, Gator One," Lieutenant Landry said. "Starwood pilots will take over the frequency for takeoff. Starwood One, you're cleared for takeoff. Get your ass in the air quick, buddy. We're coming up right behind you."

"Roger, Starwood Two. Star One is outta here."

The engines revved higher, and Salam could feel their sudden liftoff in the pit of his stomach. The helo seemed to be struggling, even without their fuel load. It was the thin air.

"Floor this mother," he yelled.

Proctor fired out the bay nonstop. A gang of *muj* made a suicide run toward them, firing wild. Proctor tried to hold them off. One gangly *muj* with an AK popped up out of nowhere, coming up from underneath the helo. He stood right outside the open bay, his chest level with the deck. He swung the barrel of his rifle into the interior of the helo and opened fire. Salam fired simultaneously, riddling the man's head and killing him instantly.

"Captain!" Salam heard Corporal Canfield's screeching cry. He looked into the cockpit and saw the pilot slumped against the blood-spattered window, blood trickling from his neck. Rudge held the stick from the copilot's seat. The helo started to rise faster, but it was teetering. Canfield clawed Rudge's seatback, holding on for dear life.

"Move!" General Monroe shouted. He pushed past Salam and hauled Canfield out of his way by the scruff of the neck. He got half his ass into the pilot's seat, shouldering Jenks aside, and took the stick. The deck pitched backward violently. Salam fell on his hip and slid into the photographer's legs. Monroe leveled off quickly, and the helo started to rise faster as enemy fire clinked into the metal hide underneath.

The man's got his wings, Salam thought, staring at the back of Monroe's head. I just hope he flies better than he shoots.

Starwood One hovered over the angry mob, taking more gunfire and sounding like an old tin can.

Come on, General, Salam urged. Get us the fuck out of here!

IO

SWEAT POURED DOWN Monroe's brow, getting in his eyes. He had to force himself to keep his touch light on the stick. Helo controls are more than hair trigger—you didn't move the stick, you just *thought* about moving it and that was enough to control the craft.

He wanted to spit the taste of the fumes out of his mouth, but he didn't dare divert his attention from the controls. His head spun with concerns for the safety of everyone on board, for the man bleeding out next to him, for Zyrous Mohammed and the diplomatic fallout his assassination could cause. Would the warlords really try to pin this on Monroe and the United States government? The notion was insane, but he couldn't think about that right now. He had to fly this goddamn helo, but its response was sluggish and difficult. He felt as if they were dragging a dump truck.

He could feel the jolt of bullets in his feet as they hit the underside of the fuselage. Captain Salam and Sergeant Proctor did their best to hold the *mujahadeen* at bay, but hostile fire came in from multiple directions.

The flight engineer had his hand poised to take the stick. "Do you want me to take over, General?" His voice was extraordinarily deep and booming, his accent unmistakably deep South.

"No," Monroe shouted back. "I have it."

Monroe reached over to the bleeding pilot, yanked his headset off, and managed to get it on his own head one-handed.

"This is General Monroe at the controls in Starwood One," he said into the microphone.

He could see the closest fortress wall on his right. The helo had risen even with the battlements but couldn't seem to get high enough to clear them. Monroe swung the helo ninety degrees to the right so that he faced the wall. "Come on," he grunted, working the helo to work harder. Another six feet—that's all he needed to clear the top of the wall.

He concentrated on the controls in front of him. He had to block out everything else and get in the zone. He remembered conjuring up this same kind of intensity back in Vietnam whenever he had set up a sniper shot in a concealed hide. Nothing else mattered, just the task at hand. Even if Armageddon breaks out all around, a professional must remain an island of calm and precision. He just does the job he's assigned.

Monroe glanced out the window to his side and saw something that made his stomach knot. Starwood Two hovered twenty feet off the ground but with its fuel line still attached to the bladder. A puddle of fuel darkened the dusty earth around it, still more full than empty despite the bullet holes.

"Starwood Two! Cut your fuel line! You are still attached to your bladder. Repeat, cut your fuel line!"

The corporal who'd been cowering behind the copilot's seat popped up and gazed out the windshield. His face crumpled like a piece of paper, horror filling his eyes. As the flight engineer of Starwood Two, maintaining the bladder had been his job. Apparently no one else on board had thought to detach it.

Starwood Two kept rising, taking up more of the fuel line, but eventually it would run out of lead and the bladder would keep it from rising any farther.

"Starwood Two!" Monroe shouted. "Do you read me? Starwood Two, you're still tethered to the bladder. You must detach it immediately."

Monroe glared at Corporal Canfield. "How do they do it? How do you detach that line?"

Canfield had fucked up badly, and he wouldn't look Monroe in the eye. His face red and clenched, he looked everywhere but at Monroe.

"This is an order, Canfield," Monroe yelled. "How do you detach that line?"

"Sir," Canfield shouted over the noise of the beating rotors, "y-y-you can only do it from the outside, sir. That's the only way."

Monroe looked to Rudge, the other engineer. "Is there another way?" he shouted.

But as Monroe asked the question, he noticed something down on the ground, a lone *mujahadeen* fighter down on one knee sighting down the barrel of a grenade launcher aimed at Starwood Two's bladder.

Monroe quickly maneuvered his Starwood One, spinning it so that the open bay faced the man. "Take that man out!" he shouted into his microphone. "Salam! Proctor! The soldier with the grenade launcher. Take him—"

Too late. A grenade shot out of the tube and sailed across the courtyard, leaving a wispy trail in its wake. It hit the bladder dead on, the explosion igniting the fumes. A column of fire and black smoke shot into the air and enveloped the Starwood Two. The fiery craft teetered and pitched, then a second, sharper-sounding blast shattered the air and rocked Monroe's helo. Starwood Two's near empty fuel tanks erupted. They must have been full of fumes, optimum condition for maximum damage. Chunks of metal and burning debris rained down on the *bazkashi* field. The rotor blade detached and sailed like a spear into the main body of the *mujahadeen*.

The Afghani soldiers scattered, crashing into one another as they ran from the descending hull of the burning helo. Monroe saw it go down. It happened in an instant yet the moment seemed to stretch on into infinity, like a horrible memory. The helo pitched forward and dropped nose first, the tail rotor still spinning but useless. Flames streaked the sides of the hull and sparks plumed from the tail like a falling meteor. It spun as it descended, as if it wanted to drill itself into the ground, but when it crashed, the ground didn't give, crushing the nose. The tail snapped off, flipping over onto the main rotor stump, attached only by a hinge of sheet metal. Monroe felt the violent shock wave reverberate through his body. He immediately thought of Lieutenant Reilly and Brie Richards and the Berets. The collision must have sent them all hurtling toward the cockpit.

Oh, Jesus, he thought.

"General," Rudge shouted to him, pointing toward the wall. "You can clear it now, General. We can go."

Monroe nodded, immediately getting back in the zone. Starwood Two had crashed, survivors highly unlikely. His job now: Getting Starwood 1 out of there. He turned the helo and faced the wall head-on. Unfortunately enemy rounds had turned the windows at his feet into intricate spider-webs, impossible to see through. "Salam, Proctor, watch my bottom," he said into his headset.

Monroe worked the stick and moved the helo forward. Glancing over his shoulder he could see the two Green Berets on the deck, Proctor holding Salam's ankles as he hung out the bay, eyeballing the underside of the craft.

Salam's voice came through Monroe's headset: "You look good, general. Keep it coming."

Monroe guided the helo forward slowly. "What's my clearance?"

"About two feet. Keep her level."

Monroe willed himself to stay calm. His brain, not his hand, had to work the stick.

"Keep her coming," Salam said. "You're looking good."

Suddenly Monroe felt enemy fire peppering the sheet-metal skin of the helo, and he jerked the stick ever so slightly. The helo lurched forward in response. He heard a loud scraping noise.

"Salam! Talk to me."

"Your port landing skid knocked off a piece of the wall, General. Don't worry. They'll send you the bill."

"Cut the jokes, Salam, and get your head inside the craft."

"But you need my eyes on—"

"I said get your head inside, captain. I need you alive."

"Yes sir," Salam said.

But Monroe knew from the smart-alecky tone of Salam's voice that the insolent son of a bitch hadn't moved, but Monroe didn't dare look over his shoulder to check. Did Salam want to get shot? Monroe thought as he worked the stick. Or did he want Proctor to get shot and drop him? Suicidal sons of bitches, all of them.

Salam's voice came over Monroe's headphones, "The skids are over the wall, General. You're good to go."

Fuck you! Monroe thought. Salam had disobeyed a direct order and stayed outside the helo.

The regrouped *mujahadeen* fired up at them full force. Monroe remembered the man with the grenade launcher and hightailed it away from the fortress, fearing a repeat of the downing of Starwood Two. Monroe managed to get the Pave Hawk moving despite the high altitude. He headed straight toward the nearest mountain, then banked sharply west toward the downward slope and the route they'd taken to get here.

He glanced at the patch on Rudge's sleeve to get his rank. "Which way, Corporal? What's our best option?"

Rudge leaned forward and tapped the fuel gauge with his finger. Empty. Most of their fuel had been off-loaded, and it must have taken quite a bit to get her off the ground.

"We have to find someplace to land, General," Rudge said. "Fast."

Monroe didn't like Rudge's know-it-all tone. Rudge looked like a plow boy from the middle of nowhere but spoke with the kind of supercilious politeness that Southern blacks had made their own.

"Where do you suggest we land, Corporal? Find me a place."

Rudge just looked out the windshield as if the answer should have been obvious. There was no place to land. The rocky landscape sloped precipitously for as far as Monroe could see. It leveled off a bit in places, but he couldn't see any clearings that would do them any good.

Salam stuck his head in the cockpit. He'd overheard Monroe's question through his headset. "The road," he said, pointing to a steep and bumpy dirt road that led up to the fortress. "It's our only option."

"The tribesmen will be on us in no time if we land there," Monroe protested. "Find someplace else."

"General," Salam said, "there is nowhere else."

"There has to be somewhere else, and I'm going to find it." Monroe revved the engines and put the helo into overdrive, skimming over the treetops.

"General, what're you doing?" Salam said.

Rudge tapped on the fuel gauge again. "Slow down, General. You're eating up fuel."

Monroe ignored them both and picked up speed. He kept thinking about the man with the grenade launcher and all the other men down there with grenade launchers. He had to get as far away from the fortress as possible. He would go around the mountain to the other side where he imagined there would be a treeline and that's where he'd find a clearing large enough to land. A clearing with a pine-needle floor. They could camouflage the helo with pine branches, then hole up there until reinforcements arrived from Gardiz.

"General, there are no clearings this high up," Salam said. "I checked the maps before we set out."

"General, *please* slow down," Rudge said with a crying note in his voice. "We'll have less than five minutes of fly time at this rate of speed."

"General!"

"General!"

Rivulets of salty sweat snaked into Monroe's eyes. He swiped his brow with the back of his hand, then tore off his headset. He didn't want to hear them. They confused him, and anyway they didn't understand. He had to get as far from the enemy as possible. Salam's option—landing on the road—would get them killed, and Rudge worried about only the machine, not the situation. Monroe would make the helo perform. There'd be a clearing on the other side of the mountain, and he'd find it.

But as he rounded the mountain, Monroe's heart sank lower and lower. No clearings in sight. The trees thinned out, showing more rocks and boulders and cliffs and ravines. The sun shone in his eyes, mocking him.

"General!" Rudge pointed to the oil pressure gauge. The needle sank steadily.

The engine started to miss, engaging and disengaging. The needle on the fuel gauge dipped below the empty mark. The engine wheezed, and Monroe's heart leapt. They started to lose altitude.

"General!" Salam and Rudge kept yelling. "General! General!"

The engine conked out completely, and the noise level suddenly decreased to near silence. The rotors still spun, but only by virtue of autorotation, the air passing through them from below.

Their rate of descent increased. They fell faster than they were moving forward. Monroe could maintain a degree of control over the craft as long as the rotor kept spinning. The landing would be hard, but if they were lucky, it wouldn't be a crash.

Jane Norcross squealed as the nose pitched forward. Pine branches cracked as they brushed the treetops. Salam and Rudge stopped shouting at Monroe. He looked for the best spot for a hard landing even though he couldn't adequately control the craft anymore. They were going down. He could feel their breakneck speed. He braced for the crash.

Corporal Canfield clenched his face and squeezed his eyes shut. Rudge and Salam grabbed whatever they could find. Jenks, the pilot, was unconscious, maybe dead. The photographer let out a fearful yelp. Proctor roared, "Fuck!"

Starwood Two slammed into trees, splintering branches as it hurtled toward the ground.

"Oh, Jesus!" Monroe murmured.

GET OUT! Get out! Get out! Monroe heard his own voice shouting in his head. Have to get out of the helo, get everyone out. His eyes fluttered open, and to his surprise he saw the sky. He could smell the wreckage, but he was on his back on the ground outside the craft.

He pushed himself up on his elbow, and his head started to throb as if he'd been whacked with a baseball bat.

"Easy, General. Not too fast. Lie back down." Captain Salam hovered over him, supporting his head.

"Not necessary, Salam," Monroe said, his voice cracking. "I'm fine."

"But you might have suffered a concussion, sir. Let me check your eyes." Without asking for permission, Salam raised Monroe's eyelids in turn with his thumb.

"I'm all right," Monroe said, but he let Salam finish his cursory examination.

"You seem okay," Salam reported. "Is anything broken?"

"I don't. . ." Monroe moved his arms and legs. He was sore as hell, but everything appeared to be functioning. "Where's everyone else? What happened?"

"Jenks is dead," Salam said. "He might have died before we crashed. For his sake, I hope so. He's pinned inside the cockpit. We're having a hard time getting him out in one piece."

Monroe just stared at Salam, trying to make sense of all this. He'd been in the cockpit with Jenks. He should have been pinned inside, too.

"Corporal Rudge yanked you out of the pilot's seat before we hit. He saved your life, sir."

Monroe looked around at the charred ground and smoldering debris. Forty yards of skid marks led up to the wreck, indicating that the helo must have come in at a fairly flat trajectory. The landing skids were gone, and the rotor was mangled. The hull was on its side, wedged up against the base of a small jagged cliff that had sheared off hunks of metal before the helo hit an outcropping it couldn't slide past. The windshield was smashed, the nose crumpled.

Rudge sat on the ground farther away from the wreck than Monroe, cradling his head. Canfield sat with him, picking glass out of his scalp. Blood trickled down the side of Rudge's dark face.

"Is he all right?" Monroe asked.

"A few cuts," Salam said. "He'll be okay."

"What about the others?"

"Bumps and bruises, mostly minor stuff," Salam said. "Vitelli the intel officer might have fractured his wrist, and a bullet grazed Proctor's leg, but it's no big deal. We were lucky."

Unlike Starwood 2, Monroe thought. He pulled himself up into a sitting position, and suddenly his head started to spin. He felt nauseous. He closed his eyes and stayed very still.

"General?" Salam said.

"One minute." He needed a moment to get it together.

"Yes sir," Salam said.

Gradually the vertigo subsided, and Monroe's stomach settled down. He opened his eyes and saw Sergeant Proctor off to the side wrapping the intel officer's wrist. Rudge cradled his head as Canfield spoke softly to him. Salam on one knee stayed by Monroe's side.

The photographer, Monroe suddenly thought in a panic. Where was she?

"Salam," he blurted. "Ms. Norcross. What happened—?"

"I'm right here, General."

Monroe looked over his shoulder. Jane Norcross knelt on the ground behind him, going through her camera bag, checking her lenses and filters, tossing out the ones that had cracked. She pulled the cap off a long-range telephoto lens and inspected the glass. "Shit!" she said and heaved it at the rocks. She'd set aside the salvageable pieces on the ground in front of her—two Nikons, a few lenses, some filters, a lot of film.

"Are you all right, Ms. Norcross?" Monroe asked.

"Better than you," she said, not even looking at him. She made no attempt to hide her foul mood.

"General?" Salam said, lowering his voice. "We can't stay here. The *muj* will be out looking for us. We have to get moving."

Monroe squeezed his eyes shut and forced himself to focus. Yes, of course. Salam was right. They had to prepare for further aggression from the *mujahadeen*, but how and when and where? He couldn't process all this information.

"Sir," Salam said, "would you like me to take command until you feel up to it?"

"Shit!" Jane Norcross flung a red filter into the sky as if it was a Frisbee. It crossed the sun and colored the light as it flew by, distracting Monroe.

"Sir?"

Monroe stared blankly at Jane.

"Do you want me to lead until—?"

"No," Monroe said abruptly. "I'm in control." He picked himself up and got to his feet. His head felt light, but the others didn't need to know his condition. The dizziness would pass, he told himself.

"Sir, I think you should take it easy," Salam said. "You were just unconscious."

"Thank you for your concern, captain, but I'm fine now. Have you assessed our resources? How many guns do we have? How much ammo?"

Salam seemed a little taken aback by Monroe's direct questioning, and that angered the general. What did the man think? That Monroe had never led a field unit?

"Sir, we have two M4A1s, two MP5-A5s, three nine-millimeter sidearms, and one concussion grenade. We have about a thousand rounds for the fives. About half that for the rifles. Oh, and we also have the sniper rifle the warlords gave you. There are seven rounds in the magazine."

"Distribute the weapons to the men. I assume the intelligence officer is the least experienced with a weapon. Give him a sidearm."

Salam frowned. "General, these men are not combat ready. None of them know much about using a weapon."

"Terrific." Jane's deadpan, sarcasm. "Soldiers who can't fight. I feel *real* safe."

Monroe ignored her comment, but he could feel his face getting hot. Flight crews and intelligence officers are not trained for combat per se. He knew that.

"These soldiers have all been through basic training," he said to Salam, trying to recover. "What they don't know, you and Proctor will show them."

"But, sir, this is no time for remedial coursework. I suggest we move out right now, go to higher ground."

Vitelli the intel officer, his right wrist bandaged, climbed into the open bay of the wreckage, disappeared for a minute, and climbed out again. He was carrying a satellite phone, which looked more like an ordinary black attaché case, and a device that Monroe didn't recognize, a small metal box the size of a shoe box with two lenses protruding from one side. Monroe scanned the horizon on the high side of the mountain and noticed Sergeant Proctor crouched on a small cliff overlooking the wreckage. He was standing guard, watching for signs of enemy approach.

Vitelli walked toward Monroe. "Sir, I was able to salvage a sat phone and this." He held up the black metal box with two lenses embedded in it. He had an unmistakable New York accent.

Monroe focused on the box. "And that is. . . ?"

"A SOFLAM, sir. Special Operations Forces Laser Marker. It's for—"

"Yes, I know what it is," Monroe said, cutting him off. In fact he should have known what it was because he'd reviewed its specs before it was funded for development. A very useful field tool. A man could use it to mark a target—a bunker, a compound, a tank, whatever—from long range with an invisible laser dot. When air support arrived, they located the dot and pinpointed their ordnance on the designated target. SF loved it. They could pick off enemy targets like sitting ducks—as long as they had available air support. Many of the men who used it compared it to playing a video game—not exactly Monroe's notion of proper military attitude.

"Is the SOFLAM operational, Corporal?" he asked Vitelli.

"It looks okay, but I'll have to try it out to be sure." He looked to Salam, as if Salam would give him the order to try it out.

"Corporal," Monroe said, "you were addressing me."

Vitelli screwed up his face and gave him a strange look.

Typical New Yorker, Monroe thought. All attitude.

Jane had wandered into their circle, holding one of her Nikons.

"Sir," Salam said, "I strongly suggest that we quit this area and move on to higher ground as soon as possible. Staying here is not a good idea."

"Why not?" Jane asked.

Monroe ignored her. "I strongly disagree, Captain. Search planes will locate us sooner if we stay with the helo."

"But, sir, if we come under attack—"

Monroe overrode him. "If that happens, we'll use the helo as a bunker. It will provide more cover than anything on this terrain."

"But, sir, the *muj*—"

Monroe overrode him again. "We will set up here, Captain! Is that understood?"

Salam pursed his lips and glared at Monroe, but he didn't say a word. Monroe liked it that way.

Proctor shouted from his perch. "*Muj* in Toys coming this way. Less than half a mile and they ain't watching the speed limit."

"Distribute the weapons, Captain," Monroe said. He called out to the three corporals. "Vitelli, Rudge, Canfield. Get a weapon and get into the helo. Prepare for engagement with the en—" He stopped himself before using the word *enemy*. He would try to talk to the *mujahadeen* and defuse the situation before it deteriorated any further. "Ms. Norcross, I want you inside the helo as well."

"No thanks, General. I have to get some shots," she said.

"I said, get in the helo."

"Hey, I'm not one of your 'men,' okay? I don't *take* orders."

He scowled at her. "Your press card won't afford you any protection with this bunch," he said, mimicking her sarcasm. "I don't think they subscribe to your paper. If I were you, I'd collect my gear and get in the helo."

The sound of revving engines and thunking axles on rough roads started to fill the air like a swarm of cicadas. When Jane heard that, she didn't object any further. She quickly gathered up her functional equipment and ran for the helo. Rudge waited by the helo to help her climb up to the bay. Suddenly Monroe realized that the men inside the overturned helo wouldn't be able to see out the bay to defend their position. With the helo on its side, none of them, not even Rudge, would be tall enough.

"General, what's the plan?" Salam asked pointedly. "What do you want Proctor and me to do?"

"You. . . you're both SF. You know what to do."

"Excuse me, sir."

Proctor shouted, "Here they come! Take cover!" He scrambled down from the ledge and found a crevice for himself behind the crumpled nose of the helo. He held his weapon braced to his shoulder, ready for a firefight.

"Salam, you take that position," Monroe said, pointing to the helo's bent tail. "Take cover and do not fire until you hear from me. Is that understood?"

"What if they split their force and come at us from the rear as well?"

"You heard my orders, Captain," Monroe snapped. "Go!"

Reluctantly Salam ran to the helo and took his position.

"I need a sidearm," Monroe shouted to Rudge, who sat on top of the hull, holding an assault rifle.

Mudge took the 9mm sticking out of his own waistband and handed it down to Monroe. He made eye contact with the general as their fingers touched. He seemed to want to say something but didn't.

Monroe had no time for this nonsense. "Do not fire until I say so," he said to Rudge. "Make sure everyone inside understands that."

"Yes sir," Rudge said with a melancholy note in his voice as if Monroe were a poor fool who just didn't know any better.

The roar of the trucks got louder. Monroe stuck the 9mm in his belt at the small of his back. He then thought better of it and shifted it to his front. A concealed weapon would not show trust. He intended to negotiate with the *mujahadeen*, explain to them what he'd seen just before Zyrous had been shot, explain that he and his party were innocent, that they were all still allies, and that the American government would help them locate and apprehend those responsible for the assassination.

He glanced at Salam. He would need the captain to interpret. But just as he was about to call to Salam, four beat-up white pickup trucks overloaded with armed *mujahadeen* came bounding over the rough terrain, each one swerving to a stop and kicking up dust in the small clearing. Monroe backed up against the helo.

"Hold your fire!" Monroe shouted to his men. He didn't want any itchy noncoms or hell-bent Berets jumping the gun.

He held his hands up where they could be seen. Nearly twenty Afghanis stood in the open—some in the beds of their trucks, others on the ground—all with their guns trained on him. Salam and Proctor had their guns trained on them.

"Salam," Monroe called out, keeping his voice as even as he could, "translate for me."

"Yes sir," Salam said.

"Not necessary, dude." Another voice came from behind.

Monroe looked over his shoulder and saw Yusef standing on the ledge over the helo where Proctor had been. He had at least a half-dozen grizzly fighters with him and they all had automatic weapons pointed down at Salam and Proctor and into the interior of the helo.

Yusef grinned from ear to ear. "So what's that they say in American movies? The jug is up?"

"That's *jig*, asshole," Proctor growled.

"Really?" Yusef said. "Okay, the *jig* is up." He stopped grinning. "Assholes."

More trucks arrived, and more Afghanis crowded around, each one with an assault rifle. This was not what Monroe had planned.

12

SALAM WATCHED as the *mujahadeen* forced Monroe to kneel in the back of one of the shitty little pickups with his fingers linked on top of his head. They shoved Salam in next. Three of the bastards stood behind the truck with their AKs pointed at his back. They'd taken all their weapons, of course, and put them in another truck. The *muj* put Proctor and Vitelli in with Salam, Rudge and Canfield with the general. Ms. Norcross had a separate truck all to herself. The *muj* had thrown down a blanket for her. Salam wondered if she realized that the blanket wasn't for her comfort. The locals considered all women unclean, and they didn't want her leaking menstrual blood all over their vehicle. They'd probably burn the blanket once this was all over.

All over... Salam pondered the concept. He wondered when that would be.

"Look at that," Vitelli said in disgust, nodding at the helo. "They're picking it clean. Like a Thanksgiving turkey."

The *muj* were all over the wreck, crawling around inside, ripping off anything they could get their hands on.

"Did they get the SOFLAM?" Proctor asked.

"Yeah," Vitelli said. "They gave it to that guy Yusef."

"You should have destroyed it, dickwad," Proctor said.

Vitelli's eyes shot open. "We need that. How else could we—?"

"*We* don't have it," Proctor said. "*They* have it. SOP. Never let the enemy have your goodies, because you know sure as shit that they'll use 'em against you."

"But—"

"Save it for a VA shrink." Proctor wouldn't even look at him, he was so disgusted.

"Did they find the sat phone?" Salam asked.

Vitelli nodded. "They found the other one we had, too."

"Great." Salam shook his head.

"Yeah," Proctor grumbled. "Making calls on our fucking tab. Barbarians, that's what these fucking people are."

They watched as *mujahadeen* hauled equipment out of the helo's open bay. They took everything they could yank out of it, including the cockpit seats.

"Animals," Proctor muttered.

But what came next silenced them. A *muj* perched on top of the hull reached down and strained to lift out Lieutenant Jenks's lifeless body. When he got Jenks's chest onto the ledge, he grabbed the pant legs and got the rest of him out. The man called out for help, but when it didn't come fast enough, he just slid Jenks over the side, the body crashing to the ground in a loose-limbed heap.

"Fuckers!" Proctor shouted out in anger. "Fuckers! You don't treat a man like that!"

One of the *muj* guards jabbed Proctor in the back with the muzzle of his rifle.

"Eat me!" he said, shrugging it off.

Salam's guts roiled as he watched this. Two *muj* picked up Jenks by the arms and legs and dragged him to Jane Norcross's truck, heaving him in the back. Initially she turned her head away, but to Salam's surprise she immediately looked down at the body. Her face didn't register any of the emotions he'd expected. She stared at Jenks, taking it all in. She was bearing witness. Salam was impressed.

Yusef, who stood on the rocky ledge, overseeing the salvage operation, called out to his men in Dari. "Finish up. Let's go."

The *muj* inside the hull scrambled out and found places in the pickups. One by one the engines started up until they hummed as one, spoiling the mountain serenity. The trucks started to pull out, turning around and heading back up the dirt road. Two of the guards jumped in with Salam, Proctor, and Vitelli. The trucks ahead and behind were full of *muj* with their guns trained on the three Americans. Monroe's truck, which was similarly guarded, went ahead of theirs. The truck with the photographer and the body brought up the rear. No one guarded that one.

A half-hour later the convoy of pickups arrived back at the fortress. As soon as Salam's truck passed through the high arched gate, he spotted the pile of bodies in the middle of the courtyard near the blackened wreck of Starwood Two. He smelled burnt plastic, burnt rubber, and burnt flesh, and his stomach clenched like a fist. Bile burned the back of his throat. The convoy veered toward the pile—on purpose, no doubt—to give the surviving Americans a good look.

The *muj* had lined up the charred remains on the ground, shoulder to shoulder, face up. Salam had a hard time making out who was who, but Lieutenant Reilly's red hair had somehow survived the flames. Salam could identify Brie Richards's body only by her size.

"Shit!" Vitelli said. "What the hell's that all about?"

"It's an insult," Salam said, barely containing his fury. "Afghanis bury their dead the same day. Leaving a body out in the open like this is a sacrilege. They're defiling our dead and rubbing our noses in it."

"Oh." Vitelli's face was pale. No doubt he wanted to look away, but he couldn't. No one could.

"Do they still make napalm?" Proctor growled. "That's what these cocksuckers deserve."

Salam looked past their guards to the other trucks. General Monroe stared at the bodies, his face hard as stone. Corporal Rudge bowed his head. Salam thought he might have been crying. Canfield looked totally spooked. If he'd had more hair, it would have been standing on end.

Salam looked for the photographer. Her face was immobile, staring hard at the bodies. Salam would have expected a woman to be hysterical, but Jane obviously wasn't like most women. She wasn't human, Salam thought.

Two *muj* jumped out of the cab of her truck and went around to haul Jenks's body out. They slid him out by his legs and let him drop to the ground. They dragged him toward the pile, picked him up by his arms and legs, and started to swing him—one, two, three! They sent the body hurtling onto the pile, where it landed on top of Reilly's, its limbs bent and cocked like a discarded marionette.

A commotion started up at the far end of the courtyard. Salam squinted to see. A small group of *muj* ran toward the pile, hooting and screeching like banshees. As they came closer, Salam could see that at the center of the group, two men carried a headless goat carcass by the legs, its hair matted with its own rancid blood. The men who surrounded the goat carriers cheered them on as they took a running start and heaved the carcass high into the air and onto the pile. It landed on top of Brie Richards's and stayed there.

General Monroe's voice cut though the clamor of the jeers and cheers. "No!" he bellowed. "No! No!" He just kept shouting "No!"

Too little, too late, Salam thought bitterly.

The *muj* ignored the general and continued their zombie celebration.

"I think he's losing it," Proctor said.

Salam kept his mouth shut.

"You. You come," one of the guards said to them with typical gruff *muj* charm. He and his buddy emphasized the point by prodding them with the barrels of their AKs. "You come!" the man repeated.

"Yeah, yeah, we heard you," Salam said, getting up off his knees. He kept his hands on his head and moved to the end of the bed.

"You come! You come!" the *muj* insisted.

Salam stepped down onto the ground, followed by Proctor and Vitelli.

"You come!" The guards prodded them with their guns, corralling them toward Monroe, Rudge, and Canfield. All the Americans had their hands on their heads.

"Are you all right?" the general asked as they approached. His eyes darted from Salam to Proctor to Vitelli.

"No new injuries, sir," Salam said. But he wouldn't exactly say they were fine and dandy.

"Who do you think we deal with now?" Monroe asked. He was blustery and take-charge all of a sudden.

"Hard to say who's in charge now that Zyrous is out of the picture," Salam said. "Raz Khan was Zyrous's second in command, but he doesn't have as much sway with the other warlords. Maybe we should start with Yusef since he's leading this posse."

Yusef stood in the back of one of the pickups, triumphantly overseeing the rounding up of the Americans.

"Okay, let's start with him," Monroe said.

Salam called out, "Yusef! Yu—"

The butt of an AK smashed into Salam's shoulder blade. He turned quickly and saw the *muj* who'd done it. The blow didn't do any damage, but Salam wanted to strangle the little raghead motherfucker. "You come!" the man squawked. "You come!"

More of them gathered around, and more AKs prodded them to move. "You come! You come! You come!" They sounded like parrots.

The Americans had no choice but to walk, swept along by the crowd surrounding them.

The general suddenly looked panicked. "What about Ms. Norcross? Where is she?"

Salam turned around and looked over the heads of the mob. Two *muj* guards marched her off in another direction, pushing her from behind. She made eye contact with Salam, looking for help.

Salam caught Yusef's eye. "What about the woman?" Salam shouted. "What're you gonna do with her?"

Yusef just smiled, showing his teeth. "You come!" he said, mimicking his own people's accents. "You come!"

13

RAZ KHAN and Yusef sat at a rough-hewn table in Khan's quarters inside the fortress. The room was small, the walls made of rough mud bricks that constantly flaked, leaving lines of fine dirt along the stone floor. The SOFLAM and the two sat phones taken from the Americans' helicopter lay on the table. The lone window in the room looked out on the courtyard. Outside, torches burned along the fortress walls, casting shadows across the *buzkashi* field.

Khan looked at his lieutenant's face, debating with himself. Should he tell Yusef or not? He trusted Yusef, but he could not afford to have this revealed. Still, Yusef had always been loyal. He talked a lot, but he didn't gossip. He used his nonstop chatter for confusion and distraction. Khan studied Yusef's eyes for a long moment, then made his decision.

"You should know," he said in Dari. "I have made a deal with"—he nodded toward the mountains to the east—"*them*."

Yusef looked puzzled at first, but then his eyes widened as he realized who Khan referring to. He leaned forward, his face inches from Khan's. "Al Qaeda?" he whispered.

Khan frowned. He didn't want to hear their name mentioned, not even in whispers. He raised his hand and extended all of his fingers. "Five million US dollars for Monroe alive."

Yusef's eyes widened. "They will pay for the general?"

Khan nodded. "Having an American general in their custody will be great propaganda for them. They say it will humiliate the 'Great Satan' and unite their people around the world."

"Do you think it will?"

Khan shrugged. "I don't care if it does or it doesn't. All I care about is the money."

For once Yusef was speechless. He tried to digest what he'd just heard, but he didn't need to understand. Khan had already thought this through.

With Zyrous gone, he needed to secure his position as the new leader of his tribe. He would have to buy the popularity that had come so naturally to Zyrous. He would also have to buy weapons, more modern weapons, to keep the other warlords in their places. He had already put out feelers to Russian arms dealers. If things worked out the way he envisioned, the northeastern section of Afghanistan would be his. No sharing of power, no coalitions, no American-backed government. Just him.

"Where is Monroe now?" Khan asked. "With the others?"

"Yes," Yusef said. "They're all in the turret." He nodded toward the turret in the western corner across the courtyard, a hulking black shadow against the night sky.

"Where is the woman?" Khan asked.

"In the turret as well. By herself. The men are together."

Khan stroked his beard. He contemplated how he would separate Monroe from his men and how he would get Monroe out of the fortress without interference from the other warlords. He laid his hand on the SOFLAM. "Does this work?" he asked.

Yusef nodded.

"You can operate it?"

"Yes. I've seen the Americans use it before. These, too." Yusef opened up one of the sat phone cases and put the receiver to his face, pretending to be making a call. "Yes sir," he said in English in a perfect New York accent that was very close to Vitelli's. "Everything is A-okay up here. Nuttin' to worry about at all, sir. The general is in good hands, and the warlords are happy as hell to have him here."

Yusef smiled, eager for approval for his performance.

Khan couldn't tell one American accent from another, but he knew from the astonished faces on every American who had ever heard Yusef that his ability with English was astounding. Khan smiled and nodded. Yusef's smile widened, not realizing that Khan's pleased expression had nothing to do with him.

Five million US dollars, Khan thought. State-of-the-art weapons. And a new country. All his.

General McCreedy sat at his desk in the Pentagon, holding the phone receiver to his ear. Senator Frye and Alan Hooper occupied the tufted green leather chairs on the other side of his desk. A color photograph of the president and McCreedy on a duck hunting trip hung on the wall behind the general.

Hooper took out a pen and scribbled something on a yellow Post-it. He peeled it off and pasted it on the desk right in front of McCreedy. Put him on speaker, the note said.

The general nodded and pressed the speakerphone button. His secretary's voice came through the speaker. "General McCreedy, I have General Graydon on line three."

"Thank you, Doris." McCreedy pressed the button for line three.

"Bill?" McCreedy said. "Are you there?"

"Yes, General, I'm here." Graydon's voice came back over the speaker. It wasn't the best connection, but it was good enough.

"Bill, I just wanted to check in with you regarding Jackson Monroe. I assume he got there all right."

"Yes, General, he arrived last night at twenty-one hundred." McCreedy, a five-star, called Graydon by his first name while Graydon, a three-star, had to respect McCreedy's rank.

The senator stared at the speaker. Hooper drew cubes on the Post-it pad on his knee as he listened.

"And did he make it to the tribal conference?" McCreedy asked.

"Yes sir, he did. We just got confirmation from the intelligence officer with his party that they're 'A-okay.'"

"Good," McCreedy said, looking at Senator Frye.

Hooper kept his head down but nodded and allowed himself a small grin.

"Any reports about how the conference is going?"

"No, sir. Not yet."

"I'm sure it's fine. Zyrous Mohammed has been solid for us. I expect he and Jackson will get along famously."

"Yes sir. I'm sure they will."

"I'm glad to hear everything is going smoothly," McCreedy said. "If there's anything I can do for you on this end, just let me—"

"Sir, there is one thing I'd like to get off my chest if I may."

The senator's mouth drooped. The lobbyist looked up from his doodling.

"Yes, Bill, what is it?"

"Sir, I realize that Monroe is not the most enthusiastic supporter of Special Forces, but I find his disregard for my men's expertise difficult and, worse, demoralizing to the Green Berets under my command."

McCreedy cocked an eyebrow. "Can you be more specific, Bill?"

"General, it's not my intent to go telling tales out of school. My problem is with Monroe's attitude. He can feel any way he wants about SF, just don't denigrate my men."

"You're absolutely correct, Bill. Our men in the field deserve no less than total support from the officer class. If the problem persists, please don't hesitate to write me a report on the matter."

Hooper pinched his nose and chuckled silently.

"If it happens again, I will do that, sir," Graydon said.

"Bill, you stay out of the heat now."

"I will do my best, sir. Thank you."

"So long, Bill."

McCreedy hung up the phone, and the crackling speaker suddenly went silent. Senator Frye steepled his fingers against his thin lips. Hooper nodded, his brow furrowed, as he processed all of this. The other two men waited for his assessment. Hooper, the acknowledged tea-leaf reader of their group, always knew which way the wind was blowing before anyone else even felt a breeze.

Hooper looked up and stared at their faces in turn. Then his face relaxed. "Monroe's on track. Nothing to worry about here," he said. "Anybody want lunch?"

14

THEIR CELL WAS more like a cave with bars. No windows whatsoever. The only source of light came from a kerosene lantern on the other side of the bars where a guard crouched against the wall, leaning on his upright AK. Monroe stared at the guard's face, looking for a shine in his eyes to see if he was awake, but in the dim light, he couldn't see much. The man could be like a viper, perfectly still but wide awake and ready to strike at a moment's notice.

Monroe and his men were in similar positions scattered around the cell—sitting on the floor, their backs to the walls, motionless but not asleep. Salam and Proctor sat shoulder-to-shoulder with their elbows on their knees, hands dangling. Opposite them, Rudge sat with his long legs stretched out. Next to him, Canfield had his legs crossed, cradling his head in his hands. Vitelli stood by himself, his hands clutching the bars. He hadn't sat down yet.

Monroe slid over to get closer to Salam, keeping his eye on the guard. He kept his voice down just in case the guard understood English. "When day breaks, I'm going to ask for a meeting with Raz Khan. I think I can make him see some sense. The coalition has a lot to lose if they keep us captive."

Salam and Proctor just stared at him, the lantern flame picking up the gleam in their eyes.

"What about our people, sir?" Salam said with an edge in his voice. "Four Berets, two pilots, your lieutenant, and a civilian are out rotting in the courtyard. Are we supposed to forget about them? In the name of diplomacy?"

"No, Captain, we are not going to forget about them," Monroe said, "but our first priority is our release. And that's something that I'm going to have to negotiate."

"These people are animals. You'd have better luck negotiating with dogs."

"You're out of line, Captain."

"With all due respect, sir, I think I deserve to be out of line. This wouldn't have happened if we'd had a full A-team with us."

"I disagree." Monroe stared him down.

"Duly noted, *sir*."

"You are out of line, Captain. You fail to see the big picture—"

"You're damn right I don't see the big picture. Seeing the big picture isn't my job, sir. My job is protecting lives, individual lives, little lives."

"Captain, I realize you're under a lot of stress, but we all are, so let's just pull together."

Monroe caught Proctor rolling his eyes.

"Do you have a problem, Sergeant?"

"No sir. No problem, sir."

"Good. Let's keep it that way." Monroe turned back to Salam. "Now, as I was saying, I will negotiate with Khan. . ."

Salam started digging into the leg pocket of his cargo fatigues. "Forget negotiation, sir. *Baksheesh*. Bribes. That's what these people understand." He pulled out a shrink-wrapped packet of hundred-dollar bills and slapped it on the ground between them. "Sergeant Proctor and I have $150,000 between us. That might be enough to buy our way out of here."

Monroe wanted to punch Salam in the face, he was so angry. "Captain, I gave you a direct order to leave that money behind."

"Yes sir, you did. I'll accept all consequences when we get out of this hellhole. But in the meantime, let's get the fuck out of here so we can come back with reinforcements to kick some serious ass and retrieve our dead. Then you can court-martial me."

"Is *that* how you would handle this, Captain?" Monroe fumed. "Is *that* how you would resolve this situation? This is—"

"General Monroe," Proctor interrupted. "*Muj* coming."

Two *mujahadeen*—one armed, one not—approached the bars. The guard scrambled to his feet, and the man without a weapon, who was clearly in charge, instructed him to level his weapon at the prisoners.

With two assault rifles pointed through the bars, the leader unlocked an ancient padlock on a long hasp that extended along the wall outside of the cell farther than a prisoner could reach. He unfolded the hasp and opened the portal in the bars.

The man pointed at Monroe. "Come," he said. "You come."

"Stay put, sir," Salam said out of the side of his mouth. "Make them come in."

Salam gripped Monroe's sleeve, and Monroe was outraged at his presumption. He tried to ease his arm away from Salam, but the captain wouldn't let go.

"Trust me," Salam said.

"*You come!*" the lead *muj* insisted. "*You come!*"

The man stammered in anger. Salam tightened his grip on Monroe.

Rudge sat up straight. Canfield lifted his head, looking scared. Vitelli's body stiffened.

The lead *muj* didn't have any patience for nonsense. He snapped his fingers at the two guards and ordered them into the cell.

"Beautiful," Proctor whispered with satisfaction.

The three *muj* came in. The leader stood over Monroe. The guards stood next to him in front of Proctor and Salam with their rifles pointed down at Monroe.

"*You come! You come!*"

In an even voice Salam said, "Now."

Salam and Proctor acted in unison, taking one guard each. In a single motion, they deflected and grabbed the rifle barrels, tugging them forward and pulling the guards off balance. From a sitting position, Salam delivered a round house kick to his guard's kidney. Proctor was more direct—straight kick to the balls. Rudge jumped to his feet and blocked the leader from running out. Salam stood up and used the rifle butt to bludgeon the leader and the guard whose gun he now had, bashing them repeatedly until they were unconscious. Proctor got to his feet, grabbed his guard by the scruff of the neck, and rammed his head into the wall. The man fell over into a heap.

"We need some help over here," Salam said to Canfield and Vitelli as he knocked off the leader's turban and started to unravel it. "Rip some strips from their clothing and tie them up. Make sure they're gagged. And be quick about it." Canfield and Vitelli hesitated. "Hurry up!" Salam barked, and the men finally got it in gear.

Salam knelt over one of the guards, tearing strips of cloth. "We have to find the photographer," he said. "We stick together as a unit."

The quickness of the Berets' actions stunned Monroe, and Salam's taking charge humiliated him. "And what if we do find Ms. Norcross? Then what, Captain?"

"Then we do whatever we can to get out of here, General."

"We are vastly outnumbered here."

"All the more reason to get moving, sir."

"And what if—"

Salam cut him off. "We do what Berets do, sir. We improvise."

Monroe held his tongue even though he had plenty to say. This was no time for an argument.

Salam and Proctor tied up the guards with the skill and speed of rodeo riders tying up calves. Salam finished quickly and jumped to his feet. "Let's go, let's go," he said, moving toward the bars, and motioned for the others to get out of the cell.

Monroe waited for all the others to get out first. As he ducked his head and stepped through the portal, Salam started to give more orders, but Monroe overrode him. "Let's stick together. We'll start from the top of the turret and work our way down—"

Salam interupted. "With all due respect, sir, we're not looking for Rapunzel. The *muj* wouldn't take her up to the penthouse suite."

"And why's that, Captain?" Monroe was seething.

"Because in this country, sir, women are about on par with livestock. And an American woman is worth even less. If this place has a hole in the ground, that's probably where she'll be. I suggest we work our way *down*, sir."

Proctor nodded in agreement.

"All right," Monroe conceded. "Let's start downstairs. And I hope to God you're right, Captain."

"I hope so, too, General."

Salam and Proctor had the AKs. Salam took the point while Proctor covered the rear as they entered the winding stairway in a tight pack. The stairway was narrow and claustrophobic, and it was impossible to see more than a few feet ahead or behind. Monroe was wedged between Rudge and Vitelli. "Don't push," he whispered back to Vitelli, but someone up ahead admonished him with a sharp *shush*. They had to maintain silence. Monroe knew that, but he'd thought it would be safe to whisper in the cramped confines of the stairway. Apparently his voice had carried, and now he felt embarrassed.

When they finally filed out onto the next landing, Monroe exhaled his relief. From what they'd seen on the way up to their cell, the turret didn't have many rooms. This floor had another cave-like cell and a room with a closed wooden door. The cell was dark. Salam stepped closer to the bars. He ground the toe of his boot into the gritty floor, hoping to stir anyone who might be inside. He did it again. No reaction from within. If she was in there, she was dead, Monroe thought.

Proctor stood at the wooden door, waiting for Salam. Proctor took the side away from the hinges and pointed his rifle at whoever might be on the other side while Salam reached for the handle. It didn't open easily, and Salam had to put some muscle into it. When it finally gave way, it only opened a few inches. Cold air whistled in. Instead of finding a room on the other side, Proctor looked out at a view of distant silhouetted mountaintops against the night sky. This end of the fortress was built on a precipice so it was a straight drop into a dark abyss. Only the indistinct outlines of the jagged rocks far below gave them any sense of how high they were. Way too high to jump.

Salam signaled for them to move on. Monroe braced himself for the next stairway down. Vitelli waited for him to take his position behind Rudge, but Monroe motioned for him to go ahead and took the next-to-last position in front of Proctor, hoping the sergeant wouldn't tailgate the way Vitelli had. Thankfully, he didn't.

On the next floor, they found the same layout—a cell and a closed door. The men clustered around the bars of the cell as Monroe emerged from the stairway. He could hear Jane Norcross's voice. "Don't leave me here, damn it!" Rudge and Canfield tried to shush her.

"General," Salam whispered, motioning him over. "She knows you. Calm her down, she's making too much noise."

Jane seemed more than scared. "General! Don't you people leave me," she ordered, "Come on!" Monroe took her hands through the bars.

"Sshhh," he said. "We're going to get you out of there. Just quiet down."

She pulled her hand away. "I don't need my hand held, I need to get out of here," she hissed.

Rebuked. Monroe stiffened, embarrassed and unsure of what to do.

The lock on this cell was the same as the one on theirs, a long, padlocked hasp that extended along the wall outside the cell. It was loose, and Proctor worked it up and down, trying to yank it out of the crumbling wall with his bare hands, but it wouldn't give.

"Let me try," Rudge said, nudging Proctor aside. Rudge didn't look much bigger than Proctor, but whereas Proctor was a beefy white guy with a hockey player's build, Rudge was pure plowboy muscle. He worked his fingers under the hasp, patiently rubbing away the deteriorating mortar until he could get a good grip. He braced his boot against the wall and put his back into it, not yanking the way Proctor had but keeping up a steady pressure. It started to give, the metal squealing. Rudge stopped only long enough to adjust his grip, then started pulling again. The old metal bolts holding the hasp were thicker than his fingers, but they started to lose to his determination. When they finally gave way, Rudge lost his balance and almost fell on his ass, but he caught himself and held onto the hasp, which would have made a clattering racket if it had fallen to the stone floor.

Salam opened the door and pushed his way in as Jane tried to get out. He went to the small window in the cell, which had flat bands of rusty iron blocking an escape. Proctor followed him in.

Jane dashed out. "Finally. Thank you," she said and left it at that.

"General," Salam called to him in a stage whisper. "Look at this."

Proctor moved aside so that Monroe could see, but he smelled it before he saw it. The window overlooked a horse pen one story below inside the courtyard. Even in the cold mountain air, the odor of urine and manure was pungent. A small fleet of vehicles were parked nearby, mostly the ubiquitous putty-colored Toyota pickups.

Salam gripped the iron bands to see how secure they were, but they didn't budge.

"Get Rudge," Proctor said.

They waved Rudge into the cell.

"Think you can do anything with this?" Salam asked.

"Let's see," the big man said. He wrapped his long fingers around the bands, tested them and frowned. Monroe felt it was useless. They'd have to find another way. But Rudge wasn't through yet. "Stay back, please," he said.

He backed away from the window, calculating the distance, then raised his leg and kicked at the bands with his boot. The mud cement started to crumble on the first blow. Rudge set himself up and delivered a second blow. More crumbling mortar. He made noise, but he didn't rush, so it didn't sound urgent or alarming. He set himself up again and delivered a third kick. He must have had the kick of a mule times ten, Monroe thought, because the bands came loose on one side of the window and vibrated with the impact.

Rudge stopped and inspected the bands.

"We don't need perfection," Monroe whispered impatiently. There was something about Rudge that Monroe didn't like, the way he behaved—so deliberate and conciliatory—more like a butler than a soldier.

Rudge looked to Proctor. "Would you give me a hand here?"

Rudge gripped the high side of the iron bands, and Proctor took the lower section.

"You can count, sir," Rudge said.

Proctor obliged. "On three. One . . . two . . . three!"

They pulled together, putting their backs into it like a pair of dray horses pulling a heavy load from a dead start.

The iron bands squeaked and complained, emitting a high pitch as the two men moved slowly in unison.

"Good enough," Salam said when the opening was sufficient for a man to pass through. He gathered everyone into a tight circle. "Okay," he whispered, "we're gonna do this fast but not stupid. Now who knows how to hotwire a truck?" He looked directly at Canfield.

"I do," Canfield said sheepishly.

"So do I," Proctor said.

"Me too," Vitelli said.

"I'm glad to see we have so many reformed juvenile offenders among us," Salam quipped. "Okay, we're gonna jump down into the horse pen. Don't worry, Ms. Norcross, it's not a long jump, and the horseshit will break your fall."

Some of the men snickered.

"Enough," Monroe said, glaring at Salam.

"Don't worry, Captain," Jane said. "I'm not afraid of horseshit." She gave it right back to Salam, putting up a ballsy front, but Monroe sensed nervousness in her voice.

Salam started giving assignments. "Vitelli, Proctor, and Rudge will jump first in that order. Get to the trucks and find ones you can hotwire. Also, look for weapons while you're at it."

"Yes sir," they all said.

"Canfield, you go next. Then Ms. Norcross and General Monroe. I'll cover the rear. Now everybody, listen up, especially those of you who haven't taken paratrooper training. You're only jumping one story, but you can still get hurt. Keep your legs together and knees bent to absorb the shock. Roll over in the shit if you have to. Better that than breaking a leg. Is that understood?"

"Yes sir," the men said.

Jane was strangely quiet. Having a civilian woman with them was definitely a problem and an irritation for Monroe.

"Watch out for the horses," Salam said. "And don't jump till you see that the man in front of you has cleared the area. Once you're on the ground, stay close with the others. Get in a truck with either Sergeant Proctor or Corporal Vitelli. You two are driving. Canfield, you wait for me. I'll be driving with you."

"Yes sir," Canfield said. He sounded jittery.

"Drivers, get your people on board first, then start your engine and go. The main gate is open. I can see it from here." He pointed across the courtyard to the southern wall. It was in fact open and large enough to drive a tank through. Monroe suspected that whatever archaic gate mechanism it had was now inoperable and had been for some time.

"Okay, any questions?" Salam said.

"Sir," Canfield said, "what if the *muj* see us before we get to the trucks?"

"You just pray that doesn't happen, Corporal," Salam said. "Any other questions?"

No one said a word. Monroe had to admit, Salam was doing a good job, even if he didn't like Salam's style.

"All right," Salam said. "Is everybody ready?"

"Damn," said Jane under her breath, "I wish I had my camera."

15

SALAM STOOD BY THE WINDOW, like a jump coordinator on a paratrooper mission. Vitelli crouched on the narrow sill, looking down and hesitating.

"It's only horseshit, Vitelli," Salam said. "It won't kill you."

"I'm waiting for the horses to move," he said.

"You don't need a fucking airstrip, for chrissake. Go!"

Vitelli stalled for a few more seconds, muttered something in Italian—a curse from the sound of it—and jumped. Vitelli made a wet sound on impact, which pleased Salam. The mud and manure mixture was soft and deep, a good cushion. As Vitelli slogged his way to the fence, the sturdy mountain horses made way for him.

Proctor squeezed his big frame onto the sill and jumped right away. No fanfare, no hesitation. Rudge climbed onto the sill next. He looked down and waited for Proctor to get out of the way. "Jesus Lord, help us all," he murmured, then jumped. He made a bigger sound when he hit because he fell on his ass. Salam watched carefully to see if he was hurt, but the big man just picked himself up and waded through the shit.

"Canfield," Salam prompted. "Hurry up!"

Canfield stepped forward and reluctantly got up on the sill.

"Wait for me by the fence," Salam said. "When you get down there, smear your face with mud. You're too white. A *muj* with a peashooter will pick you off at a hundred yards."

"Mud, sir?"

"Mud, shit, motor oil, I don't give a damn what you use. Just black out your face. That's an order."

"Yes sir." Canfield jumped. Because of his size, he hardly made a sound at all when he landed.

"Ms. Norcross? Are you ready?" General Monroe asked.

Monroe went to take her elbow then reconsidered. Salam took her by the upper arm.

She shrugged him off. "Let go," she snapped at both of them. "And stop calling me Ms. Norcross, for chrissake. It's Jane."

"You got it, Jane," Salam said. "Just step up on the window and jump. It's all clear. The horses are staying away."

She climbed into position, and jumped before Salam even gave the signal.

Salam looked down to see if she'd landed all right. She stood up to her calves in manure, pumping her legs, trying to work her way out of it.

"Is she all right?" Monroe asked.

"Yes sir, she seems to be doing okay." Salam kept his eye on her. She moved fast, already at the fence.

"Okay, General, your turn."

But in that moment Salam saw something he didn't like, and he threw his arm across the window to hold Monroe back. Down below Jane opened the gate of the pen. What the fuck was she doing? Just climb over the fence, he wanted to yell to her.

She led one of the horses out, one hand on the animal's nose, the other holding a fistful of mane. She clearly knew how to handle a horse.

"What the hell is she doing?" Monroe said.

Salam had a bad feeling about this. "Excuse me, General. I think I'd better go first."

"Salam—" Monroe said, but Salam had already climbed onto the sill and jumped.

He stayed loose as he dropped and kept his knees bent, so much so that he ended up kneeling in horseshit when he landed. He got to his feet and high-stepped toward the gate, shoving horses out of his way as he went.

Jane, already outside the pen, straddled her mount.

He wanted to yell at her, but he couldn't. He'd draw attention.

She held onto the horse's mane in lieu of reins and a bridle, kicking the animal's flanks with her heels. The horse trotted, and she kept urging him on, kicking him relentlessly. By the time Salam reached the edge of the pen, Jane's horse had started to canter across the courtyard, heading for the main gate.

Fuck me! Salam thought. Fuck me and fuck you, too, lady!

Salam reached out and grabbed the mane of the horse closest to him.

Monroe saw it all unfolding from up in the turret. Salam led a horse out of the pen, hopped onto its back, and spurred it on, getting it to break into a run. He went after Jane who was already out of the fortress.

The other men, unable to hotwire the trucks quickly, just wanted to get out too. They started grabbing horses for themselves, following Salam's lead. This was insane! They needed trucks, not horses.

Monroe stepped up onto the sill and immediately jumped down. He hit harder than he'd expected, his knees slamming into his chest and momentarily knocking the wind out of him.

Across the pen Rudge gathered up horses for the others, finding the biggest ones for himself and Proctor. Vitelli found a horse for himself and mounted it. "Y'all just hang on and don't be shy about giving him your heel if he slows down," Rudge told Vitelli. "The horse will follow his buddies."

"How do you know?" Vitelli said.

"That's the way horses are," Rudge said. "Now go!" He slapped the rump of Vitelli's horse, and it took off toward the main gate.

Monroe slogged his way toward the rest of the men. "Release those horses immediately!" he said in an angry whisper.

But Proctor and Rudge didn't hear him. They mounted and wasted no time getting under way. Rudge clicked his tongue and held the manes of both his and Proctor's horse, guiding them out into the courtyard. Proctor looked totally helpless on top of a horse. Rudge looked over his shoulder at Canfield. "Just get on," he said. "Don't worry. He'll follow us."

"Halt!" Monroe said in a stage whisper. "Stop where you are."

But Rudge and Proctor were too far away, picking up speed. Canfield glanced back at Monroe, having heard him, but he proceeded to get on his horse anyway.

"Get off that animal, Corporal," Monroe said, wading closer.

Canfield's brows slanted back in confusion. "But, sir—"

"Get off the horse," Monroe repeated.

Canfield looked at Rudge and Proctor as they trotted across the courtyard, approaching the main gate. "With all due respect, sir—"

"I don't want to hear it, Canfield. Get off the horse on the double." What the hell was wrong with this kid?

Canfield watched as Proctor and Rudge passed through the gate. "With all due respect, sir," Canfield said, his voice cracking, "Captain Salam said we should stay together, and it looks like the captain changed the plan. He said we were running out of time, and... and... I have to go, sir." He spurred his horse and kept spurring it, making it gallop in pursuit of the others.

"Canfield!" Monroe hissed. "Canfield!"

But it was no use. Canfield was already well into the courtyard and out of earshot.

A horse nudged Monroe's shoulder, and he shoved it aside. He hated horses. He'd tried riding a few times and detested the experience. Everything associated with riding involved filth and stink. Besides, the constant jostling up and down always threw his back out. Cavalry today meant airships.

Monroe walked toward the fence to get out of the manure. He moved around the horses, careful not to get behind any of them. Horses kicked when startled from behind, and he had no intention of adding that to his list of bad horse experiences. But as soon as he made it to the fence, he heard a voice. Someone called to him.

He looked up, and a flashlight shone into his eyes. It came from the window they'd jumped from. Instinctively he froze. If he didn't move, he might blend in with his surroundings. But the horses around him moved restlessly, which probably made him obvious to the person with the flashlight.

The man in the window started shouting. Monroe didn't understand his language, but obviously he was alerting others that there'd been an escape. Monroe threw his hands up to show that he had no intention of fleeing. He wanted to negotiate with them. If he could sit down with Raz Khan and the other warlords, they could work something out. Of course, they'd have to take some responsibility for the downed helos and the Americans who had perished, but the deaths could be interpreted as unfortunate casualties in the general chaos that followed the assassination of Zyrous Mohammed. This need not jeopardize America's relationship with the Northern Alliance or Monroe's purpose in coming here. He would not let anything that had happened here taint Frye-Yoder's chances of—

A shot rang out, and Monroe ducked behind a horse. The horse to his left whinnied and fell to its knees. In the dim light, Monroe could see a shiny black stream oozing from the horse's flank. He heard a second shot. The man shouted again, and someone from across the courtyard shouted back, sparking a frantic dialogue. Other bodiless voices joined in. The flashlight swept the pen, looking for him. He gripped the mane of the horse he'd ducked behind, trying to keep it near him. More voices added to the clamor. The beam of light found his hands on the horse. It stopped and probed for Monroe's face. The man in the window screamed to the others. "He's here!" he must have been saying. "I found him! He's in with the horses!"

Monroe's heart pounded. He kept thinking about negotiation, trying to visualize his way to an agreeable solution, but the notion now seemed ridiculous.

16

THESE PONIES ARE UGLY AS HELL, Salam thought as he raced along a moonlit trail, but they sure can run. He kept spurring his horse on, working his heel kicks into his posting rhythm. Up ahead, Jane ran like the devil on her dappled gray mount. The trail sloped downward, which accelerated their pace. He hoped it would work in his favor so he could catch up to her. If the trail turned into an incline she'd be able to put more distance between them, being lighter. He had to catch her before the terrain changed.

A field of boulders opened up to his right, a wall of sheer rock on his left. He could tell from the occasional sharper clack of his horse's hooves that they passed over stretches of rock along the otherwise dirt path. These patches made him nervous. If the nag lost his footing and took a spill, it could be disastrous for both of them. But Salam couldn't stop now. He had to catch Jane. If she got away from him, she'd be on her own out here, and if the *muj* found her, no telling what they'd do to her. Leaving her to die of exposure and starvation would be the kindest outcome.

A cloud cover passed over, but the moon reflected enough light for Salam to just barely see Jane and her horse. The woman really could ride, he thought. No doubt about that. At this crazy pace she'd take a spill and go down with her horse. She'd suffer broken bones, head injuries, maybe worse. And no way to call for Medevac transport. Even if a helo could get up here, the *muj* would probably shoot it down. Carrying her out would be nuts, though Salam had a feeling Monroe would insist that they try. Escaping from this nightmare would take all they had, and they didn't need an anchor. No, he had to catch her.

The trail leveled off a bit but still sloped downward. The rock wall on his left disappeared, replaced by a rocky field that mirrored the one on his right. This was his chance. He could catch up to her here.

He bore down on his horse, leaning into its neck like a jockey, as he kept spurring the animal on. The AK he'd taken from the guard had come loose from his shoulder, bouncing freely at his side. He didn't dare adjust it and risk breaking his stride. He moved up fast on her. Only two and a half lengths separated them now.

"Stop!" he shouted to her. "Ms. Norcross! Jane! Slow down—"

Suddenly his heart jumped into his throat as the dirt trail turned into uneven rock and his horse slipped. The horse's rump took a quick dip, but to Salam's amazement, the little nag kept its footing and hardly lost any ground. His heart slammed in his chest, but he kept pouring it on. He had to catch her.

"Slow down!" he yelled to her. "Slow down, goddamnit!"

He regained the distance he'd lost, but she and her horse didn't let up at all. "Slow down!" he shouted.

She ignored him. Or maybe she couldn't hear him.

"Slow down," he shouted louder. "Slow down, you fucking cunt-licking bull-dyke bitch!"

She looked back over her shoulder and glared at him. "Fuck you, asshole!" she screamed back.

Looking back at him slowed her down. He hadn't let up on his own pace and so he caught up with her in seconds. Running almost neck-and-neck, he reached out to grab her, but she threw her arm out and backhanded his arm away. The blow did nothing to him, but it slowed her down further.

"Leave me alone, you fucking stupid dick," she yelled.

But he already had a fistful of her horse's mane, slowing his horse down and slowing hers at the same time.

"Let go!" she yelled. "Let go!"

He ignored her and pulled both horses to a halt. He kept his grip on hers, knowing that she would bolt again if he gave her half a chance.

"Let go!" she screeched and hammered him over the head with her fist.

The blow angered him more than it hurt. When she tried it again, he blocked it with his forearm, and their arms crashed, bone on bone.

"Fuck!" she cursed in pain. "Let go of my horse!"

"Shut the fuck up!" he roared in her face. "*SHUT UP! SHUT UP! SHUT UP!*" He kept saying it, using his words like a pugil stick, pounding her with them until she settled down. People who have never gone through Basic Training aren't used to being yelled at like that.

"Look," she said. She breathed hard, struggling to be coherent. "Look. We have to go. . . Too dangerous here. . . We have to—"

He overrode her: "Just shut the fuck up and listen. I'm talking."

"But—"

"Shut up and listen!" he shouted. "I need you."

"You. . . what?" She looked puzzled.

"You obviously know how to ride," he said. "I've got men back there on horseback and they don't. Go back and help them. Just tell them what they need to know to get those horses moving."

"Where?" she said. "Where do you want us to go?" She calmed down and seemed to be willing to cooperate, which surprised him.

"About a quarter mile back the trail branches off and heads higher into the mountains. Bring them up that way."

"Why higher? Don't we want to get out of here?"

"The *muj* will be out looking for us. They'll probably assume that we'll try to get out off this mountain as fast as we can and get back on the main road."

"Oh. . . I see. . . I guess."

"Just trust me. And don't go crazy on me again. I need you to round up the others and get them on that trail. Rudge can ride, and he's helping Proctor. I don't know about Vitelli and Canfield. They're city guys so I doubt that they know what they're doing. Make sure they all get on the right trail. Do you understand?"

"I understand." In the shadows he couldn't read her expression in the shadows, but she sounded coherent.

"Okay, let's go." He released his grip on her horse.

"What about General Monroe?" she asked as she brought her horse around. "Is he with the others?"

Salam hadn't even thought about Monroe. "Don't worry about him," Salam said. "Just get to the others and do it fast. We're gonna have first light soon and that means they're gonna be out looking for us. I'll scout out a place where we can hole up for a while." He spurred his horse to get moving.

"But what about the general?" she called after him. "Do you think he can ride?"

Who cares, Salam thought. His horse broke into a canter, and he didn't look back.

Mortified, Monroe sat on his stupid horse, leaning over its neck and holding on tight. He kept sliding off the side. Jane rode next to him, holding the manes of both horses and keeping his horse under control, which she had to do because on its own his nag seemed to have only two speeds, slow as shit and breakneck. The others all rode up ahead on the trail, and from what Monroe could see, they had apparently gotten the hang of riding these infuriating beasts. Canfield's horse in particular seemed to love him because that animal did whatever Canfield wanted.

"Over here!" Salam called to them. About fifty yards up the trail, Salam sat on his horse near the mouth of what looked like a cave. He waved his arms so he could be seen.

"This way," Salam shouted. "Over here."

The others guided their horses up to the cave. Jane slowed down her horse and Monroe's followed suit. When they came to a stop behind Canfield's mare, Jane looked over at Monroe. "Do you want me to take your horse for you?" she asked, but he didn't answer. He just jumped off and held onto the mane for himself. He didn't like the pitying cast of her eyes or the solicitous tone in her voice.

"Everybody inside. Horses, too," Salam said, waving them into the cave.

One by one they all filed in, but Monroe hung back. He wanted to be last. "I counted seven trucks in pursuit," he said to Salam. "They took the road down the mountain—"

"I know, General," Salam said, interrupting him. "I could see them from up here."

Monroe didn't like his know-it-all attitude. "Captain, do we have a problem here?"

"General, can we discuss it inside? I think we should be out of sight." He looked up at the sky as if Monroe didn't realize that the sun had come up and they could be seen.

Monroe bit his tongue and stepped into the cave, yanking the horse's mane to get it to move. It felt twenty degrees cooler inside, dark but not impenetrable. Actually, the farther inside he got, the lighter it became. A small opening in the roof of the cave cast a shaft of light into the interior, illuminating their faces.

"What is this place?" Jane said. "An Al Qaeda summer timeshare."

No one laughed. They were all exhausted, too tired for clever comebacks.

Salam squeezed past with his horse. "Put the horses all the way in the back so they won't run out. There's a little water trickle back there they can drink from."

When the horses were squared away, they reassembled near the shaft of light.

"Okay, listen up," Salam said to the group. "Let's take inventory. Did anyone recover anything from the trucks?"

Vitelli took an M4A1 assault rifle off his shoulder and held it out to Salam. "I believe this is yours, Captain."

Salam took the weapon. "Thank you. Anything else?"

Proctor set down two battered ammo boxes. One had "US Army" stenciled on it; the other showed significant rust. He slid their tops off and checked the contents. "God loves us, Captain," he said with a smile. He tipped the rusty box to the light. It was about a quarter full. "Five point four five millimeter. AK ammo." He rattled the other box, which was almost full. "Nines. Anybody pick up my MP5?" When no one responded, he looked disappointed. "Well, I guess these won't be much use to us."

"I'd rather have the AKs anyway," Salam said.

"And why's that, Captain?" Monroe said.

"It's a better weapon, sir."

Monroe wanted to dress him down for criticizing an American-made weapon, but suddenly he felt a wave of exhaustion, too tired to argue. Besides, Salam was right. The AK was a better weapon, unfortunately.

"Anybody get anything else?" Salam asked.

Rudge unhitched the rifle from his shoulder, the sniper rifle that Zyrous Mohammed had presented to Monroe. Rudge held it out to him. "General," Rudge said in his slow deep voice, "this is yours."

Monroe took the rifle. He checked the magazine. Five rounds and one in the chamber. Just six shots. What good was it?

"I found these, too," Rudge said. He pulled two mini grenades out of his pocket and held them out. A concussion and a smoker.

Salam looked at them. "You hang on to them, Corporal."

"Yes sir," Rudge said.

"Okay, here's the deal, people," Salam said. "We've got firepower, we've got water, and we've got transport. We will get ourselves off this mountain, but obviously we cannot travel by daylight. So we will stay here until dark and move out then. Get comfy and rest up. You'll need it. Any questions?"

The only sounds came from the horses snorting and clomping their hooves.

"Okay then," Salam said. "Get settled and try to sleep. I'll stay up and take the first watch."

"I'll take second," Proctor said.

"I'll be third," Rudge volunteered.

Monroe considered volunteering himself but knew that wouldn't be appropriate given his rank.

"Canfield, you take the last shift," Salam said. "You've still got making up to do."

"Yes sir," Canfield said. He was looking down at the ground.

"Okay, everybody find a place and go to sleep."

"Yes sir," the men said. Their subdued response reflected their mood. But Salam had done the right thing in telling them unequivocally that they would get off the mountain. They had to remain hopeful that this could be accomplished. Worrying about their odds of survival would be counterproductive. The commander calculates the odds, not the soldiers.

"Sir," Salam said, moving in close and speaking softly, "did you want to speak with me?"

Monroe studied Salam's face, his square jaw, his keen eyes. He did want to have a talk with Salam, but he really had no reason to. Salam was doing his job and doing it very well. Monroe had nothing to criticize, which irritated Monroe. The captain's competence pointed up all of Monroe's deficiencies. He'd been a snake-eater once himself but was no longer. He was brass, and he was soft. Somehow he'd thought he would have handled himself better in a situation like this.

"Sir?" Salam prompted.

"It can wait, Captain," Monroe said wearily. "We'll talk later. Get some rest."

"Yes sir."

Monroe wandered off to find a place where he could lie down. No one had slept at all last night, so they all must have been as tired as he was. The others had already found rocks flat enough to bunk down on.

Rudge saw that Monroe didn't have a place. "Sir," he said, getting up, "take this place."

"Lie down, Corporal," Monroe said with a frown. "I'll find a place for myself." Rudge's version of respect verged on obsequiousness.

"That's all right, sir. Please, take it."

"No thank you, Corporal."

Rudge had put himself in an awkward position. He couldn't exactly lie down and fall asleep with the general standing there. Monroe recognized his dilemma but did nothing to remedy the situation. He hated the way Rudge always looked at him with those expectant eyes. Such a childish, demeaning expression on a grown man.

"May I ask you something, Rudge?" Monroe said.

"Of course, sir."

"Why did you retrieve the sniper rifle? Didn't you realize it would be useless without sufficient ammo?"

"I . . . I didn't think about that, sir. I just saw it in the truck and I knew it was yours, so I took it."

"Were there any other weapons you could have taken?"

"No sir. I didn't see any." Rudge was nervous.

"Did you take the sniper rifle because you thought perhaps it would curry some favor with me?"

Rudge's eyes shot open wide. "No sir. That's not what I was thinking at all. I was just thinking we needed weapons and I saw it there on the seat of the truck and I took it. That's all."

Monroe just stared at him. "Rudge, do you think we share some kind of special bond here because we're both black?"

Rudge's lips parted. He didn't know how to respond to that.

"Let me tell you something, Rudge. We are not 'brothers,' not that way. You are a soldier like every other man here, and I am an officer. That's about as complex as our relationship gets. Now if you think we should be sharing confidences, that I should be your father-figure, that I should somehow treat you differently, then you are very wrong."

"No sir. I know that, sir. That's not what I expect."

"I have been in the Army for thirty-four years, Rudge, and I can honestly say that I have never concerned myself with racial issues. Race has never held me back in the Army. In fact, it worked the other way. That's why I don't waste my time with it."

"Yes sir." Rudge sounded unsure.

"I'm not telling you how to feel, Rudge. I'm just telling you not to expect me to feel the same way you do. Do you understand what I'm saying?"

"Yes sir."

Monroe doubted that he did, but at least the man had been put on notice. The only brotherhood that existed in Monroe's Army was soldier to soldier, not black soldier to black soldier.

"Get some rest, Rudge."

"Yes sir."

Monroe moved toward the rear of the cave and located a flat perch. As he lay back and tried to get comfortable, he could see that Rudge was still sitting up, staring at him. Monroe ignored him and closed his eyes.

16A

"WHAT THE FUCK?"

Jane's voice woke Monroe. He looked toward the wall where she'd been sleeping and saw her up on her elbows. Then he saw the assault rifle pointing down at her. His eyes adjusted to the shaft of light that illuminated the interior of the cave, now golden with the setting sun. Armed intruders had come into the cave, four of them, and they all had assault rifles trained on the Americans. In dress, they looked no different from the *mujahadeen* who had been at the fortress conference, but these men had longer beards. They seemed different somehow—grimmer, more serious. They didn't speak or attempt to communicate in any way. Monroe took that as a bad sign.

He looked for Salam, but the captain wasn't on the flat rock where he'd laid down.

"Over here, General."

Monroe followed Salam's voice to the rear of the cave where he stood among the horses. His 9mm sidearm protruded from his waistband over his belly; his utility knife hung in its sheath on his hip. He held his hands up, palms facing out.

"Did you hear them coming?" Monroe asked, trying to figure out how Salam knew to get up.

Salam's eyes pointed toward the mouth of the cave. An intruder Monroe hadn't noticed before held Canfield from behind with a leather cord cinched around his neck. They must have taken him by surprise while he'd been on watch.

"Who are these men?" Monroe asked.

"Qaeda," Salam said, "Ms. Norcross was right."

"How do you know?"

"The long beards, the way they're acting. . ."

"Why aren't you talking to them?"

"I'll try, but . . ."

"But what?"

"We're the infidels, and these guys have only one goal. You know what I'm saying?"

Monroe looked around the cave. He counted five of them. But were more outside?

Canfield's face turned purple-red as his captor tightened the cord around his neck. He groaned and strained. "Relax, Canfield," Monroe said. "Don't fight against him."

"I think he knows that," Jane said sarcastically.

"Ask them what they want?" Monroe said to Salam.

"Like it's not obvious?" Jane said.

Monroe glared at her. "Please be quiet and let us handle this."

"Because you've done a good job the past twenty-four hours?"

Salam spoke to the men, repeating his question in all the languages he knew.

Vitelli didn't move a muscle, petrified. Proctor sat hunched over on his rock, his elbows on his knees, eyeing the enemy from under his brow, his rifle just out of reach. Rudge lay on his side, his face turned away from the muzzle pointing at his head.

None of the Qaeda soldiers responded to Salam. They remained stone-faced with death in their eyes.

"So why don't they just kill us?" Jane's voice quivered despite her attempts to be tough.

"They're waiting for someone," Salam said. "That's my guess. Probably their commanding officer."

"Maybe we'll be able to talk to him," Monroe said.

"Highly unlikely. They're just waiting for him to give the order. The fun can't start without him."

"Just give me the word, Captain," Proctor said in a low growl. "I'm ready."

"Stay put, Sergeant," Monroe said. "We don't have a chance this way."

"We don't have a chance, period," Jane said.

Monroe looked toward the mouth of the cave, unsure how the commanding officer's arrival would affect things. It could mean a chance to make a deal. More likely it would mean instant execution.

"Rudge," Salam said, "you got that smoker?"

"Yes sir. Right in my hand."

"No," Monroe said, "Wait for their CO."

"That would be a very bad idea, sir," Salam said dismissively. "Proctor, try to keep the friendly fire to a minimum, okay?"

"I'll try."

Canfield groaned. The bastard holding him tightened the cord in gradual increments, killing him slowly.

"Okay," Salam said in an even, conversational tone, keeping it mellow for the Qaedas, "I want everybody to stay put. Stay right where you are. Except for you, Proctor."

"Okee-dokee," Proctor said pleasantly.

"But—" Monroe started.

Salam spoke over him. "No time for talking. Canfield's fading."

Monroe glanced at the barely conscious corporal. Another fucking casualty, he thought, feeling angry and helpless.

"Rudge, you're the man," Salam said. "I'm gonna talk to these guys in their language, try to distract them. You pull the pin behind your back and just drop it on the floor. Keep your movements small. Nothing dramatic."

"I understand," Rudge said.

"Captain," Monroe said, keeping his eye on the Qaeda soldier closest to him, "what are you going—?"

But Salam ignored him and started to speak to the invaders in one of his languages. Monroe's heart pounded. "Don't look at Rudge," he said to the others. "Stare at our captors."

Salam picked up his pace, jabbering faster. He seemed to be pleading with them.

Monroe checked the eyes of the intruders as Salam became more animated. They stared hard at Salam, annoyed with his impertinence.

Monroe didn't dare look toward Rudge.

Then Monroe heard it before he saw it—the smoke grenade dribbling along the floor in the middle of the cave. Suddenly it went off with a deafening *thwump*. Yellow smoke immediately created a wall that divided the cave as it started to take over the entire space.

Salam slapped the rumps of the horses. "Ha! Ha!" he shouted. The animals, already in a panic from the sound of the grenade, kicked and whinnied and jostled, desperate to escape. They bolted and ran for the exit. The stampede rushed through the thick smoke, knocking the Qaeda soldiers out of their way.

"Salam!" Monroe yelled.

"Stay put!" the captain shouted. "Everybody!"

Monroe looked up and through the choking smoke he saw Salam's legs disappearing through the light hole in the roof of the cave. How in God's name did he get up there? Monroe wondered.

Gunfire echoed off the hard walls, but Monroe had no idea who fired it.

"Stay down!" Proctor yelled. "Stay down!"

But Monroe didn't listen. He got up off his perch and felt his way toward the mouth of the cave.

Proctor, who seemed to be in front of Monroe, kept yelling for people to stay down. Another blast of auto gunfire assaulted Monroe's ears. Monroe couldn't see much through the smoke, but Proctor appeared to be flushing out the cave. Monroe stumbled forward, covering his nose and mouth with his sleeve.

He could hear people coughing as he stumbled out of the cave. A dead horse lay across the exit, and Monroe had to step over it. Canfield, writhing on the ground, coughed his lungs out, clutching his throat. Proctor, also on the ground, fired his weapon from the prone position at a fleeing soldier.

Monroe blinked and rubbed his irritated eyes, searching for Salam. A gunshot went off. Salam turned toward it. A Qaeda fighter fell to the ground, a smoking bullet hole in his chest. Salam stood nearby, arm extended, holding his sidearm. Two other Qaeda soldiers lay motionless in the dust at his feet.

Another Qaeda rushed out of the cave, shoving Monroe aside. Eyes tearing and disoriented, the man swung his rifle around, aiming it at Monroe.

Monroe's heart shot into his mouth. This was it, he thought.

But the shot he heard didn't come from the Qaeda soldier. It came from Salam's 9mm as the captain rushed up and shot the man through the head from three feet off. The man's legs buckled, and he fell on his face. His turban tumbled off revealing cropped black hair soaked with blood.

The last intruder continued running down the mountainside, dodging boulders, running for his life. Proctor stood up and tracked him, his rifle to his face. One... two... three single shots rang out. The running man finally fell and tumbled out of control until his body rammed into a boulder and flopped over on its back, dead.

Salam went to the mouth of the cave and yelled inside, "It's safe now. Come on out."

Vitelli, Rudge, and Jane wandered out, coughing harshly, waving smoke away. Stunned, Monroe stared at the dead bodies on the ground, all of them Salam's kills. The captain had initiated the action, climbed out through the light shaft, intercepted the Qaeda fighters as they fled from the cave, and personally taken out four of the five intruders. The blood in the hair of the man who had taken the headshot glistened in the sun. Monroe couldn't take his eyes off him.

Jane coughed as she came up behind Monroe. She nodded toward Salam, who knelt over Canfield, checking his neck. "That guy," she said through her coughs, "deserves a fucking medal."

Monroe looked away and didn't say a word.

17

THE CLIP-CLOP of hooves walking down the rocky trail filled the cold night. Fortunately the horses hadn't run far when they fled from the cave. The moon wasn't as bright as the previous night, but Salam worried that they would be seen, especially on the open stretches where the rock walls disappeared and left them walking on open terrain. Proctor was on point with Rudge close behind in case Proctor's horse got hinky and he couldn't handle her. Salam took the left wing, Vitelli a few lengths back, took the right. Salam glanced back and saw Monroe's silhouette bouncing on his horse, second from the end in front of Canfield, the long sniper rifle hitched over his shoulder. Monroe had insisted on carrying it himself, and Salam thought he looked pretty silly. A sniper rifle with only six rounds was pretty laughable. Proctor had started calling him "Deep Six" behind his back.

They had waited until dark before setting out from the cave. Salam wanted to lessen the chance of running into enemy forces out here. He'd considered waiting until midnight, but that would have decreased their travel time. They'd taken the Al Qaeda fighters' weapons, but with no food, Salam wanted to get out of these mountains as soon as possible.

"Captain Salam," Jane called to him. "Captain Salam."

He reined in his horse so he could fall back. She rode behind Vitelli and in front of General Monroe. "Keep your voice down," he said to her in a whisper. "We don't know who's out here."

She lowered her voice to a testy whisper. "Do you know where we're going? Where are we heading? What's the goal?"

"At the moment we're heading northwest," he said, just as testy, "because that's the way the trail down the mountain goes. The goal. . . Jane"—he still hadn't gotten used to calling her by her first name—"is to get to a friendly village, if there still is such a thing, or even better, run into an American or allied unit—British, Australian, whatever—and hope that they have a sat phone we can use."

"That seems like a pretty nebulous plan to me," she said.

"Well, I'm open to suggestion if you've got any ideas."

She didn't respond, but he could feel her glaring at him, though he couldn't see her face all that well in the dark. Salam expected Monroe to say something, but the general hadn't said much since their encounter with the Qaeda fighters. He seemed to be in a mood.

"Excuse me," Salam said to Jane and spurred his horse past hers and Vitelli's to his former position.

They walked at a steady pace, and the sound of the clopping hooves became mesmerizing. Salam eventually lost track of the time. Five minutes could have passed or a half hour or anything in between. He had no idea. He came out of his trance when the trail narrowed, high rock walls on either side, forcing them to ride single file. As they moved on into the ravine, it grew darker, the night sky just a slit overhead.

"Proctor," he whispered to the front, "what do you see? Is there a way out of here?"

"Hard to tell, Captain. These things usually do open up at the other end."

Salam didn't like this. They were fish in a barrel down here.

The trail narrowed even further. He could touch the walls without extending his arms all the way. This was bad, he thought. They couldn't turn their horses around if they had to. He thought about turning back, hoping these little beasts could be persuaded to walk in reverse, when he noticed that the sky started to open up. The walls shrank in height as they continued, getting shorter by the step. The end of the ravine had to be close. Thank God, he thought.

Then he heard Proctor's voice in a low whisper. "Oh, shit."

"Proctor," Salam whispered back, "what do you see? Proc—"

Salam saw something that shut him up. On top of the wall to his right, which was even with his head, he saw hooves, a lot of them. He looked up and saw dark shapes against the sky—riders, six of them, maybe more. He saw rifle barrels, too. Not exactly pointed directly at them but none pointed up. Who the hell were these guys? Salam wondered. And why were they waiting here like this? If they'd intended to ambush, they would've done something by now.

Salam could hear the riders talking. "Who are they?" one of them said in Pashto.

The other riders mumbled in response.

Pashtuns, Salam thought and immediately assumed that they had been at the conference in the fortress. Even if they hadn't, word of the assassination might have spread already.

"Keep moving," Salam said to his people in a soft, even voice. "Just keep moving." If the shit hit the fan, he didn't want them trapped down in that narrow space.

The Pashtuns muttered and gestured at the strangers, getting louder and more animated as the Americans started to emerge from the ravine. They commented on the size of the two big men, Proctor and Rudge. Salam and Vitelli guided their horses out, and the Pashto chatter increased. When the Pashtuns saw the Americans' guns, they raised their own. Proctor already had his AK leveled and Vitelli quickly raised his, a sudden movement Salam wished he hadn't made.

"Who are you?" one of the Pashtuns shouted in Pashto. "Speak!"

"Who are *you?*" Salam responded in their language. "What do you want?"

"Are you Taliban? And do not lie under the eyes of Allah," the Pashtun leader said.

Salam breathed a little easier. At least these men didn't seem to be gunning for a pack of assassins.

But then the muttering and gesticulating increased again as Jane rode out of the ravine. "Why do they have an unholy woman with them?" Salam heard one of them say. Unholy to them because her head was uncovered and her arms were bare.

"Stop!" the leader ordered.

"Why?" Salam shot back. "We haven't done anything to you." He tried to stall. General Monroe and Canfield hadn't made it out of the ravine yet.

"Stop now!" the leader shouted. Salam heard the clack of their weapons as the Pashtuns raised them and took aim.

"We have done nothing to you," Salam repeated. He looked sideways and saw Canfield and Monroe stepping out of the ravine. Salam and the others had pulled their horses together facing the Pashtuns. Monroe and Canfield joined the group.

"Everybody dismount," Salam ordered. "Keep your weapons, but try to look friendly."

"Sorry," Jane said sarcastically, "I didn't go to charm school." Fear registered in her voice despite the attitude.

"Keep your mouth shut, Jane," Salam said, getting off his horse. "It just riles them up to hear a woman talk. They don't know what to make of you."

"Yeah, well, screw them," she muttered under her breath.

All the Americans got off their horses. Monroe handed his mount off to Canfield and went over to Salam. "What do they want?" Monroe said. "Ask them."

"Yes sir," Salam said, but he didn't say anything to the Pashtuns.

"What are you waiting for?" Monroe said.

Salam lowered his voice. "I've dealt with these people before, General. You never ask them anything directly. That's just an invitation for evasion or an outright lie. Better to let them talk first."

The Pashtuns stayed on their horses, silently staring at the Americans who just stared back. A horse snorted, another stomped the dirt with its hoof.

"This is ridiculous," Monroe said. "Talk to them."

"I want them to come to us, General.

"Stop playing games. Just find out what the hell they want."

The Pashtuns grumbled at Monroe's sharp tone.

"Please keep your voice even, sir. And don't say much. Never assume that the *muj* don't understand English. Enough of them do."

"That's being paranoid, Captain."

"That's being smart, General."

"What did you say?" Pent-up, slit-eyed anger dripped from Monroe's words.

The anger in his voice incited the Pashtuns. One of them started complaining loudly to his comrades. "That's them," the man said in Pashto. "I'm telling you. That's them!"

"*Who* do you think we are?" Salam said, trying to bully them. "*Who?*"

The leader got down off his horse. He walked up to Salam and stared him in the eye. Even in the scant light of the moon, Salam could see the shine of his oily, sunburnt complexion and the glint in his deep-set eyes. He glanced at Monroe for only a second before returning his attention to Salam.

"You are the ones," he breathed, his voice a low croak. "You are the ones who murdered Zyrous Mohammed."

"Fuck!" Canfield said as soon as he heard Zyrous's name.

The others had picked up on it, too.

"Take it easy," Salam said to his people. "Stay calm."

"We did not kill Zyrous," Salam said to the Pashtun leader. "We saw it happen. It was someone else. A sniper."

The leader looked at Monroe and focused on the sniper rifle on his shoulder. "You. . . tell. . . lie," the man said in slow, deliberate English. His men had their guns squarely trained on the Americans.

"Easy," Salam said to his people. "Just take it easy." It would be their five AKs, Salam's M4A1, and Monroe's old blunderbuss versus six of whatever the Pashtuns had. He and Proctor could certainly create some havoc, but who knew how effective the corporals would be. And Monroe—forget about it. No, this was not a firefight they could afford to get into.

"Don't shoot," Salam said to the Pashtuns. He pointed to the leg pocket of his cargo fatigues. "I have something you'll want." He slowly unbuttoned the flap and pulled out a shrink-wrapped packet of hundred-dollar bills, $10,000 worth.

The Pashtuns grumbled. They probably couldn't tell what it was in the dark.

Salam dug his thumbnail into the plastic and tore off the wrapper. He fanned out the bills so they could see what he had.

The Pashtun leader's eyes widened. His men creaked in their saddles as they leaned forward to get a better look.

"Salam," Monroe snapped, "I gave you a direct order not to use that money."

"Yes sir, you did," Salam said, keeping his eyes on the Pashtuns.

"Then goddamnit, explain yourself. You disobeyed a direct order," Monroe fumed.

The Pashtuns started shouting, not to each other but at Monroe. Even though they didn't understand English, they intuited that Monroe didn't want them to have the cash.

"Sir," Salam said, "I respectfully suggest you calm the hell down before we end up a bunch of casualties like Starwood Two. Do you understand what I'm saying, sir?"

"Who the hell are you to talk to me like that, soldier?"

Salam's eyes darted back and forth between Monroe and the Pashtuns. Their leader mounted his horse but not to leave. His men spread out on horseback into a semicircle. Salam looked from one man to the other. Six muzzles stared back at him.

"Look at me, Salam," Monroe shouted.

"Sir, this will have to wait."

"I said, look at me!"

"Captain," Proctor said, "just give me the word."

"Don't shoot," Salam said. "Nobody shoot." Fucking Monroe was a loose cannon, he thought. What the hell was wrong with him? Didn't he realize that he was making a bad situation worse?

The Pashtun leader yelled, "Put down the money and put down your guns."

Yeah, right, Salam thought. They'd take the cash—plus the rest of the cash that he and Proctor had stuffed in their pants—then take them captive and bring them back to the fortress for execution. Or maybe they'd just do it Afghani-style—shoot them here and take just the heads as proof of their deed.

"Captain!" Monroe shouted. "I'm talking to you."

"Put down the money!" the Pashtun leader yelled.

"Captain! I'm addressing you."

"Put down your guns!"

"Oh, fuck," Vitelli said. He dropped his rifle, snatched the wad of bills out of Salam's hand, and in one continuous move threw them up into the air. The bills scattered and flew, falling to the ground like autumn leaves.

The sight of free-floating money made everyone jump. The Pashtuns leapt off their horses and dove for the bills. Even the leader got on his knees, scooping up hundreds.

"Go!" Salam shouted. "Take them!"

He and Proctor were already in motion, kicking heads and doing knee drops on Pashtun backs. Rudge joined the fray, throwing his body over the leader and pinning him flat to the ground. Canfield took a flying leap, feet first, and knocked another Pashtun onto his belly, taking the man's rifle away in the process. Even Vitelli, as prissy as he was, jumped in, kneeing one Pashtun in the face, following it up with a gun-butt strike to the back of the head that knocked the man out cold.

"Vitelli," Salam said, "where'd you learn to fight like that?"

"I came from a bad neighborhood."

"It must have been a pretty rough place."

Vitelli shrugged, thrusting his weapon at one of the downed Pashtuns, knocking the man flat. "Yeah, I did some things," Vitelli said.

The Americans confiscated the Pashtuns' rifles, and Jane picked up an AK for herself. They encircled the Pashtuns and forced them to sit on the ground, back to back, fingers linked on top of their heads.

"Get undressed," Salam ordered in Pashto. "Hurry up. Take off your clothes."

They grumbled among themselves, but Salam stepped forward and put the muzzle of his rifle into the leader's eye socket.

"Salam," Monroe reprimanded, but Salam ignored him and pressed harder.

The leader whipped his head away, squinting against the pain in his eye. "Do what he says," he told his men bitterly.

The men begrudgingly complied, taking off their jackets, long vests, and voluminous pants.

"Pakuls and turbans, too," Salam ordered, pointing at their headwear. "Disguises," Salam said to his people. "Come on, everybody take a costume. It's Halloween."

Monroe sputtered furiously, "Salam, this is not how the United States Army—"

"Sir," he yelled over the general, "this is how we are going to get out of these mountains. We need these clothes if we're gonna pull this off."

"Let's get one thing straight, Captain," Monroe said. "You may be in command of this unit, but I am in command of *you*. Do you understand me? I am going to hold you responsible for any breach in protocol and any violation of the rules of engagement. Officially the Afghani militiamen are our allies. You will not treat them like the enemy."

Jane stepped in. "Are you on Mars, General? What the fuck is wrong with you? These people are not our allies. They want to *kill* us."

"Ms. Norcross, this is none of your business."

"Saving my ass *is* my business," she replied. "You're a fancy pants general who doesn't know shit. I'm with Salam."

Monroe looked at the other men. Canfield and Rudge had already started putting on the Pashtuns' clothes. Vitelli picked through the piles, looking for something that suited him. Proctor and Salam kept their weapons trained on the Pashtuns, waiting for the others to finish dressing so that they could have their turn. Jane walked over to a pile, snatched up a *pakul,* looked Monroe in the eye, and jammed it on her head in defiance.

Salam grinned. You go girl. She said things that he and the rest of them couldn't.

Jane and the general glared at one another, neither one backing down. Monroe was being a dick, but Salam still felt bad for him. From the very beginning none of this had gone down the way the general had wanted. Now he was taking shit from a female civilian half his age.

Monroe glared at Salam. "You are on notice, Captain," he said.

"What're you gonna do?" Jane said. "Send him to his room?"

He scowled at her for a moment, then stooped down and snapped up a few articles of clothing. He stomped off to the area behind their horses.

Canfield, Rudge, and Vitelli took up their rifles and guarded the Pashtuns while Salam and Proctor got re-dressed. None of them took a complete *mujahadeen* outfit because most of the *muj* wore outfits that mixed traditional garb with US Army surplus. Rudge had taken a blousy shirt and long vest, but on him they were almost snug. Vitelli found a turban, and with his dark complexion, he could almost pass as a *muj*. Canfield was wearing M.C. Hammer pants and a *pakul*. Salam and Proctor kept their camo flak jackets but dressed them up with patterned scarves that were as big as shawls. By the time the two Berets were finished dressing, General Monroe returned to the group.

Jane let out a howl despite herself. She covered her mouth and started laughing out of control as soon as she saw Monroe.

He wore a tribal scarf wrapped around his neck as if he were a little kid bundled up by his mother for a cold winter's day. The sight of the turban on Monroe's head had Jane in stitches, and the men pressed their lips together to keep from bursting out into laughter. Monroe wore the Pashtun leader's blue-gray turban pulled down low over his brow. It looked like an elephant dropping enveloping his head.

"Here," Jane said, going over to him. She loosened the scarf and draped it over his shoulders the way the *mujahadeen* wore them. She then rearranged the turban so that it sat on his head with more dignified tilt.

"I'm not much for hats," Monroe muttered with a frown. "I don't have a hat head."

"No kidding," she said.

The men couldn't hold it in any longer. It started with Canfield and Vitelli, then spread to the others, including the Berets. They doubled over, laughing out of control. In fact Monroe's outfit wasn't all that funny, but it afforded a much-needed opportunity to release the tension they'd been under since the assassination.

"Canfield! Vitelli! Rudge!" Salam barked to get them back on track. "Are you watching these prisoners?"

"Yes sir," Rudge said. He'd been watching them the whole time. Vitelli and Canfield moved closer to the prisoners and took up positions around them. Salam wanted to distract them all from the general. Monroe's little *muj* fashion disaster wasn't for their amusement.

Out of the corner of his eye, Salam saw Jane talking to Monroe. He couldn't hear what the general was saying, but he did hear her say, "No hard feelings?" It pleased Salam to see them making up. This trek was going to be hard enough without internal strife.

Salam mentally ticked off what had to be done next. Tie up the Pashtuns but not so tight that they couldn't free themselves after a while. Blindfold them so they wouldn't see which way the unit went. Take their horses so they couldn't pursue. Take whatever food they had. Continue along the trail. Start looking for shelter before dawn—

"Fuck me." Proctor's hushed voice carried through the chilly air. "Captain."

Salam looked around—a line of *muj* on horseback on the next ridge, black silhouettes on a dark background less than a hundred yards off. Salam did a quick count—at least two dozen of them that he could see. Their horses stomped and snorted, spewing hot breath from their nostrils. The men didn't move. Salam couldn't see their faces, but he could feel them staring back at him.

A voice flew out of the night, one word in Pashto, as sharp as the crack of a starter's pistol: *"Attack!"*

18

MONROE DIDN'T NEED A TRANSLATION. The horseman's bark conveyed his meaning, and the sight of twenty-plus mounted *mujahadeen* simultaneously spurring their horses to run confirmed it.

"Get on your horses," Monroe shouted to his people.

"Let's go, let's go," Salam yelled at the same time.

The two men exchanged quick glances. They could not afford any confusion in leadership. "I'll take it from here," Monroe said to Salam.

"But, General—"

"Ride, Captain."

Salam started to object, but the sound of pounding hooves changed his mind. "Yes sir," he said. "I suggest we take the Pashtun horses. They have saddles." He ran toward the pack and mounted the nearest horse with a clean bounce step.

Monroe ran, too, and mounted a horse but far less gracefully. Jane found a horse for herself and the other men soon followed. "I can lead," she shouted.

"Captain Salam! Sergeant Proctor!" Monroe called out. "Take the rear positions. Hold your fire until you hear from me. The rest of you follow Jane. Go!"

She spurred her horse, moving quickly from a trot to a canter, Canfield and Vitelli right behind her. Rudge held back, waiting for the general.

"Rudge, go!" Monroe shouted.

But Rudge just looked at him. "I'll wait for you, sir."

An irrational flash of anger passed through Monroe, who took offense at the corporal's implication that he couldn't take care of himself. Monroe knew he should have been touched that the man would willingly risk his life for his commanding officer, but everything Rudge did irked him.

"Get moving, Corporal," he said. "Go!"

Rudge spurred his horse and went first, but he kept looking back to check on Monroe and his new mount. Monroe tried not to let on that he felt only marginally more confident on a horse with a saddle and a bridle.

The *mujahadeen* horsemen screamed as they charged, emitting ear-piercing shrieks meant to intimidate. The Americans galloped single file along a downhill trail. The *mujahadeen* hadn't gained any ground on them because they had to cross the shallow ravine. Monroe leaned into his horse's neck, forcing himself to stay loose above the waist, using his legs to steady himself on the animal. He fought the urge to tighten his grip on the reins, not wanting to give the horse any unintended signals. If his horse slowed down, Proctor and Salam would run right into him and cause a pileup.

The moon had moved higher in the night sky, smaller but brighter than it had been earlier. Monroe could see Rudge's face as he turned around yet again. He could also see Canfield and Vitelli up ahead. Jane at the front of the pack a dozen lengths away spurred her horse like a jockey. But did she have any idea where she was going?

"Stay out of the ravines," he shouted to Rudge. "Pass it forward. Tell her to stay out of the ravines."

Rudge repeated the message twice to Vitelli, who shouted it to Canfield, who yelled it to Jane. She made no indication that she'd heard it, which worried Monroe. They could dead-end in a ravine and be trapped.

A wide ravine came up fast on the left, and she passed it up even though it was wider than the trail they were on. She'd gotten the message, Monroe thought with relief. More importantly, she was taking orders.

A shot rang out, a crack in the night. A second and a third followed. Monroe looked back, and his horse suddenly swerved. Monroe's stomach bottomed out, certain that he and the animal would spill, but the horse righted itself and regained its gallop. His sudden movement must have jerked the reins to one side, telling the horse to turn. Thank God the animal knew better than to run off the trail. Monroe tried looking back again, moving more carefully this time. More single shots came. The lead *mujahadeen* horseman took shots at them, but since his fellow horsemen were also in single file on the trail, only he could fire.

"General," Proctor called out. "Permission to fire, sir."

"Denied," Monroe said.

Proctor closed the distance between them until his horse's nose almost touched Monroe's horse's flank. "General, we can take out the lead man and cause a pileup."

"Permission denied, Sergeant."

"But, General—"

"I said no! Don't ask me again."

Proctor fell back and passed the general's orders on to Salam.

Monroe knew the Berets hated him right now, but they didn't see the big picture. Afghanistan's only chance for lasting independence rested with the Northern Coalition. For that reason it had to be preserved. The warlords already thought the Americans had killed Zyrous Mohammed. Killing more of their people would only reinforce that wrong headed notion. And the seven of them had no chance against thousands of mountain-dwelling *mujahadeen* on their own turf. It would be a diplomatic disaster for the United States and suicide for them personally.

The lead *mujahadeen* kept firing single shots. The trail suddenly went into a steep decline, winding to the left. Monroe's horse had to drop his rump to stay on his feet.

"Don't slow down! Don't slow down!" The message traveled back from the front of the pack, going from man to man. But they had already slowed down, the horses crowding on the narrow pass. Monroe's horse inched up on Rudge's, and Proctor fought to keep his mount from bowling into Monroe's from behind. Proctor nosed his horse alongside of Monroe's to avoid a collision.

Monroe looked toward him and noticed a wet sheen on Proctor's pants along his thigh.

"Sergeant," he yelled, "you're bleeding."

"Don't concern yourself, General," Proctor said, barely containing his sarcasm. "It's nothing, sir."

It had better be nothing, Monroe thought. They couldn't afford injuries.

The trial curved sharply to the left, so much so that Monroe couldn't see the *mujahadeen* horsemen anymore even though he could still hear their pursuing hooves behind him. To Monroe it felt like a toboggan run, barreling down a chute, just hanging on and praying.

After a few moments the trail started to level off and widen, the rocks not as high along the shoulders.

He heard instructions being passed back from the front. "Don't slow down! Run! Run!"

Monroe raced with the pack. The trail opened up onto a clearing—an open field, relatively level and remarkably free of boulders, the earth soft and purple-gray in the moonlight. The horses fanned out into the open space and ran seven abreast, the *mujahadeen* horsemen still on the trail and out of sight.

"Run!" Jane shouted. "Run!"

Monroe watched her. He admired her skill as a rider, but fear and hysteria made her wild. He scanned the landscape ahead. She spurred them all on to run like hell, but where were they running to? On open ground the *mujahadeen* would eventually overtake them. The field stretched on for another two hundred yards to a stand of pine trees where the terrain sloped up again. Monroe could make out truck-sized shapes among the trees. Boulders, he guessed. Good cover in case of a skirmish. He hoped it wouldn't come to that, but if the horsemen persisted, a firefight might be inevitable.

Monroe assessed his options as he bore down on his galloping mount. Another incident involving Americans and Northern Coalition fighters could irreparably damage the United States' relationship with the warlords. But as commanding officer of this unit, his primary responsibility was the survival of the people under him. Yet if he did allow his men to fight back, and it got out that he had ordered SF troops to engage in combat, would that diminish his effectiveness at the congressional hearings? Would it hurt the bill's chances of passage? Would he have to bow out? What would that do to his career? Plenty of military careers had stalled for reasons that couldn't be helped, but Monroe didn't see himself as corporate window dressing for one of those Fortune 500 companies that hire retired military leaders for their contacts rather than their abilities.

But these people were his responsibility, he kept thinking. He had to do his utmost to keep them alive.

Suddenly Captain Salam raced his horse around the charging line and cut in front of everyone, forcing the horses to slow down. "Stop!" he yelled. "Stop! Stop right now!" He pointed at a makeshift wooden sign stuck in the dirt in the middle of the field. Monroe wouldn't have noticed it until he'd passed it if Salam hadn't pointed it out. Crude lettering in yellow paint. Under the first line written in one of the native languages, Monroe read "Beware Mines" in terse English.

They all abruptly pulled their horses to a halt, raising a cloud of dust. Monroe looked back. The horsemen emerged from the trail and burst onto the field, spurring their horses to gallop. Several of them started firing their weapons.

Monroe felt panic rising in his chest, unsure of what to do. They couldn't get off the field fast enough to evade the horsemen. A firefight on open ground would be a slaughter for his outnumbered forces, and at this point negotiation wasn't an option. How could he get them to talk when they were already shooting?

"Dismount," Salam shouted as he jumped off his horse. "Get off your horses. Do it! Now!"

The others listened to him, even Jane. Monroe dismounted last.

Salam brought his horse around by the bridle, pointed it across the field, and slapped its rump, shouting like a cattle driver in the animal's ear. The horse took off through the minefield. Salam grabbed Vitelli's horse and did it again.

"No!" Jane screamed, running over to stop him. She hung on his arm, but he shrugged her off and went for Canfield's horse.

"No!" she shrieked, coming back at him. Proctor put her in a bear hug to keep her from interfering.

Salam slapped Canfield's horse and sent it galloping through the minefield after the others. He turned to the group, pointing to the field. "Run in their footsteps," he shouted. The fresh hoofprints appeared as dark scallops on the purple-gray surface. "Hurry up! Go!"

Salam set Proctor's horse loose, and Rudge did his own, then Jane's. She struggled to get free of Proctor's grip, cursing like a sailor.

"General, your horse," Salam shouted.

Monroe snapped out of it, positioned his horse, and smacked its rump. It fussed but didn't run, and Monroe had to hit it again harder before it would go.

The horses ran wild and reached the middle of the field in no time. They converged and ran together in a pack.

"General, run," Salam yelled. He and the others had already started across the field, even Jane, stepping carefully into the hoofprints, moving faster as they got the hang of it. The horsemen came up fast, all of them firing their weapons. Monroe had to hustle, keeping his head down to make sure he stepped where the horses had already gone.

Boom!

Monroe looked up and saw one of the horses in a twisted position six feet in the air. It had stepped on a mine and let out a horrific noise, one that Monroe never imagined could come from a horse. It landed with a bounce and detonated a second mine, sending a geyser of gore into the moonlight.

Jane emitted a gut-wrenching howl for the poor animal, reaching out as she ran. Proctor had to haul her back in line by the scruff of the neck to keep her from stepping on virgin dirt.

Salam's raspy shouts could be heard over the commotion. "Move! Move! Move!"

Monroe felt that he should be doing something, but it took all his concentration to make sure he stepped only in the hoofprints.

Another explosion up ahead buffeted his chest. He looked up to see a horse doing a backflip and landing on its head. It lay motionless in the purple soil.

As he picked up his pace, he could hear Jane crying, her anguished moans carrying across the field. Bullets tore up divots around his feet. He moved faster but couldn't help glancing back.

The *mujahadeen* had stopped at the edge of the field, surveying it from their saddles. The mines had dissuaded them from pursuing. They kept firing their weapons, but halfheartedly. Monroe had expected them to deliver a barrage of bullets, but under these conditions their kill rate would be low. They'd probably decided to save their ammo for better opportunities, he figured.

One by one Monroe and his people made it to the other side of the field. They didn't break their stride until they were into the trees and behind the boulders.

"Get out of sight and stay down," Salam yelled as he intercepted the stragglers, pushing their backs as they ran by.

Monroe, the last one to come off the field, received a shove from Salam, and instantly he saw red, offended that a captain would dare treat a general with such disrespect. But he kept on running until he found cover behind a huge boulder, crouching down beside Proctor and Rudge. Angry, out of breath, embarrassed, and disgusted with himself, Monroe knew that he couldn't have done what Salam had just achieved. Salam had led them out of danger. Salam could do everything, it seemed.

The horsemen kept firing across the minefield. A few bullets ricocheted off the rocks, but they came at long intervals. Rudge looked at Monroe, giving him those pitiful eyes again. The sound of the bullets chinking into the rocks annoyed Monroe; he wanted them to stop. He wanted to stop them himself.

He unhitched the sniper rifle from his shoulder and checked the chamber. He hugged the rock and got to his feet.

"Easy, General," Proctor said.

"Shut up, Sergeant," Monroe snapped.

He positioned himself on the curve of the boulder, his rifle pointing over the top. He squinted through the scope, found the man he thought was the leader, and took aim. Clamping his jaw and clenching the butt to his shoulder, he squeezed off a shot, holding the position and watching his target through the scope. He waited, but his target didn't fall off his horse, and none of the horsemen stirred. He must have been far off his mark.

"Sir," Rudge said, "the captain says we should save our ammo for sure shots."

Monroe stared at Rudge, smothering his anger. Then he caught the look on Proctor's face, the sergeant staring at him disapprovingly.

"Is there a problem, Sergeant?" Monroe asked.

"None, sir," Proctor said. "None whatsoever."

19

"NO FIRES," Salam said to Canfield. The captain kicked the small pile of dry brush that Canfield had collected.

"But, sir, we're freezing," Canfield protested.

"Why don't we just put up the Bat Light?" Salam said. "Then we can tell *all* the *muj* where we are."

"Oh. . ." Canfield dropped his head. "I understand, sir."

They all huddled under a ledge of overhanging rocks in a large ravine about a quarter mile from the minefield. The bitter cold consumed their thoughts. Rudge kept looking up at the dark sky, wishing out loud for sunrise, but he'd have to wait several hours for that. Vitelli and Jane sat on the ground with their backs to the wall, hugging their knees for warmth. Canfield paced, stomping his feet and rubbing his arms. Proctor lay on his side with his pants down below his knees as Monroe attended to his wound. Without a medical kit, Monroe had to improvise, tearing strips from his voluminous black pants and tying the wound tight to stop the bleeding. The bullet had sliced into the flesh on the outside of this leg, just above the knee—hardly the "scratch" that Proctor had described. He had a gash two fingers deep with bone showing.

"Do you think you can walk on it?" Monroe asked.

"Yes sir. I'll be fine, sir."

"Save the SF machismo for the lady, Sergeant. Just give me an honest assessment."

Proctor grimaced. "I can walk on it, sir. I am not a liability. If it becomes a problem, I will tell you. . . sir."

"Be sure you do, sergeant." Monroe finished tying off the wound.

In the meantime Salam had gathered the three corporals. "Listen up," the captain said. "I'm gonna cut to the chase with you. Our chances of getting out of here are slim to nil unless you three can shape up and show some stellar qualities that I haven't seen in you yet. I apologize if

I hurt your feelings, but right now I don't give a flying fuck about your feelings. All I care about is that you men turn into snakeeaters ASAP. I want you to eat bullets for breakfast and shit 'em back out for lunch. If you can do what I know you can do, then we stand a chance. Not a great chance but a chance."

"Yes sir," Rudge said.

Canfield mumbled the same.

Vitelli stayed silent.

"I have to commend you, Vitelli," Salam said. "You thought fast and threw down that money. That saved our hides."

Vitelli shrugged. "I've seen it work on the street back home. The sight of money fucks people up."

"You know how to think on your feet," Salam said. "Now get over yourself and get your hands dirty, and you'll really be worth something."

Vitelli screwed up his face. "Whattaya mean?"

"I mean, start paying attention to the unit, not just your own sorry ass. Get involved. You see a guy at risk of getting shot, start shooting, give him some cover."

"I wasn't trained for that."

"You did Basic, you've seen war movies, you know enough. Just get with the program, okay?"

"Yeah, okay, whatever."

"Not 'whatever,' Corporal. You do it or you die. Understand?"

Vitelli scowled at him. "Yes sir," he finally said.

Salam turned to Rudge. "Rudge, you're a good man, but you are too methodical and too goddamn slow for this unit."

"I'm sorry, sir."

"You are not fixing helos here. Precision is secondary to initiative."

"Yes sir."

"I want you to grow fangs, Rudge."

"Yes sir."

"You're not getting me, Rudge."

"Yes sir. I am, sir."

Salam narrowed his eyes. "Rudge, I want you to say 'fuck.'"

"Sir?"

Salam raised his voice. "Just say it, corporal."

Rudge hesitated. "Fuck, sir."

"Say 'motherfucker,' Rudge."

Rudge looked uncomfortable. "Motherfucker, sir."

"Say 'cunt-licker.'"

"Sir, I—"

"Say it!"

"Cunt-licker."

"Say 'ass-sucker.'"

"Ass-sucker, sir."

"Now say, 'I hate those motherfucking, cunt-licking, ass-sucking *muj* who are trying to blow my ass off.'"

Rudge looked like he was in pain.

"Say it!"

"I hate. . . those motherfucking. . ."

"Go on. 'Cunt-licking.'"

"Cunt-licking, ass-sucking *muj* who are trying to blow my ass off."

"Well done, Rudge. Now say it in your own words. And make it just as nasty."

Rudge took a deep breath. "Sir, I want to find every *muj* on our trail, cut off his dick and make him smoke it."

"Not good enough."

"I want to cut their fucking heads off and go bowling."

"You can do better."

"I. . . I want to rip their motherfucking spines out," he shouted, "and beat them to death with it, then. . . then I want to pray to God to come down from on high and bring these ass-sucker heathens back to life so I can *motherfucking do it again, sir!*" Rudge's chest heaved. A nervous smile played over his thick lips.

"Excellent, Rudge. I think you're getting it."

"I am, sir."

Salam turned his gaze on Canfield. "Corporal Canfield."

"Yes sir." Canfield was standing at attention.

"There is a phrase that comes to mind when I think about men like you, Canfield. Young, dumb, and—"

"Full of cum," Canfield finished.

"That's exactly what I mean about you, Canfield. You're a premature ejaculator. You're unfocused. You're jacking off all over the place."

Canfield frowned. He didn't know how to respond to this.

"Canfield, I want you to start thinking before you go off half-cocked. I want you to think about everybody else in this unit, not just yourself. I want you to get your attention-deficit-disorder ass under control and contribute to the effort. If I have to babysit you, Canfield, I'm just gonna fucking shoot you. Because I am not gonna risk my neck to save a walking liability. Do you understand what I'm telling you?"

"Yes sir."

"You are a liar, Canfield. I know right well you do not understand what I'm telling you."

"Sir?" Canfield looked like he was about to cry.

"Suck it up, Canfield. If I see so much as the beginning of a tear in your sorry eyes, I *will* shoot you."

"Yes sir." Canfield pressed his lips together and put a clamp on his emotions.

"Remember, Canfield, you are on probation in my book. You fucked up back at the fortress. You let your team down. Then you fucked up at the cave. Now you have to make up for it. Big time."

Canfield's lower lip trembled.

"You *can* make up for it, Canfield." Salam lowered his voice and looked him in the eye. "I believe you can do it, Canfield. You can redeem yourself. . . if you try."

"I will try, sir. No sir, I'm sorry, sir. I will not just try. I will *do* it. I *will*, sir. I *will*."

Monroe looked at Proctor, who had a proud smile on his face. SF proud. Salam was a good motivator and a natural leader. Better than Monroe. The men probably realized that.

Monroe stood up and looked down at Proctor. "Stay off that leg as much as you can, Sergeant," he said lamely.

"Yes sir." Proctor's attention went right back to Salam.

Monroe walked off, clamping his hands under his armpits for warmth. He moved away from the others and walked farther into the ravine. He wanted to be alone for a while.

"General?" Jane walked up behind him.

"Yes?"

"General, what's— Wait a minute," she said. "Do I have to keep calling you 'General'? Considering the shit we've been through, can't I just call you Jackson or Jack or. . . what do your friends call you?"

"If you had cancer, would you call your doctor by his first name?"

"If he was the one who gave me cancer, yeah," she said.

He ignored her jibe. "I wouldn't," he said. "I'd want a professional treating me. And I would regard a professional *as* a professional."

"Don't flatter yourself, Jack. You'd be the first guy I'd vote off the island."

He scowled at her. "You may be a civilian, but this is an Army unit. Rank matters, and it will be respected."

I've heard that one before. The West Point rap."

"What would you know about West Point?"

"My brother went there. Remember?"

"What was his branch?"

"Infantry. He fought in Desert Storm."

"I'm impressed. Any cadet who picks Infantry is a true warrior. He's not a five and flyer. He's not thinking about a career *after* the Army. The Army *is* his career."

"Yeah, that's my brother. Total gung-ho. He's stationed in Iraq now. Won't be happy till he does something to get himself a Congressional Medal of Honor."

"Do you know what that entails?"

"Bravery, I would hazard to guess."

"A *selfless* act of bravery. Risking your own life to save others. It doesn't happen often."

"Like Salam at the cave?" Her gaze wandered toward the captain.

He followed her eyes and stared at Salam, who was still talking to the corporals.

"So you gonna put him up for one?" she asked.

"A Congressional Medal? Right. I think we have other things to worry about right now." Inside Monroe seethed with envy and anger with himself for feeling the way he did. He should have been the one leading like Salam.

"So what was your branch?" Jane asked.

Monroe paused. "Aviation," he said. "You were about to ask me something before we got off topic."

"Well, I was just worried about you. You look kind of—I don't know—peeved."

"Well, of course, I'm concerned about our situation. I'd say that's pretty natural, wouldn't you?"

"It's more than that," she said. "Salam is really pissing you off, isn't he?"

Monroe felt a flush of embarrassment. He didn't think it was that obvious. "Why do you think the captain is. . . upsetting me, as you put it?"

"General, you can drop the big shot routine. The networks aren't watching, Brie is gone, and I don't have a camera. You're just another Indian to me."

"Captain Salam is doing a commendable job," Monroe said. "So the answer is no, he's not pissing me off."

Jane gave him a wry grin. "You're full of shit, Jack." She used his first name only because she knew it bothered him so much.

"Pardon?"

"I'm a visual person," she said. "All I know is what I see, and when I look at you, I see someone sitting on his emotions, someone about to explode."

"Are you a photographer or a psychologist?"

She looked him in the eye. "We're never gonna make it out of here, are we? Salam's putting up a brave front, but I can see the truth in your face. It's hopeless. Admit it."

Could she really read that much from his demeanor? She'd sized up the situation accurately. Unless command in Gardiz sent out rescue units, their chances of survival would be dismal. But she didn't need to know that.

"It's not hopeless," he said to her. "When you stop breathing, that's when it's hopeless. Now if you'll excuse me, I'd like some time alone, please."

He turned his back on her and walked along the rock walls of the ravine into the darkness.

Nearly an hour had gone by when the general finally returned, and Salam could see trouble coming. Monroe had that "higher" look, the expression common to all high-ranking officers when they come up with "The Plan," a smugness combined with divine inspiration as if God had spoken to them directly and given them exclusive rights to the solution to all their mortal problems. The Plan could be massive troop movement or a way to keep maple syrup from turning to water in desert heat so that every American fighting man could have his flapjacks the exact same way he remembered them from back home. Invariably the Plan was either nothing new or some harebrained, jerry-rigged Rube Goldberg notion that anyone with half an ounce of sense and more than a day's worth of real field experience could see wouldn't work from the get-go.

Monroe walked right up to him. "Captain Salam," he said, "I'd like to talk to you."

"Yes sir." Oh, shit. Here it goes.

Monroe laid his hand on Salam's shoulder and led him away from the others, who obviously smelled trouble, too, because they perked up like nervous deer. Except for Proctor. As usual he conveyed his suspicions through his sneer.

"I've been considering our options," Monroe began. "I think that when day breaks we should continue on without stealth or concealment."

"But, sir—"

"Let me finish. The *mujahadeen* have been pursuing us because we've been running. They can attack because they know they can always say that they didn't know they were firing on Americans. If we proceed in the light of day, they won't be so quick to engage and risk censure from the international community."

"Sir, these people don't care—"

"I'm not finished, Captain," Monroe overrode him. "Now if these people persist in engagement, we will stand a better chance of being spotted by rescue units during the day than at night. But I'm confident that if we walk in the light, they will not attack. Do you have any input?"

Salam took a long breath before he spoke, wishing he knew how to phrase this better, but he didn't so he just said it. "Sir, this plan is impractical. The *muj*, the warlords, Afghanistan in general, they doesn't give a damn about the international community."

Monroe furrowed his brows and frowned. "Well, I disagree."

"Sir, I don't mean to criticize you, but. . . your plan is. . . crazy."

Monroe trembled with anger. "Your level of insubordination is astounding," he said, struggling to hold his temper. "I don't know how you managed to sneak your way through—"

Salam turned his back on Monroe and started to walk away. He didn't want to get into it with Monroe. But before Salam could take a second step, Monroe shoved him hard from behind and nearly knocked him over. "Don't turn your back on me, you asshole. Not unless you want trouble."

Salam just stared at him over his shoulder. He couldn't believe this. A three-star calling out a captain?

"Now turn around and face me," Monroe said through gritted teeth, "and you just listen."

Salam didn't move a muscle. "Fuck you. . . General."

20

JANE COULDN'T BELIEVE IT. Monroe had flipped out, challenging Salam to fight. Real schoolyard stuff. She moved in closer, fascinated by the whole situation, dying to see how this would play out. Oh, for a camera! If she were betting, she'd put her money on Salam—he had the training, the skills, the physique—but Monroe couldn't be counted out because he had something else. He had the fire. She could see it in his eyes.

The general shoved Salam again, but Salam barely moved. He had turned around to face Monroe, ready for it this time. Monroe yelled, "Don't patronize me, Salam."

Salam stared at him, his face rock hard. He would not let himself be goaded into striking a general, but Jane could see that he was dying to. The glint in his eyes reminded her of a lit fuse. No telling when he would go off.

The two men had moved in closer and now stood a foot apart. Salam had his back to the wall. They eyeballed one another, each one wanting the other to make the first move. But Monroe's stare wavered when he glanced at Jane and the others. The audience concerned him. They'd witnessed him making the challenge; now he had to follow up on it or risk losing face. Jane shook her head in amazement. So juvenile. Monroe wanted to impress the others. He had to prove that he had the bigger *cajones*.

"Excuse me, ma'am." Rudge squeezed past her and went up to them. "Sirs," he said, ever conscious of his rank, "it's not my place to interfere with superior officers, but I don't think you two should be—"

Monroe shouted, "Mind your own fucking business, Rudge. Step back."

"Whoa," Canfield said under his breath.

"You hear that?" Vitelli said with mean glee.

She couldn't wait to see where this was going to go.

"Rudge," Proctor called out. He sat on the ground, his wounded leg stretched out flat. "Rudge," he repeated with a warning note in his voice.

Rudge looked back at Proctor but didn't move. Rudge wore his morality plainly. Officers squaring off like schoolkids did not align with his sense of right, wrong, and practicality. He couldn't just stand by.

Monroe shouted again. "I said, step back, Rudge. Step. Back." He glared at Rudge, and Jane wondered if Monroe would take him on next.

"Do not talk to my soldier that way," Salam said.

Monroe's eyes bugged out of his head. "*Your* soldier? *Your* soldier? Who the hell do you think you—" The general lunged at Salam, not even bothering to finish his sentence. He grabbed Salam by the jacket with his left hand and threw a punch with his right, catching the captain in the face.

Salam's head snapped back, but the blow apparently didn't do much damage because he shrugged out of the general's grip and threw his arms around him in a bear hug, intent on keeping Monroe from throwing another punch. Monroe grabbed the lapels of Salam's jacket and threw his leg behind Salam's, trying to trip him and bring him down. But Salam saw what was happening, and he lifted the general off his feet, preventing the throw.

Monroe countered by going for the pressure point under Salam's nose, hooking his thumb under Salam's jawline and pressing the knuckle of his index finger against the upper lip. Salam let go and slammed his elbow into Monroe's arm to get the general's hand off his face, then swung his elbow back, smashing it into Monroe's cheek. Monroe reeled back, squinting and wincing.

"Stop now," Rudge yelled. "Please!"

But they ignored him. Monroe blinked as he backstepped into the ravine wall. Salam stalked him, staying close.

"Are we through, General?" he said.

Monroe felt his cheek for broken bone. "No," he said.

"Have it your way."

"I will."

Monroe threw his leg out, trying to sweep Salam's legs out from under him, but Salam avoided the sweep by stepping in and grabbing

Monroe by the face and pushing him back. Salam's hand shook. He had the opportunity to bash Monroe's head against the wall, but he held back.

Suddenly Salam let go of Monroe's face and hunched over in pain. Monroe's right hand was balled into a fist. He had delivered a dead-on punch into Salam's solar plexus.

"You're patronizing me, Salam. Don't. Just fight."

"No sir," Salam said, gasping for breath. "I won't do that."

Monroe lunged, arms out and fingers spread, intent on getting Salam on the ground, but Salam surprised him, grabbing his jacket and twisting his body, going with Monroe's momentum and throwing the general down hard on his back. The fall knocked the wind out of Monroe, and Salam didn't waste any time, jumping on top and pinning him.

But Monroe didn't waste any time either, raising his knee to meet Salam's groin as he went for the pin. Monroe took the brunt of Salam's falling weight, but the excruciated expression on Salam's face made Jane wince. Monroe pushed him off and he rolled onto the ground, doubling over.

Monroe's face was frightening, crazy vicious. He wanted to punish Salam. As Salam got to his knees and shook his head, trying to get his eyes to focus, Monroe struck again, jumping at him, but Salam saw him coming and reacted, taking Monroe's balance and throwing him down hard on his belly as if he were as light as a scarecrow. He then leapt onto Monroe's back and crawled on top, using his knees to pin the general's arms to his body and linking his fingers around Monroe's forehead and pulling back, poised to snap Monroe's spine.

"You fucking little snot-nose motherfucker!" Salam whispered in a hiss.

Monroe's mouth hung open, the whites of his eyes blazing, helpless to fight back, grunting like a cornered animal.

"I'm gonna kill you, you pompous son of a bitch. I don't give a fuck what happens to me. We'll be better off without you." Salam increased the pressure.

Monroe howled.

"Rudge," Proctor shouted, "stop them. Hurry up. That's an order."

Rudge rushed over to pull Salam off the general, tossing the captain aside as if he were a bale of hay. Monroe, furious, scrambled to his knees and lashed out, flailing his fists at Salam, who deflected the wild blows and pulled Monroe close by the front of his jacket, flipping him onto his back. But Rudge grabbed Salam by the shoulders and hauled him off before he could do anything to Monroe.

"Sergeant Proctor says that's enough," Rudge said.

Salam just looked at him, breathing hard, lying on the ground on his side.

Jane couldn't imagine what would happen if Rudge ever lost *his* temper. The man was a titan.

Monroe slowly climbed to his knees, facing away from Jane. She saw him reaching for something, a flat rock the size of a steam iron. He picked it up.

"Salam!" she shouted. "Look out!"

Monroe raised the rock high, his crazed eyes focused on Salam's head. Salam could only raise his arms to protect himself. But Rudge snatched Monroe's wrist and stopped the rock's descent.

"Let go of me, Rudge!" Monroe shouted.

A pained look contorted Rudge's face, but he didn't let go.

"I said, 'Let go,' Corporal," Monroe snarled. "I am giving you an order."

Sweat coursed down Rudge's face.

"I said, *Let go!*"

Rudge's lips trembled, but he held fast to Monroe's wrist. "Don't make me break your arm, sir," he said, straining to get the words out. He shook Monroe's hand as if he were choking a snake. Monroe let go of the rock, and it hit the ground with a *thud*.

Suddenly another rock, this one the size of a bowling ball, hit the ground near Monroe's rock with a deeper *thud*. All eyes went to Salam, thinking he'd tried to retaliate, but Salam looked as surprised as everyone else. Another rock fell from the sky, this one even bigger. It landed inches from Rudge's leg, bounced a foot high, and crashed into the stone wall of the ravine, knocking out a few chips.

"Heads up!" Proctor shouted.

Jane looked straight up to the lip of the ravine, fifty feet above her head. Boulders rolled over the side, free-falling straight at her. Instinctively she hugged the wall, pressing her back flat against it. A boulder crashed inches from where she stood and bounced wild, colliding with the wall right next to her. Her heart started to pound, thinking that her rib cage, her hips, something would have been crushed beyond repair if she'd been standing just two feet to her right.

"Hug the walls, people," Salam shouted. "Stay flat."

But they were already doing that.

She looked up again. More boulders toppled over the edge. She pulled her head in just in time to avoid a glancing blow.

She could hear voices up there, men shouting in a foreign language. She looked to Salam, then Monroe, whose eyes had changed. The mania had disappeared, replaced with uncertainty.

She shouted to Salam, pointing up with her eyes. "What are they saying?"

Salam screwed up his face, trying to make out their words. "They're Tajiks. I don't know their language." He looked sideways at Monroe. Anger and resentment smoldered in his eyes.

More boulders tumbled over the side. Jane watched them fall, clutching her breath, not knowing how or where they would land.

"Stay alert," Salam shouted.

"No shit," Jane said, her eyes glued to the ledge above.

Still more boulders came tumbling down. They came in waves, five or six all at once, then a pause before the next onslaught.

When the next lull came, Jane noticed that Salam's eyes bored into Monroe. "What do you think, sir?" he asked pointedly. "How should we proceed?" It wasn't a question. It was an invitation to fuck up.

Monroe opened his mouth, about to respond when Canfield yelled, "Heads up!" his voiced high and strained.

Jane looked up. Another bunch of boulders fell. They hit the ground in a ragged bass drum beat, bouncing in all directions, clacking against the stone walls like giant billiard balls. Her heart leapt with each crash. It would just a matter of time before someone got crushed.

"General Monroe?" Salam shouted angrily. "How should we proceed, sir? Tell us, sir."

"Look out!" Canfield screamed.

Another barrage fell from the sky.

Monroe clung to the wall and braced for the impact just like all the others.

Salam shouted at him. "Tell us what the fuck we should do, General. You tell us!"

21

IT FELT LIKE CAMBODIA—not hot and humid or overgrown with vegetation, but to Monroe, the feeling was the same. Trapped. Thirty-four years ago he had been injured, lost, and alone inside Cambodia, crawling through the jungle, hoping everything he'd been told wasn't true, that the mission he'd been sent on did not exist, would not be acknowledged, and rescue inside Cambodian territory would not be provided. He'd felt completely abandoned. And that's how he felt right now as boulder after boulder rained down on them. He and his people had been abandoned.

"Sir?" Salam shouted. "What are your orders, sir?"

Monroe's gaze shifted from Salam to Jane to Canfield's scared eyes. Rudge pressed his body against the wall as best he could given his size. Proctor tried to do the same, struggling to stand up straight on his wounded leg. Vitelli stayed with him, standing by in case he needed support.

"Sir?" Salam shouted.

Monroe didn't answer. They had been abandoned. Command in Gardiz should have done something by now. A search plane should have been circling, rescue units should have been dispatched. No. They'd been abandoned.

A boulder struck the ground at his feet, bounced straight up, and flew toward his face. He moved just in time as it hit the wall head high.

"Sir?"

Monroe looked at Jane. She's holding up well, better than Canfield, he thought. Maybe she's just resigned to our fate. Abandoned and doomed.

"Sir?" Salam yelled, his voice getting shriller. "What do you want us to do, sir? Do you want me to take over? Tell me."

A boulder struck close to Monroe's foot, startling him. Fear gripped his chest. He nodded.

"Is that a 'yes,' General?"

Monroe nodded again. He knew he was in no shape to lead. "Yes, take over."

Salam slid closer to Monroe so he wouldn't have to yell. "I'm gonna need you, sir. Proctor's in no shape, and these other three are worth shit."

Monroe's eyes widened. "Need me for what?"

"Judging from the number of rocks that come down each time, I'd say there are about a half dozen men up there. Unless they're working in teams."

"But why the caveman tactics instead of firearms?" Monroe asked.

"Saving ammo is my guess. But it could be a tribal thing. The Tajiks are on the outs with the coalition. Killing your enemy with rocks instead of bullets is like rubbing your nose in it."

"Why do they think we're their enemy?"

"We must've wandered into their territory. Trespassing is reason enough to kill somebody in these parts."

"What do you propose, Salam?"

"You and I are going up there to mount an ambush. If the terrain is as rocky as it has been everywhere else in this area, we'll have more than adequate cover."

Monroe's heart thumped, uncertain if he could do this.

"Follow me," Salam said.

Monroe's legs felt like lead as they inched along the wall, watching the sky for new attacks, timing their movements as they slid past Jane so as not to get crushed. Monroe looked for signs of their attackers, but they stayed clear of the edge and didn't show their faces. He wondered when they would finally get tired of hauling boulders and take a peek to see if they'd scored any hits.

As Monroe came up to Proctor pressed against the wall, he glanced down at the sergeant's leg. Dried blood had darkened his pants, but the tourniquets had apparently stopped the bleeding. He looked alert, but he kept his weight on his good leg.

Salam put his face up to Proctor's. "I want you to coordinate the others. I want you and the corporals to start firing up at the enemy, but time it so that it coincides with the falling rocks. Don't waste fire. Just let them know that we're here and we're not going to be sitting ducks. Keep them distracted while the general and I get out of the ravine."

Proctor glanced at Monroe and looked surprised. "But I can——"

"Yeah, I know you can when you're not injured," Salam said, "but you are and so you can't. Just follow my orders and make sure these numbskulls don't waste all our ammo."

"Yes sir." Proctor called to the corporals. "Rudge, Vitelli, Canfield. Grab a weapon."

The assault rifles they'd stolen from the *muj* leaned against the wall right where they'd left them, undisturbed by the falling rocks. Salam took an AK-47 and inspected it in between quick glances up. Monroe picked the American M4A1, and did the same, checking the weapon while keeping an eye out for rocks.

Canfield snatched one of the available AKs, and Rudge took the other. Proctor had kept his AK by his side all along, and he had it pointed up, watching the lip of the ravine. Vitelli reached for Monroe's sniper rifle, but Monroe stopped him.

"Don't use that one unless you absolutely have to," Monroe said. "There are only a few shots left and we don't have ammo for it."

Vitelli nodded and took another rifle.

"Use your bullets wisely," Proctor shouted to the men. "Shoot only when you see the rocks *starting* to fall. In other words when those bastards are near the edge. Let's let 'em know we're here."

"Gonna bust a motherfucking cap in these motherfuckers' motherfucking asses," Canfield said.

Rudge just looked at him as if he were from another planet. "What're you *talking* 'bout?"

Canfield snorted a mocking laugh. "Shit, Rudge. I'm from Dee-troit. I'm blacker than you are."

"I don't think so," Rudge said. He watched the edge of the ravine, straining to make out the ledge line against the dark sky. A barrage of rocks suddenly came into view, already halfway down.

Canfield started firing, a three-shot burst followed by another, then another. "Whoo-eee!" he yelped, adrenaline gushing. "Who's your niggah, Rudge? *I'm* your niggah! Me!" He fired off two more bursts.

"Canfield!" Proctor shouted. "Save your fucking ammo, dickwad."

"Yes *sir!*" Canfield shouted back with glee, pumped for the kill.

Rudge shook his head. "I don't know what's got into you, boy, but you ain't nobody's niggah. You just a white boy from Dee-troit who happened to live near black folk."

As Monroe passed Proctor, he said, "Try to keep them under control, Sergeant."

"I will do my best, sir. But, sir?"

"Yes?"

Proctor nodded toward Jane, a silhouette against the wall. "What about the woman, sir?"

Monroe paused. "Get her a rifle. She can't be worse than these guys." He moved on, sliding along the wall right behind Salam.

"Do you have a plan, Captain?" Monroe asked.

"I will when we get to the top," he said and left it at that.

Monroe kept moving, his eyes straining to make out what was in front of him. Bursts of gunfire sounded from behind, but gradually they became fainter, telling him how far they'd gone. It sounded as if the Tajiks had decided to return fire, but only single shots spaced far apart.

As he and Salam kept walking, the ravine narrowed. The gunfire seemed more distant. They trudged up an incline. Soon the path ended, blocked by huge boulders. Salam started to climb.

Monroe touched his back to stop him. "One minute, Salam. We have to talk."

Salam turned around and faced Monroe. "General, we don't have time for a twelve-step program right now. You hate my guts, and I'm not too thrilled with you. But we need each other, so let's just play nice and get the job done."

Monroe nodded. "Agreed."

They mounted the boulder, Salam going first. When they got to the top, they inspected the terrain, jagged with rocks and boulders. Monroe tried to locate the Tajiks, but he couldn't see much in the dark. The faint pops of sporadic gunfire indicated that they were about a hundred yards away. He and Salam would have to double back along the high ground to pinpoint the enemy. Using hand signals, Salam gave Monroe the plan. They'd make a wide circle and approach the attackers from the rear.

Without a word, they moved on, staying low as they scuttled up and down easy boulders. They came to the crest of a high point and peered over. The cloud cover started to break up, and in the moonlight they could see the attackers in the distance—*mujahadeen*, seven of them with their horses tethered nearby. To Monroe these men looked no different from all the other *mujahadeen* he'd encountered so far, even though their language had identified them as Tajiks. Three of them struggled to roll individual boulders to the edge. Another three had rigged a rope sling between two horses and urged the animals to pull a boulder the size of a hog. They made slow progress, moving inch by inch over the jagged terrain. The seventh man straddled his horse, supervising.

"Fucking barbarians," Monroe cursed under his breath.

Salam frowned at him and put his finger to his lips. They surveyed the landscape for the best route to the Tajiks' position. The ridge they were on was a fairly direct approach of moderate rock-climbing, but it was the highest point in the vicinity. They would be spotted before they got close enough to mount an effective ambush. Salam tapped Monroe's forearm and pointed over the edge of the boulder they were on to a dirty path about fifteen feet below them. It seemed relatively flat and appeared to go in the direction of the Tajiks. Probably a horse path, Monroe thought.

Salam put his face to Monroe's ear. "I'll hang over the side. You climb down my body. Can you handle jumping the rest of the way?"

Monroe immediately thought of broken ankles and twisted knees—his own. "Can *you* handle the jump?" he asked.

"I used to jump off roofs when I was a kid," Salam said. "No problem."

Monroe didn't like the risk of having one, possibly two men injured from a high fall. That would be disastrous. But then he looked over at the Tajiks driving their horses to drag the hog rock. Bursts of gunfire echoed out of the ravine. Someone was wasting ammo again, probably Canfield. No time to consider an alternate plan.

"Let's go," Salam said as he slid his body toward the edge of the boulder. He felt around until he found a knobby outcropping that would support his weight. He linked his fingers around it and lowered his body over the rounded edge, his rifle on his shoulder. He jerked his head impatiently for Monroe to get moving.

Monroe maneuvered his body to the edge next to Salam, then mounted his back and lowered himself down, gripping Salam's belt. Gravity suddenly pulled him down further, and he hugged Salam's knees, Salam completely supporting Monroe's weight. Despite the cold, sweat dripped from Monroe's forehead into eyes. He loosened his grip slightly but slipped faster than he expected, stopping with a jolt at Salam's ankles. He felt his pulse racing, certain that he was going to pull them both down. But the captain held fast. Monroe paused to collect himself, his arms shaking. He looked down but couldn't see the path. The clouds had covered the moon again.

"Go," Salam whispered.

Monroe figured it couldn't be that far of a drop, but thoughts of broken bones and twisted ankles stole his nerve.

"Go!" Salam hissed. "I can't hold you forever."

No turning back now, Monroe thought. He willed himself to grab Salam's ankles in his hands despite his shaking. He released the tension in his muscles and lowered himself to a dead hang. He sucked in a deep breath and let go.

He fell straight down, and his paratrooper training kicked in, bending his knees to absorb the shock and rolling to his side. The path was all rock and he hit hard, banging his ribs. He thought he might have broken one or two, but so what? Broken ribs were minor, he told himself.

He scrambled out of the way and stage-whispered up to Salam. "Go!"

Salam dropped, a dark shadow falling down the side of the boulder. He bent his knees and rolled just as Monroe had, his AK clacking against the rocks.

Monroe got to his feet and went over to him. "Are you all right?"

"I'm fine." Salam got to his feet.

Monroe thought about his ribs. He didn't feel any pain, but adrenaline could override that. If he had broken a rib, he'd feel it later, and it would make breathing difficult. Not to mention the risk of internal bleeding if a fragment punctured something. But he couldn't worry about that now.

Salam led the way, leading with his rifle. Monroe stayed close, his rifle also at the ready. They stepped carefully in the dark, more carefully as they got closer. The sound of a loose rock underfoot could alert the *mujahadeen* to their presence. The path grew steeper, taking them back up to the ridgeline. The gunshots became louder. Judging from the sound, Monroe imagined the *mujahadeen* just on the other side of the ridge. A knobby boulder ten feet tall stood between them and the attackers. It would be an easy climb. Monroe looked to Salam for the go-ahead to proceed.

Salam whispered in his ear. "Hold your fire until I give the order."

Monroe nodded and started to climb. He didn't know how Salam wanted to handle this. Fire to kill, or just scare them off? Having been attacked, they had the moral imperative to retaliate with full force, but would that be the wise thing to do? Would a counter attack against these Tajiks jeopardize America's standing in Afghanistan?

Monroe followed Salam up the rocks and positioned himself next to the captain, both of them peering over the crest of the ridge. Three Tajiks drove the horses, three rolled boulders over the side by hand, and the one on horseback occasionally fired down into the ravine—same as before. Except for the man on horseback, the Tajiks seemed jittery and agitated despite their favorable position. The horses pulling the boulder had reached the precipice. The men unhitched them from the sling and called to the three rock rollers to help them push the hog boulder over the edge. They all strained and struggled, but they made some headway, moving it forward incrementally. Monroe felt that he and Salam had to do something before the Tajiks got that boulder to the edge.

Monroe thumbed his weapon's safety to the off position and rolled his eyes toward Salam. The thought of it stuck in his craw, but he was waiting for orders.

Salam leaned into Monroe's ear. "Take out one of the men on the ground. I'll take the man on his horse. Let's take out two and scare off the rest. Without a leader, they won't be very effective."

Salam aimed his AK. Monroe did the same with his rifle, getting one of the rock pushers in his sights.

"On my word," Salam whispered.

Monroe wondered if this was the right decision. Maybe they should eliminate the whole unit. What if the survivors ran back to Khan's forces and revealed their location? But a massacre would lend credence to the assassination charge. He let Salam make the call, ashamed of himself for not facing it himself.

Monroe tracked his target. The leader and one more would send a message. These weren't battle-hard warriors. They were amateurs, throwing rocks like Neanderthals. Scare them off but send a message, Monroe decided. Salam had made the right call.

"Fire," Salam said in a full voice.

They pulled their triggers simultaneously. Monroe fired once, then once again. Salam fired a short burst.

The leader pitched back and toppled off his horse. Monroe scored a hit as well. His boulder pushers abruptly stood up, spun on one foot, and stumbled backward over the edge. He made no sound at all until his body hit bottom with a dull thud that echoed out of the ravine.

The remaining Tajiks fell into chaos, firing their guns in several directions, unable to determine the source of the attack. All five of them tried to hide behind the hog boulder, but when they realized it wouldn't protect them all, they ran for their horses and fled into the night as fast as they dared along the dark path.

Someone down in the ravine—Canfield probably—fired like mad on full auto, having heard the increased gunfire up above. Monroe watched the Tajiks riding off, disappearing into the darkness.

Salam let out a long breath. "I hope that scares them all the way back to Tajikistan."

Monroe grunted. He didn't know how to feel about all this. He felt as if he'd failed somehow.

Another burst of gunfire sounded from the ravine.

"Come on," Salam said. "Let's get back before Canfield wastes all our ammo."

22

"LOOK! LOOK AT THIS! Do you see what the Americans have done?"

The five Tajik fighters routed by the Americans talked all at once. They stood outside in the courtyard of the fortress, angrily pointing down at their dead—their leader and one of their brothers. That morning they had returned to the sight of the ambush to retrieve the bodies, carrying them back to the fortress and laying them in the dust, so that they could show Raz Khan what the Americans had done.

Khan stared down at the dead men, his expression grim. Hajji stood at his side, and he kneaded the boy's shoulders as if they were worry beads. The charred wreck of the Americans' helicopter lay on its side near the far wall. The morning sun warmed the American bodies laid out in the dirt near the center of the courtyard, flies already swarming around them.

The loudest of the Tajiks stepped forward and stood right in front of Khan. "What are you going to do?" he demanded. "You want us to be part of the coalition, then show us what you can do for us. *Do something!*"

Khan tuned him out and kneaded the boy's shoulders harder. He still hadn't sorted all this out. General Monroe had gone from being an opportunity to a potential disaster. Khan might have to forgo the price on Monroe's head to maintain his position as Zyrous Mohammed's replacement. He did not have the full support of all the warlords. They had to be courted and placated.

The Tajiks clamored for his attention. "First, they kill Zyrous," the loudmouth said. "Now they are killing more of our people. *Our* people! And yet you do nothing! You do not listen, you just play with this boy!"

Khan cocked a fierce eyebrow at the man but held his tongue. He started to walk, circling around the dead men. Instinctively Hajji walked with him, Khan's hand never leaving his shoulder.

The blood had congealed around the dead men's bullet wounds. The one with the broken body had taken several bullets to the chest. The other man, the leader, had a single head wound that had blown out a chunk of his head upon exiting. The flies had just found his brains. A new feast, Khan thought, glancing over at the American bodies.

Monroe, Monroe, Monroe, he thought. You have left me with a hard choice. If I capture you and sell you to Al Qaeda, the other warlords will grumble and rebel if they find out. However, if I can maintain control of the coalition, I can quite possibly equal that ransom over time with aid money from the American Army, which spends on the coalition like a desperate old man courting a young whore. But can I afford to let you and your people live, Monroe? What did you see from the stage when Hajji pulled the trigger? What could you possibly tell your superiors that will do any good for me? Two helicopters down, eight Americans dead, including the woman journalist. No, Khan thought, this will all be bad if it becomes known. The American government must never know.

The loudmouth Tajik nipped at Khan's heels. "Raz Khan," the man said, "you do not answer. Does that mean you do not care about the murder of Tajiks? If this is true, we will make sure that our people know. We cannot follow a man who cares nothing for us."

Across the courtyard Yusef emerged from the barracks. Khan watched him as he strode into the courtyard, cocky even in the way he walked. Cocky but valuable.

"Raz Khan," the loudmouth said, waving his arms at the dead men, "you dishonor their memory with your silence."

The other Tajiks grumbled in chorus.

Khan kept his eye on Yusef, who smiled broadly as he walked, as if Allah had shared a divine confidence with him alone.

"Raz Khan, you are no leader," the loudmouth bellowed. "You are not a worthy successor to Zyrous Mohammed. Zyrous would have listened to us. He would have *done* something."

Khan stared hard at the man, but the man didn't flinch, nor did the other Tajiks. They had no fear or respect for him.

No, Khan thought, making up his mind in a flash of understanding. This cannot happen. He could not lose this position. He would not let Monroe do that to him.

Yusef stepped toward the group, but before he could deliver his greeting, Khan cut him off. "Do you have the American equipment? The satellite phones?"

Yusef gave him a puzzled look. "Yes, of course. What would I do? Give them away?"

"Do you know how to use those kind of phones?"

"Yes."

"Can you make a call to the Army headquarters in Gardiz? An official call?"

"I could do that. I've been listening to their transmissions."

"Can you speak as an American?"

Yusef grinned. "Sure can," he said in English.

Khan caught the loudmouth's eye and nodded his assurance. He walked away from the Tajiks, taking Hajji and Yusef with him. "We have much to do," he said softly to Yusef.

"Whatever you need, General," Yusef said.

"We must eliminate a problem."

Hajji winced in silent pain. Khan didn't realize how hard he was digging his fingers into the boy's shoulder.

General Graydon stood over First Lieutenant Lynn McNabb as she sat at a computer in the communications center on the base at Gardiz. She had been the officer on duty when the message came through less than fifteen minutes ago. Tall and buff with straight blond hair that barely covered her ears, McNabb had attended the Academy. She'd been with the base from the beginning, and Graydon knew her to be cool and confident both on and off the job. When she put in a call to his office and asked him to come over, he knew it had to be something serious.

"Sir, this is the entire communiqué," she said. "It came in via sat phone." She typed the codes into her keyboard, and a sound bar appeared on her monitor. Voices came from the speakers.

"*Starwood 1 to Bigmouth Bass. Starwood One to Bigmouth Bass.*"

"*We read you, Starwood One.*" Lieutenant McNabb's recorded voice.

"*Bigmouth, we are requesting air support ASAP. Repeat, we are requesting air support as soon as you can get it here.*" He gave the coordinates for the air strike. "*We will have the target laser-marked.*"

"*Who am I speaking to, Starwood One?*"

"*Corporal Frank Vitelli.*" The accent was unmistakably New York City.

"*State the reason for your request, Corporal.*"

"*Talie unit spotted crossing a valley between two big mother mountains.*"

"*Is that a confirmed sighting, Corporal?*"

"*I didn't ask to see their driver's licenses.*"

McNabb had been unfazed by the smart remark. "*State your reasons, Corporal.*"

"*Orders from General Monroe. The Talies crossed over the Paki border. Captain Salam says he's been tracking them for a week.*"

"*I'll submit your request and get you an answer by twenty-two hundred.*"

Graydon glanced at the clock on the wall. *Twenty-two hundred hours* was less than an hour away. Monroe wanted a night strike.

"*Make it snappy, sweetness. The ragheads are on the move.*"

"*What's their mode of transport?*" McNabb asked.

"*Their smelly feet.*"

"*Save the clever banter for someone who cares, Corporal. We'll get back to you.*"

"*General's orders, my dear. And Monroe's one general you don't want to disappoint.*"

"*We'll take that under consideration,*" she said coolly. "*Over and out.*"

The tone bar on the screen had reached the end of its track. McNabb swiveled around in her seat to face General Graydon. "Should I call for an air strike, sir?"

Graydon's gut churned. *Goddamn Monroe, hot-dogging it on my turf,* he thought. The guy was already in the express lane to get his next star, and this could seal it for him. But what the hell was he doing calling an air strike when he was supposed to be on a diplomatic mission, meeting with Zyrous and the warlords? When did he decide to start chasing down Talies? And why in God's name was Salam helping him? Graydon had a good mind to ignore the request. Let the Taliban unit run, he thought. He'd have his Berets do the job later after Monroe's ass was on a plane heading back for the States.

"General Graydon?"

Graydon looked up at the clock. He didn't answer. He hadn't made up his mind.

23

CANFIELD THOUGHT he heard something. It was in the night sky, a low drone. He sat cross-legged on the sandy ground with his AK in his lap, tilting his head like Nipper the RCA dog, trying to listen. He didn't want to even think that it might be an aircraft out looking for them. After all the crap they'd been through, he didn't want to be disappointed.

He looked over at the sleeping bodies on the ground. They'd crossed the valley to the foot of this mountain, and it had taken them all day. Might as well have crossed a fucking desert, Canfield thought, annoyed that the others got to rest while he had to stand guard. Yeah, yeah, he knew it was his turn, but he needed some rest, too. He checked his watch. Shit. Two hours until Vitelli relieved him.

He listened for the drone again, but he didn't hear it. Probably his imagination, he thought. He'd heard strange sounds in these mountains before. Nothing unusual. He felt his sunburned nose and winced. It must have been as red as Rudolph the fucking reindeer. The captain had made them travel by daylight, said they had to evacuate the area where they'd engaged the Tajiks. They'd been damn lucky that no one had spotted them coming across that valley. Personally Canfield didn't like the idea of moving by day, but being the youngest of the three corporals, he counted for shit. No one listened to him.

Canfield yawned and blinked his baked eyelids, forcing himself to stay awake. He couldn't doze off, no matter what. He'd already fucked up royally with the bladder on Starwood 2 and then almost got strangled to death. He couldn't screw up again. He had to ignore the difficulties of his situation: dead tired, cold as hell, and the sound of that rushing stream fifty yards off working like white noise at the back of his head. Where Canfield came from, that stream would be called a fucking river. It had rapids. But the captain called it a "mountain stream," and a corporal doesn't argue with a captain, not when he's the hump in this outfit.

Canfield stared out into the darkness, wishing that water would just shut the fuck up. It made him want to pee, but the thought of getting up and pulling down his fly to take a whiz in the cold made him hold it. He hugged himself and rocked back and forth, trying to work up some warmth and that's when he heard it again. The drone. Far off but a little louder this time. It seemed pretty real. At least he thought it was real.

He stood up and looked over at the others, unsure if he should wake them. What if he'd imagined it? What if it was nothing? Maybe the sound of the rapids echoing off the mountain mimicked a turboprop drone.

But it could be real. It could be an aircraft. Then they should do something. Start a fire, signal to it. How else would the plane find them in the dark? He jogged over to find Captain Salam. Canfield decided it would be best to wake only the captain just in case.

Canfield moved carefully in the dark so as not to step on the others. He found Salam asleep on his side and crouched down beside him. "Captain," he whispered and touched Salam's shoulder.

Salam's eyes shot open. "What's wrong?"

Monroe woke up as soon as he heard Salam's voice. He'd been sleeping on and off, waking up periodically to check on Canfield, making sure that the kid hadn't fallen asleep. Monroe sat up and waited until his eyes adjusted to the darkness. He saw Salam getting to his feet, Canfield with him.

Stiff from the cold, Monroe stretched his legs and rotated his head before he got up. But as he listened to the cricks and clicks in his neck, he noticed something else, a sound, a drone in the sky. He froze and homed in on it. The sound seemed to be traveling toward them. He furrowed his brow and looked up, searching for night lights on an aircraft. The sky showed a spattered canvas of stars but no moving lights. He focused on the sound, trying to identify it.

Definitely a turboprop, he decided. Not a jet. It had the low rumble of a cargo craft, like a C1 transport. The warlords didn't have their own aircraft, certainly nothing like that.

He stood up and scanned the sky. The drone increased in volume. Why would Gardiz send a C1 all the way up here? It's not a rescue craft. And where were the lights?

That's when it dawned on him. The realization went through him like ice water. Mother of God, he thought.

"Wake up!" he yelled. "Everybody up!" He ran toward the others. "Get up and run! Run!"

Monroe shook them from their sleep one by one.

"Get up, Jane," he said, shaking her hard. "Get up now! Hurry up! Run!"

"What is it?" she gasped, startled by the abrupt wake-up. "What?"

A high whistle screamed out of the sky followed by an ear-shattering explosion that came so close it knocked Monroe off his feet. Jane screamed. Clumps of dirt and shards of rock rained down on them.

A second ordnance struck even closer, tearing up a different plot of terrain and igniting the scrub ten yards off.

"What the fuck?" Proctor cursed, his face lit by the fires.

"Spectre!" Monroe yelled. "Run and scatter. Don't stay together."

"What?" Jane said as Monroe pulled her to her feet.

"Just run. By yourself. Don't stop. I can't explain now."

The men, however, didn't need an explanation. They only needed one word: Spectre. A C-130 gunship specially equipped for night raids. Monroe knew it well because he'd been on the Pentagon committee that oversaw its development. A monster with wings. The Specter ran without lights. The crew wore night vision goggles and located their targets with the help of SOFLAM, invisible laser markers operated by ground troops. Its motto: "Death Waits in the Dark."

Monroe scanned the terrain as he ran, looking for the bastard who had their SOFLAM, using it against them. Khan, he thought. Fucking Khan!

"Scatter!" he yelled at the running shadows around him. "Don't stay together."

The Spectre also had thermal sensors that could locate individuals by their body heat and coordinate with its two rapid-fire M61 20mm Vulcan cannons.

The shock wave of another explosion shoved Monroe from behind. More scrub caught fire casting a flickering light across the field. Monroe could see Proctor hobbling double-time. Vitelli sprinted in the distance. Monroe couldn't see any of the others.

Besides the Vulcans, the Spectre carried an L60 40mm Bofors cannon and an M102 105mm howitzer and plenty of rounds for each weapon. Enough to kill seven people a thousand times over.

The boom and clack of the cannons shouted down from the sky. Monroe zigzagged, hoping to give the thermal sensors more data to process, slowing down the gunfire. He looked up, searching for the Spectre, but he could only hear it. The roar of the gunship's four turboprops reached a crescendo as it swooped by, then quickly tapered off. The Spectre would be circling back for another run. It had to because all of its armament was on one side. A big craft like that, nearly 100 feet long with a wingspan over 130 feet, would need a few minutes to make the turnaround.

Monroe ran to Proctor and positioned his shoulder under the sergeant's armpit on his injured side to help him run. "Has anyone been hit?" Monroe said.

"Don't know, sir," Proctor said, breathing hard. "I've seen Vitelli and Rudge."

"Jane?"

"Haven't seen her."

The roar of the Spectre diminished to a drone. Monroe could hear the gurgle and rush of the rapids again.

"Now I know why the Talies call it 'raining death,'" Proctor said.

But Monroe didn't hear him. He had an idea.

"Go to the stream, Sergeant. Jump in and stay submerged as much as you can."

"Excuse me, sir?"

"The cold water, Sergeant. The thermal sensors won't be able to locate you under cold water."

"Yes sir."

"Tell anyone you find. Get under the water and stay under as long as you can."

"Yes sir."

Monroe left Proctor and ran toward the nearest running figure he could find. Rudge.

"Go to the water. Jump in and stay under," he yelled.

"Yes sir," Rudge shouted back.

"Tell anyone you see."

Monroe raced in the direction where he'd last seen Vitelli, hoping that he could catch up with him. He wanted to find Jane. She wouldn't know what to do. If she hunkered down, she'd be dead. She might already be dead, he thought. He had a feeling that Canfield might do the same, grab his head and freeze. Most of all Monroe wanted to find Salam. They needed him.

"Vitelli! Salam!" he shouted into the darkness, hoping he'd be heard. "Go to the wat—"

But the drone became a roar again, coming up behind him. The Spectre had circled back. The surface of the rapids shimmered in the firelight, off to his right, maybe fifty feet away. Monroe changed tack and headed straight for the water, running hard. His chest hurt, but he didn't think about that. He had to get under the water.

The turboprops blared across the field. The Spectre swooped into position to create its theater of destruction. A high whistle overrode the racket. Incoming ordnance. Monroe strained to run faster, forcing himself to change directions every third step to defeat the thermal sensors. The round hit somewhere behind him, the explosion throwing him forward. He fell, tumbling out of control onto the rocky ground. He gave no thought to injury, picked himself up, and kept running, making a beeline for the water. He could see the shore close by.

The cannons rattled and clacked. Rounds tore up lines of turf all around him. He kept running, running hard, hoping to God the others had gotten the message, that they had already made it to the water.

His boot sank into mud. His next step splashed into shallow water, barely up to his ankles. He kept running. Another explosion knocked him off his feet and sent him flying. He landed in the rapids on his back, frigid water rushing over him, into his ears, eyes, and mouth, pounding his head. The shock of the cold delivered a jolt like electricity, then knocked the wind out of him. But he had to keep going and get into deeper water. The thermal sensors would find him here. He gulped for air, then dove under, swimming toward the middle of the stream.

Even underwater he could hear the deafening roar of the Spectre. He waited for ordnance to find him, but he felt nothing. He thought the Spectre had passed, but he stayed under and kept swimming, his chest burning, crying out for oxygen.

He stopped swimming to check the depth of the water; his feet didn't touch bottom. His lungs felt as if they were in a vise. He had to get some air. He swam up and broke the surface, gasping and mostly swallowing water as the rapids rushed over him, grabbing him like hands and carrying him downstream, dunking him along the way. He tried to relax and take a breath whenever the rapids allowed, but his mind raced out of control. Where was the Spectre? Where were the others? Had any of them survived? Could they all swim? He could see the burning scrub in the distance, but water rushing over his head blurred his vision, getting in his nose and dragging him farther downstream.

He breached the surface and whipped the water off his face. "Stay under!" he shouted to the others, hoping they'd hear him. "Stay under!"

Please stay under, he thought as the rapids grabbed him from below.

24

SENATOR FRYE'S thin lips contorted into a stern frown. "Where the hell is he?" he said in a hushed voice. "Why hasn't he gotten in touch?"

Alan Cooper sat next to him on the picnic table, General McCreedy across from them in the inner courtyard of the Pentagon where staff members usually took their lunch and coffee breaks in good weather. Each man had a paper coffee cup in front of him. The sun shone brightly, but a chilly breeze had kept most people inside today—perfect for Frye, McCreedy, and Cooper because they wanted privacy. Hooper always cautioned them against electronic bugs in their offices, mainly because he used to install them around Washington himself in his younger days.

General McCreedy took a sip from his cup. "Walter, you're getting worked up for nothing," he said to the senator. "If something were wrong, we'd know about it. General Graydon sends in regular status reports twice a day."

"But we haven't heard from Monroe directly," said the senator. "He said he'd check in and give us a progress report. The hearings begin in a week and a half, for chrissake."

Hooper stirred sugar into his coffee. "It would be helpful to know how he's doing with the warlords. I could get the pre-spin going, put our friends in the press on notice."

McCreedy sneered. "What friends in the press?"

"We have a few," the lobbyist said. "All well-placed and very valuable. But you have to prime the pump if you want a gusher."

Senator Frye scowled. "We have to start thinking about a Plan B. Who else can we get to testify?"

Hooper raised his eyebrows. "Well, we have General Cuddy and Colonel Vickers. Cuddy's not the most dynamic speaker and he's only a one-star. Vickers doesn't have as much rank as I'd like, but he's young and good-looking. Trouble is, he's a little *too* buff. People might confuse him for a Special Forces commander and that would work against us—"

"I'll do it," McCreedy said. He seemed to be preempting any other suggestions.

Hooper flashed a nervous smile. "With all due respect, General, your image is. . . well, not as smooth as Monroe's."

McCreedy frowned. "Meaning?"

"Meaning your image, your persona—it projects Old Think. Do you know what I mean?"

"Yeah, I know what you mean. I look like an old fart and Monroe looks like a movie star. Right?"

Hooper sighed. "Essentially, yes. Image counts for everything. No one pays any attention to substance."

"Then why don't you hire Harrison Ford to testify? Or better yet, Tom Cruise." McCreedy was leaning on his elbows, glaring at Hooper who, as always, took any sign of hostility in stride. He'd long gotten used to people hating him.

"Don't take it personally, general," Hooper said. "We all have our individual strengths."

"And weaknesses." McCreedy gave Hooper a hard look.

"Drop it, Bill," Senator Frye said. "Alan knows what he's doing. We have to trust his expertise."

McCreedy huffed. "Expertise is in the results."

"I absolutely agree," Hooper said. "And I've been thinking. Losing Monroe might not be such a bad thing for us."

The senator and the general both stared at him skeptically.

"What do you mean, 'losing Monroe'?" McCreedy said.

"Well, let's just suppose," Hooper said, gesturing with both hands, "and I don't mean to be morbid, but let's just suppose that Monroe was injured or even perished in Afghanistan while under the care of a Green Beret unit. That would certainly be a black eye for Special Forces. I'm not wishing it, but. . ."

McCreedy shook his head, flabbergasted. "Hooper, we are talking about a three-star general in the United States Army. Jackson Monroe is not expendable. He's a valuable member of the military community."

But the senator nodded slowly as he digested the idea. "Jackson takes one for the team," he said, trying out the notion.

"So to speak," Hooper said. "And that would be a situation where we *could* use you at the hearings, General."

"Oh?"

"You're pretty good at conveying righteous indignation," Hooper said with analytical cool. "I wouldn't want you to come right out and *blame* Special Forces, but a pointed eulogy for a dead general with strategic mentions of the Berets who were with him would certainly illustrate our point that these guys are not the be-all and end-all of military effectiveness. If you know what I mean."

A smile crawled across McCreedy's face. Senator Frye's thin lips stretched to a tight grin. They saw the possibilities.

"*Gentlemen.*"

The three men looked up simultaneously and saw Secretary of Defense Riordan in a black pinstripe suit walking toward their table with a paper cup in his hand, the tail of a tea bag fluttering in the breeze. Retired General Vandermeer stood at the condiment bar nearby, pressing a plastic lid on a jumbo cup of coffee. He ambled toward the table and caught up with Riordan. Vandermeer wore a light-gray suit with a visitor's pass clipped to his pocket. He and Riordan went way back, and Riordan valued his counsel. Both men held Special Forces in high regard and supported the concept vigorously.

Vandermeer took a sip from his cup. "Have any of you heard from Jackson?" he asked with a cordial smile. "How's he doing over there?"

"Fine," McCreedy said. Frye and Hooper kept their mouths shut. The senator didn't want to let on that he had any particular interest in Monroe, and Hooper as a civilian had no business knowing anything about Monroe's mission in Afghanistan other than what had been printed in the papers.

Vandermeer grinned at them. He knew what they were up to, and they knew that he knew. But as long as they didn't put their cards on the table, they could all remain civil. Secretary Riordan, however, played by different rules.

"I hear you're planning to use him to push the bill," he said bluntly. Sunlight glinted off his glasses.

The senator looked at him but said nothing. Hooper started stirring his coffee again.

"He might be called to testify, yes," McCreedy said. As a member of the Joint Chiefs, he had experience standing toe-to-toe with Riordan.

"Good move," Riordan said. "I'd sure as hell use Jackson if I had him."

McCreedy worked up a good-natured chuckle. "You make it sound like a competition, Mr. Secretary."

Riordan pressed his lips into a frown. "Football is a competition," he said. "This is a war."

McCreedy's brows bunched into a knot. "Excuse me?"

"The stakes are high; that makes it a war," Riordan stated flatly. "A war for the future of the American military. No, I take that back. A war for the future of American *sovereignty*."

"That's an interesting viewpoint," McCreedy said.

"It's not my *opinion*, General. It's *fact*." Riordan used words like fists.

Hooper caught McCreedy's eye, warning him to tread cautiously. McCreedy had a temper, and Hooper didn't want him blurting out something that could be used against them later. McCreedy wanted to get his shot it, but for once he picked up on Hooper's hint and kept his mouth shut.

The breeze died down, and the silence suddenly became the elephant in the room.

General Vandermeer finally spoke up. "Did you know that Jackson was a cadet at the academy when I was CO there?"

"Is that so?" the senator said.

"I brought him in—kicking and screaming, I might add." Vandermeer smiled at the memory. "It was a tough row for him to hoe in the beginning, but he graduated top of his class. When he was a firstie, I swear he could have led a division all by himself. He was that good."

"Impressive," Frye said.

Hooper nodded in silence.

A disgruntled grimace had settled on McCreedy's face and stayed there.

Riordan remained an inscrutable presence, an unmovable mountain.

"So how *is* Jackson making out with those warlords over there?" Vandermeer asked.

No one said a word. The elephant sat on the table.

"I'll meet you inside," Riordan said to Vandermeer. He walked off without saying goodbye to the others.

Vandermeer nodded to them and followed Riordan into the building.

Frye, McCreedy, and Hooper raised their cups and all sipped at the same time.

The bodies of the two slain Tajiks lay side by side on the wooden stage in the courtyard of the fortress, tightly wrapped in black shrouds and ready for burial. Torches lit the entire courtyard where the warlords and their minions had gathered to hear Raz Kahn, who stood on the stage with the bodies. The slain Tajiks would have to be in the ground before the sun came up or else it would be a sacrilege and a dishonor to their memory. On the far side of the courtyard, more torches had been jammed into the dust where the dead Americans lay rotting. The cool night air kept the stink down.

Over three hundred *mujahadeen* crowded around the wooden stage, looking up at Raz Khan, who held a bullhorn in his hand. Hajji and Yusef stood at the front of the crowd at Khan's feet. Hajji's huge unblinking eyes caught the light of the flickering flames as he stared up at his master.

"We have been betrayed!" Khan shouted into the bullhorn. He hammered the air with his fist. "The Americans say they are our friends, but they have *betrayed* us."

The fighters grumbled and murmured. Khan looked down at Yusef and caught his eye. Yusef raised his eyebrows, encouraging him to continue.

"The Americans killed Zyrous Mohammed. Killed him where I stand right now on this stage. They martyred him. But they will not martyr me. I cannot die because my mission from Allah is to avenge the murder of Zyrous Mohammed."

The crowd stirred. Some shouted in assent. A contingent at the rear began to chant: "Zyrous! Zyrous! Zyrous!"

"The Americans have also murdered our Tajik brothers," Khan shouted, pointing down at the bodies.

The Tajiks in the crowd roared and wailed, unashamed of their sorrow and outrage.

Yusef widened his eyes, urging Khan to continue in this vein.

"We are different peoples from different tribes, but to the Americans we are all the same," Khan said. "To them we are targets for their assasinations, battlefield slaves to do their bidding."

The grumbling became more agitated.

"But they are right. We *are* all the same."

Shock rippled through the crowd. Many jeered.

"We are all the same," Khan continued, "because now we are *one*. . . *one* against the United States, *one* against the Americans who have slaughtered our brave men, *one* against the global dictatorship that wants nothing more than to take Afghanistan from us for their own purposes. They want to control us. They want to *own* us!"

The crowd roared. Many of the *mujahadeen* hammered the air, following Khan's lead.

"But we. . . will. . . not. . . have it!" Khan bellowed.

Hajji covered his ears, the crowd cheered so loudly.

"General Jackson Monroe and the other American soldiers who killed Zyrous Mohammed will meet the same fate as their comrades." Khan pointed a condemning finger at the bodies across the courtyard. "Dead and dishonored."

The chants from the back took over the whole assembly: "Zyrous! Zyrous! Zyrous!"

Khan himself joined in, his voice through the bullhorn taking the lead: "Zyrous! Zyrous! Zyrous!" It cut him inside to be chanting the name of the man who had stood in his way for so long, but to get the warlords' support, he had to do this. It also hurt him that he had to abandon his original plan, capturing Monroe alive and selling him to Al Qaeda for five million dollars. But he knew that with power, money would come. He looked down at Yusef, who nodded with a sly glint in his eye as he chanted along with the others.

Khan shouted over the chants. "We must find General Jackson Monroe and avenge these deaths. Monroe must die! He must join his rotting friends!" Khan extended his arm and pointed at the pile of corpses again.

Mujahadeen broke away from the crowd and ran across the courtyard, snatching up stones and clumps of dung along the way, hurling them at the bodies. The missiles came in a hailstorm, littering the area around the death pile. The chanting gave way to cheers and roars. Tribesmen fired rifles into the air. Determined faces screamed in the firelight.

On stage Khan's face remained fierce for the public, but Yusef couldn't contain his delight. He knew Monroe was already dead.

25

THIS IS NOT GOOD, Rudge thought. Not good at all.

He sat on the ground, huddled around the fire that he and Canfield had built, rubbing his arms and trying to control the shivering, but water still dripped from his clothes, and he could see his breath. Canfield sat right next to him, shoulder to shoulder, trying to share some body heat. Vitelli hugged his knees, chin on his chest. Proctor lay on his side closest to the fire. He had a fever, his eyes were glassy. Rudge could see Proctor's exposed wound, purple-red and puss-white at the edges. God only knew what bacteria he'd picked up in that water.

Jane sat on Rudge's other side, her hair sticking out in all directions. She kept looking at Proctor's face, had even felt his forehead once, but she clearly had no experience taking care of someone else.

But Captain Salam upset Rudge most. Salam stared into the fire, his expression dazed and hopeless. He hadn't said more than a few words since they'd dragged themselves out of the rapids. Actually no one said very much; they were too tired, too cold, and too disgusted to talk. But Rudge knew that they couldn't just sit here. They had to do something. They had to look for the general.

"Do you think we should go look for him?" he said, breaking the silence.

No one answered. Their eyes stayed on the fire.

"I think we should look for him," Rudge said. "Leave no man behind." He stared at Salam, waiting for a reaction. Leave no man behind, the motto of the Ranger Mountain Brigade, another SF group like the Berets. Rudge wanted Salam to agree or disagree or maybe reprimand him for invoking another group's motto. He wanted Salam to do *something*.

"I think we should look for him," Rudge insisted. "It's our duty."

"I think," Proctor said, his words flat and slow, "I think we should frag the bastard."

Vitelli raised his head. "Yeah, we should fucking whack him, the motherfucker."

Jane made a face at him. "Who are you, Tony Soprano?"

He gave her a dirty look. "Monroe should be whacked for getting us into this mess. This is all his fault."

"Well he didn't shoot Zyrous Mohammed. I'll give him that," said Jane.

"But he cut our unit in half," Proctor said. "With a full unit we could have gotten out of there. . . all of us."

"What about you, hip-hop?" Vitelli said to Canfield. "You think we should go looking for Monroe? Or just leave him to die. . . or go looking for him and then kill him?" Canfield shrugged. "I dunno."

"Whattaya mean, you don't know? You're the white-boy gangsta. Don't you want to put a cap up his ass or something?"

A humorless grin passed over Canfield's face as he shook his head before burying it in his arms again.

"Can't ask you, Rudge," Vitelli said. "You're the president of the Jackson Monroe Fan Club. You think he shits ice cream."

"I never said that."

"You don't have to. I can tell from the way you act around him. You're, like, in awe."

"You don't know what you're talking about."

"Aw, come on, Rudge. Be honest. It's a black thing. You're both brothers, so you're gonna stick up for the guy."

"Doesn't work that way, Vitelli."

"It does where I come from." Vitelli stared him in the eye, challenging him.

Rudge stared right back, but he held his tongue.

"You got something to say, Rudge? Say it."

"Seems like you got enough to say for everybody, Vitelli. Just keep talking."

Vitelli's expression turned nasty. "What's that supposed to mean, Rudge? Huh?" He started to get up off the ground.

Rudge just stared at him. All of a sudden Vitelli had grown balls.

Vitelli went to the fire and picked up a thick branch, holding it by the unburned end. Flames licked the other end. He turned the point down so that the flames grew higher.

Rudge watched him, ready to jump to his feet. He could move fast when he had to, despite his size.

Vitelli sauntered over toward Rudge with the burning stick in his hand. Canfield slid away from the big man, not wanting to get burned. Vitelli walked slow and cocky but kept his distance. Rudge got off his butt and stayed in a crouch, but apparently that was too sudden a movement for Vitelli because he jabbed the burning branch at Rudge's face, forcing him back onto his ass. Rudge raised an arm to protect himself. Vitelli jabbed at him again. Burning cinders rained down on Rudge's chest and legs.

Rudge rolled over onto his hip and threw his legs out, ready to mule-kick Vitelli if he got any closer. Go 'head, motherfucker, he thought. Burn my boots. See what I care. You'll be tasting Army-issue leather till next Christmas.

Vitelli grinned with mean delight. He jabbed again just to watch Rudge flinch, teasing him to kick. But when Vitelli attempted a deeper thrust, Rudge hammered the back of Vitelli's knee with his heel.

"Hey!" Vitelli yelped as he fell forward. He braced himself with his hands but held onto the burning branch, trapping it against the ground. "Cocksucker!" he cursed as he swung it like a sword, whacking Rudge's leg. Sparks flew, but Rudge's pants were too wet to burn.

When Vitelli saw that his attack had done nothing to the big man, he scrambled to his knees and raised the stick over his head, about to slash Rudge across his face. Rudge instinctively raised his arms to protect himself.

"That's enough!"

All eyes turned toward the voice in the dark. Vitelli, startled, dropped the branch.

General Monroe emerged from the shadows like something rising to the surface of a murky lake. His *mujahadeen* clothes hung on him like wet rags.

"General," Jane said, "where were you?"

He stepped into the light and hunkered close to the fire. "The rapids carried me downstream about a half mile," he said. "Fortunately I saw the fire, figured it was probably you."

"You all right?" Rudge asked.

Monroe nodded, rubbing his hands and staring into the fire. The vacant look in his eyes alarmed Rudge. Monroe's military starch had been washed away. The general seemed like just another wet, exhausted—and scared—soldier.

"Do you want me to put the fire out?" Rudge asked, figuring that he'd say it would give away their position, but Monroe shook his head.

"The Spectre's gone," he said wearily. "Khan's fighters probably figure we're history. They won't hang around if they know 'raining death' is in the area."

He looked at Salam. "What's our status here, Captain?"

Salam opened his mouth, but nothing came out at first. He coughed to clear his throat. "Sir," he said, "no new injuries, but the ordeal on the rapids—well, you know."

"Do we have any weapons?" Monroe asked.

"Yes sir. All weapons are accounted for."

Monroe stared down at Proctor's infected wound. He didn't have to ask. He just sighed. "I have something I want to say."

Vitelli threw the branch back into the flames.

Monroe paused and looked at them one by one. He seemed to be having a hard time getting started. "I. . . I owe you all an apology. My faulty decisions got us here. . . and got the others killed. . ." He fell silent, and the crackling of the fire suddenly seemed very loud. "I—" he started again. "I'm unfit to lead a combat unit. I've been out of it for too long. Captain Salam is in charge. Completely. I trust his judgment, and I will not interfere—"

Salam's mouth hung open. "But, General—"

"Captain Salam, you have the training and the experience to lead us out of here. I'm conceding leadership of the group to you. You are the commander."

The fire crackled. No one knew what to say.

Jane spoke up. "Are you fucking shitting me, General? You're giving up your rank to Salam?" She said what everyone else was thinking.

"There's a difference between rank and leadership," he said quietly.

"I don't get it. What're you saying? That you're gonna take orders from a captain?"

The firelight played off his face. "I am going to do whatever is necessary so that we survive this. I will defer to Captain Salam and do whatever he deems necessary."

"In-fucking-credible." She shook her head in disbelief.

"General," Salam said, "I don't know if I can—"

"If you can't, no one else here can. I'm asking you, Salam. Lead us out of here."

"General, I'm not sure if *anyone* can pull that off. I—"

"Huah!" Proctor said, his voice weak and gravelly. His eyes shone wet in the firelight.

"Huah!" Rudge said.

"Huah!" Canfield echoed.

Vitelli furrowed his brow but finally gave it up. "Huah!" he said.

"Huah!" Monroe said.

Everyone stared at him in shock, except for Jane who frowned at them all. "This male bonding shit is all very touching." She looked at Salam. "You're in charge now, Captain. What's the fucking plan?"

Salam looked her in the eye. "We get out of here. That's the fucking plan."

"Huah!" the men said in unison.

25A

"WHAT DO YOU THINK?" Monroe whispered into Salam's ear. They and the rest of the unit crouched behind a ridge overlooking a tiny camp. The noonday sun brought the temperature up to summertime levels. Hungry and near exhaustion, they'd been walking since dawn.

Salam stared out at the three dirt-streaked canvas tents that made up the camp, assessing the situation. "We need to rest and regroup," he said, almost to himself. "We might be able to get some rations from these people. But we don't know who they are."

Two women tended to an iron pot suspended from a log tripod over an open fire. It could be goat stew they were cooking or they could have been boiling their laundry. Salam couldn't tell because the wind blew the other way. Small children tended to chores directed by their mothers, mostly carrying things in and out of the tents. But where were the men? Salam wondered. He saw only one horse, a sway-backed old nag. Three tents should mean three families. Maybe the men had taken the horses and gone somewhere. But where?

"Who are they?' Monroe asked.

Salam shook his head. "Hard to tell from just looking at them. There are nomads who live in these mountains. People with no particular allegiance to the tribes."

"You sound dubious."

"Suspicious," Salam said. "It's how you survive in this country."

Monroe held his tongue. Salam had been treating him like a newbie all morning, and Monroe had been having second thoughts about handing over command of the unit. Salam's SF style didn't exactly jibe with Monroe's. He'd also stopped addressing Monroe as "sir." He reminded himself to leave the ego out of it.

"We can take some of their food and leave immediately," Monroe suggested.

"Maybe," Salam said tersely.

"What do you mean, 'maybe'?"

Salam rolled his eyes toward Monroe. "Did you give me command of this unit?"

"Yes."

"Well, then let me lead."

"I just—"

"There was plenty I wanted to say to you back at the fortress, but I didn't. I kept my yap shut. Now I expect you to do the same."

Monroe felt his face flush. "I'm sorry. Continue." This was not going to be easy.

Salam stared him in the eye. "I will."

He signaled to the corporals to meet him below the line of the ridge, out of sight from the camp. "You too," he said to Monroe.

Salam stepped quietly down the dusty incline to meet the other men. Proctor joined them, Jane helping him walk. His wincing face told his story. They huddled together.

"Okay, here's the deal," Salam said. "We're gonna pay a little visit to these people. Rudge and Canfield will go down the ridgeline and approach from the left flank. Rudge, you circle around to the rear. Vitelli and General Monroe, take the right flank. Vitelli, you circle around toward the rear on your side. I'll take the forward approach. Proctor, you stay on the ridgeline and provide cover."

"What am I supposed to do?" Jane asked with attitude.

"Set the table," Salam said sarcastically. "You stay with Proctor and stay out of sight."

"But I can shoot, too."

He looked at the AK in her hands. "Do not discharge your weapon unless you are personally threatened or Sergeant Proctor gives you permission."

"But—"

"No buts. Now stop talking."

She gave him the finger, but he ignored her.

"Now listen up," Salam continued. "This camp is not a Holiday Inn. We are not staying. Think of it as our own little Afghani 7-Eleven. We grab some food, look for medical supplies, then we motor. These are women and kids, so don't get greedy. Leave them something to eat. But if you so much as see a weapon, you take that person out. No hesitation. They'll know who we are as soon as they see us, so if they show guns, that means they don't like us. And if that's the case, we don't like them. Do you understand?"

"Yes sir," they all murmured. Except for Monroe.

Salam looked at him, waiting for a response. "Yes. . . I understand."

"Good. Now take your positions. On my signal we converge."

The band dispersed, and Monroe moved off with Vitelli toward the right flank. Monroe could feel Vitelli's eyes on him. Did he think that they were equals now? That the general was just another soldier? Or perhaps he saw Monroe as an oddity. The used-to-be general. Monroe didn't know what he was. A failure, that's what.

They walked to the end of the ridge, then climbed to the crest, their boots sinking into the soft ground. Monroe checked his weapon. He had one of the extra AKs. He'd lost his sniper rifle in the rapids.

The aroma of whatever was cooking on the open fire wafted toward them in the breeze. Monroe's stomach growled. He couldn't identify it as anything he knew, but that didn't matter. He'd gladly eat whatever he could get at this point.

Vitelli held his rifle one-handed with the butt propped on his hip as he looked toward Salam, waiting for his signal.

"Two hands on your weapon," Monroe reminded him.

"Yeah, right." Vitelli didn't look at him, and he didn't listen either.

Monroe thought about insisting, but he didn't have the energy. He just wanted something to eat. He looked over toward Salam as he climbed over the soft dirt of the ridge, his arm raised, his eyes on the women below. Salam pointed forward, giving the others the signal to go.

Rudge stepped over the ridge and headed down the incline toward the village. Canfield came running up from the rear. Monroe moved in as well. Vitelli took his good sweet time. Monroe would say something to him about his lackadaisical attitude later. Or he'd tell Salam, so that he could deal with it.

A little girl carrying a tightly packed load of laundry on her head spotted the intruders first. The square pack fell to the ground as her eyes widened. The two women tending the pot noticed the American and started clucking like frantic hens. A third, older woman emerged from one of the tents. She snapped orders to the others, pointing here and there. The younger women gathered up the children. Monroe counted five kids in all—four girls and a little boy.

Canfield broke into a run, dashing toward the cooking pot. The women scattered, shooing the children out of his way. He lowered his face to the pot. "Stew," he shouted. "Some kind of meat."

"What kind?" Vitelli shouted.

"Who cares?" Canfield said. " I'll eat camel butt if I have to."

"Shut the fuck up!" Salam reprimanded.

He approached the older woman with his rifle pointed down but kept the other two women in his peripheral vision.

Vitelli headed straight for the pot. Canfield already had his fingers in it, trying to pick something out without getting burned. Monroe wanted to yell at them both.

Rudge watched Salam's back. He had a clear view to at least one of the tents. Monroe moved forward so that he could cover the other two.

Salam spoke to the women. He seemed to be trying out different languages and dialects without much success. The old woman jabbered back at him, but there didn't seem to be any give and take between them.

Vitelli turned toward one of the younger women. "Hey, Suzie-Q, you got any spoons we could use?" He reached out to her, and she recoiled from his touch. She stumbled over one of the children and fell to the ground, screaming her head off and clawing at the scarves around her neck and head. She pulled her neck scarf up to cover her face all the way to the bridge of her nose and pulled her head scarf down below her brow until she had just a slit to see through. She kept screaming. The other young women stepped back and did the same with their scarves.

"Oh, shit!" Salam said.

"Talies!" Proctor shouted from the top of the ridge.

Salam snarled at Canfield and Vitelli, "Get out of that fucking pot and pay attention."

But while he yelled at them, a figure rushed out from behind the tent closest to Monroe. A teenage male jerked to a stop ten feet from Monroe and stood frozen with a rifle in his hands. Monroe focused on his face. He wore a black turban and a sparse, silky beard. Monroe guessed that he'd never shaved in his life. The boy's eyes broadcast his fear. He couldn't have been much more than thirteen, Monroe thought. Same as his own son.

"Get him!" Proctor shouted from the ridge.

But Monroe didn't raise his weapon. He couldn't.

The kid suddenly raised his rifle and leveled it on Monroe.

Monroe held up his hand, palm out. "Easy, son—"

Auto fire drowned out his words. The boy collapsed to his knees, then doubled over and clutched his gut, his face twisted in pain. He still had the rifle in his hands. A second burst of fire threw him into the dirt, rolling him over twice until he stopped on his belly. His eyes didn't move.

Monroe looked up toward the source of the gunfire, Proctor on the ridge, peering down the barrel of his rifle.

"Heads up!" Proctor yelled.

Another teenager ran between the tents. The three women screamed in grief and outrage. The boy held a pistol in his outstretched arm, firing wild. A bullet ricocheted off the iron pot. Vitelli and Canfield hit the dirt. Salam had his back to the boy, who hadn't noticed Monroe off to the side. Monroe could take him out. He raised his weapon and aimed but didn't take the shot.

Proctor didn't hesitate. Auto fire ripped through the kid. Pepper holes riddled his shirt and jacket. His black turban flew from his head, and his face instantly turned into raw meat. He must have died in midair as he ran, but his body kept going. He crashed into the dirt near the fire in a loose-jointed heap.

"Cover the women," Salam shouted, wheeling around. He yelled at them in one of his languages, ordering them to get facedown on the ground. Canfield pointed his rifle down at them.

"Don't hurt the kids," Jane screamed from the ridge.

"Rudge!" Salam shouted. "Rip down those tents."

"I've got you covered, Captain," Proctor shouted.

Salam moved like a demon on fire, yanking down one tent, then another, dragging the canvases through the dirt and stomping on them to flush out any other gunmen. Rudge followed his example with the third tent.

"Careful!" Jane shouted. "There could be little kids in there."

Salam whipped the downed tents to the side, revealing an assortment of possessions. Clothes, food, cooking utensils, a shortwave radio, another AK, and other personal items littered the ground. The women cried and wailed, reaching out to gather up the children from their prone positions. Salam snatched up the AK and hitched it over his shoulder, then started looking for rations. "Take the flatbread and the goat jerky," he said, "but leave them half."

"Can we take some of the stew?" Canfield asked.

"Leave it," Salam said. "It could be poisoned."

"What? It smells okay to me."

"This could be a setup, numb-nuts. Women and kids out by themselves? Easy pickings, right? Too easy. It could be a trap. This shit happens out here."

Canfield looked disappointed. "But if this is a trap, where are the men?"

"Who knows? Maybe we got lucky. All I know is we're not gonna be here when they get back. Now hurry up and grab some food so we can get out of here."

Vitelli and Rudge scrounged through the items on the ground, stuffing what they wanted into their shirts.

Monroe hadn't moved. He stared transfixed at the face of the first boy who'd been killed. A crude doll made out of sticks and hay and scraps of fabric lay on the ground next to the boy's foot. Monroe couldn't take his eyes off it. He felt sick to his stomach.

Salam walked up to him. "You too," he said, nodding down at the mess on the ground. "Help out with the salvage so we can get out of here."

"I'm sorry," Monroe said in a raspy whisper. "I choked."

"Well, don't let it happen again," Salam said as if Monroe's failure didn't particularly concern him. "Hurry up with the food. We gotta get going."

The doll crunched under Salam's boot as he walked away.

26

YUSEF'S EYELIDS DROOPED WITH FATIGUE. Sitting close to the fire on this cold night lulled him toward sleep. The others obviously felt the same way. He scanned the tired, burnished faces of the ten men under his command. They'd been up for too many hours, racing from the fortress to find Monroe and his people in the valley, then calling Gardiz by sat phone for an air strike and using the SOFLAM to target the Americans. He kept the laptop-sized sat phone and the SOFLAM in a gray hard-shell case by his side. He had aimed the SOFLAM himself. The display of destruction the little machine had brought still amazed him as he thought back on it. He had heard about the "raining death" many times but had never seen it for himself.

The man who had been chosen to stand guard sat cross-legged on a boulder nearby, hunched over the assault rifle in his lap. He looked just as tired as they all were, but Yusef didn't care if the man dozed off. The Americans were dead, he thought. They should all take the opportunity to rest because tomorrow would be a busy day. At daylight they would return to the valley and search for proof of Monroe's death. Yusef prayed that the general's head was still intact. Khan had renegotiated with his Al Qaeda contact and gotten them to agree to pay a portion of the ransom money for Monroe's head as long as the features were recognizable. Two million dollars US for Monroe's head on a stake. As Yusef spread out his blanket and lay down on his side facing the fire, he imagined Monroe's bullet-riddled body sprawled out somewhere in the valley like a dead *buzkashi* goat.

He motioned to his men. "Rest now," he said, gesturing for them to spread out their blankets for the night.

The men immediately complied, wrapping themselves in whatever clothes and blankets they had, crowding around the fire like dogs.

Yusef called to the man on guard. "Stay awake as long as you can, then wake somebody else to replace you."

The guard nodded.

Salam saw the guard nodding. He was crouched behind a boulder, thirty yards away. Monroe crouched next to him. Rudge lay flat on his belly behind a low rock ten feet to Salam's left. Vitelli and Canfield crouched behind another rock farther back. All of them had smeared their faces and hands with mud, even Monroe and Rudge, because black skin can reflect light, too. They were all armed with AK-47s except for Salam, who had retained his M41A. Salam had ordered them not to fire unless he gave the command.

He looked back toward the line of scrub seventy-five yards behind them. Proctor and Jane hid back there. Proctor's fever had spiked, and though he was more than willing to contribute, he didn't have the energy. Salam had left Jane in charge with an AK and three hundred rounds.

Salam couldn't see the enemy's campfire from here, but he could see the embers rising behind the guard perched on the boulder. Stupid, he thought. That fire had drawn them straight to this pack of *muj*. It had taken Salam's unit less than three hours to find them, and that was with his men taking turns helping Proctor walk.

Salam made eye contact with each of his men. It felt strange having Monroe looking at him this way. But the general had insisted that he lead, so that meant Monroe had to follow. Still, Salam had to wonder how effective Monroe would be. He'd choked back at that Taliban camp. No reason to believe he'd do any better here. The man might have had it once upon a time, but he sure as shit didn't have it anymore.

Salam had already given the unit his plan for a SF-style ambush. He'd ordered them to communicate via hand signals only, even after they'd made contact with the enemy. They knew how many *muj* they had to deal with, but the *muj* wouldn't know how many attackers they had on their ass. By keeping silent, Salam's people would keep the enemy guessing.

Salam had also ordered them to refrain from using their weapons unless absolutely necessary. Gunfire would alert other *muj* in the area, and Salam didn't want them sending in reinforcements. Besides, Salam's people had to conserve their ammo.

Salam looked over at Rudge who waited for the go-ahead. Salam glanced over his shoulder. Canfield and Vitelli had their eyes on him. He looked at Monroe but couldn't read his bland expression. Scared shitless no doubt, Salam thought. Well, that was his problem. Salam had planned it so that Monroe's participation wouldn't make or break this operation.

Salam raised his hand, middle and index finger extended and pointed up. He waited and listened. Nothing unusual, just the distant crackle of the enemy's campfire. Time to go. He snapped his wrist and pointed his fingers forward.

Rudge quietly got to his feet and moved in a crouch, toting his AK. Monroe moved out to join him. They would circle around to take the left flank. Vitelli and Canfield would cut a wide path around the boulders to hit the right flank. Salam would give them two minutes to find their positions. He watched the second hand sweep the face of his wristwatch, his eyes darting left and right to check on his men. At the two-minute mark, he left his cover and headed straight up the middle toward the guard.

He stepped carefully, shifting his weight slowly from his heel to the ball of each foot, to make the least amount of noise possible, keeping his eye on the guard. He didn't see any movement from the guard. He could be sleeping, but Salam knew that could be a dangerous assumption. The closer he got to the guard, the slower he moved. He had to blend with the darkness. He had to be invisible.

When Salam got within twenty feet, he just stopped and watched. The man hadn't moved in fifteen minutes, then suddenly he rubbed his nose with the back of his hand. Salam didn't move. The man was very much awake. Salam hoped to God that his men remembered what he'd told them. Patience is key. It might take hours for him get to the guard. They just had to wait until he did. He worried that Canfield or maybe even Vitelli would get squirrelly and then trigger happy.

Salam didn't need to check his watch at this point. Berets know time by instinct. Every fifteen, twenty minutes, he took a slow step forward and froze. Any more than that might be sensed by the guard. Moving twenty feet would be like crossing a continent. Salam knew it might take two hours before he got within striking range. But he also knew he couldn't take any longer than that because the sky would start to lighten before dawn.

Patience is key, he told himself.

But four steps and nearly an hour later something happened. The guard stood up and stretched.

Hold your positions, Salam said mentally to his men. Steady.

The guard hitched his rifle over his shoulder and climbed down from the rock. Was he going to take a piss, Salam wondered, or was he going to get someone to relieve him? As soon as the man disappeared from sight, Salam moved fast, crossing the rest of the distance to the boulder and crouching under its lip where he wouldn't be seen from the top of the rock.

Salam listened carefully. He heard a man's voice, but he couldn't make out the words, not even the language. Was it the guard trying to rouse someone? Or was it his replacement complaining that he'd been sleeping so nicely when he'd been awakened? Salam wanted to whip around the boulder and empty his clip into the sleeping enemy. But making that much noise would be a big mistake. Instead he waited until he heard footsteps dislodging loose pebbles from the boulder as the guard—or the *new* guard—took his post.

The pebbles gave Salam an idea. He reached down and felt around for a good-sized stone. He rejected a few before he found the perfect one for his purposes—flat and about a quarter pound in weight. He waited twenty minutes. The guard had to get settled in. Boredom and monotony had to breed disgruntled skepticism. Salam picked his target, an area off to his left crowded with tall boulders. He positioned the stone in his hand, then flung it side-armed, aiming not too far and not too close. He listened for the impact. It sounded as if it hit packed dirt, then bounced into rock. Good enough to arouse the guard's suspicions unless the mother was deaf or a total fuckup.

Salam peered up over the edge of the boulder. The guard—a new man—stood up, staring in the direction Salam had thrown the stone.

Salam moved around the base of the boulder. He saw the man in profile focused on the distance, not the area immediately around himself. Salam quickly leapt up onto the boulder and tackled the man from behind, straddling his back and pinning his arms to his sides. Salam linked his fingers around the man's forehead and yanked up, snapping his neck in two sharp cracks. It all happened so fast the man didn't have a chance to yell. Dead before he knew it.

Salam stood up and faced the firelight, raising his arm and signaling to the others. They emerged from the shadows one by one—Vitelli, Canfield, Rudge, Monroe. They moved fast but didn't run, just as Salam had instructed them. Salam counted the sleeping bodies. It would be five against nine. The initial kills had to be fast and sure. The remaining *muj* would be awakened by the slaughter. The Americans had to change the odds fast and leave no opportunity for a rally.

Salam jumped off the boulder and used his rifle butt as a bludgeon, mashing the head of the nearest sleeping man. Canfield and Vitelli did the same. Rudge grabbed a sleeping *muj* by the beard and whipped his head against a boulder over and over again, like a baseball in a sock. Salam didn't expect Monroe to get his hands dirty, but the general shocked him when he snatched a knife from the belt of a sleeping *muj* and slit his throat, then moved on and did the next guy. The gore glistened in the firelight, Monroe's knife hand slick with blood.

The other *mujahadeen* woke up and saw the intruders. They called out to one another in warning. One man jumped to his feet and reached for his rifle, but Rudge kneed him so hard in the groin the man's feet left the ground. Rudge looped a length of his *muj* scarf around the man's neck and pulled. The man tried to struggle, but it did no good. Rudge looked like the Hulk, his arms pumped, his huge jaw set. The man's legs gave out, but Rudge held him up by the scarf until he stopped struggling.

Canfield and Vitelli worked as a tag team. Canfield quickly pinned one of the *muj* down before he had a chance to get up, pressing his AK into the man's throat. Vitelli then used the butt of his rifle to make gravel out of the man's rib cage, stopping only to kick him a few times in the gut, showing his street colors. Canfield's unrelenting pressure on the man's windpipe ultimately did him in.

Monroe tangled with a fierce *muj* who had gotten to his rifle. Monroe grabbed the barrel and pointed it up and away from himself as he slashed the man's face, cutting through his eye. The *muj* released his weapon and clutched his bloody face. Monroe plunged the blade into the side of his neck. Blood spurted in an arc, falling into the fire with an angry hiss. Despite his wounds, the man fought on. Monroe stayed on top of him, intent on finishing him off.

Salam went to help Monroe, but another *mujahadeen* popped out of nowhere and grabbed Salam from behind, pressing a dagger to his throat.

"Fucking bastard," Yusef cursed in Salam's ear.

Salam deflected the knife hand, but Yusef held on to the weapon and brought it back to Salam's neck, his eyes on fire.

"Now you will suffer, my friend," he said.

"No, *you* will suffer," Monroe said as he came up behind Yusef and grabbed a fistful of the man's oily black hair. Monroe hauled him back, but instead of slitting his throat, Monroe reached around and stuck the knife into Yusef's gut up to the hilt and ripped a line through his flesh from left to right. The blade bunched Yusef's clothes as it traveled. When it hit bone and wouldn't go any farther, Monroe changed course and headed north, ripping upward *seppuku* style. Yusef collapsed to his knees, his eyes screaming. Monroe stood over him, his arm dripping blood, and watched Raz Khan's right-hand man writhe in pain on the ground. A throat slash would have been quick death; gut wounds are slow and painful.

Salam stared at the general, shocked and impressed. Monroe stood there, his eyes on his quarry, the fire illuminating one side of his face like a moon. A beast in the night, Salam thought.

The others gathered around. Yusef gurgled and choked and clutched at phantoms as he slowly bled out. The Americans stood over him and silently watched him die.

27

"I WISH I HAD A FUCKING BEER," Canfield grumbled.

"I wish I had a fucking keg," Vitelli muttered.

The unit had taken refuge under an overhanging ledge on a cliff that towered over a barren valley. A dry hot wind blew in from the valley, negating the effects of the shade. The men who had taken part in the ambush looked like animals after a feeding frenzy, their faces caked with mud, their clothes stiff with *mujahadeen* blood, still intoxicated by the kill. Monroe caught himself staring into space, brooding along with them, but he forced himself out of the trance, realizing that they'd reached a dangerous crossroads. Their actions against Yusef's unit had put them on the divide that separated humanity from savagery. They could all easily drift onto the dark side and become a pack of wild mongrels, a curse that has plagued soldiers throughout time.

Monroe studied the faces of the soldiers around him. They'd fallen silent, their faces drawn and surly, their eyes drained. Monroe knew he had to do something to pull them back from the edge, to get them back together as a unit.

He cleared his throat and broke the silence. "There was a time, not so long ago, when I was at Fort Bragg." Monroe spoke somberly, he had the group's attention.

"I called down for a vehicle. I was alone in my office—no assistants, no secretary around—and I had to make the call myself. The phone rang a few times and a guy answered, 'Motor Pool.'

"I need a vehicle for an officer ASAP," I told him.

Rudge watched and listened, slowly drawing a line in the dirt with the toe of his boot. Vitelli cracked his knuckles.

Monroe proceeded: "'Well, here's the deal,' the soldier told me. 'We've got three kinds of officer-class vehicles down here. We've got Jeeps for the captains. We've got the Hummers for the majors and colonels. And we've got khaki-colored Escalades with mini-bars, and four speeds in reverse for your candy-ass generals who only know how to lead from the rear."

"What was that last part?" I asked.

"Four speeds in reverse for your candy-ass generals who only know how to lead from the rear."

"'Oh, really,' I say. 'Do you know who this is?'"

"'Nope,' the soldier says."

"So I tell him, 'This is Lieutenant General Jackson Monroe!' Now, this guy is probably quaking in his boots."

"So, the guy says, 'General Monroe, do you know who *this* is?'"

Monroe stopped and made eye-contact with each of them. "And I say, 'No, I don't.'" A sly smile came over Monroe's face.

"And the soldier says, 'Well, so long candy ass!' And he hangs up."

Jane actually laughed, the others managed smiles. They had heard it before.

"Guess you don't like my joke," Monroe said with a mock frown.

But then Salam broke up, hissing like a radiator, and gradually they all started to laugh. The joke wasn't that funny—Monroe knew that—but the sound of their laughter triggered more laughter. Each one of them was happy to see everyone else happy, and that kept the laughter going. Even grumpy Proctor had tears spurting out of his eyes. Monroe finally relaxed. They'd connected with one another again. They'd stepped back from the divide.

"Okay," he said when they started to quiet down. "Let's try to get some rest. We deserve it."

Jane couldn't stop looking at Monroe. A red sunset lit his face, making him look like an ancient, exotic god of war. They all slept on the ground, except for Vitelli, who stood guard on a flat rock overlooking the valley twenty yards off.

Lying on her side facing Monroe, she couldn't get a handle on her feelings. It had been six hours since they'd bedded down, but she hadn't slept well in that time, waking up frequently, trying to sort it all out, going over what had happened the night before.

Morally she opposed all killing, and yet she made her living as a war junkie. She followed the action wherever it took her, and for a photographer, nothing compared to armed conflict. She'd faced these contradictions before. She'd fretted over them long ago, made peace with the basic hypocrisy of her chosen profession, and filed it away. Every photojournalist lived with moral duplicity tucked away in a bottom drawer of the soul. But that's not what bothered her right now. In one of her waking periods she'd figured out that she'd been trying to put this situation into that category to make it easier to deal with, hoping she could just forget about it. But watching Monroe sleep with the glowing light bathing his face, she had to admit that she felt something else, something neither moral nor professional. . . something personal. She'd suddenly found herself attracted to the man. Two days ago he'd been a stick-up-the-ass military edifice. But now he was a killer, a predator, an alpha. Now he was hot.

She stared at his lips. She wanted to kiss him. Not because she loved him—God forbid—but just to see what it would be like. His dirty and sweated-through clothes clung to his body and showed off more of his physique. The man had a good body—and not just for a fifty-three-year-old. But the physical part didn't matter as much as the man himself—and not his bullshit words, his actions. He'd swallowed his pride and gotten down and dirty with his men. He'd killed with his bare hands. He'd inspired the whole unit. She wondered what it would be like to fuck him.

The scratch of a boot in the dirt stole her attention. She looked past Monroe and saw Rudge staring at her as if he knew what she was thinking. Down-home, Southern-fried, church-on-Sunday Rudge wouldn't approve of her curiosity. Especially because he also had a thing for Monroe—not a sexual thing, he was too straight-laced for that—but a protective thing. He wanted to be Monroe's guardian angel, and he wanted Monroe to be like God or something. So far Monroe seemed to be put off by Rudge's cow-eyed kowtowing. But that hadn't stopped Rudge. Guardian angels don't give up easy.

She stared back at him, and he didn't look away. What the hell did he think? she wondered. That she was going to corrupt Monroe? Lead him into sin? Christ, as if being a career military man wasn't sin enough.

She closed her eyes. Maybe she could get a little more sleep before nightfall. Salam had said they'd be moving out again after dark. She'd better rest while she could.

"Hey! Hey!"

Her eyes popped open. Vitelli crouched under the overhang, going from person to person, waking everyone.

"Hey! Get up!" He shook Canfield's shoulder.

Salam sat up fast and grabbed his rifle, his face electrified, instantly ready to kill. Proctor reached for his gun, groggy and slow by Special Forces standards. Canfield jumped up like a cat, and Rudge got to his feet.

Monroe opened his eyes as if he'd never allowed himself to enter deep sleep. He sat up.

"What is it, Vitelli?" Salam said.

Vitelli grinned. "Sir," he said, "there are two trucks out there. They're driving through the valley."

"You left your post, Corporal," Salam said, reprimanding him.

"Sir, I thought this was important."

"Show me."

Vitelli led the way out of the cave, and everyone followed him. Even Proctor got up. He seemed to be a little better, more alert. His fever must have broken, she thought.

They shaded their eyes with their hands as they walked toward the sunset. Vitelli led them to his "post," a huge flat boulder that overlooked the valley. He crawled on his belly to the edge and peered over, then waved to the others to come take a look for themselves. Monroe and Salam crawled out. Jane muscled past Rudge, eager to get a look.

The valley stretched out for miles—a dry, dusty expanse. The setting sun had colored the land a dull pink. Clumps of low scrub bushes and man-sized outcroppings of rock dotted the basically barren landscape. Eighty yards or so below their position, a tire-track path cut across the valley, and two colorful Afghan trucks trudged along, heading east, the sun casting long shadows in front of them. Jane smiled at the sight of them. The Afghanis took great pride in decorating their trucks with intricate multicolored designs that included paint, tassels, pieces of mirror, odd scraps of shiny metal, and anything else that could be construed as a decoration. She considered them works of art and had done a photo essay on them on her last trip to Kabul.

"Stay low," Salam said. "Keep your heads down."

The trucks stayed close and moved at a good clip. They reminded Jane of fancier versions of the Beverly Hillbillies' dilapidated vehicle. She tried to make out the faces of the drivers, squat old men in *pakuls* and dark suit jackets over their long shirts. As they drove past, Jane could clearly see two women, one in the back of each truck. They both wore *burkhas*—one midnight blue, the other deep purple—the despised head-to-toe robe that the Taliban had forced all women to wear to cover themselves completely. Most people in the West thought that these feudal garments only came in black, but the religious zealots cared little about the color as long as it was dark. But the *burkha* had to cover every speck of skin, including the face. A tight mesh in the hood allowed limited visibility.

"We could sure use those trucks," Salam said, thinking out loud.

"Maybe they'll give us a lift," Monroe said, but the ominous way he said it implied that they should take control of those trucks with or without the owners' consent.

Salam peered through the scope on his rifle, looking east in the direction the trucks were traveling. "The valley narrows about a mile and a half from here. There's a pass." He panned back to the trucks. "They've got longer to go than we do on foot. If we hightail it, we can get to the pass before they do."

"To welcome them?" Monroe asked wryly.

Salam allowed himself a slight grin. "Something like that. If you agree, that is."

"You're in charge, Captain."

Jane noticed that a lot of the bitterness between Salam and Monroe had dissipated overnight. They'd forged a bond, it seemed, and tempered it in *mujahadeen* blood.

"Okay, let's go for it." Salam said. He turned to Jane. "Do you mind staying back with Sergeant Proctor again?"

"Sir, I'm fine," Proctor blurted. "I feel like a little marching. Get the kinks out."

Salam gave him a frank, assessing look. "Okay," he said, then turned back to Jane. He looked doubtful. "It's double-time over rough terrain. You think you're up for it?"

"You're asking me as if I'm the one with the bum leg. Of course, I'm fucking up to it."

The men stared at her. She could have choked on all the testosterone in the air.

The trucks slowed down as they entered the pass. Their dangling decorations jangled as they bumped over the ruts. The trucks dipped and swayed and seemed dangerously close to tipping over, but they never did. Functional shock absorbers did not exist on Afghan trucks. Every rut and rock in the road produced a frightening bang and jolt as if an axle had snapped in half, but the trucks kept on going, their motors humming like bumble bees with bad coughs.

The road curved sharply to the right. Suddenly the lead driver saw the line of armed strangers blocking the way and slammed on the brakes. The second truck had to swerve to the right to avoid rear-ending the first truck. A cloud of dust rose from their tires and drifted toward the pack of Americans wearing *mujahadeen* hats, jackets, and shirts over their camo fatigues, their clothes streaked with red dirt from their slide down the steep embankment into the pass. They kept their rifles pointed down.

Salam stepped forward, keeping his eye on the driver in the lead truck, who was gray and grizzled but not as old as they'd originally thought. Same with the other driver.

"Come out of your trucks, please," he said in Dari. When he got no response, he repeated it in Pashto. He motioned with his rifle, and they finally seemed to get the message. The drivers climbed down from their seats, but Salam wanted to see the women, too. In Afghanistan, you trusted no one.

"Everyone," he said, speaking louder. "Everyone out. Women, too."

"Yes, yes," one of the men said in heavily accented English, though it appeared that he didn't really know the language. He hunched his shoulders, bowed his head, and smiled obsequiously.

The women stepped down from the beds of the trucks but didn't venture forward. Stepping in front of a man could easily earn a woman a beating in this country. They stayed silent and ghostly in their *burkhas*.

"Rudge, Vitelli," Salam said. "Check the trucks."

The corporals walked around to the truck beds, leading with their rifles.

A stiff breeze blew through the pass, raising a new cloud of dust.

"What's that smell?" Jane said, making a face. She stood at the rear of the pack, behind Proctor and General Monroe.

Salam smelled it, too. Vinegary, kind of like something rotting. He imagined dead bodies.

Vitelli suddenly jumped out of his truck. "Nobody fucking move!" he shouted. He pointed his rifle at the Afghanis, moving quickly from one to the next. "Don't move a fucking muscle!" he screamed.

"Corporal, what's the problem?" Salam shouted. Vitelli had gone insane.

But Vitelli didn't answer him. "Do not fucking move!" he roared at the Afghanis.

But the woman in the midnight blue *burkha* did move, the billowing fabric betraying her, and Vitelli started shooting, riddling her body with automatic fire. She collapsed inside the *burkha* as if the earth had opened up and swallowed her, leaving only the garment.

"Christ, Vitelli!" Salam yelled. "What the fuck is wrong with you?"

But Vitelli ignored Salam and rushed over to the other woman, ripping the purple *burkha* off her back, almost pulling her down with it. "Put your hands up!" he shouted like a mental patient. "Put 'em up! *Now*, goddamn it! *Do it!*"

The person under the *burkha* wasn't a woman. It was a man in a dirty white t-shirt and khaki shorts. An Uzi submachine gun hung from his neck on a black nylon web strap. He kept his hands in the air, arms bent at the elbow.

"Watch the other two!" Vitelli screamed. "Get 'em down! On the ground!"

Salam and Proctor converged on the drivers. "Down! Down! Down!" they shouted, prodding the men with their rifles. Rudge covered the former "woman" while Vitelli yanked the *burkha* off the dead body— another man with a submachine gun around his neck.

"Shit, Vitelli," said Salam, "How did you—"

"Hang on. I'll show you," Vitelli said as he bounded into the truck bed with his gun leveled. Salam could hear him rummaging around, turning things inside out. He jumped back out, holding something in his hand. It looked like a fresh five-pound elephant turd loosely wrapped in plastic.

Salam reared his head back from the stink when Vitelli showed it to him.

"What the fuck is that?"

Vitelli had a know-it-all smirk on his face. "Opium, sir. Raw paste. It's the base for heroin."

Monroe came closer to get a better look. "How do you know, Corporal?"

Vitelli wiped off the smirk. "I've got a cousin from back home who ran a lab for some guys. He's doing time now. You don't forget this smell." Vitelli left it at that, but Salam had to wonder how involved Vitelli had been in his cousin's drug operation.

"Hey, hey," one of the drivers said. "Can I say something here?" He spoke English with a slight southern California accent.

The other two kept their mouths shut, but their disgruntled expressions betrayed their awareness of the situation. Their faces registered neither shock nor fear. Just annoyance.

"They must have a ton of this shit," Vitelli said. "It's all in barrels."

"And they're heading east," Proctor said, his anger seething. "To Pakistan maybe? For processing. Shit!"

"Look, man," the lead driver said. "We can make a deal here. We're not greedy. We can share."

"Save your breath," Salam said. "The Army doesn't do deals with people like you."

"Don't be so quick to judge," the man said. "This stuff never leaves Asia. It never goes to America. It's all for internal use."

"Don't insult me," Salam said. "We're going to burn your supply. Right here."

"No, man, don't do that," the man pleaded. "Just hear me out. We're talking millions. US dollars."

"Start unloading the trucks," Salam ordered. "Vitelli, will this stuff burn? Do we need gas—?"

A single gunshot rang out, and everyone hit the dirt. The shot echoed off the rock walls of the pass. Salam immediately started looking for a sniper hide, but then he saw Canfield still on his feet, his rifle cocked on his hip. Canfield had fired a shot into the air. He stared at Monroe, his chin tucked.

"I don't think so, Captain," he said.

The breeze tinkled the hanging ornaments on the truck.

28

CANFIELD LOOKED LIKE the devil had taken possession of his soul. He had purpose in his bearing and hot coals in his eyes. He kept his gun moving, pointing the muzzle from one man to the next.

"Hey, man," the lead drug smuggler said, forcing a little laugh and keeping his hands up, "let's not go shooting anybody else, okay? One's enough for today."

His buddies, the other driver and the guy who had been wearing the purple *burkha*, flashed big smiles at Canfield to show that they didn't mind that he'd killed their buddy.

Monroe looked grim. "Lower your weapon, Canfield."

"Hang on, General. Just hear me out. We're sitting on a gold mine here. This stuff has got to be worth millions. Am I right, Vitelli?"

Vitelli shrugged and weighed the elephant turd in his hand. "Yeah, but you gotta get it out of here. And you need a connection. Can't just sell it at the local farmers' market."

"Not sell it," Canfield said. "Barter. To get us out of here."

Salam scowled at him. "You're all fucked up, Canfield."

"The Army is not in the drug business, Corporal," Monroe said. "And neither are you."

"But, General, don't you see? This is an opportunity," Canfield said. "We can *buy* our way back to Gardiz with this stuff." He turned to Vitelli. "Tell him what this shit is worth. You must've done some deals with your cousin. Tell him!"

Vitelli dropped the turd in the dust and shook his head. "I don't know nothing."

Canfield looked to Salam. "You heard what the guy said. These drugs don't go to America. Internal use only. So who cares?"

"Canfield, you have to be the dumbest fuck I have ever seen," Salam said. "You can get heroin for pocket change in Pakistan. The same stuff costs a hundred times that in Chicago. So where the hell do you think this shit ends up? Where the markup is highest, you fucking moron."

"Rudge," Canfield said, looking for support, but Rudge wouldn't even look at him.

He looked to Jane, but she cut him off before he even got a word out. "Don't even ask," she said, holding up her hand. "Salam's right."

"I thought you were hip," Canfield said. "I thought you knew how things were in the real world."

"Yeah, that's why I don't want any part of this," she said. "Rehab is no picnic, believe me. I wouldn't wish it on anyone."

Monroe looked at her.

"Don't get all judgmental on me, okay?" she said. "It was cocaine, and it was a while ago. It's all past tense."

"I wasn't judging you," Monroe said. He shifted his gaze to Rudge. "How do you feel about all this?"

Rudge wouldn't look him in the eye.

"Corporal, I'm talking to you?" Monroe said.

Rudge finally lifted his head and met Monroe's gaze, glowering at him. "Don't look at me to back you up," he said. "I ain't your nigger."

Monroe felt as if he'd been slapped in the face. Where did that come from?

"Captain," Proctor shouted, leveling his AK on Canfield, "permission to frag this asshole to kingdom come. Permission to frag *all* these assholes."

Canfield swiveled his weapon toward Proctor, his eyes were wide with fear, but not backing down.

"Easy, boys," the lead smuggler said. "Let's not do something that'll keep us out of heaven. You know what I'm saying?"

Salam coughed up a derisive laugh, his weapon leveled. "I'd rather stand up to a firefight at close range than go along with a drug deal."

Rudge and Jane inched away from the line of fire, but the smugglers inched closer to Canfield, setting up sides. The situation deteriorated by the moment. Monroe decided he couldn't let this continue.

"All right," he said to Canfield. "You do what you want."

Canfield looked puzzled. "Excuse me?"

"You're on your own. If you want to fall in with these dirtbags and buy your way out of here, that's your decision."

Canfield narrowed his eyes. "You don't really mean that."

"Oh, yes I do," Monroe said. "You're a man. You don't need my permission to fuck up your life. Make a deal with these pirates. See how far you get with them."

"I bet he doesn't see the Paki border," Proctor said. "Not alive."

"They're just fucking with your head," the "woman" smuggler said to Canfield. "Let's get away from these nuts and we'll talk."

"Yeah," the lead smuggler said, "we'll get you out of here and cut you in. That's not a problem."

Canfield looked to Monroe, but Monroe just shrugged, wiping his hands clean of the whole affair.

Canfield held his weapon on his unit while he looked at the smugglers. He seemed to be assessing them. *Burkha* Boy still had the Uzi dangling from his neck. The smuggler who did all the talking seemed as phony as they came, all smiles and conciliation. The other driver hadn't said a word, but his cold eyes told his story. He'd slit a man's throat just as soon as look at him. Canfield would be an idiot to let his guard down for a second around any one of them. But Canfield would do anything to escape from these mountains. Young, dumb, and scared shitless.

The moment stretched into eternity. Everyone waited on Canfield. Proctor had trouble keeping his eyelids open. The march had caught up with him. His fever must be spiking again, Monroe thought. The sergeant might overreact and start shooting. Monroe tried to catch his eye, but Proctor's glassy focus stayed on Canfield and the smugglers.

Canfield's turmoil showed in his strawberry-red face. Rage and tears threatened to burst out of him at any moment. Suddenly he swiveled his rifle away from his unit and turned toward the smugglers, focusing on *Burkha* Boy. "Take off the Uzi and throw it toward me," he said. "And don't fuck around."

"Hey, whatever you want, dude. Just be cool." The smuggler took the gun from around his neck, holding it in one hand by the strap.

"Toss it," Canfield said.

"Sure, sure," the smuggler said. "But you don't want to think about this?"

"One. . ." Canfield started counting. "Two. . ."

"Hey, c'mon, man, we're just talking here."

Canfield raised his AK to his shoulder. "Three!"

"No! C'mon!" The smuggler instantly threw the Uzi away. "Okay, you happy? I did it. See? I did it."

Canfield lowered his rifle. "Thank you." He grinned like a little kid getting his first taste of control.

Canfield turned to Monroe. "Sir, I apologize," he said, his face blotched with shame. "My Dee-troit white-trash instincts got the better of me. May I rejoin the unit, sir?"

"You'll have to ask Captain Salam."

Salam glanced at Monroe. "No," he said. "You'd better ask the general. He's the ranking officer in this unit."

Monroe stared at him. "Salam, I ceded authority to—"

"And I'm giving it back, sir. I think you showed. . ." Salam left his thought unsaid, but his eyes showed his approval.

"General?" Canfield's eyes pleaded.

Monroe looked to Salam, unsure of his fitness for command.

Salam nodded to show his confidence in the general.

"Huah," Proctor said, adding his support.

"Huah," Vitelli joined in.

Monroe didn't know if he was ready for this, but the men's vote of confidence thrilled and humbled him at the same time.

"General?" Canfield repeated. "May I rejoin the unit, sir?"

Monroe nodded. "Yes, you may, Corporal." He turned toward the others. "Salam, Proctor, you mind our friends here. The rest of you search the trucks for weapons and food." He tried to catch Rudge's eye, but Rudge had turned away, walking toward the trucks. Monroe wanted to get things right with him.

The Berets corralled the smugglers, ordering them to sit back-to-back on the ground in a tight circle so that Salam and Proctor could keep an eye on them. In the meantime Rudge, Vitelli, and Canfield rummaged through the smugglers' cargo.

Rudge found an H&K 9mm MP5-A5 under the seat of the lead truck and a 9mm Beretta pistol under the seat of the other. Vitelli came back with an M16A2 heavy-barrel assault rifle.

Canfield jumped out of his truck. "Hey, look what I found!" He held up an M203 grenade launcher.

Salam looked at Monroe, who shook his head in disgust. All US Army-issue weapons and all current models.

He walked over to the lead smuggler. "Where'd you get these weapons?"

"We found 'em."

Monroe wanted to strangle him with his bare hands. Instead he walked over to Rudge and took the Beretta out of his hand. He racked the slide and checked the barrel as he walked back toward the smuggler.

"Hey, listen—" the smuggler started to say.

Monroe lifted the gun to the man's face and fired three shots into the ground inches from his ear.

The man winced and covered his ear. "Mother*fucker!*" he yelled. The others tried to scuttle away, but Salam and Proctor prodded them back into place with their gun barrels.

Monroe pointed the pistol at *Burkha* Boy. "Where did you get the weapons?"

"I don't—"

Monroe lowered the pistol and shot the man in the foot. The smuggler opened his mouth in a silent scream as he watched blood pool around the hole in the top of his scuffed boot.

"I'm going to ask you again. Where did you get these weapons?" The muzzle hovered over the man's shaking knee.

"Are you fucking crazy?" the smuggler screamed. "I'm an American! You can't shoot *me!*"

"The United States has been waging a war on drugs for many years," Monroe said. "You are an international drug dealer. Therefore, as an officer in the United States Army, I am at war with *you*. Now"—Monroe positioned the muzzle directly over the man's kneecap—"do I have to repeat the question, or do you remember it?"

"All right, all right," the smuggler squealed, tears springing from his eyes. "It was a guy in the mountains—"

"A 'guy'?" Monroe said with the pointed tenacity of a drill instructor. "What guy? We're all guys."

"Just let me finish." Blood gushed from his foot. Sweat dripped down his face. "A warlord. His name is Raz Khan."

"Raz Khan sold you these weapons?"

"Most of them. Yeah."

Proctor growled. "Goddamn cocksuckin' motherfucker! We give him guns as part of the coalition and he turns around and sells 'em. Fuck him! Fuck him and his whole motherfuckin' tribe!"

The smuggler shook all over. "He told us his men didn't like American weapons. They like Russian stuff better."

"Look at me," Monroe said, turning the man's chin with the barrel of the pistol. He rested the muzzle on top of the man's knee. "What else did he sell you?"

"What do you mean, what else? Ammo. He sold us ammo."

"What else?"

"Nothing."

"I said, *what else?*" Monroe pulled the trigger, but the gun jammed. He scowled at the Beretta as he partially disassembled it to correct the jam, working with such skill and purpose, the smuggler started to whine in anticipation of getting shot. "Noooo..." the man moaned, his face deep red beneath the stubble and grime and sweat. "The base," he said. "Raz Khan sold us the base."

Monroe slapped the slide back into place. "The what?" he said.

"The stuff in the trucks, the dope. He sold us the opium base. Half a ton of it."

Monroe shouted to Vitelli. "How much heroin would that produce, Corporal?"

"A lot, sir."

"Enough to destroy a neighborhood?"

"More than one neighborhood," Vitelli said.

Monroe ground the muzzle of his gun into the man's knee. "Where did Raz Khan sell you this shit?"

"His village," the smuggler said, hyperventilating with fear. "Over there." He pointed to a mountain in the distance. "On the other side of that mountain."

Monroe said nothing as he processed this information.

"You are a terrorist," Monroe finally said to him. "Exporting narcotics to the United States and poisoning American lives is an act of terrorism as I see it. You are all terrorists."

The wounded smuggler melted into a puddle of anguish. "Take the base, man," he said. "Just let us go. You can have the junk."

Monroe snorted a mocking laugh. "That was my intention all along. The question is, what do we do with the three of you? Any suggestions?"

"Just let us go. Please. We won't come back. Ever."

Monroe let out a long breath and looked over at Salam and Proctor. He shifted his eyes back to the smuggler. "We could eliminate the threat of future attacks on United States security here and now."

Proctor nodded gravely. Salam's face had turned to stone.

"But," Monroe continued, "that would be playing judge, jury, and executioner, which might be the Afghani way, but it is not the American way. Therefore, we will destroy all of your product, seize your weapons and most of your food, and take one of your trucks. The three of you can have the other truck, and you can go on your way."

The other two smugglers grumbled. The taciturn man who hadn't said a word yet finally spoke. "We show up empty-handed on the other end. . . " He let his words trail off. Obviously the consequences of that would be severe.

"That's your problem," Monroe said. "I want those trucks unloaded ASAP, and you two are going to help," he said to the uninjured smugglers. He turned to the enlisted men. "Work with them, but keep your eye on them. Make one pile."

"Captain," he said to Salam, "do we have any way of siphoning off gas from the trucks?"

"Sir," Canfield spoke up, "there's a rubber hose in the truck I searched."

"Good," Monroe said. "When you're finished unloading, I want you to douse the drugs with gasoline. Take it from this truck." He pointed to the nearest truck. "That'll be theirs."

"Aw, c'mon," the wounded man whined, "we won't make it to the border without a full tank."

"Then I guess you'll have to go somewhere else."

"But—"

"Case closed." He turned to Salam and Proctor. "Berets, secure the area."

"Yes sir," they said.

Monroe then went to work, helping the men unload. It took twenty minutes to unload the opium base and make a pile. Rudge and Canfield then worked together using the rubber hose to douse the base with gasoline.

"Vitelli," Monroe said, "move our vehicle out of harm's way." He pointed in the direction the smugglers had come from.

"You three get going," he said to the smugglers. "On the double. Go!"

The smugglers sneered and complained, but they didn't waste any time clearing out, helping their wounded buddy into the bed of their truck. The other two jumped into the cab. The starter whined, and it took several tries before the engine kicked over, but as soon as it did, the truck lurched forward and picked up speed, grinding through the gears until it moved out at a good clip.

Monroe watched it depart, the long rays of the setting sun at his back. "Corporal Canfield," he called out.

Canfield came rushing over. "Yes sir."

Monroe found the grenade launcher on the ground and handed it to Canfield. Monroe indicated the truck with his eyes. "Take it out," he said.

Canfield held the grenade launcher as if he didn't know what to do with it, but he knew exactly what the general wanted. "Sir, I..." he said. "I've never killed anyone."

"Give them one warning shot, count to five, then hit the truck."

"But, sir—"

"Do it, Corporal. Those are drug dealers. They're not going to change their ways."

Canfield's eyes bulged. "Yes sir."

The others gathered around as Canfield got down on one knee and positioned the weapon on his shoulder, squinting down the sights.

"Fire," Monroe ordered.

Canfield hesitated, then pulled the trigger. A grenade sailed out of the tube with a hollow *fwoop,* leaving a wispy trail of smoke in its wake. It hit the dirt fifteen feet to the truck's left, lifting the vehicle onto two wheels. The truck fell back down with a jolt, the driver braking hard.

Monroe started to count, "One... two... three... four..."

"Five," Canfield said.

Fwoop!

A moment later the second grenade entered the interior of the truck bed and exploded, instantly setting the roof on fire. It burned for half a minute before the gas tank exploded, sending a plume of fire and black smoke into the red sky. The smugglers had wisely abandoned the vehicle after the warning shot, running as fast as they could away from the explosion. The wounded man hobbled painfully on one foot, his buddies having left him behind.

The soldiers cheered as the sun sank behind the mountains, and the burning truck became the brightest spot on the landscape. Only Jane didn't cheer, but like the others, she couldn't take her eyes off the billowing black smoke and raging flames.

Monroe turned his attention to the pile of opium base. The vinegar smell combined with the gasoline fumes to produce an overpowering stench. He looked to his men.

"Who has a light?" he asked.

29

IN THE DAWN LIGHT the village seemed uninhabited, which made Monroe suspicious. The only movement came from the penned horses shuffling their hooves. Monroe watched the cluster of flat-roofed huts from behind a bush. He and his unit had been here for hours, just watching. Earlier Monroe had counted about thirty men—mostly Pashtuns, but a few Uzbekis, Baluchis, and Hazaras, too, according to Salam. Monroe had seen Raz Khan and the boy Hajji emerge from one of the larger huts. Monroe wanted to spare the child if at all possible.

The village campfires had gone out long ago, but he could see thin trails of smoke coming from several of the small structures. Monroe imagined the huts as being crowded and overheated inside with gangs of *mujahadeen* sprawled out on the floor around an indoor fire.

He exchanged glances with Salam, who was by his side. "What do you think, Captain?" he whispered.

Salam gave him a sly look. "You're in charge now. I'm just taking orders."

"You're second-in-command. I expect your input."

"Even when you're not gonna like it?"

"*Especially* when I'm not going to like it."

"Great. I can't wait to tell a three-star he has his head up his ass."

Monroe's expression turned serious. "I want you to know that I'm putting you up for a Congressional Medal of Honor when this is all over."

"Forget about that. I didn't do anything."

"You did everything. You rescued us from those Qaeda fighters back in the cave. Single-handed. Not to mention everything else."

"Seriously, General. I don't need a medal. Please."

Monroe just stared at him. "Fuck you," he said. "You're getting one." He returned the sly look.

Salam smiled and shook his head. He knew the medal talk was just Monroe's way of giving him props—but he appreciated that.

Finally they had an understanding.

Monroe looked over at the rest of the unit hiding in the underbrush. He had ordered silence, but words weren't necessary. They knew what they had to do. Hit the enemy hard and fast. Do a quick search for more opium base. If they find any, destroy it. Take the horses and rations. Don't hang around.

With the weapons they'd taken from the smugglers, they had more arms than they needed. Monroe carried the H&K MP5-A5 as well as an AK. He'd given Jane one of the smugglers' Uzis with strict instructions to use it only if she absolutely had to. He'd warned her that fighting a war is a lot different from covering a war. The Uzi wasn't known for being an accurate weapon, but since she had no real experience with firearms, it really didn't matter. He'd told her that if she came under attack, she should start firing and keep firing. Given the gun's rapid rate of fire, she might get lucky.

He glanced over at her crouched down behind another bush with Vitelli and Proctor. Monroe worried about her. She didn't say much, but she had a risk-taker's personality. War wasn't about risks; it was about certainties. Overwhelming manpower and a clear means of escape—the keys to victory, in his opinion. But in this situation they had neither so they had to go with what they had in spades—brains and guts. From here on, this operation would be an SF extravaganza. Okay, maybe war *was* about risks. Grant and Patton certainly thought so.

Monroe's focus shifted to Proctor, another wild card. He pushed himself despite his injury. But the wound had become infected, and he kept fading in and out, listless with fever, then back to normal a few hours later. A tough son of a bitch running on sheer willpower. But how long would that last? And what if he faded out at a crucial juncture? In Monroe's mind, Proctor couldn't be counted on. Despite the man's abilities, he would not be an essential component in Monroe's planning.

All eyes were on Monroe, waiting for him to give the word to infiltrate the village, but something else bothered him. Why didn't Khan's people have a guard posted? Were they that certain of their security? It didn't make sense. If they sold drugs in quantity and had a large amount of cash from the smugglers, surely they knew they could be targets. And what about the Taliban threat? Why would Khan be so lax?

For the umpteenth time, Monroe weighed his options. They could pull back, abandon the area, and leave Khan for a later date. But that in itself could be risky. If the *muj* discovered them, they'd attack, and Khan had the numbers. Monroe's unit would be slaughtered.

Right now they had the element of surprise, which would even the odds.

And there was another factor. They had a moral obligation to decimate Khan and his troops. In Monroe's mind, Khan had become an international criminal, a drug lord as well as a renegade warlord—and most likely an assassin.

The murder of Zyrous Mohammed had been gnawing at Monroe since it happened. He'd replayed the scene in his mind a hundred times over—the muzzle flash on the parapets, Zyrous's gory head wound, his blood soaking the dry planks of the stage, the frantic escape, the downing of Starwood 2. Certainly Zyrous had enemies—any man in his position would—but he had led the coalition without opposition for two years. By all accounts he'd been a popular leader. Taliban or Al-Qaeda infiltrators could be responsible, but who else would have wanted him dead? A lean and hungry man, Monroe thought. A man who felt he was being passed over. A second in command who longed to be on top. Raz Khan.

Monroe predicted the future. In the coming weeks, Khan would present himself to the world as the rightful heir to Zyrous Mohammed. The international community would recognize him as the new leader of the Northern Coalition. If that were to happen, he'd be untouchable. Monroe couldn't let that happen. Strategy always trumped mere tactics, but the great war theorists—Sun Tzu, Musashi, von Clausewitz, and all the others he'd studied at the Academy—had fought in times of honor. Unfortunately Monroe did not live in a time of honor. He lived in an age of terrorists and drug lords. Expedience had taken the place of wisdom. Monroe had to strike now because they might not get this opportunity again. If they waited, Khan would be a harder target—maybe an impossible target. Monroe scanned the faces of his unit, then stopped at Salam, locking eyes with him. Monroe gave the nod. They would attack.

Salam signaled for everyone to move forward. They knew what to do. Proctor and Rudge would take the right flank. Salam and Vitelli would take the left. Monroe and Canfield would circle around to the rear. Jane would cover the forward position. The flanks would go from hut to hut, mowing down as many of the enemy as they could before they had a chance to get organized. The rear guard would stand by for support and take care of any *mujahadeen* who tried to flee from the village. Monroe doubted that any of the enemy would flee in Jane's direction because of the steep terrain, but if they did, she'd have adequate cover there and men on the flanks would rush in to help.

Monroe hoped his men fully understood the unspoken directive: no survivors. Obviously they couldn't let Khan live, but they couldn't afford to leave any witnesses either. Khan should not become a martyr in public opinion. He hoped Jane understood as well, but if she chose to report this event, Monroe felt certain that every man in the unit would stand together and deny it. It might be wrong, but it was necessary.

If she or any of the men gave him resistance on this point, he already had his argument formulated: If you had the opportunity to kill a Hitler or a bin Laden or any other mass murderer before he reached his deadly pinnacle of power, would you do it? Would you squelch his existence so that his hateful ideas could never be conveyed?

They moved carefully in the dark, measuring their steps so as to make no sound, a sniper skill Monroe had learned in Vietnam. He and Salam had instructed the unit in how to preform it. They moved slowly, shifting their weight carefully from heel to toe, thinking about every movement they made. It would take an hour or more to get to the village, a quick trip for a trained sniper.

Canfield came up next to Monroe. He looked scared, but Monroe had come to realize that he always looked scared. The young corporal had matured more in the past four days than he had in twenty years. He'd fought off temptation and showed courage and decision. He still had a long way to go, but Monroe was proud of him for the effort.

Monroe pointed and led the way, taking the left-hand track behind Proctor and Rudge. He and Canfield soon branched off the path and made a wider circle around the village. The father they got from enemy ears, the faster they moved.

Monroe glanced back at Canfield, who stayed close, rifle pointed down but ready. The darkest part of the night had passed, and the sky had lightened slightly, enough to see twenty feet in front of them. They moved from boulder to bush, stopping momentarily at each one to listen and reassess. They heard nothing.

Monroe could feel the sweat gathering in his armpits and at the small of his back despite the cold. The thrill of fear buzzed in his chest, but he considered it a healthy feeling. Too much fear blinds you to reality, but a small controlled dose keeps you alert, and in the field alert is alive.

Thin trails of smoke from the village striped the sky. Monroe couldn't see the huts from behind the boulders, but the smoke gave him the enemy's position. He watched for any increases in the rising smoke, which would have meant that someone was awake, stoking a fire.

They pressed on, Monroe keeping Canfield from moving any faster than they should. Wired and anxious, Canfield wanted to rock and roll. Young people hurry to get things done and over with. But in war hurrying can be fatal. Monroe would show him the value of patience.

They left the cover of one boulder and moved at Monroe's deliberate pace toward the next one fifteen feet away. They stopped again, paused and listened, then moved on. Walking, stopping, listening. Walking, stopping, listening. The sky had grown lighter by the time they'd finally made it around to the other side of the village. Soon the landscape would be a gray monochrome in the predawn light.

Monroe led the way as they moved forward toward the village. They stopped when the rooftops of the huts became visible. Monroe found a hide for them in the notch formed by two touching boulders. They'd wait here and listen for the action to begin. It would be a little while, Monroe estimated. The others wouldn't be in position yet.

Canfield looked at him, his expression as hopeful and pathetic as a puppy's. Monroe nodded and smiled and touched his shoulder. You're doing fine, son, he thought.

He peered through the space between the boulders at the rooftops and the chimney smoke. Any time now, he thought.

Then he heard it—gunfire in short bursts like a splash of cold water in the face. Monroe could feel Canfield's nervous electricity. He touched the young man's arm to settle him down. The *mujahadeen* shouldn't know they were here. Not yet.

More gunfire reverberated through the rocks in three-shot bursts, but Monroe frowned. He didn't like what he heard, that it only came from one side of the village, the left flank. In his mind he saw Proctor and Rudge clearing huts, but what happened to Salam and Vitelli? They had to have heard the gunfire, and their orders were to start as soon as they heard engagement, no matter who started it. Monroe had a bad feeling about this.

"General," Canfield whispered, "what's wrong?"

"Stay here," Monroe whispered back. "Don't show your face until I call for you. Do you understand?"

Canfield nodded.

Monroe moved out from behind the boulders, leading with his weapon. He walked slowly in a crouch toward the village. He listened for more gunfire, *wished* for more gunfire. He wanted to hear a firefight. He wanted to hear his people initiating the ambush. The eerie silence spooked him. He had to see what was going on down there.

He found a boulder with a low incline and mounted it, proceeding cautiously. As he shifted his weight from one foot to the next, a piece of rock scaled off. He lost his balance and had to drop to one knee on the unforgiving surface to catch himself. He felt no pain immediately, but he knew he'd feel it later after the bruising started. But that didn't concern him. His men, his unit, Jane—that's what concerned him.

He inched farther up the incline, slowly, slowly, knowing that with every step forward he became more visible to the enemy. First he could see the rooftops, then the huts, then the ground that they sat on. He scanned the area carefully, moving up a little farther until he could see the center of the village. He saw heads, a lot of them. His hands tightened on his weapon. He kept inching up. Then his stomach bottomed out when he saw the whole group. His unit sat on the ground, hands on top of their heads, surrounded by armed *mujahadeen*. The plethora of rifle barrels pointed at the captives created a lethal sunburst. There seemed to be more enemy fighters than Monroe had previously estimated.

He strained to make out the faces of his people, fearing that there had been casualties. He looked for Jane first, afraid that she would have been singled out for unique punishment simply because of her gender, but he quickly spotted her between Proctor and Vitelli. Rudge sat next to Proctor, but Monroe didn't see Salam. He moved up a little more, hoping that Rudge had simply blocked his view of Salam. They couldn't lose Salam, he thought. They needed him more than anyone.

"Stop!"

Monroe turned around toward the voice. Four *mujahadeen* on the ground at the base of the boulder pointed their rifles up at him.

Where the hell did they come from? Monroe wondered angrily. These men couldn't have been asleep in the village. They must have been waiting in the outskirts. Monroe and his people had been suckered.

"Stop! Stop!" one of them shouted in heavily accented English as the others jabbered in their native tongue. The man kept repeating the word, thrusting the air with his rifle every time he said it. Probably the only word he knew. Monroe knew what he wanted: Drop the weapon, put your hands up, and come down off the boulder.

Monroe raised his hands and faced them. He gestured that he would put down his weapon. Holding it by the barrel, he lowered it gently and set it down on the boulder.

"Come!" the man shouted. "Come!"

The other fighters shouted angrily as well, but Monroe didn't understand the language. With his hands in the air, he started to come down off the boulder. His mind raced, trying to figure out what he would do next and how he would do it without Salam. He hoped to God nothing had happened to him.

Monroe heard something and looked up. Canfield stood on a boulder twenty feet away, his AK in his arms, his face broadcasting scared determination. He swung his barrel toward the four *mujahadeen*, but they opened fire before he could get off a single shot.

Canfield's arms flung open, the rifle flying from his hands. His body jerked violently. He took several gut and chest shots and one through the cheek. He pitched forward and rolled onto his back, clinging to the boulder in suspended animation for a moment like a man crucified upside down, blood coursing from his cheek into his hairline. Another burst of fire helped gravity topple his body from the rock. He fell into a heap, his head arched back unnaturally like a dead deer at the side of the road.

Monroe's gut ached as he stared at the young man. Young, dumb, and full of cum, he thought. I told you to stay put, Canfield. I told you, goddamnit!

But inside Monroe blamed himself. He was the CO. It was his duty to protect that man.

"Come!" the *mujahadeen* yelled. "You come!"

The others shouted at him, too, thrusting their gun barrels at him.

30

THE WIND HAD PICKED UP, and Monroe had to squint to keep flying grit from getting into his eyes. He ignored the prodding of the rifle barrel at his back and walked at his own pace down a dirt path that led to the village. The man behind him jabbed harder, but pain didn't register. Monroe thought about Canfield and his parents, wondering if the young man had been married or engaged. He tried to remember if he'd ever noticed a wedding band on Canfield's finger.

His captors shouted at him, demanding that he go faster. Someone shoved him from behind. He stumbled but didn't fall. Once they'd entered the village, Monroe could see the men crowded around the center. He wanted to see his people, see their condition. He wanted to see Salam alive.

The crowd of *mujahadeen* guarding the unit didn't make way for him. Monroe had to peer over their heads.

"Over here," Jane called to him as he passed.

A gust of wind howled in Monroe's ear as he searched for Jane's face. She sat on the ground with the others. Beneath the hair blowing across her face, her eyes betrayed, the fight still in them.

His men remained silent, solidarity in their eyes. Even aloof Vitelli looked like he'd finally gotten with the program.

Monroe pressed his lips into a terse smile and nodded to them, but his eyes searched for Salam. He tried to see around Rudge, hoping to see Salam. Monroe let out an involuntary sigh when he didn't see him.

Was Salam married? Did he have children?

Someone shoved Monroe from behind again and pointed him toward a space between two small huts. The largest hut in the village stood just beyond. Two fighters guarded the door. One of them shouted through the open doorway when he saw them coming. Someone inside shouted back, and the guard conveyed the message to Monroe's captors. The guards took Monroe by the arms and led him roughly into the hut.

Inside Raz Khan sat at a table with two older men in *mujahadeen* garb. Two younger men holding folding-stock autoloaders stood at the back wall. The boy Hajji sat at Khan's side, sipping hot *chai* from a small pottery cup. Khan and the two seated men had similar cups.

Khan lifted his cup to his lips and stared up at Monroe, his face showing nothing. But the faces of the two lieutenants brightened as soon as they recognized Monroe. They looked to Khan, seemingly asking for his okay to be delighted.

Monroe focused on Khan, waiting for him to make the first move. Khan set down his cup and stared at it in his fingers. The room became silent. The guards remained stone-faced, and the lieutenants turned grim. So did Monroe.

The boy tugged on Khan's sleeve, and Khan leaned toward him. Hajji whispered something in Khan's ear. Khan smiled, his eyes crinkling, and whispered something to the boy.

Khan looked at Monroe. "Hajji wants to know if you are a warlord from America."

"What did you tell him?" Monroe said.

"I said, yes, of course you were."

"Tell him you're wrong."

"Am I?" Khan's gaze became keen.

"I am not a warlord," Monroe said.

"Only in your mind, General. But, of course, that is an American national failing, the inability to see from another's point of view. You and your president obviously cannot see your country's presence here from an Afghani's perspective."

Anger rose in Monroe's throat. "My government has spent billions of dollars to secure the independence of—"

Khan waved him off. "Money! That is the only thing that matters to Americans. Freedom, independence, loyalty—to you they are only a means to acquire more money. Another flaw in the American character."

"And money means nothing to you?" Monroe's eyes blazed, but he sat on his temper. "Why are you selling drugs then? Why are you selling the arms that American taxpayers have given you? It's not for the money?"

Khan scowled. "You do not understand. You are incapable of understanding."

"I understand greed and corruption," Monroe said. "I understand a leader who doesn't give a shit about his people."

Khan slapped the table so hard the tiny cups spilled, one rolling onto the floor. "You understand *nothing!* I can get money if I deliver *you.* But look at me. I don't want wealth. I don't need fancy cars and palaces and fine clothing. I am a warrior. For me, money is only respect. That is its value to me."

Monroe scoffed. "Save the high-minded bullshit for someone who might believe it. You're out for yourself, Khan, just like most of the other warlords."

"Another American trait! Deliberate ignorance of history. Do you know anything about this country? Did you know that for hundreds of years Afghanistan has been trampled by other nations for their own gain?"

"I'm well aware of your history."

"Then you should realize that whatever money I can earn for my tribe empowers them. It will keep us alive. It will preserve us as a people."

Monroe just stared at him. He started to clap his hands slowly. The guards tensed, not sure what he was up to. "Very stirring," Monroe said. "This has to be the first time I've ever heard of a kidnapping and ransom presented as an act of patriotism."

"American sarcasm," Khan said with a scowl. "Another clear sign of your national insincerity."

Monroe flexed his fists. "Insincerity?" he repeated. "The United States has given the Northern Alliance its unqualified support. We helped you drive out the Taliban dictatorship. We're keeping terrorists outside your borders. But you have the nerve to say that we're 'insincere'?"

"Yes, you—"

Monroe cut him off. "I'm not finished!"

Hajji's mouth dropped open. The others in the room stared at Monroe in disbelief. None of them had ever heard anyone talk to Khan this way.

"We have given you our know-how, our weaponry, our best men, and our loyalty," Monroe continued. "It's not unreasonable to expect the same degree of loyalty from *all* the members of the Northern Alliance." Monroe's eyes narrowed and honed in on Khan. "But I guess loyalty is something you don't know much about, Khan. If you did, we'd still have Zyrous Mohammed around."

Khan slapped the table again and jumped out of his seat. At the sound of Zyrous's name, the lieutenants started chattering, and the guards became agitated. Khan barked out orders to the men, gesturing with his arms. He seemed to be quelling dissent before it started.

Two of Monroe's captors took him by the arms and led him to a chair, shoving him into it. Three men surrounded him, their weapons pointed at his face.

"I will get my ransom money and I will get respect," Khan said to Monroe. "And whatever Al Qaeda does with you, I hope you suffer long and hard."

Khan stomped out of the hut followed by the two lieutenants. Hajji lagged behind, staring at Monroe, his usually inscrutable face twisted into a mask of intense curiosity.

31

"CLOSER," Rudge said. "You, too, Jane. We have to protect this man."

Jane nodded and moved in closer to Rudge and Vitelli, who huddled around Proctor, sheltering him from the brutal wind. Despite the chilly gusts, Rudge had taken off his jacket and draped it over Proctor like a blanket. Proctor's fever had spiked again, and he'd become semiconscious. His wound looked nasty, iridescent green around the edges and oozing pus. If it weren't for the wind, it would be covered with flies, Jane thought.

The *muj* had put them in a filthy livestock pen. Khan's fighters surrounded them on all four sides, leaning on the split-rail fence, staring at them as if they were zoo animals. Jane noticed one man who carefully picked his teeth with a twig as he stared at them. For some reason, she hated him more than the others, maybe because he paid so much attention to his goddamn teeth. She gave him the finger, but he didn't react. None of them did. They didn't understand what it meant.

"Don't get them riled up," Vitelli said, wincing against the sandblasting wind. "We're not in a good position here."

"No shit," she said.

Vitelli gave her a snotty look, and she gave *him* the finger.

"Sweet Jesus in the morning," Rudge uttered as he looked off into the distance.

Jane followed his gaze until she saw what he saw. "Oh, my God," she mumbled.

"Damn. . ." Vitelli said.

Muj fighters opened the gate in the fence. Two guards held Salam by the arms. They shoved him in and slammed the gate closed. He stumbled forward, tripped, and went down on one knee but got right back up and walked toward the others without looking back. An angry red welt showed under one eye.

"Captain," Rudge said, "we thought—"

"I was dead," Salam said, cutting him off. He struggled to keep his fury under wraps. He didn't want to give the *muj* the satisfaction of seeing him angry.

"What happened?" Vitelli said. "Where'd they take you?"

"To Starbucks," Salam grumbled.

"The attitude doesn't help," Jane said.

Salam and Jane exchanged glares. "No. It doesn't," he said.

Salam got down on his knees and inspected Proctor's wound. He carefully moved Proctor's ripped pants so he could get a better look. Proctor flinched and winced, irritated by the lightest touch.

"Anybody got a knife," Salam said with grim resolution. "We might have to amputate before it kills him."

"Oh, fuck you!" Jane exploded. "Do you have to be so goddamn dramatic?"

"Do you know what gangrene is?" he said, staring her down. "Do you?"

"What are you, John Wayne?" she said. "Amputating a leg in the middle of a pigsty. How fucking manly!" She jerked her thumb at the *mujahadeen* gawking at them. "How about asking them for medical supplies first? Don't you think that would be a better idea before you start cutting?"

"I've already asked," Salam shot back. "In three fucking languages."

"So what the hell were you doing with them?" she said.

Salam's face tightened. "They had to show me something. They said Khan wanted to make sure I saw it."

"What?"

"Canfield's body."

"Oh, fuck!" Vitelli said.

Rudge's face crumpled, his forehead creasing. "Canfield, Canfield, Canfield," he murmured sorrowfully.

Jane suddenly felt like a piece of shit. "How did it happen?" she asked.

"How do you think it happened?" Salam said. "He got shot. That's how soldiers die in battle. They get shot or they get blown up. Does that answer your fucking question?"

"Easy, Captain," Vitelli said, trying to calm him down. "She doesn't know."

"Well, she should. After what we've been through, she should know, goddamn it."

"I'm sorry," she said but with an edge, as if she expected him to apologize, too.

The wind blew in their ears, filling the silence. Proctor groaned. He started shivering, his teeth chattered.

Salam rubbed his eye sockets with the heels of his hands. "We have to stop shittin' around. We have to pull together." He craned his neck and surveyed the perimeter of the pen. He counted seventeen *muj* in all, pretty evenly distributed on each of side of the square pen.

"Did any of you manage to hang on to a weapon?" Salam said. "Anything?"

Vitelli and Jane shook their heads no.

"They took everything from us," Vitelli said.

Rudge said nothing, an odd look on his face. "Pull in close," he said under his breath. "Cover me."

"Cover *you?*" Vitelli said. "A billboard couldn't cover you."

Rudge grimaced as they squeezed in closer. He kneeled in the dirt and pulled down his fly.

"What the fuck?" Vitelli said.

Rudge looked down to avoid Jane's eyes. He reached inside his pants and dug deep, sticking his arm in halfway up to his elbow. He pulled it out again, quickly adjusted himself, and pulled up his fly. He looked all around at the *mujahadeen* to make sure they hadn't picked up on what he'd been doing before he opened his hand.

Jane's eyes widened.

"Holy shit," Vitelli said in a hushed voice.

Salam grinned.

An M61 frag grenade nested in the middle of Rudge's big palm.

Vitelli turned to Salam. "So what do you think, Captain? What can we do with it?"

Salam's grin faded. He pressed his lips together, his brow furrowed. "Grenades have a small kill zone, about a fifty-foot radius from the point of detonation. These assholes are too spread out to get them all."

"What if we throw it where most of them are?" Jane said. "Like over there." She pointed at a corner of the pen with her eyes. "Then we make a run for it, grab some of their rifles, go—"

He cut her off. "The other ones all have AKs. They'll shoot us down before we make it to the fence."

Vitelli shook his head. "Too bad we can't get them all on one side," he said glumly. "Blow all those motherfuckers up together."

"Yeah, wouldn't that be nice," Salam said. "But it ain't gonna happen."

"Sheeet. . ." Rudge groaned in despair, closing his hand around the grenade.

"Hang on," Jane said. "I have an idea."

32

MONROE STARED at his hands spread out on his thighs, looking for signs of shaking. His nerves felt like severed high-tension wires. The two guards that Khan had left behind watched him without blinking, impassive but vigilant. Two others stood right outside the door. The guards might have noticed his jitters, but they would never let on that they did. Only Khan could enjoy the mean pleasure of mockery and derision. Followers just followed orders.

Monroe's fingers felt numb. The wind howled outside the hut, but he didn't feel the cold. He felt the fear. Fear of many things. . . so many he couldn't sort them out in his mind.

The fear of dying surprised and shamed him. A warrior should be ready to die at all times. That's what frees a man to act. But he couldn't stop thinking about his wife, his son, his daughters, his mother, his sisters, his staff at the Pentagon, and he wondered what would happen to them if he died. How would they be affected? Would they be able to carry on?

Of course they would, he kept telling himself. People don't stop breathing just because a person close to them dies. Life goes on.

But a greater fear gripped him, the fear of the damage that Al Qaeda could cause with him in captivity. He imagined a videotape of his torture and execution broadcast around the world. An American general humiliated and slaughtered like a cow. Americans would be dealt yet another psychic blow, and more importantly terrorists around the world would be heartened by the event. Fence sitters would commit to Al Qaeda's cause. Moderate factions would be radicalized. Al Qaeda's numbers would swell. Sympathizers around the world would lend support.

No, Monroe thought. He couldn't let that happen. He had to prevent it. He had to die *now*. He had to deny them the opportunity of filming a torture video for worldwide distribution. He took a long slow breath. Was he ready? Did he have the warrior mind set? No, not really. But that didn't matter. *What* he did mattered, not how he felt about it. He had to do it. There were no other options.

One of the guards grunted something, and Monroe snapped out of his ruminations. He looked up and saw Hajji stepping through the doorway. The boy had the immobile face of a mosaic icon, impossible to read. His emotions—if there were any—lay trapped below the surface.

The other guard said something to the boy, and he responded curtly. The guards said no more and looked straight ahead, having apparently been reprimanded in some way. The boy seemed to enjoy some sort of rank by his association with Khan. He stared at Monroe but kept his distance, staying by the wall as he moved into the room as if Monroe were a captive tiger, mesmerizing but dangerous.

Monroe flexed his hands as a plan formed in his head. He had to die, only the guards would prevent him if he tried to do it himself. But if he attacked Hajji, the guards would have to do something. If he could somehow get his hands around the boy's throat, they might have to shoot him to save the warlord's beloved companion. But how could he get to the boy? At this distance the guards would surely stop him before he reached Hajji. Still, he had to try. Monroe steeled himself for what he had to do.

"I have to get up and stretch," he announced, even though he knew they didn't understand him. "I'm going to stand up." He extended his arms over his head and started to stand, thinking he could get closer to Hajji that way, but the guards rushed in and shoved him back into his seat. If he tried it again, he feared that they would tie him up. He couldn't let that happen.

He looked around the sparsely furnished room, searching for something that would lure the boy closer to him. A round table, several chairs, not much else. A small cabinet against the wall behind him held a radio, a plastic liter-sized bottle of water, and a newspaper clipping in a scratched Plexiglas frame on top of a copy of the *Koran*. The clipping showed a photograph of Raz Khan on horseback surveying a cadre of *mujahadeen*.

Monroe didn't bother to ask for permission. He reached back, lifting his butt out of his seat, and took the holy book and the picture frame. The guards didn't react until they saw what he took. They must have assumed he wanted the water.

He opened the *Koran* and stared down at the pages of unfamiliar script. He fingered a page and felt bad about what he intended to do to the word of God, but he had no choice. He ripped out the page and crumpled it in his hand.

Hajji's eyes widened. The men yelled at him.

Monroe tore out another page, crumpled it, and tossed it on the floor.

The men yelled again, but their tone rang an empty warning of what would happen if he continued. He ripped out yet another page, rolled it into a ball, and threw it at Hajji.

The boy raised his hands and recoiled as it bounced off his wrist.

Monroe did it again. Hajji moved farther away, ducking behind one of the guards.

Shit! Monroe thought, his heart slamming. He had wanted chaos to erupt so he could lunge at the boy.

He threw down the *Koran* and stomped on it, grinding his heel into the leather cover, crushing the hand-sewn binding. The guards jabbered and shook their heads, apparently remarking on Monroe's craziness rather than showing outrage at the sacrilege. Hajji peered at him blank-faced, waiting to see what he would do next.

Monroe had miscalculated their religious fervor. Yes, they were Muslims, but they weren't religious fanatics like the Taliban. They had been opposed to the Taliban.

Monroe's shoulders slumped, and his mind raced. Impulsively he thought about rushing the guards, attacking *them* instead, but once he thought it through, he rejected that idea. They would subdue him, maybe knock him out, but they wouldn't kill him. Khan wanted him kept alive.

Suddenly Monroe felt terribly exhausted. He couldn't think straight. No other possibilities came to him.

His arms went limp, and he slumped forward with his elbows on his knees, the plastic frame dangling from his fingers, about to drop. Khan's face in the newspaper clipping looked back at him. The noble warlord on a dappled gray steed. Khan the statesman and hero. An "allied warlord," according to the caption.

What fucking bullshit! Monroe thought. The man is a pedophile, for God's sake. Monroe lifted the frame and stared at the picture for a moment. . . then spat on it.

Hajji gasped. His mouth fell open in shock as he pointed an accusing finger at Monroe. Tears welled in his eyes, and it took a moment before he could get a sound out. Finally he emitted an ungodly screech, his words drowning in a tide of braying emotions. He pumped his arm, pointing insistently at Monroe, screaming at the guards.

Monroe had defiled the image of his beloved protector, the fucking child molester, and that put the boy into a frenzy. Bile rose in Monroe's throat. He coughed it up and spat it out at Khan's image.

Hajji howled like a tortured animal. He balled his fists and pounded the hip of the guard closest to him, demanding that they punish the defiler.

Monroe had hit a nerve. He stared into the boy's face, flushed red and wet with tears. The sounds coming out his contorted mouth expressed pain beyond his years.

Monroe's heart beat harder. He glanced at the guards' rifles. Hajji told them to shoot. The men resisted, their faces showing panic, unsure if they should carry out his demands or not. Then Monroe lifted the photo over his head about to throw it down.

Hajji screamed as if someone were stabbing him.

Monroe closed his eyes. God forgive me, he thought.

33

JANE STOOD UP and started walking toward the fence that enclosed the livestock pen.

Salam frowned. "What the hell're you doing?" he called after her, shading his eyes from the setting sun

She turned around to face him but kept on walking backward, the wind blowing her hair across her face, spears of sunlight jutting around her body. "You want these guys all on one side?" she said. "I'll get them all on one side." She turned around and kept walking.

The *mujahadeen* loitering along the sides of the square pen watched her with both interest and contempt, curious to see what she would do but offended by her brazen body language and indecent clothing by their standards. She tilted her head and exaggerated the swing of her hips as she walked. The men grumbled and gestured their opinions to one another.

"What has gotten into that woman's head?" Rudge said. "They'll shoot her down sure as shit if she keeps that up."

Vitelli stared at her butt and shook his head. "Why'd it take her so long to get the stick out of her ass?"

Even Proctor in his listless state sensed that something was up and raised his head to check it out. A deeply puzzled look crossed his pale face as he blinked and squinted to focus on Jane's swaying silhouette as she walked toward the setting sun.

"Fucking sick in the head," Salam grumbled, shading his eyes with his hand. He could barely see her in the strong glare, but then he saw the shadow of her overshirt as she whipped it off and let it flutter in the breeze.

The *muj* grumbled disapprovingly, but the ones who faced the sun gradually moved to the other side of the pen so that they could see.

Jane stopped walking about twenty feet from the gathering group of *muj* at the edge of the pen. Salam couldn't make out their expressions, but he didn't have to. They were men—Afghani men—so he knew how they thought. To them, Afghani women served only two purposes: manual labor and making babies, preferably male babies. But Western women were sluts and whores in their minds, objects of lust and deliciously forbidden sacrilege.

The gang of perverts jostled and craned their necks to get a good view, and their heads partially blocked the sun for Salam. He saw Jane from behind crossing her arms to grab the tails of her long-sleeved t-shirt. She pulled it off in one quick move. The *muj* let out a collective roar of shock, outrage, and glee. The stragglers rushed to the side of the pen where the sun would be to their backs. She tossed the shirt over her head, and the wind picked it up, swirling it in circles. No one paid any attention to her shirt. They all focused on her white tank top, wondering if that would be the next to go.

"Lord Jesus," Rudge murmured. "The devil himself must've gotten into that woman."

"*I'd* like to get into that woman," Vitelli said, his eyes glued to her ass.

She shook her hips and did a Mick Jagger cock walk for the *muj*, going overboard to be sexy. "I feel like a fucking idiot," she said in a loud sultry shout, knowing that the *mujahadeen* didn't understand a word she said. "But you cocksuckers think this is the hottest thing since camel shit." She pulled the tails of her tank top out of her pants, and some of the men started to clap a heavy rhythm.

"Sure thing, you fucking ragheads," she said. "Keep thinking what you're thinking in your little perverted, lice-ridden heads. Keep thinking you're gonna get a good look at my boobs. Keep thinking about 'em. Not that they're anything to write home about, you fucking idiots. They're only B cups!" she shouted, tilting her head from one side to the other, prancing the way she figured strippers did.

"Think she'll take it off?" Vitelli said.

Proctor struggled to keep his head up so he could see.

Salam couldn't take his eyes off her either. A big grin had taken over his otherwise grim, snake-eater expression.

Jane circled around her section of the pen, high-stepping in a tight figure eight. When her back was to the *muj,* she made eye contact with each of the men in the unit. "My eyes, assholes," she shouted. "You look at my eyes!"

"I'm trying," Vitelli shouted back.

"Fuck you, Vitelli," she said and turned her back on them. She smiled for the *muj* and fingered the hem of her tank top suggestively, mesmerizing the bastards.

She made another figure eight, facing the unit again, homing in on Salam. "I've got 'em all in one place for you," she shouted. "So do something."

"Yes, ma'am," Salam shouted back as she turned toward the *mujahadeen* again. They jeered and cheered, condemning her and urging her on at the same time.

"Rudge," Salam said. "Give me the grenade."

Salam sidled up to Rudge, who retrieved the grenade from inside his fly and surreptitiously handed it over. Salam wrapped his hand around it and held it inside his open jacket.

Jane came around for another figure eight. "I'm losing my patience here," she said, glaring at Salam. "They're all right there. Do something!"

"Get ready to dive back this way," Salam said, smiling like a horny fool to disguise the seriousness of his instructions.

"I know that," she said. "You think I'm stupid?"

She turned back toward the *muj* and lifted her tank top as high as her ribs. They shouted their delirious outrage.

When she came back around, Salam called to her. "On your signal. I'm ready." He had his finger on the pin, visualizing how he'd switch the grenade to his right hand, pull the pin, count down—three, two . . . — then heave it at the sons of bitches.

"I hear you," she said, staring at Salam and looking scared for the first time. Her hands gripped the tails of her tank top, her midriff exposed. "On my signal."

"What's the signal?" Salam called out.

But she had already turned away from him to face the *muj*.

"Think she'll really do it?" Vitelli said.

And then she did, whipping the tank top over her head.

Salam could see the whites of the bastards' startled eyes. He switched the grenade to his right hand and pulled the pin.

"I'm not showing them anything else," Jane yelled impatiently.

Salam counted mentally. *Three. . .*

"Jump!" he shouted.

Two. . .

34

THE PICTURE FRAME FELL from Monroe's hand as he heard the explosion outside. The two guards reacted like startled cats, but Monroe stayed focused on what he had to do—get the boy to approach him so he could grab him and hurt him, giving the guards no choice but to kill Monroe. As soon as the frame landed on the dirt floor, Monroe stomped on it, crushing it under his boot, grinding it into the dust.

Hajji screamed and cried and pointed. He wanted the guards to do something, but the commotion outside had distracted them, their heads turned toward the open window.

Monroe lifted his foot off the frame and spat on the photo of Khan. He worked up more saliva and did it again.

Hajji screamed louder, demanding retribution.

Come on, boy, Monroe urged mentally. Come closer. You're mad. Come hit me! Come closer!

Engines roared to life outside. Shouts and cries. But Monroe forced himself to ignore all that. He would not let it distract him from his task. He had to die.

The two guards moved closer to the window, staring outside. Monroe saw his chance to lunge at Hajji and force their hand, but a sudden crash right outside the window sent the guards bolting for the door. As they ran, Hajji snatched one of their guns. The guard protested, but he and his partner didn't stop going toward the door. Hajji trained the weapon on Monroe and barked something at the guards through his tears. They paused for only a moment, then raced out the door.

Monroe stared into the boy's face, his brain running in two directions. He wondered what had spooked the guards. Was the compound under attack? And what about his unit? Were they being rescued? Was it something else entirely? The *mujahadeen* typically fired their weapons whenever they celebrated things. The explosion had sounded like a grenade. A celebratory blast? Maybe some great dignitary had arrived. Someone from Al Qaeda here to take him away? He couldn't wait, then. He had to get Hajji to shoot him. Either that or he had to get the gun away from the boy so he could do it himself.

Sweat coursed down Monroe's face like the tears on Hajji's. He stood up and took a step toward the boy, his legs rubbery, his hands shaking. He knew he had to die, but an intellectual decision is easy. They did it all the time at the Pentagon. Carrying it out is the difficult part. Wars aren't won on paper. They're won in the mud. Blood in the mud. The blood of men. The time had come to be a man, he told himself. He had to die.

"Kill me," he said to the boy. He intended to shout and sound abusive, but it came out as a strangled rasp. "Kill me!" he repeated, louder this time, but it still didn't sound the way he wanted. He took another step forward, moving like a deep-sea diver out of the water, his feet encased in lead, his head weighed down by an enormous brass helmet. "Do it!" He wondered if he'd actually said it out loud. It might just have been his voice in his head.

Hajji pressed the gunstock to his cheek, smearing it with his tears. He trembled, his finger poised over the trigger. Monroe knew he could do it. Khan had taught him. So why did he hesitate? He'd been trained by a killer. Why wouldn't he do it?

Monroe tried to take another step, but his feet wouldn't move. Humiliation washed over him like a dousing rain. How could he ever have thought of himself an officer, a soldier, a man? He could certainly talk the talk—they all could back at the Pentagon. But this is where it mattered, in the field. He only had to get a boy to pull a trigger—a simple mission—but Monroe didn't have the guts. Just lunge at Hajji, make him think he's in peril, make him shoot. The kid appeared to be an emotional wreck and angry as hell. He'd do it if pushed. But *Monroe* had to do the pushing. The brain said "Go," but the body didn't listen. He didn't have the guts. His piss-poor little life meant more to him than the security of the entire United States of America—no, the entire world!

One miserable little life. Thirty-four years in the Army and what had he learned about service? Absolutely nothing.

Monroe closed his eyes to get the child's image out of his mind. He could do this, he told himself. He just had to get his mind straight. He'd been taking the coward's way, hoping that the boy would do it for him. Passive thinking. Wishful thinking. A soldier doesn't wish; he *acts*. He doesn't wait for others to act first. Monroe didn't need Hajji. He needed Hajji's gun. Get the gun, do the job. That's the mission. Now do it.

He opened his eyes and focused on the rifle. He breathed slowly, deeply. His body felt lighter. He imagined the videotape that Al Qaeda would make of his execution, imagined it broadcast on Al Jazeera, the less gruesome segments broadcast around the world. He let it play in his mind to dispel the lesser thoughts of family, friends, and colleagues, the thoughts that would make him immovable again. He stepped forward, his eye on the gun and the muzzle he would put under his chin. He took another step and held out his hand.

"Give it to me," he said to the boy in a firm voice. "Give me the gun."

The gusting winds outside buffeted the hut, shaking the walls.

"Give it to me, Hajji."

The boy's eyes widened when he heard his name coming out of Monroe's mouth. He froze, terror in his face.

Voices yelled outside. Another distant blast drowned out the wind for a moment.

Monroe reached out for the rifle, his fingers inches from the barrel.

Hajji trembled.

"Give it to me, son." A tear emerged from the corner of Monroe's eye. "Let me do it. Don't put this on your soul. I'll do it."

Engines revved, louder than before. Horns blared.

Monroe wrapped his fingers around the cold steel barrel and pulled. Hajji put up some resistance, but Monroe pulled firmly, sliding the automatic weapon out of the boy's clammy fingers. Hajji finally let go completely, and the rifle swung into Monroe's hands. Hajji raised his arms and covered his face, terrified, certain that Monroe would shoot him.

"Go!" Monroe said harshly, gesturing toward the door. "Get out of here! You don't need to see this."

The racket outside came closer, but Monroe's awareness of it existed in a far compartment of his mind.

"Go, I said," Monroe snarled, kicking Hajji in the rump. He didn't want to hurt the boy; he just wanted him to leave. "Go!" he raised his voice, kicking him again. "Get out! I want to die alone."

Finally Hajji dashed for the door, looking over his shoulder as if expecting a bullet in the back. He ran without looking and crashed into the imposing figure of Corporal Rudge, who had just stepped into the doorway, an AK in his huge hands.

"General," Rudge said, looking from Monroe to the scared boy to the general again. Hajji squeezed past him and fled from the hut. Rudge looked at the rifle in Monroe's hands and seemed puzzled. "General," he said, "we have secured transport and weapons." He looked at Monroe's rifle again. "Let's go, sir."

Monroe nodded to Rudge, unable to speak. He'd prepared himself for death, but now he had to be a commander again, a real commander. He nestled his index finger inside the trigger guard.

"Show me the way."

"Yes sir."

Rudge ran out the door and headed down an embankment off the path. Monroe followed him, the sound of automatic gunfire cutting through the crisp breeze. The sun had set, taking the color out of the landscape before darkness set in. Two vehicles sat parked on the dirt road at the bottom of the embankment—a troop carrier and a cream-colored Toyota pickup. Vitelli stood behind the open door of the pickup, firing an assault rifle back toward the village. Salam did the same from behind the front fender of the troop carrier. Someone else in the back of the troop carrier fired as well. At first Monroe thought it might be Proctor, hoping that he'd made a miraculous recovery, but as he got closer, Monroe could see Proctor flat on his back in the bed of the pickup, Canfield's lifeless body next to him. Had Proctor died, too? Monroe felt a gnawing pang at the core of his being, the feeling that commanders suffer whenever they lose one of their troops. Jesus God, he thought.

Rudge dropped to a crouch as he ran down the hill, firing his AK up at the hidden *mujahadeen* taking potshots at them from behind the huts above. The unit used up a lot of ammo to provide cover for Monroe and Rudge, and Monroe feared that they'd be left wanting later; but whenever enemy fire picked up, he pointed his rifle up the hill and talked back until their chatter subsided.

Steady fire came from the back of the troop carrier, more than necessary. When Monroe reached the truck, he peered around the canvas side and saw Jane down on one knee, clutching an AK tight to her shoulder, spitting out three-shot bursts at mechanical intervals.

"Slow down," he said. "You're wasting ammo."

She just stared at him. The power of the weapon was new to her, and like any first-timer, she was under its spell.

"I thought journalists were supposed to remain neutral," he said.

"Not when my ass is on the line."

Monroe nodded. That's what it came down to, he thought. Their asses on the line. Fuck politics, diplomacy, and policy. American lives were at stake. They had to do whatever they could to save themselves.

Enemy chatter started up again. Rudge, Jane, and Monroe responded simultaneously, sending the *muj* back into their holes.

Monroe shouted to Salam, who crouched behind the front of the troop carrier. "Drive, Captain. Get us out of here."

"Yes sir," Salam shouted back.

Monroe provided cover fire so that Salam could abandon his position and get to the cab.

"Rudge," he said. "You go with Vitelli."

"Yes sir."

"Tell him to drive like there's no tomorrow."

"Yes sir."

"Go."

Rudge hightailed it over to the pickup as Monroe provided more cover fire, Jane mimicking him with her weapon. Rudge made it to the passenger side of the pickup and motioned for Vitelli to get behind the wheel. The small engine came alive, and the tires kicked up dust as they took off down the road. Enemy fire picked up again. Rudge leaned out the window, firing back as they sped off.

The troop carrier's larger engine turned over with a cough and a low rumble. "Get in, General," Salam shouted from the cab.

Monroe hopped onto the bed and got down on his belly. "Get low," he shouted to Jane. "Like this."

She imitated him, rifle pointing out. The troop carrier started to roll, slow at first, Salam grinding gears until he built up some speed.

"Shit!" Jane said.

Monroe saw what she saw—headlights flashing up on the hill. Four, maybe five sets of them. They bounced over the rough terrain as they headed out of the village.

"They're coming!" Jane said in a panic.

"Yes, I can see that," he said.

The sky had darkened quickly, making the approaching headlights seem like menacing insects on the move.

Monroe shouted toward the cab. "Get this thing moving, Captain. Floor it!"

At the top of the hill four small pickups mounted the road. Another troop carrier brought up the rear. Monroe could hear the distant pops of gunfire. In the darkness he couldn't see any of the men in the trucks, but he imagined the vehicles loaded to the gills with armed *mujahadeen*.

Jane started firing.

"Stop!" he yelled. "You're not going to hit anything from this distance. Make your shots count."

Her eyes were wild as she stared at him. "Then what do we do? Shoot out their headlights? Or the tires. Shoot out the tires?"

"It's dark, we've got headlight glare in our eyes, and there's no clear angle for a tire shot."

"But we should try," she said excitedly. "Maybe we'll get lucky."

He set his jaw and gave her a look. "Jane," he said, "this isn't a movie."

35

THE ENEMY VEHICLES caught up quickly. The lead *mujahadeen* pickup followed so close, Monroe could make out the faces of the men in the cab. They barreled down the dirt road in single file. The troop carrier's tires suddenly slipped on soft dirt and fishtailed, sending Monroe and Jane rolling into one another. They scrambled to get back into firing position.

Jane clutched her AK the way a mother clutches her baby in a burning building. "We're gonna have an accident," she said nervously. "We're going too fast."

"Not fast enough," Monroe said. "They're right on us."

The shoulders of the road sloped down into dangerous gullies that wouldn't allow passing. The *mujahadeen* in the bed of the first pickup focused intently on the back of the troop carrier, but the men had stopped firing once they'd caught up. Monroe could only assume that they'd recognized him, and Khan had ordered them not to kill the American general because he was the prize, worth more alive than dead. Monroe guessed that they wouldn't even risk shooting out the tires for fear of killing him in the resulting crash.

But Monroe had lost concern for himself. He only worried about his unit. Khan's men outnumbered them at least four to one, from what he could see. If they continued with this insane chase, eventually the road would end or they'd run out of gas and they'd be caught. And what would happen then? He imagined the charred bodies of the Starwood 2 passengers. At least they'd died quickly, he thought. Monroe's group probably wouldn't be so lucky.

Monroe racked his brain for a plan, but he had limited information to work with. He hadn't seen Vitelli's and Rudge's pickup since they'd started out. Probably racing in front of the troop carrier, out of sight and somewhat safe from enemy fire, he guessed. But this single-file chase prevented Rudge from being any help in fending off the *muj*. Same with the drivers, Salam and Vitelli. That left just two guns on the enemy—his and Jane's.

"Jane, listen to me," Monroe said. "We're going to cut this caravan short."

"Huh?" She held her rifle in a death grip, her expression frazzled and frenetic, her eyes glued on the *muj* truck on their tail.

"Jane, pay attention. I need you."

"I hear you. What the fuck do you want me to do? Just tell me."

"On my signal, I want you to shoot at the men in the back of the truck. Start shooting and keep shooting until I tell you to stop. Do you understand?"

She glanced into his face. "You want me to kill them?"

"By all means. I'll handle the men inside the cab."

"Got it."

He doubted that she did, but the resolution in her voice gave him hope. She would do what he asked. "Okay, on my word," he said as he squinted down the barrel of his rifle and focused on the driver.

The *muj* shouted as soon as they saw Monroe taking aim. The driver, his face frantic, laid off the gas and opened up some space between the vehicles.

"Fire!" Monroe shouted.

Jane pulled the trigger and held it down, wrestling with the weapon to keep it trained on her targets. Gunfire ripped over the roof of the cab, sparking over the sheet metal. The men in the bed instantly dropped out of sight. Some of them must have been hit, but Monroe paid no attention to them. He stayed focused on the driver. He fired a single shot that spider-webbed the windshield; his second blew it out. He held down the trigger and peppered the interior of the cab, but by now the truck had started veering to the right. Blood streaked the driver's immobile face; he slumped over the wheel. The head of the man in the middle tipped back lifelessly. The *muj* in the passenger seat reached out desperately for the steering wheel, but it was too late.

The pickup's front wheel dipped into the gulley. The rear end flew up and tossed two of the men in the back into the air, but before they landed, the front fender crashed into a boulder. The rear end of the truck flipped over the front end, landing upside down, blocking the road and crushing a few unfortunate *mujs*. The second pickup in line braked and turned hard skidding on the soft dirt road. The wheels skimmed the roadside, and though the driver tried to avoid it, the momentum took the pickup over the road's edge—slowly it went over and then tumbled down the ravine. The third truck in line rear-ended the first truck ahead of it, hitting it so hard its rear wheels bucked off the ground. The fourth pickup and the troop carrier saw the pileup and managed to stop before they killed themselves too.

As the Americans' troop carrier pulled away, Monroe could see *mujahadeen* swarming around the lead truck, straining to shove it into the gully to get it out of the way. He looked at Jane.

"Good job," he said to her.

"I think that might have been you, not me." But she was pleased nonetheless.

"I'm going up to talk to Salam."

She nodded and squinted into the darkness as the skewed headlights of the *muj* trucks still beamed from the tangled collision.

Salam wisely hadn't slowed down. A small sliding panel separated the cab from the bed. Monroe opened it and squeezed through headfirst, getting himself settled into the passenger seat.

"How're we doing, General?" Salam asked without taking his eyes off the road.

"Just keep driving," Monroe said. He assessed the rugged landscape in front of them. No telling where Khan's men might pop up. The darkness unnerved him as they careened downhill on a treacherous surface with weak headlights that gave them no more than fifty feet of visibility. He looked for Vitelli and Rudge but couldn't see their pickup. If they had stopped for some reason, they'd all be shit out of luck because at this speed the troop carrier's braking distance far exceeded their visibility.

"General." Salam pointed to the dashboard. A pair of night vision goggles had slid into the corner of the windshield and gotten wedged there. "I tried to drive with them, but it was too disorienting," he said.

Monroe grabbed the goggles and peered through them. The landscape suddenly became visible under a wash of engine-coolant green. Boulders dotted the land on either side of the road. Going off road would be insanity. Under these conditions, Salam would never be able to avoid a collision. Monroe tracked the road ahead. He could see Vitelli and Rudge's pickup about a quarter mile up ahead. The road headed toward a ravine. It appeared to lead right into it with no opportunity to turn off. He scanned ahead to the foothills of the nearest mountain, looking for a connecting road, but there didn't seem to be one. But something did catch his eye on a cliff that overlooked the ravine. He adjusted the focus on the goggles to zoom in on the area.

On a wide ledge he could see movement, human figures like walking shadows. He zoomed in even closer, and the figures began to show some detail. He counted three standing figures as well as other shadows that could have been men sitting in a group on the ground.

"Do you see anything, General?" Salam asked.

"Maybe," he said as he honed in on the standing figures. He didn't see a campfire, but he didn't expect to. He did notice brief glints and flashes coming from the figures. Flashlights? Maybe reflections off the lenses of scopes. One figure stood out more than the others. Monroe stared at him until his eyes started to water.

Salam glanced over at Monroe, wanting to hear something hopeful.

Monroe kept his eyes on that one figure, willing the person to move so that he could see something else and hopefully pick up a clue as to who these people were. Please be American soldiers, he thought.

The man just stood there. Monroe imagined him talking to the other standing figures. Eventually the darker figures moved, but this man didn't. Monroe chewed on his upper lip as he waited.

Finally the figure moved, and his back became more fully illuminated, picking up light from some minimal source that only the goggles could detect. Monroe's pulse raced. He stared and blinked and stared again to be as certain as possible before he said anything. He could see the desert camo pattern on the man's pants and jacket, and his scalp seemed to glow through a high and tight like a lantern. He's a blond, Monroe thought, hoping that he wasn't just imagining this. Those could be Americans up there. But he had to be sure.

He kept staring, concentrating on the other figures. One of them became more animated, gesturing with his arms as if he was telling the others a story or a joke. Suddenly the man became very animated, and Monroe recognized what he was doing immediately, a wobbly-kneed touchdown dance. The man even feigned spiking an imaginary football in the end zone. His buddies high-fived him. Monroe smiled so hard it hurt. He had no doubt now. These had to be Americans.

"Captain," Monroe said, keeping the goggles to his eyes, "I think there's a rescue unit nearby, and I'm willing to bet they're out looking for us."

Salam clenched his fist. "Fucking A!" he blurted, then glanced at Monroe. "Sorry, sir."

"Fucking A is right," Monroe said. "We're heading right for them."

The boulder fields on either side of the road had suddenly transformed into craggy rock walls as they approached the ravine. In the dim yellow glow of the headlights, the walls started growing higher.

Salam looked concerned. "General—?"

"This leads into a ravine," he said. "Keep going. It'll get us closer to the rescue unit."

Monroe bent his head and looked into the side mirror. He saw no vehicles in pursuit. He sucked in a long breath and prayed that this road led out of the ravine on the other side. If it didn't, they'd be trapped.

36

THE CLIFFS GREW HIGHER, and the road narrowed as they raced into the ravine. The walls slipped by in a blur, so close Monroe could have struck a match against them. Salam had eased up on the accelerator, dropping down to sixty mph. Monroe leaned forward and looked up through the windshield, trying to locate the ledge where he had seen the rescue unit. It was difficult focusing the night goggles from this position, and Monroe soon stopped trying. He couldn't pinpoint the ledge, which had to be at least three stories above their position. He estimated that they would soon be moving under the unit's camp.

A large rock in the road forced Salam to veer suddenly to the left.

"Shit!" he cursed as his side mirror scraped the rocks, shattering glass and twisting the metal tubing.

Monroe looked into the mirror on his side and saw nothing but darkness behind them. "They're not on our tail anymore," Monroe said.

Salam pressed the brakes, slowing to a near crawl. "This doesn't look good," he said. The cliffs had closed in tighter. On the right they stood nearly vertical. On the left they sloped at a forty-five-degree angle.

"I wonder if Vitelli was able to squeeze through," Monroe said.

Salam looked doubtful. "If this road goes anywhere."

Monroe nodded. Most likely a dead end, he thought. He looked through the windshield with the goggles. The cliffs on the right went straight up for at least one hundred feet. The terrain on the left sloped up at least a third of a mile to the top. That would clearly be the easier climb.

"Look," Salam pointed up ahead.

The tan-colored Toyota backed up the road. Rudge knelt in the bed, waving to them frantically, signaling for Salam to stop. Salam pressed the brakes and pulled to a halt as the Toyota's cracked brake lights flashed. The two vehicles stopped less than twenty feet apart.

The Toyota's lights flashed off as Vitelli got out of the cab. Rudge stepped down from the bed, making the springs dip and rebound. Monroe stared at Proctor, looking for signs of life. Monroe opened his door, but it crashed against the cliff wall, and he had to twist his body sideways to squeeze out. He shut the door and slipped around the fender, heading for Proctor.

"How is he?" he shouted to Rudge. The wind howled through the ravine, making it difficult to hear. Monroe moved past Rudge to get to the injured man.

Rudge raced to keep up with Monroe. "He's moaning, General," he shouted over the gusting wind. "He's running hot. Doesn't respond much when you talk to him."

Monroe hopped into the back of the truck. Proctor's eyes were glazed-over slits. A white crust had formed over his lips. Monroe felt his forehead and the clammy side of his neck. He was burning up. Monroe glanced over at Canfield's body. His skin had turned yellow and waxy. Cramps gripped Monroe's stomach. This shouldn't have happened, he thought. He was responsible for this.

"General?" Salam stood at the gate of the pickup with Rudge, Vitelli, and Jane. "We need a plan, General." He said it respectfully, but his tone indicated that he thought anything they tried would ultimately fail.

Monroe scanned their faces. Their collective hopelessness hung over them like a stench, and Monroe began to smell his own despair. He looked down at Canfield's angelic face. He seemed even younger in death. Monroe felt hollow, as if his innards had been ripped out of him. He had let these people down. This was all his fault.

"General?" Salam repeated, raising his voice over the wind.

Monroe looked at him. My responsibility, he thought. I have to do something. Even if it fails, I will do *something*.

Jane gripped her AK in both hands, wired, ready to go. She pointed up at the cliffs. "Salam says there are Green Berets at the top of this cliff. Why don't we call to them? All of us together."

Vitelli tapped her on the shoulder. "With this wind, they'll never hear us."

"And dressed like this I'm not so sure I want them to," Salam said, opening his arms to show his long Afghani shirt and baggy pants. "Those guys look down here, what're they gonna see? A *muj* troop carrier, a *muj* Toy, and a bunch of people dressed like *muj*. We don't know what their orders are. They might start shooting at us."

Monroe looked past his people, staring at the road they'd come down, then scanned the rocky slope opposite the cliffs. Khan's troops could be circling around and moving in, using the rocks and the darkness for cover.

"General," Salam said, "I propose that I scale the cliff and alert the Berets of our presence and condition. They could rappel down and—"

Monroe shook his head. "No time," he said. "We're sitting ducks here." He pointed to the long slope. "Khan's men could infiltrate this area on foot within the hour and we wouldn't know it. The wind, the darkness. . ." He shook his head again.

"Why don't we all climb up?" Jane said. "I've done some rock climbing."

Salam scowled at her. "Where? The gym?"

"And in Utah," she spat back, "I'm a 5.13 climber, asshole. What are you?"

Salam ignored her but a 5.13 climber was definitely fucking better than he would ever be. "Sir," he said to Monroe, "if I start out at first light, it won't take me that long to get up there. I can—"

"Can't wait for first light. You'd be a stationary target for them." Monroe stared out at the slope, wondering how long it would take Khan's troops to get into position for an attack. He tried to come up with an option for escape, but it seemed hopeless. Still, they had to do something to save themselves or die trying.

He looked from person to person, assessing their individual capabilities. Finally he spoke, "Jane is right. We're all going up, a free climb."

Vitelli made a face. "Excuse me, General?"

"We're all going up," he repeated. "Before first light."

Rudge and Vitelli stared up at the cliff simultaneously.

"General," Vitelli said, "I'm an intelligence officer. I've never been trained in climbing. I don't know how to—"

"You'll learn," Monroe said, not letting him finish. "Jane is going to teach you."

Vitelli made no further objections, with a woman in charge it would be hard not to get in line.

Monroe looked at Rudge. "Corporal?"

"I'll do whatever I have to, General," Rudge said. "But what about Sergeant Proctor?"

Proctor hadn't moved since Monroe had checked him. The sergeant blinked and rolled his head to the side. A glimmer of life flickered dimly in his eyes.

37

DANGEROUSLY HIGH WINDS whipped through the ravine, forcing Monroe to squint. He gripped the small ledges and spurs on the face of the cliff, his fingers aching so badly they felt like huge stiff claws, not even part of his own body, just tools to keep him from falling. Salam had gone up first, then Jane and Vitelli. Monroe followed with Rudge bringing up the rear because of his size. Salam feared that his weight could destroy footholds on the way up, depriving the others of good opportunities. None of them had discussed the possibility that Rudge's weight could bring him crashing to his death. They all knew the risks, Rudge included.

They had no ropes or climbing equipment of any kind. Jane had given them a five-minute primer that even Salam found useful: relaxing into the wall, distributing weight, and finding and moving to the right hold. And most important? Keep looking up and stay confident. Then she insisted all of them, including General Monroe, leave their boots and climb in socks, "It will mean cold and pain," she said, "And it will save your life."

At the end of the lesson, Monroe had added a historical note for them all, "Twenty-three hundred years ago, Alexander the Great and a contingent of his army free-climbed at night in winter snow, with weapons, silently. It was not so far from here, either. That bold move gave them victory."

They free-climbed now, each person straining to see the one in front of him or her in the near total darkness, memorizing the steps, reaches, and pull-ups that their predecessor had used. Salam first discovered the footholds and handholds, feeling his way in the dark.

Monroe reached up with his left hand and felt around until he found a ledge large enough and strong enough to hold him as he pulled himself up. He moved with great care and deliberation, unwilling to give the gusts a chance to peel him off. He positioned his left foot on the rocky knob where his hand had been. This would be a mental challenge as well as a physical one for all of them, requiring that they concentrate on every move their predecessor made.

Monroe kept his eye on Vitelli, watching what he did and how he did it. Vitelli would have had the advantage of being slender and light if not for the persistent wind. A strong gust had already threatened to twist Monroe out of a handhold, so he took his time now. Salam had estimated that it would be about the equivalent of a five-story climb and, by Monroe's reckoning, he'd covered about half that distance, Salam even more. Vitelli stopped to probe with his foot for a toehold that Jane must have found and Salam before her. Monroe had no choice but to stop and rest.

He looked down at Rudge and saw the whites of the man's eyes staring up at him. "Don't look down, General," he said. "It don't help."

Monroe worked up a tight smile. "Don't worry about me, Rudge."

"I do worry about you, sir."

"That's not nec—" Monroe stopped himself and changed his brittle tone. "Thank you, Rudge." He wondered why he'd been so hard on the man. Was it because he was black? He recalled Rudge's heat-of-the-moment remark about not being Monroe's "nigger." That had been bothering Monroe, but he didn't know how to apologize to a man below his rank.

He looked up at Vitelli, who took his time getting into position.

Monroe glanced down again. He could barely make out Canfield's body in the back of the pickup. It looked like a chalk-mark outline at a crime scene, a form without details. They'd moved Proctor into the back of the troop carrier, where he'd be shielded from the winds and out of sight. If he stirred and Khan's men saw it, they might shoot at him out of spite.

Monroe looked up at Vitelli. He seemed to be stalled, his hands and feet still in the same positions. The gap between him and Jane had widened. "Vitelli," he said. "What's wrong?"

Vitelli's voice sounded shaky. "I can't do it, General. I can't find anything. My feet are killing me."

"If an old man like me can do it, you can do it. My feet are killing me too. Go!"

"I can't, General. I'm afraid I'm gonna fall."

Monroe could hear the cold fear in his voice. "Call to Jane and Captain Salam. Tell them to hold up." Vitelli had to imitate their steps exactly so that Monroe and Rudge could do the same.

Vitelli called to the pair above, but his voice blew away in the gusts.

Monroe shouted up himself. "Jane! Salam! Hold up! Hold up!"

Vitelli joined in, shouting with him. Jane, a body length higher than Vitelli, stopped. It was too dark for Monroe to see Salam.

Had Vitelli been watching her? Monroe wondered. Did he remember what she had done to get where she was?

"Vitelli," Monroe said, "you have to keep moving."

Rudge shouted from below. "What's the problem, General?"

Monroe looked down at him. "Hang tight, Rudge."

"That's all I can do, General."

"Vitelli," Monroe said, "listen to me, son."

Vitelli's legs shook badly.

"We're gonna do this together," Monroe said. "I'm right here."

Vitelli didn't respond.

Monroe wished to hell he knew Vitelli's first name. "Vitelli, look at me. Look at me."

"I can't. I'm gonna fall."

"Trust me, Vitelli. You can do this. It's not a big deal. You get to the top of this cliff, you're home free. Salam will be up there to help you over the edge."

"I can't do it," he wailed.

"I think you can," Monroe said, trying hard to be encouraging. "Think about going home, seeing your family, your friends. Think about that home-cooking, Vitelli. What does your mother cook? Spaghetti and meatballs, veal parmigian—"

"Stop trying to bullshit me," Vitelli shot back, half angry, half anguished. "My mother's dead, and she was a lousy cook anyway."

Monroe grimaced, embarrassed that he wasn't handling this better. He should know how to deal with a situation like this. He should know how to motivate a soldier, how to lead him, make him feel safe.

"I'm half Irish," Vitelli said moodily.

"What's that?" Monroe said.

"I'm only half Italian," Vitelli said. "I'm Irish on my mother's side."

"Okay," Monroe said, perplexed as to how he could use this information. "I guess I shouldn't even mention corned beef and cabbage."

"You can mention it," Vitelli said. "She did that pretty good."

Monroe noticed that the shaking in Vitelli's legs had subsided somewhat. Monroe had to keep him talking. "Sounds like you miss your mom," he said.

"She had cancer. Breast. . . She smoked."

"I bet she fought it, though. She was Irish, after all."

"Fought like hell. Doctors gave her a year. She took four."

"She must have been a hell of a woman."

"Damn straight."

"What would she have done in this situation?" Monroe asked.

"Oh, be real, for chrissake!" Vitelli snapped. "She was a woman."

"Jane's a woman. She's doing it."

"Jane's different. She's practically a dyke."

Monroe let that one pass. "You said your mother was a fighter. Aren't you one, too?"

Vitelli laughed nervously. "You trying to con me, General? I don't like being conned."

"I'm trying to help you, Vitelli. I'm trying to help all of us."

Vitelli didn't respond.

Monroe gave him a minute before he said anything. "Vitelli?"

"Go around me." He seemed to be crying. "Just go around me. Leave me."

"I'm not going to leave you," Monroe said.

Rudge spoke up. "Getting kind of cold down here, General."

"I know you're there, Rudge."

Vitelli screamed in anguish, "Just leave me, goddamnit! I'll come up by myself when there's more light."

Monroe opened his mouth, about to list all the logical reasons why Vitelli wouldn't last that long—the cold, the wind, the *muj*—but he realized that would serve no purpose. Vitelli's emotions had taken over. Monroe had to appeal to him on that level. "I'm coming up," he said.

"You gonna pass me?" The strain in Vitelli's voice betrayed his true fear that he would be left behind.

"No, I'm not going to pass you," Monroe said. He knew he couldn't even if he wanted to. "I'm going to help you." He boosted himself up another two feet and wedged his boot into a small outcropping of rock, putting some weight on it to test its strength. Satisfied that it would hold, he reached up and put his hand on Vitelli's heel.

"Put some weight on my hand," Monroe said. He had to get Vitelli to trust him so that he'd try to move.

"I can't," Vitelli said.

"You can," Monroe said.

"No. I can't."

Monroe's lower back started to spasm, but he forced himself to ignore it. "Vitelli, do you want me to start talking about home cooking again?"

Vitelli laughed despite himself. "Please. You don't have to."

"Then listen to me. All I want is to help you. Try to reach the next handhold. I'll brace you from down here."

Monroe's mouth felt bone dry. If Vitelli slipped and fell into Monroe, they'd both go down. Probably Rudge, too.

Vitelli got quiet again. "Are you sure about this?" he finally said.

"I'm sure. I'll hold you."

Monroe applied a small amout of pressure to Vitelli's heel to show that he would be strong for him.

"What's your fear, Vitelli? Tell me."

"I. . ."

"What? Let's talk it out."

"I'm afraid of fucking up. I don't want to let the unit down."

"You won't let us down. I know you won't."

"I don't do things the way other guys do. You know what I'm saying, General?"

"I'm not sure I know what you mean."

"I'm Army, yeah, but I go against the grain. I'm intel. I do my own thing, basically. I'm not a combat guy."

"You mean you don't think you're a team player?" Monroe guessed.

"Something like that."

"You don't want people to see you fail, is that it?"

"Yeah. . . I guess. . . "

"So you try not to play the game to avoid being humiliated."

"Don't analyze me, okay?"

"I'm not analyzing you, Vitelli, I'm relating to you. I was like that once a long time ago."

Monroe thought back to his tour in Vietnam. He'd had the classic sniper personality—aloof, unfriendly, self-sufficient, and self-possessed. He only trusted the voice in his head, his own. It had been a hard transition, going from combat sniper to firstie at West Point, where General Vandermeer's voice eventually assumed equal volume with his incessant internal monologue.

"Vitelli, I don't want to hang out here all night," Monroe said evenly. "And I know you don't want to either. So just trust me. One step at a time. Get a solid handhold and start feeling around for a place for your foot. That's all you have to worry about right now. One hand, one foot, the other hand, the other foot. You just do that till we get to the top."

"I—"

"Don't tell me you can't."

"I. . . I'll try."

"Go ahead. Put your weight on my hand if you have to."

Monroe could see the silhouette of his arm reaching up. "That's it," Monroe said. "Start pulling yourself up and looking for a place for your foot."

Vitelli pulled his foot out of Monroe's hand. He scraped the rocks, searching for a foothold. "I've got one," he said and immediately put his weight on it, reaching for the next handhold.

"Test it first," Monroe cautioned. "Put your weight on it slow—"

"Fuck!"

The rock Vitelli stood on broke off. Monroe braced himself as soon as he heard it. Vitelli lost his hand grip and dropped several feet. Somehow Monroe caught him, sandwiching Vitelli's legs between the cliff and his own chest. Vitelli held on to something, but Monroe didn't know what. Monroe supported most of Vitelli's weight.

Vitelli's legs shook, his breath wild and ragged.

"Hold still," Monroe said. "Don't squirm."

Pain radiated from Monroe's lower back. If Vitelli made a sudden move, they'd probably both go tumbling down.

Rudge shouted up to him. "Are you all right, sir?"

"Yes, we're okay," Monroe said. His back spasmed like crazy. He feared that his legs would give out. He didn't know how long he'd be able to hold Vitelli.

"Vitelli," he said. "Start feeling around for solid ledges. We can't stay like this."

Vitelli shuddered. "I... I can't."

38

JANE SHOUTED UP TO SALAM. "Something happened. I heard rock breaking. Vitelli's not behind me."

Salam glanced down at her, more than a body length below him. She was the better climber, but he had to go first, for good reason. He reached up and could just about touch the edge of the cliff. He hadn't heard any signs of trouble from below, but with the wind blowing in his ears, he wasn't surprised. He'd been concentrating on getting himself up.

"Can you see them?" he shouted to Jane.

"Not really. Just shadows."

Salam peered down the side of the cliff, looking for signs of victims, but he couldn't see a thing in the dark.

"What should I do?" she asked.

"Keep climbing," he said without hesitation. She didn't know enough to do any rescuing, not under these conditions, and he didn't have any equipment. He needed help.

But that presented another problem, one he'd been thinking about ever since they'd started climbing: how to get over the edge of the cliff without getting shot? The reason he had to climb first. He imagined the Berets up there zipped into their individual portable shelters for the night—all except for one man who had to stand guard. If Salam couldn't identify himself fast enough or that guy got jumpy, Salam could end up being a casualty. He looked down into the black void. He had no choice. He would have to take that risk.

"Jane," he said, "if anything happens to me, you identify yourself to the guys up there. Do it loud and do it a lot until they understand you're not *muj*, you're an American."

"What do you mean, 'if anything happens'?"

Salam deliberately ignored the question. She didn't need to know everything. An imagination running wild can keep a person from thinking clearly, and she needed her wits about her. They all did.

Here goes, Salam thought. He reached up for the crust of earth right over his head and tested it for stability. He eased himself up, searching for a new foothold. Dirt crumbled under his boot and sifted down the side of the cliff. He kicked through the dry dirt, digging for solid rock. When he found it, he pushed himself up. He could see over the lip, but he couldn't see the Beret unit. Obviously they wouldn't camp on the edge of the cliff. They must be farther away, he thought, behind boulders and brush that would provide a wind shield.

Salam found a foothold for his other foot and climbed up, getting his elbows and forearms onto the ledge. The muscles in his arms felt like burning ropes, his hands torn and bloody. His feet released their footholds, and his legs hung loose. He pressed his palms into the ledge and hauled himself over the top. He quickly rolled away from the precipice and sat on his butt, leaning back with his arms braced behind him, head hanging on his chest as he caught his breath.

He crawled back to the edge and called down to Jane. "Are you secure where you are?"

"I wouldn't use the word *secure*," she said.

"I mean, are you hanging by your fingernails?"

"No, I'm okay."

"Good. Just stay there until I come back."

If I come back, he thought.

He stood up, slung his rifle around to his back, and raised his arms over his head in the surrender pose. He started walking away from the edge, staring into the darkness, looking for the unit.

Don't shoot, asshole, he thought, mentally talking to the Beret on guard duty, wherever he was.

He had to make his presence known and make sure they understood he was an American, but he didn't exactly know how to do that. Well, no time to be modest, he thought and immediately started to sing at the top of his lungs. "'Wake up, mama! Turn your lamp down low! Wake up, mama! Turn your lamp down low!'" The Allman Brothers' version of "Statesboro Blues." Unfortunately he didn't know any other words. "Captain Louis Salam," he shouted. "Fifth Special Forces out of Fort Campbell, Kentucky. Now stationed in Gardiz under General Graydon. Does anybody hear me? You assholes all sleeping? Jerking off? What?"

He stopped to listen. He heard only the wind.

"I'm Captain Louis Salam," he repeated, identifying himself again. "I've got a situation, and I need some help over here. Does anybody hear me?"

He stepped cautiously, knowing that he could very well be walking into a shit storm. The fact that it would be a friendly-fire incident didn't make much difference to him. Dead is dead.

He repeated his name, rank, and unit, listening for a reply, but he got no response. The wind whistling in his ears mocked him.

He approached a group of boulders, his heart pounding. What if the men Monroe had seen weren't Berets? What if they were really *muj*? Or Qaeda? Or Taliban? What if they were American troops, but they'd had some prior experience with Yusef and his collection of American accents? What if they thought he was Yusef? They'd plug him for sure.

"Is there anybody here?" Salam shouted as he stepped between two boulders higher than his head. "Can you hear—?

A flashlight shone in his eyes, blinding him. He threw his hands up higher, waiting for the bullets.

"Relax, Captain," a familiar voice said. "We hear you."

The light moved off his face. As his eyes adjusted, Salam could make out their shapes and the face of the closest man.

"Perez, you motherfucker," Salam said, his heart still pounding but a smile of intense relief on his face. "Why didn't you say something?"

Captain George Perez of Team 807 stepped forward, clutched Salam's hand, and clapped him on the back. "We were beginning to think you'd switched sides, buddy."

The other soldiers gathered round. Salam swallowed the lump in his throat. He jerked his thumb behind him. "I've got four people on the cliff, freestyling it. They need help."

Captain Perez didn't have to say a word to his men. They immediately scrambled to get their rappelling gear.

"One of them is General Monroe," Salam said.

"No shit," Perez said, showing some surprise. "Can the old guy climb?"

It suddenly struck Salam that Perez's perception of Monroe matched the one he'd had until a few days ago. Jackson Monroe, the executive general. Funny. Salam didn't think of him that way now.

"Butch Proctor has a bad leg wound," Salam said. "He's in the back of the troop carrier at the bottom of the cliff."

Perez nodded. "We'll get him. Anyone else?"

"Yeah. A casualty. Corporal Canfield. You'll see him. He's in the back of the pickup."

Perez touched his shoulder. "We'll take care of it," Perez said. "We'll get him home."

Salam nodded, unable to speak. He flexed his aching hands as the dark silhouettes of the Berets rushed toward the edge of the cliff, their boots clomping over dry dirt. He just wanted to sit down and not move for a long time, but he couldn't do that yet. He willed his legs to move and started to trot after the Berets. He had to see this job through.

"No," Monroe shouted over the wind as he shook his head.

A Green Beret sergeant had just rappelled down the side of the cliff and hung even with him. Another Beret was on his way down.

"I'm Sergeant Lanning, sir," the Beret said to him. He held a nylon web crotch belt. "I'm going to put this belt around you, sir, and then—"

"No, you're not, Sergeant," Monroe said.

"But, sir—"

"Take care of the others first. Get the wounded man in the truck down below."

The other Beret slid down the side of the cliff and stopped at Vitelli. The Beret reached out and started to put a crotch belt on Vitelli.

"No!" Monroe shouted. "Leave him be."

The Beret looked confused. "But, sir—"

"I said leave him. Just stand by."

The Beret's silence expressed his opinion of Monroe's order.

Vitelli shivered in fear, Monroe still holding him up.

"Vitelli, listen to me," Monroe said. "This man can haul you up if you want, but if you don't do it yourself, you will be an old man and you'll still be beating yourself up about this. If you don't do it, in your mind you will live on this cliff for the rest of your life."

"I… I can't," Vitelli said.

"Yes, you can. And you know I'm right. It will haunt you. Now this man will stay with you. Won't you, Sergeant? What's your name, sergeant?"

"Makefield, sir."

"Sergeant Makefield will stay right with you. He will give you the belt, and he will catch you if you slip, but you have to do it yourself, Vitelli."

"I… I—"

"Don't talk, Vitelli. *Do*."

Vitelli didn't answer.

"I'm here for you, man," Makefield said as he strapped the belt around Vitelli. "I'll catch you if anything happens. The rig will hold us both."

"I… I… I'll try."

"Here," Makefield said. "I'll give you some light." He switched on the snorkel flashlight clipped to his flak jacket. "How's that?"

"Better," Vitelli said.

"How far to the top, Sergeant?" Monroe said.

"Twenty-five, thirty feet, sir. It's not that far."

Monroe kept his mouth shut. Vitelli hadn't responded all that well to his cheerleading. He'd let Vitelli take that information and come to his own conclusions. Vitelli had to decide for himself.

Vitelli's body seemed to relax a bit once the belt was on. "I can grab hold of you if I need to?" he asked Sergeant Makefield.

"Anytime. Don't worry."

"Point the light where I'm going. I can't see where to put my hands."

Makefield obliged, and Vitelli reached up for a handhold.

As Vitelli hauled himself up, Monroe felt that burden melting off him. The pain in his back subsided a bit. Vitelli found a new foothold and separated entirely from Monroe. Makefield kept talking to him, assuring him that they'd make it to the top, pointing the light wherever Vitelli asked. Vitelli wouldn't have to live with failure.

Monroe looked down over his shoulder. "Rudge? Are you still with us?"

"Got no choice, General. You're stuck with me."

Monroe had to laugh. They would make it out of there. They really would. The joy he felt made him giddy.

"Rudge, I want to tell you—"

A sharp *clack* three feet from Monroe's head stopped him cold. Rock fragments stung the side of his face, and falling pieces trickled down the cliff.

"What the hell—?" Rudge said.

But Monroe knew.

"Cut the light!" he yelled up to Makefield. "Cut it now!"

Clack! More stinging rock shards. This one had come even closer. Only the wind had saved him, blowing the bullet off course.

"Sniper fire," Monroe called out. "No lights. Eyes toward the cliff. The snipe will pick up the whites of your eyes."

They had to get off that cliff ASAP. With six people hanging out in the open, something would eventually give off a reflection—a metal clip, a face, a hand. The sniper had their position. He'd taken two shots, trying to find zero.

"Makefield, take him up. Now."

"I'm going, I'm going," Vitelli shouted, and indeed he was. He reached up and felt his way, digging in for footholds, hauling himself higher without hesitation.

Vitelli had needed the right incentive, and apparently the fear of getting shot did it for him.

Makefield stayed by his side, but Vitelli climbed like a monkey.

Monroe looked down. "Come on, Rudge. Let's go." He looked past Rudge and suddenly saw Proctor in a body harness floating in air by himself. The Berets at the top of the cliff pulled him up. As he came even with Monroe, the general looked for signs of consciousness, but he couldn't see much in the dark. Monroe spun him around so that he faced the cliff and guided him until he floated out of reach.

"General?" Rudge said. "I think we should—"

"I'm going." Monroe stopped watching Proctor and starting looking for a new foothold.

39

KHAN HAS TO GO, SALAM THOUGHT.

Salam leaned over a tall boulder, peering through a pair of binoculars. Khan's men had set up camp on a flat clearing across the "ravine," five hundred yards from their position. In the predawn light, Salam could see that the ravine they'd driven into was actually a ravine at the bottom of a much larger gorge. Smoke rose from a campfire hidden behind a stand of high bushes. He could see several of Khan's men in plain view, one of them taking a piss in the dirt. They all had their rifles with them. Salam adjusted the focus when he came to Raz Khan, an easy person to spot because of the small figure by his side. Khan faced the gorge, staring out, and Salam felt that Khan stared right at him, reading his mind.

The fucker has to go, Salam thought. "Too fucking dangerous alive," he murmured to himself.

"That's exactly what I was thinking," Monroe said.

Monroe had startled Salam, coming up behind him like a ghost. Snipers walk softly, he thought. Monroe must not have lost the knack.

"Sorry, sir," Salam said. "I didn't know you were there."

"Relax, Captain. You have a right to your own opinions. Especially when they are correct." Monroe gazed across the gorge with his own pair of binoculars.

Neither of them had gotten any sleep since the rescue. Rudge and Jane had caught a few winks, but Vitelli paced like a cat, too wired to rest. The Berets practically had to sit on him to keep him out of sight. They'd all feasted on the Berets' rations. Sergeant Makefield had dressed Proctor's wound and given him antibiotics for the infection. They'd called for air support to drive off Khan's men before a rescue helo would come to pick them up. Salam still couldn't get over the fact that they had traveled more than a hundred miles from the fortress in five days. The incident at the fortress seemed so long ago.

"Air support should get here soon, sir," Salam said.

"Mmmm." Monroe acknowledged him, but he was preoccupied, still staring through the binoculars. He looked at his watch. "Who's the best sniper in this A-team?" he asked.

"I believe that would be Sergeant Hartman," Salam said.

"I assume he has his rifle with him?"

"I'd be very surprised if he didn't."

Monroe looked through the binoculars again. "Get Hartman and Rudge. Tell them I want to see them. And make sure Hartman brings his weapon. I want to borrow it."

Borrow it? Salam thought. He looked at the general, wanting to make eye contact, but Monroe kept the binoculars to his eyes.

"The problem is the boy," Monroe said. "We can't risk taking a shot with him next to Khan."

Rudge and Hartman crouched close to the campfire, nodding and soaking up everything Monroe said. Salam focused on the sniper rifle in Monroe's hands. Monroe had taken it from Hartman and hadn't given it back, holding it on his knee. What did he mean, "We can't risk taking a shot"? He couldn't be thinking of taking the shot himself. He'd missed a stationary target at half this distance when he'd competed with Khan at the fortress. Hartman was trained and ready. Let him take the shot, for chrissake.

"Rudge, you can refuse this assignment if you want, but here's what I propose."

Rudge's eyes grew big as softballs as Monroe presented his plan.

"I need a decoy," Monroe said. "If you put on my *mujahadeen* outfit—the scarf, the turban, the baggy pants—and then go out into the open, Khan might be tempted to take a shot at what he thinks is me. He fancies himself a marksman, and now that he can't have me alive, I'm sure he'd prefer me dead. Hopefully setting up his shot would separate him from Hajji long enough for me to get a shot or two off before he could retaliate. But it's entirely up to you, Rudge. You can refuse."

Rudge remained silent for a moment. "How much Kevlar can I have?"

"We'll pool all the vests we have. We'll cover as much of you under your clothes as we possibly can."

"Except my head," Rudge said. "He's got to see a black face, right?"

Monroe nodded. "Obviously that's why I asked you."

Rudge turned to Hartman. "No other people of color in this unit?"

Hartman shook his head.

"You know, General," Rudge said, "I wouldn't want anyone thinking I got this job through Affirmative Action."

Monroe had to chuckle. "If anyone complains, I'll set 'em straight."

Rudge rubbed his eyes with his thumb and forefinger. He sucked in a deep breath and let it out as a resigned laugh. "How do you like that?" he said, flashing an ironic grin. "I guess I am your niggah."

"You don't have to do it, Rudge. No one will blame you."

Rudge gazed off in the direction of Khan's position, his breath visible in the cold air. He started to nod. "Okay, I'll do it," he said.

Monroe clasped Rudge's shoulder and gave him a tight-lipped smile. "I will do my absolute best to keep Khan from getting a shot off."

"You'd better," Rudge said. "Else you'll be answering to my mama."

They shared a laugh, the kind of laughter meant to mask the gravity of a situation. Salam didn't like any of this. Monroe's ego had gotten out of control. An out-of-practice sniper in his fifties taking the shot instead of a trained elite soldier in his twenties? Insanity! Salam couldn't bite his tongue on this one.

"General," Salam said, "may I have a word with you?"

"Of course, Captain."

"In private."

Rudge picked up on the cue. "I'll go scare up some vests," he said.

"I'll give you a hand," Hartman said.

The two soldiers stayed low as they walked toward the area where the Berets had camped.

"I'm listening, captain," Monroe said.

"Sir, I... May I speak freely?"

"Hurry up, Salam. We don't have much time. Air support's on the way."

Salam frowned. "This is fucked up, sir."

"Pardon?"

"This is totally fucked. Hartman should take the shot. He's a trained sniper—"

"So am I."

"But he's on active duty as a sniper. He's younger. His eyes are probably better—"

"I'm taking the shot. End of discussion."

"But, sir, this is crazy. What if you miss?"

"That's negative think."

"*What if you miss?*" Salam insisted. "What about Rudge? He's gonna be the one with his ass on the line."

"He will be protected. Taking out Khan is important. We've all agreed on that."

"Khan's a sniper, and snipers are cowboys. He'll go for the headshot. You'll do the same."

Monroe stared him in the eye. "Do you have anything constructive to add to this plan?"

Salam didn't flinch. "I don't want any part of this plan."

"Then get the hell out of the way."

Salam stayed in his face. "Is that an order, sir?"

Ten minutes later Rudge stood out in the open, twenty feet from Monroe's hide behind a low boulder. Rudge wore Monroe's black *muj* pants, his black-and-white patterned scarf, and his gray turban as well as five Kevlar vests—one on his torso and one wrapped around each of his limbs. To Salam's eye he looked like the Michelin Man, and Salam wouldn't be surprised if Khan recognized a decoy and refused to take a shot. Unless he decided to kill Rudge out of spite and contempt for the Americans.

Monroe wore Rudge's XXL fatigues, the sleeves and pants rolled up. The A-team, Jane, and Vitelli had taken positions behind the other boulders and bushes to watch Rudge and Monroe. Salam crouched down behind the same rock as Monroe, binoculars hanging from his neck. The wind blew into Salam's face, not as strong as the night before, but it would still be factor.

Salam couldn't contain himself. "Sir," he said in a low voice, "I'm asking you. Please let Hartman take the shot."

Monroe did not disrupt his position, rifle butt to his shoulder, stock to his cheek, his eye to the scope. "That discussion is over, Captain."

"Be logical, General."

Monroe didn't respond. When setting up a shot, the slightest movement, even his lips moving, could throw him off.

Salam considered pushing Monroe, grabbing the barrel, physically preventing him from taking the shot. It would be the end of his military career, but under the circumstances it might be the right thing to do.

He peered through the binoculars across the gorge and saw Khan pushing Hajji away, pointing at a spot several feet away. The warlord went down on one knee, a rifle in his hands, about to take his position on the ground when the boy walked up to him. Khan shook his head and pointed at the spot where he wanted the boy to stand. Hajji obeyed and didn't move.

Salam glanced at Monroe, so still he could have been part of the boulder.

Through the binoculars Salam saw Khan reprimanding Hajji, shaking his arm and scolding the boy, who had moved off his spot again to get closer to Khan.

Monroe waited for the boy to get out of the way, but he couldn't wait too long. If Khan got down on his belly, he would be a much more difficult target.

Salam focused on Hajji. His slumped posture expressed his unhappiness.

Stay right where you are, kid, Salam thought. Don't listen to Khan. Keep these crazy bastards from shooting. Be a pain in the ass like a regular American kid. Be stubborn. Stay there.

Slowly Hajji turned and walked back to the place where Khan wanted him to be.

Salam looked over his binoculars at Rudge, who went down into a squat position as if he were looking at something in the dirt. Salam went back to the binoculars.

Hajji stopped walking and looked back at Khan. Khan stood up and shooed him away like a bad dog. Hajji ran a few steps, then stopped and stared at Khan.

Khan shook his head, annoyed with the boy. He got down on one knee again and paused to sight down the barrel and work the bolt.

Rudge stood up. He had his back to the gorge. The wind had died down.

That man is gonna be a corpse in two minutes, Salam thought. He just couldn't hold his peace. He turned to Monroe. "General—" he said.

Crack!

Monroe had pulled the trigger. The sound of the report hit Salam like a punch in the head. He lifted the binoculars to his eyes and saw Khan on one knee. Suddenly a burst of crimson mist replaced his head. His body fell back. Hajji took a step toward him but couldn't bring himself to go all the way. The spatter had reached him, turning his dun-colored jacket a brownish pink.

Salam looked at Monroe, who had held his firing position, his eye to the scope. Finally he picked his head up. "Rudge," he called out. "Get back here. On the double."

He turned to Salam. "They might have other sharpshooters," he said. "You never know."

Salam stared at him, dumbfounded.

Some of the Berets had been watching through their own binoculars, and the news spread to the others. Raz Khan was history. They began to clap and cheer.

Rudge jogged back to a tall boulder and took cover. "Thank you, General," he called out. "My mama thanks you, too."

The Berets gathered around Rudge, clapping him on the back as he tore off the turban.

Salam couldn't stop staring at Monroe. "How?" he said.

"I practice pretty regularly," Monroe said without bragging. "I've kept up with it."

"But you lost the competition at the fortress."

"On purpose."

Salam screwed up his face. "I don't get it."

"I wanted Khan to win," Monroe said.

"Why?"

"Never show your true strength until you really need it. That's a good thing to remember, Salam."

Salam nodded, letting it sink in. "Right. . . Oh, by the way, good shot."

"Thank you."

Salam heard the distant drone of approaching aircraft. Air support would be here imminently. Salam looked out across the gorge. Khan's men had already started hightailing it out of there. One of them picked up Hajji like a sack of grain and carried him away from Khan's body.

Jane came running over to their position and crouched between them. "Congratulations, General. I just wish I'd had a camera."

"Next time," he said with a world-weary grin.

"So I guess that's it," she said. "Khan's dead, we're rescued. It's all over."

"Not quite," Monroe said. "We still have something to do." He looked up at the sky as the first F-16 roared down through the gorge.

40

A MILLION STARS dotted a midnight blue sky that stretched to forever. In the mud-brick shelters within the fortress walls, *mujahadeen* soldiers slept fitfully on makeshift bedrolls laid out on the dirt floors. The tribesmen who had come for the conference six days ago had departed. Only fighters from Raz Khan's tribe remained, the men most loyal to him. Angry and distraught because they'd lost their leader, they understood their precarious position. With no one to replace Khan, they could easily come under attack from other warlords who perceived them as a dangerous and lethal force without direction.

But Khan's men still had American weapons to barter, they still had entire tons of opium base to sell, and they still had Kahn's links to Al Qaeda, which paid for bombings and assassinations inside Afganistan. They could more than get by.

Long past midnight, they slept. None of them heard the sound of the approaching turbo props.

The propellers of the AC-130H Spectre beat heavy, droning with intent, singing the dirge before the deaths. The gunship couldn't be seen except for its dark silhouette blocking out the stars as it circled the fortress and banked, pointing its guns at its target, the quarters within the fortress.

A young *mujahid* who had been roused by a nightmare heard the Spectre's engines. He stared in panic at the small window in the crowded room. Embers glowed orange through the grate in the black iron stove in the center of the room. None of the other men stirred. The engines seemed so close, for a moment the young man thought it might be a helicopter landing in the courtyard. He grabbed his AK and stepped over his brothers, rushing outside to investigate. As soon as he stepped out into the courtyard, rolling flashes of howitzer rounds swept through the barracks next door. Walls shattered, and mud bricks vaporized. Fires flared. Startled from sleep, men screamed and cried out. The young *mujahid* froze as he beheld the terrible spectacle, but a moment later his life ended abruptly, his skull crushed by flying bricks.

The rapid-fire twenty-millimeter Vulcan cannon played a treble counterpoint against the deep rhythmic explosions of the 105mm howitzers. Men fleeing from their barracks into the courtyard ran to their deaths, their bodies ripped, singed, and dismembered by the onslaught. Those who managed to avoid the initial ordnance attack ran to the gates, hoping to escape into the mountains. They ran nearly two hundred yards across open terrain. A logjam quickly formed at the nearest gate. Some men railed at the sky, cursing the Americans' infernal "raining death."

By this time the Spectre had circled and returned for a second run, adding its 40mm Bofors cannon to the symphony of retribution. The gunners on board focused their fire on the gates where the *mujahadeen* had clustered. Bodies fell like dominoes, blocking the exits for the late arrivals.

The gunship circled once again and made a third run. The Spectre's thermal detectors found the stragglers in the courtyard and those who thought they could escape by sneaking over the wall. Pinpoint gunfire handled these scrambling rainbow-colored silhouettes one by one.

On their fourth run, the Spectre's crew surveyed the scene below, firing sporadically at movement, but basically their mission had been completed. The thermal images gradually changed color from predominantly orange and yellow to green and blue as the bodies of the dead lost heat. The Spectre flew into the night over the mountains, widening its circle but standing by in case it had to be called back to tie up any loose ends.

The beating rotors of an HH-60G Pave Hawk helo came in low over the ramparts and flew into the courtyard, sweeping the grounds with its searchlights. Green Berets positioned in the helo's bay scoured the terrain with night-vision goggles, looking for movement, ready to fire before fired upon. One searchlight lingered on the charred hull of Starwood Two. The Pave Hawk circled the courtyard twice before it stopped and hovered over a spot near the ruined *buzkashi* field.

There would be no parking here, it was still a danger zone. The searchlights pointed straight down, dust flying through the beams like a plague of locusts. They focused on the pile of corpses.

A steel rescue platform on a tow line emerged from the bay and slowly dropped toward the ground. A second line flew out of the helo, beating the platform to the ground. Captain Salam, sitting on the edge of the bay, took the line in his gloved hands and pushed off from the bay, fast—roping down to the ground in a movement.

"Off rappel," Salam said into his helmet mike.

Then General Monroe, with only his hands on the rope, slid down expertly seconds later.

Both men wore goggles to protect their eyes from the flying grit. They wore helmets and body armor and carried M4A1s. Wireless headsets allowed them to communicate with the helo and one another over the racket caused by the rotors, but they had little to say. They knew what they had to do—retrieve their dead.

The *muj* had stacked the bodies like firewood. Most of the soldiers had been charred beyond recognition and looked like oblong lumps of charcoal. Of all of them only Sergeant Amberson and Brie Richards were recognizable, their faces intact, their expressions somewhat readable beneath the thick layer of dirt that had caked over them, making them look like unearthed statues. Amberson looked grim, his jaw set. Brie seemed to have died in the middle of a scream, her mouth open, deep depressions where her eyes should have been.

Together Salam and Monroe loaded the bodies onto the rescue platform two at a time, strapping them in so they wouldn't tumble out. Their deaths had been horrible enough without adding further indignity. Monroe tried to locate the name tapes on the soldiers' jackets to identify them. The only one he found that was still legible was "Jenks," Starwood One's pilot.

Monroe and Salam worked in silence, staring up as Monroe signaled for the first load to be winched up. Minutes later the empty rescue platform returned to them. They loaded the next two, strapped them in, and watched them ascend, the rotors beating down on them, the sound of the windblast broadcast through each other's headsets.

The Berets inside the helo tipped the rescue platform over the edge once more and sent it back down. Monroe and Salam sent two more soldiers back up.

The platform returned for its last run. As it approached, Salam reached up and guided it closer to the two remaining bodies, those of Sergeant Amberson and Brie Richards.

Amberson had been a big man, and his body was heavier than the others, but none of them were as heavy as they should have been. Salam and Monroe laid him on his back. Monroe arranged his legs as best he could given that rigor had set in.

They squatted down to pick up Ms. Richards, Monroe at the head, Salam at her feet. One of them could have carried her easily, she was so light, but they both did it, affording her the same respect they'd given to the fighting men.

Monroe nestled her in next to Amberson, drew the straps together, and pulled them extra tight, fearing that she would blow away. He signaled to the Berets on board, pointing up. The rescue platform rose. He held it for as long as he could to keep it from swaying in the wind.

Salam shaded his eyes against the searchlights as he looked up at the rising platform, stepping backward to get out of the glare. Monroe gathered up the tow line and held it out to him. "You go first, Captain."

"General, I think you should go first," he said, walking backward. "So I can watch your back."

"No, you go—"

Boom!

The sudden explosion knocked Monroe over.

A voice from the helo materialized in his ear. "What is your condition? What just happened down there? Repeat. What is your condition?"

Flying grit sandblasted Monroe's face as he sat on the ground. He thought that he might have lost consciousness for a moment, but the sound of the explosion echoed fresh in his head. A Claymore, he thought. He looked around for Salam but couldn't see him. Monroe jumped to his feet. He looked around and saw Salam on his back, ten feet from where he'd been standing a moment ago, bloodstains visible on his pants. Monroe started toward him, when Salam's voice in his ear stopped him.

"Mine, sir," Salam said, his voice weak. "Fucking *muj* mined the area. They knew we'd be coming back."

"Send the platform down," Monroe shouted into his headset mike. "We have an injured man down here."

The pilot's voice from above: "Are you all right, General?"

Monroe looked down for footprints in the dirt, hoping to retrace their steps and get to Salam, but the rotors had erased them.

"Salam! Talk to me," Monroe said.

"Be careful, sir... mines... fucking *muj*..." Salam's voice faded. He was losing consciousness.

"Keep talking, Salam! Tell me something. Tell me about Chicago. Tell me about your family."

"Careful, sir...," Salam mumbled.

Monroe looked around, frantic to help the captain.

"Come back up, General," the voice said. "We'll send someone else down for Salam."

"No time for that," Monroe said. "He needs help now." The bloodstains on Salam's uniform spread fast. He could bleed out in no time, Monroe thought. He needed attention now. But how could Monroe get to him without setting off another mine?

A true warrior is ready to die at any moment, he reminded himself. That's what frees him to act. Monroe decided to risk it. For Salam.

He found his rifle and took aim at the ground, firing in lines toward Salam, hoping to detonate any mines between them. The sound of automatic gunfire competed with the beating rotors. Monroe braced for an explosion—*hoped* for an explosion—but nothing came. He stopped firing when his bullet path came within ten feet of Salam. An explosion that close would finish him off.

Monroe walked his path without hesitation and continued along the last untested stretch. He kneeled in the dirt, ripped off his glove, and checked Salam's neck for a pulse. He couldn't find one.

"Salam! Talk to me! Goddamn it, Salam, that's an order."

"Be careful, General. . ." Salam murmured in Monroe's ear. "Mines. . ."

"Salam! *Salam!*"

Monroe unzipped the captain's flak jacket to find his wound, so he could apply compression. His clothes had soaked through with blood, and Monroe couldn't tell fabric from flesh.

"Salam!"

But Salam had passed. Monroe knew it instinctively. With blood-smeared fingers, he pushed back Salam's eyelids to be sure. No reaction to light. Salam was dead.

"Fuck," Monroe said quietly. He suddenly felt exhausted, as if the life had been sucked out of his bones.

The rescue platform rattled down from the sky. Monroe stood up and caught it, guiding it down next to Salam. He rolled Salam's body onto the platform and strapped him in.

"Take him up," he said into the microphone. "And be careful with him."

As the platform rose, Monroe picked up Salam's rifle, and out of frustration he fired at the field of dead *mujahadeen* across the courtyard. He kept his finger on the trigger until the weapon stopped firing.

Feeling heavy and hollow at the same time, Monroe walked toward the tow line. He stared at the hull of Starwood Two.

I could have prevented all this, he thought. If only I had listened to Salam.

He clipped himself to the tow line and signaled to be brought up. He felt the strain against his harness as his feet left the ground. As he lifted into the air, he noticed faint traces of the ash circles on the *buzkashi* field. He scanned the courtyard and saw the remains of the wooden stage where Zyrous Mohammed had met his end. He saw the turret where he and his people had been imprisoned. He saw the area on the ramparts where the sniper had fired the shot and wondered who had actually pulled the trigger. It didn't really matter, he decided, because Khan had been the one pulling the strings. Monroe looked down and saw the wet blood spot in the dirt where Salam had died.

Inside the helo the pilot looked to Monroe, waiting for his orders to depart. Monroe took off his helmet and peeled off the goggles. He stared at Salam's body face up on the deck. Monroe nodded and signaled to the pilot that they could go.

He looked around at all the bodies, then focused on Salam's dirty face.

I'm sorry, he thought. Forgive me.

41

DAWN BROKE over the airport in Gardiz. Spears of sunlight jutted over the mountaintops in the east, slicing through the gray and penetrating the open doors of the hangar where Monroe had spent the night.

When he'd returned from the fortress after midnight, Monroe insisted on overseeing the preparation of the bodies. They were first cleaned and identified, then tagged and bagged for transport to Dover Air Force Base in Delaware, the usual destination for military casualties. At 4:20 a.m. Monroe was shown to his quarters. Totally exhausted, he'd thought that he'd sleep for a month once his head felt a real pillow, but he couldn't fall asleep. His brain wouldn't let him drift off because he couldn't stop thinking about the dead, especially Salam. He imagined them alone in the hangar, zipped into white plastic body bags. Monroe got out of bed and went back to the hangar.

Leaning on the fender of a parked Hummer, he stared at them blankly, watching as the increasing sunlight reflected off the white plastic bags. Their names had been written on the bags with an indelible black marker. Except for Salam's bag, none of them seemed to have enough inside to qualify as human remains. He'd been tempted to unzip the one marked "Richards, Brie" to make sure. It could have been a pillow inside from the look of it. But his memory of her face in death stopped him. He'd been trying hard to remember her and all the others alive. If these souls planned on haunting him—and he knew their memory *would* haunt him—he'd rather live with palatable ghosts in human form rather than burnt remains.

"Jackson."

Monroe looked up, startled to hear his name. Would he be on a first-name basis with these ghosts?

He shaded his eyes and peered at the approaching figure, the rising sun providing the man with a blinding golden aura. Monroe finally recognized him when he stepped into the shade. General Graydon.

"Bill," Monroe said, feeling that he should use the man's first name since he had used Monroe's.

Graydon held a steaming cup of coffee in a white ceramic mug. "Here," Graydon said, holding it out to him. "I thought you could use this."

"Thank you." He took the cup and sipped from it. Even though it had sugar and milk in it and he usually took it black, he would drink it anyway, grateful for the caffeine boost. The warm cup felt comforting in his cold fingers.

"How'd you know I was out here?" Monroe asked as he took another sip.

Graydon smiled. "The whole base knows you're out here. News travels fast."

Monroe nodded. In that instant he felt very envious of Graydon. He seemed to have a tight command, good people under him. Nothing like the internecine bullshit Monroe had to deal with in Washington.

"I've got a folder full of messages for you on my desk," Graydon said.

Monroe looked off toward the mountains. "Wondering where I am?"

"Yeah, that," Graydon said. "And wondering if you'll make it back in time for the Senate hearings."

Monroe looked at him, puzzled.

"General McCreedy's been burning up the phone lines. Him and somebody named Alan Hooper."

Monroe stared into space. He hadn't thought about them in days.

"I guess they're worried about Frye-Yoder," Graydon said.

"Frye-Yoder," Monroe murmured. The bill had totally slipped his mind. "I'm supposed to testify," he said blankly.

"You know, you're a hero back home, Jackson. You're on all the front pages. The general who led a squad of survivors out of hostile territory and killed six enemy *mujahadeen* in the process." Graydon didn't seem to approve.

"How'd they come up with that number?"

"A British correspondent in Islamabad found a trio of American backpackers who claimed to have run into you in the mountains. They said they heard about you from Raz Khan's people."

Monroe shook his head as he recalled the drug smugglers. "Backpackers. That's a laugh."

Graydon shrugged. "The press is spinning it in your favor. We should at least be grateful for that."

Monroe sipped his coffee and nodded. More than six, he thought. He tried to imagine the faces of McCreedy, Hooper, and Senator Frye. Being with them in Washington seemed so long ago.

"I don't know how to be diplomatic," Graydon said, "so I'm just going to ask. Is there any chance you've changed your mind about Special Forces?"

Monroe met his gaze but didn't answer.

"Just thought I'd ask."

"What—" Monroe started, then changed his mind. "How soon can I get transport back to the States?"

"Whenever you'd like. Your fans are anxious to have you back."

Monroe let that comment slip. "Please set it up as soon as you can. I'll take the bodies back with me."

Graydon's smile disappeared. "Good photo op?" he said.

Monroe didn't answer. His gaze fell on the line of body bags. He became aware of the sound of vehicles on the tarmac outside the hangar. Noncoms had quietly entered the building, maintenance and repair specialists going about their business.

"I'm going to try to catch a few hours of sleep before we leave," Monroe said. "We can go directly to Dover. I'll pick up a ride to D.C. from there."

"I'll arrange it," Graydon said. "Get some rest. I'll give you a wake-up call in a few hours."

"Noon, please," Monroe said. "Thank you."

Just then Monroe noticed someone walking toward them. He heard the footsteps on the concrete floor, but the glare of the sun left the man's face a dark silhouette. It was Corporal Rudge carrying a cup of coffee.

"General," he said, saluting Monroe with his free hand.

Rudge raised his eyebrows when he noticed the cup in Monroe's hand. He looked down at the cup in his own hand. "I thought you might be wanting a coffee," he said. "I'll just bring this one back—"

"No, leave it," Monroe said. "I'll drink it."

"Yes sir," Rudge said and set the cup down on the fender of the Hummer. He saluted the generals, as he turned to leave.

"Rudge?" Monroe said.

"Yes sir?"

"Thanks for the coffee."

"No problem, sir."

"And thanks for everything else. You performed well out there. You're a warrior."

Rudge looked a little startled. "Thank you, sir." His eyes crinkled as a broad smile overtook his face. "I appreciate your saying so, sir."

Monroe returned the smile as he reached for Rudge's cup on the Hummer and brought it to his lips. Somehow Rudge knew that he took it black.

42

SERGEANT BUTCH PROCTOR stared at his wristwatch. 20:00 on Tuesday. He kept checking to keep himself oriented. He'd lost track of time in the mountains, and he wanted to get his head back on straight. The rescue happened on Friday, the bodies retrieved in the wee hours of Saturday. General Monroe had left on Saturday afternoon—just slipped away, it seemed. Proctor had been at a debriefing session when Monroe's transport departed. He'd hoped to have a few words with the general before he left.

Proctor sat by himself on a sofa in the clinic lounge down the hall from the hospital bunks. With his leg propped up on the coffee table, bandaged from his ankle to mid-thigh, he'd just been zoning out. The doctor told him he was damn lucky. Another few days up in the mountains and they would have had to amputate. He'd been trying not to think about living with a stump, but that made him think about it all the more.

Images flickered on the big TV set in the corner, tuned to C-Span, but he didn't pay much attention to it. The doctors wanted to send him back to the States to recover, but Proctor wanted to stay right here and get back to duty as soon as he was able. He didn't want to be past tense, a "was." He wanted to carry on. In memory of Captain Salam.

Proctor had no doubt that his leg would heal, but his mental state started to concern him. He kept going over the whole episode—the escape from the fortress to their rescue. He didn't want to forget any part of it, but every time he went over it, something else occurred to him, and that made him wonder how much more lay submerged in his brain and how much of it he'd unconsciously made up. He planned to have a long session with Rudge and Vitelli to get their take on what had happened, but he really would have liked to go over it with General Monroe, get an officer's perspective.

He exhaled a rueful laugh. An officer's perspective. . . Sure, generals were officers, he thought, but they weren't always good commanders.

That's how he used to think of Monroe. Brass without the brass to lead troops. Well, he couldn't say that about Monroe anymore. The general had shown that he had the stuff to do it, and Proctor had to admit, when Monroe finally got it in gear, he did it well.

"You really did it, General. And we fucking did it for you."

Suddenly Proctor realized that he'd been talking to the image on the television set. He came out of his fog, astonished to see General Monroe's face. Monroe in dress uniform, sitting at a long polished wood table, a microphone on a short stand in front of him. The legend at the bottom of the screen said, "Live Coverage: Senate Armed Services Committee Hearings on the Frye-Yoder Bill."

Proctor leaned forward and concentrated on the TV.

Monroe spoke into the mike. ". . . and my review of the current expenditures does not preclude that possibility, senator."

The image shifted to a row of senators sitting on a raised dais opposite from Monroe, like judges in a courtroom. The camera focused on the senator questioning Monroe, a long-faced man in his sixties wearing large gold-frame aviator glasses. The legend at the bottom of the screen identified him as "Senator Walter Frye—Co-sponsor of Frye-Yoder." He had a pleasant way about him, as if he were talking to an old friend. No surprise, Proctor thought. Frye supported heavy metal all the way, just like Monroe. Proctor shook his head. Bad move.

"General Monroe," Senator Frye said into his mike, "it's my understanding that you recently returned from Afghanistan."

"Yes, that's correct," Monroe said.

"Would you give us your frank assessment of the current troop situation in Afghanistan, specifically with regard to Special Forces?"

Proctor sighed. Yoder had obviously lobbed a big fat one over the plate so that Monroe could get all over it and slam it over the fence. Why didn't Frye just ask the question the way he meant it? Proctor thought angrily. *Just tell us everything that's fucking wrong with Special Forces, General.*

Monroe took a sip of water before he answered. "Senator, it's been widely covered in the press that I was involved in a prolonged incident with *mujahadeen* forces under the control of a duplicitous warlord. The reports have been varied in their accuracy. I'd like to set the record straight and let it be known that I would not be here today if it were not for the excellent work of the Green Berets who accompanied me."

"Yes, General," Frye said, "we all appreciate the efforts of the Green Berets and all the other Special Forces units stationed in Afghanistan and around the world. But do you feel that Special Forces are doing an adequate job in keeping that country secure?"

"Senator," Monroe said, "I feel that they are doing a *superlative* job in Afghanistan and should be commended for it."

"But do you think additional conventional forces might improve the situation in Afghanistan?"

"From what I've observed, Special Forces are working quite well in that country as is. Given the hard terrain and the complexity of the social structure in Afghanistan, I feel that conventional forces might prove to be a negative for our interests there."

Proctor stared at the television, his brow furrowed.

On the screen, Frye furrowed his brow as well.

"I'm not entirely sure I'm following you, general."

"Simply put, Senator, I do not feel that a reduction in Special Forces or a realignment of their command structure will benefit our goals around the world. Without question, there will always be a place for conventional forces—large standing armies well equipped with armament, vehicles, and air support. But there should also be a role for Special Operations Forces in places where the old rules don't apply. I strongly feel that there is an area that falls between conventional warfare and the kind of covert operations that are the province of the CIA. Terrorists, guerrillas, political madmen, and religious fanatics don't play by the rules. Sabotaging them covertly serves the short-term goal, but in essence it's playing the game on their level. As we've seen in the past, large-scale military operations don't always achieve the goal of flushing out terrorist commanders. This is where Special Forces come in. They're agile, they're smart, and they're effective. And they are in uniform. I can think of no better way to represent our mission globally than through our Special Operations Command."

"Holy shit," Proctor whispered.

He could hear the rumblings of the crowd in the senate hearing room. People got out of their seats to confer with one another. They'd expected Monroe's testimony to be something entirely different. The camera focused on the chairman of the committee, who banged his gavel to restore order. "Do you have any further questions, Senator Frye?" he asked.

"Just one," Frye said, his face red and angry. He looked like a pissed-off school principal. "It sounds to me, General, that you have found religion, as it were, over there. Am I correct then in assuming that you are *not* in support of the bill we're discussing here today?"

Monroe paused and leveled his gaze at Frye. "Senator, I am in support of Special Forces. I was Special Forces myself in Vietnam. I just had to be reminded."

"You didn't answer my question," Frye said testily.

"Senator, I am not in support of the bill as currently written, not as it affects SOCOM. If anything, I support an increase in the monies earmarked for special warfare."

The room erupted. People jumped to their feet. The chairman banged his gavel and called for order, but no one listened. Reporters clamored among themselves. No one could believe that Monroe had reversed his postion.

In the clinic lounge Proctor pumped his arm in the air. "You rock, General," he yelled. "You fucking *rock!*"

A couple of Berets happened to be passing by in the hallway and heard Proctor through the open doorway. They poked their heads in. "What's going on?" one of them said.

"History, man," he said with an overjoyed grin. "Fucking history."

43

THE UPROAR had died down at the Senate hearings, but the tension still thrummed through the room. Mouths might have been shut, but saucer-sized eyes stared at Monroe, flabbergasted by his sudden turnaround. Senator Frye regained his composure, even though Monroe had just punched a significant hole in his bill's chances of making it through Congress.

Monroe's testimony proceeded in a civil fashion, though it went on a bit longer than expected because the bill's opponents on the committee took the opportunity to question Monroe further in order to reinforce their opposition. At 12:40 the questioning came to an end, and the committee thanked him for his time and expertise.

Monroe leaned into the microphone. "Senators, I would like to thank you as well for your service and commitment to the country. I hope I've been of help to you."

The chairman then adjourned the hearings for lunch.

Monroe tried to catch Senator Frye's eye as he stood up, hoping to gauge the level of hostility he could expect, but Frye turned away and left the chambers. From across the room, General McCreedy stared hotly at Monroe. The man's roiling eyebrows told the tale. McCreedy looked like a furious drill sergeant with a deliberately insolent cadet.

"I want to see you *now,*" McCreedy mouthed.

Monroe met his gaze and shook his head. That wouldn't be necessary. He had made up his mind and said what he truly believed. McCreedy clearly wanted to dress him down, but McCreedy could save his bluster for a junior officer. Monroe headed down the aisle for the exit. Journalists—some of them prominent members of the press—called out to him, but he ignored them.

Out in the marble-floored hallway, reporters shoved tape recorders in his face, clamoring for a quote, but Monroe ignored them as well. A sense of urgency and time squandered propelled him through the crowd.

"General?" The man didn't shout, but Monroe recognized the voice immediately. He turned around to see Alan Hooper's round face and body, shoulders slumped, mouth sagging. The man looked so pathetic, Monroe felt sorry for him. He knew Frye and McCreedy would without question shift some of the blame onto him.

Hooper raised his palms helplessly. "What happened?"

"I went to Afghanistan to find facts, Alan, and those were the facts I found. I couldn't be anything less than honest in my testimony."

Hooper nodded, but he didn't seem convinced. Lobbyists don't believe in anything unless they're paid to believe in it.

"I have to go, Alan. You take care."

"You too." Hooper gave him a sad little wave.

Monroe continued down the hall, but when he turned a corner, he suddenly faced a phalanx of cameramen and photographers waiting for him.

"General?"

"General?"

"General?" They sounded like squawking geese as they frantically shouted for his attention. He turned on his heel and found another stairwell that led down to the ground level where his driver would be waiting for him. He pushed through the heavy wooden door and started down the marble steps.

"General!" Jane Norcross had just rounded the landing below him, a Nikon in her hand, a camera bag slung over her shoulder. She wore black slacks and a black turtleneck sweater.

"Jane!" he blurted, startled to see her.

"I missed the photo op, didn't I? *Shit!*" She slowed down and climbed the stairs to meet him. "How are you?"

She extended her hand politely. He took it and then embraced her. "How are *you*?" he asked, studying her face. "I was concerned about you."

"I'm fine. Just a little sore. But I do fit into a lot of my old jeans. I tell everyone Afghanistan was an extended extreme aerobics workout."

They both laughed, but they could tell from one another's eyes that they had much more to say. She'd made it through the ordeal as well as any of the men in their unit, and for that she had earned his respect. They had shared the kind of closeness only soldiers in combat experience. They needed to make time to talk about it.

"Can I reach you through your newspaper?" he asked.

"Sure."

"We should get together and debrief."

"Over a bottle of wine?"

"Or something stronger," he said. "Jane, I have to go now, but I'll be in touch."

"Okay," she said with a smile. "Soon."

A man's voice came from the top of the stairs. "*General Monroe?*"

Monroe would have ignored it if it weren't for the man's assertive but respectful tone. He didn't sound like a begging reporter. Definitely military, Monroe thought. He looked up and saw a young man in uniform at the top of the staircase, holding a salute. The young man had dark hair and olive skin. He wore a serious expression and one gold bar on his shoulder. Monroe had forgotten about Sergeant Major Ramos. The man had been temporarily assigned to assist Monroe in place of Second Lieutenant Reilly. Monroe saluted, and Ramos dropped his hand to his side.

"Speak, Sergeant," Monroe said.

"I just received a call from the Pentagon, sir. The Secretary wants to see you immediately."

Monroe nodded. He imagined Secretary Riordan watching the hearings on C-Span in his office, a deep disapproving frown on his ruddy face. Well, better to face the shit storm sooner than later, Monroe thought.

"Thank you, Ramos," Monroe said. "I won't be needing you for the next few hours. Get some lunch, then check in with my office."

"Yes sir."

"That'll be all."

Ramos and Monroe saluted, and Ramos went back into the hallway. Monroe turned back to Jane. "By the way," he said, "it's not Jack."

She looked puzzled. "Huh?"

"Not Jack. Jackson. You had asked me in Afghanistan what people call me."

"Oh, right. I remember."

"I'll talk to you soon, Jane." Monroe headed down the staircase.

"Hey, wait!" she said.

He turned to see her with the camera to her face. She snapped off a shot before he could object. "Don't worry," she said. "This one is just for me. . . Jackson."

44

SECRETARY OF DEFENSE Riordan's wire-rim glasses flashed in the light of his green-glass desk lamp, obscuring his eyes and making it difficult for Monroe to read his expression. Riordan sat bolt upright in his high-back leather chair, facing Monroe, who sat on the other side of the desk. Though known for being generally stone-faced regardless of his mood, Riordan never left doubt as to what he had on his mind.

Riordan used his voice like a hammer. "I'm still trying to figure out whether you *helped* us or *hurt* us today, General. That was quite a flip-flop you performed."

Monroe just looked at him, waiting for the other shoe to drop. If Riordan expected an apologetic explanation, he'd be waiting a long time.

Riordan continued, "I should be happy that you've seen the light regarding the importance of Special Forces. But. . ." He let his thought hang there for a moment. "When a man who has been so dedicated to the heavy-metal philosophy does such an abrupt about-face, it stirs up controversy and, what's worse, doubt. People start wondering why the change? Who's paying him off? What's in it for him? As you know, conspiracy theory is the national pastime in this country."

"Are you asking me to defend myself, Mr. Secretary?" Monroe said.

"Do you feel that you *have* to defend yourself?"

"No."

"Why not?"

"Honesty never needs a defense."

"Mmmm. . ." Riordan's famous frown deepened.

Monroe didn't bother to elaborate.

"I would never question your motives," Riordan said. "You have much more integrity than the company you keep...or should I say kept?"

Monroe knew who Riordan referred to, of course, but the secretary would never stoop to indicting General McCreedy, Senator Frye, and

Alan Hooper by name. McCreedy was military after all, and Frye was a duly elected official of the United States government. A lobbyist, on the other hand, was beneath his consideration.

Riordan swiveled his chair slightly, and Monroe could finally see his steel-blue eyes.

"I have a request."

"What?"

"I would like to see Captain Louis Salam recommended for a Congressional Medal of Honor."

Riordan's eyebrows raised, "And who is this Captain. . . ?"

"Louis Salam. He led the A-team that got us out of the mountains."

Riordan looked skeptical. "Specifically what did he do to warrant a medal?"

"Everything. Without him, you'd be attending my funeral right now. We would never have survived without him."

"I'm sure you're correct, but you know the rules, General. An extraordinary act of bravery performed at great personal risk must be proven to earn the medal. I'm sure Captain Salam did a commendable job, but overall excellence alone doesn't cut it. You know how many requests I get for the CMO?"

"Yes, I know. This would be a posthumous award. Salam single-handedly routed a Taliban unit, saving our unit from certain slaughter. He later lost his life retrieving our dead from the fortress. A team went in by helo, a risky situation with armed enemy survivors still in the area. He went down alone to get the bodies. I'll document those actions and considerably more."

Riordan lowered his chin. "I heard that you went down with him."

Monroe shook his head. "I was in the helo. Captain Salam went down alone."

Riordan said nothing for a moment. "That's not the story I heard."

"I was there," Monroe said.

Riordan stared at him, letting the moment stretch. "Send me a report," he finally said. "I'll review it."

"I would like you to do more than just review it."

Riordan's lips parted in surprise. No one ever pressed a point with him. "I will give it my most careful consideration," he said. "If Captain Salam performed as you say, I'll see that it happens."

"Thank you."

"So, General, what is it that you want for yourself?"

Monroe knit his brows. "I'm not following you."

"Everybody wants something, General. Whether it's reelection, Godzilla military contracts, larger consulting fees, or just more power, everybody has something they want. You don't get up before a congressional hearing, do a one-eighty, and not want something out of it. You have to want *something*."

Monroe paused before he spoke. He'd been thinking about this but hadn't had a chance to discuss it with his family. If there was ever a time to speak, it would be now. "I want to be reassigned," he said.

Riordan laughed. "You want *my* job?"

"I want one of the commands."

Riordan stopped laughing. "I was going to offer you McCreedy's position on the Joint Chiefs."

Monroes eyes widened, shocked and flattered, but then he shook his head. "I want to be in the field."

"I'm offering you a plum post here in Washington. A field command would be a step backward for you."

"Not the way I see it."

"Explain."

"I'm a soldier and an officer. I was trained to fight and trained to lead. I want to get back to that. I need to move back to move forward. At least for me."

Riordan narrowed his eyes and sized him up. "I have a feeling you're being sincere, General."

"One hundred percent."

"Do you want to be in Afghanistan?"

"If there's a place for me, yes."

The secretary pursed his lips and nodded. "I'll have to give that some thought. If that's what you really want."

"It's not just what I want. It's what I *should* do."

"All right then. I'll see what I can do. There might be an opening with SOCOM."

Is he calling my bluff? Monroe wondered. "You'd actually put an 'Old Army,' heavy-metal guy in charge of Special Operations Command?"

"*Former* 'Old Army,' heavy-metal guy. Remember, there's no truer believer than a convert."

"To me, CINCSOCOM is my idea of great work. Thank you, Mr. Secretary."

Riordan flashed a tight smile. "Don't thank me yet. You won't have it cushy like you have it now."

"Not a problem."

"What about your family?"

"We'll figure it out."

"Okay then. I'll get back to you on this. Now I have to throw you out. I have a meeting with the president in forty-five minutes, and I have to prepare."

Monroe stood up and so did Riordan. The secretary extended his hand across the desk. "I might not always have agreed with you, Jackson, but I've always respected you. Now more than ever."

Monroe shook his hand. "Thank you, sir. I appreciate it."

"And welcome back. I read the newspapers—how was it out there?"

"For us, it was the devil and then some," he said somberly.

Riordan nodded.

Monroe turned to leave. He walked to the door and put his hand on the knob, then looked back. Riordan was already engrossed in the notes and files on his desk, his face tipped down. The lamplight glinted off his glasses.

Early that evening Monroe sat at his desk in the Pentagon, trying to catch up on work, even though he'd intended to leave hours ago. The phone had been ringing nonstop ever since he gave his testimony that morning. The callers either wanted to pillory him for sinking Frye-Yoder or put his face on the dollar bill for supporting the true spirit of the armed forces. He'd heard from angry arms manufacturers and constituents from districts where those manufacturers were located. He'd heard from retired military men from all branches of the service and old classmates from the Academy, officers and civilians he hadn't heard from in years. As he packed his briefcase to leave, he scanned his desk. He had enough pink message slips to start a fire and roast a pig.

He checked his watch, 18:25. He'd sent his staff home already. The phone rang but he decided to ignore it, watching the line blink instead. Leave a message, he thought. I'll get back to you whenever. Really important calls don't come through these lines anyway. They'd use his secure cell or send someone to find him.

As he closed his briefcase and stood up to go, he noticed a framed photograph on the wall over the mahogany credenza. It had been taken on a duck hunt in South Carolina. Monroe, General McCreedy, and Senator Frye in hip waders and hunting caps, each of them holding a shotgun and smiling for the camera. I suppose that'll have to come down, Monroe thought.

He picked up his briefcase, walked through his inner office door, and locked it, then passed through the outer office and went out into the hallway, careful not to make eye contact with anyone as he strode briskly toward the elevators. Everyone wanted to talk to him about his testimony, but he just wanted to get away from that topic for a while. He'd barely seen his wife since his return from Afghanistan. He intended to go directly to the helipad, where a helo waited for him, and escape to his home in Virginia. His children would be coming home to see him. A perfect opportunity to bring up his desire to take a new assignment. As Commander in Chief, Special Operations Command, he would be based in Florida, but would spend much of his time all over the world. It felt good to want something badly again.

He made it to the elevators unaccosted, though he could feel the eyes of administrative personnel and lower ranks on him. An elevator opened, and a young black woman carrying an armload of files stepped out. Her eyes widened as soon as she recognized him. She lingered outside the elevator, staring at him.

He stepped in and pressed the ground floor button. "Good evening," he said to her as the doors closed.

The doors opened again and he made his way briskly through the maze of hallways to the door closest to the helipad. Through the glass door he could see the Bell 206 JetRanger, rotors turning, running lights growing brighter in the fading light.

"Jackson!"

Monroe turned toward the voice, knowing it instantly. "General Vandermeer."

Vandermeer stood by a window, the lights across the Potomac shining behind him. He wore a suit and tie but still had the same crisp military bearing that Monroe remembered from West Point. Vandermeer smiled at him. "I knew you'd be coming this way," he said. "I've been waiting."

"What can I do for you, General?" Monroe asked.

"I know you're in a hurry, Jackson. I just wanted to shake your hand. I want you to know that I think it's great."

Monroe clasped his hand, their grips firm but warm. Vandermeer put his other hand on top of Monroe's. Neither man spoke, but they didn't have to. Their admiration for one another could be felt in the air.

"Now get home to your family," Vandermeer said, releasing his grip.

Monroe smiled. "Yes sir." Vandermeer's approval meant a lot to him. "We'll talk soon."

"Count on it. We have plenty to discuss. But your wife's waiting now, so go."

Monroe pushed through the doorway and jogged to the helipad. He opened the side door of the helo and climbed into the copilot's seat.

The pilot, an affable lieutenant named Mark Weston, saluted him. Monroe had flown with him several times before.

Monroe put on the copilot's headset as Lieutenant Weston revved the engine in preparation for liftoff.

"Lieutenant," Monroe said, "I'd like to take the stick if you don't mind."

Weston looked at him, but before he could say anything, Monroe added, "Don't worry. I've been practicing."

Monroe's sly grin gave Weston permission to grin back. "No problem, sir."

They exchanged seats and headsets, and Monroe prepared for liftoff. He worked the stick and coaxed the helo off the ground, guiding it out over the river.

When they'd reached cruising altitude, Weston gave Monroe a sidelong glance. "If you don't mind my saying, sir, I hear you're a pretty good shooter, too."

"Lieutenant," Monroe said, keeping his eyes ahead of him, "leadership is in the details."

"Amen to that, General."

Outside the windshield, the last rosy glow of sunset diminished into the horizon. As they swept over the Potomac, Washington's pointillist grid of streetlights and headlights stretched out before them. Monroe picked up speed. He could see the White House and the Capitol distinctly in the distance as well as the Mall, the reflecting pool, the Washington Monument, the Lincoln Memorial. . . A truly breathtaking vista.

Worth fighting for, Monroe thought as he banked toward Virginia. Well worth fighting for.

FOR THE BEST IN PAPERBACKS, LOOK FOR THE

In every corner of the world, on every subject under the sun, Penguin represents quality and variety—the very best in publishing today.

For complete information about books available from Penguin—including Penguin Classics, Penguin Compass, and Puffins—and how to order them, write to us at the appropriate address below. Please note that for copyright reasons the selection of books varies from country to country.

In the United States: Please write to *Penguin Group (USA), P.O. Box 12289 Dept. B, Newark, New Jersey 07101-5289* or call *1-800-788-6262.*

In the United Kingdom: Please write to *Dept. EP, Penguin Books Ltd, Bath Road, Harmondsworth, West Drayton, Middlesex UB7 0DA.*

In Canada: Please write to *Penguin Books Canada Ltd, 90 Eglinton Avenue East, Suite 700, Toronto, Ontario M4P 2Y3.*

In Australia: Please write to *Penguin Books Australia Ltd, P.O. Box 257, Ringwood, Victoria 3134.*

In New Zealand: Please write to *Penguin Books (NZ) Ltd, Private Bag 102902, North Shore Mail Centre, Auckland 10.*

In India: Please write to *Penguin Books India Pvt Ltd, 11 Panchsheel Shopping Centre, Panchsheel Park, New Delhi 110 017.*

In the Netherlands: Please write to *Penguin Books Netherlands bv, Postbus 3507, NL-1001 AH Amsterdam.*

In Germany: Please write to *Penguin Books Deutschland GmbH, Metzlerstrasse 26, 60594 Frankfurt am Main.*

In Spain: Please write to *Penguin Books S. A., Bravo Murillo 19, 1° B, 28015 Madrid.*

In Italy: Please write to *Penguin Italia s.r.l., Via Benedetto Croce 2, 20094 Corsico, Milano.*

In France: Please write to *Penguin France, Le Carré Wilson, 62 rue Benjamin Baillaud, 31500 Toulouse.*

In Japan: Please write to *Penguin Books Japan Ltd, Kaneko Building, 2-3-25 Koraku, Bunkyo-Ku, Tokyo 112.*

In South Africa: Please write to *Penguin Books South Africa (Pty) Ltd, Private Bag X14, Parkview, 2122 Johannesburg.*